Praise for the novels of Susan Wiggs

"Susan Wiggs paints the details of human relationships with the finesse of a master."

—Jodi Picoult

"With the ease of a master, Wiggs introduces complicated, flesh-and-blood characters into her idyllic but identifiable small-town setting...."

—*Publishers Weekly*, starred review, on *The Winter Lodge*

"Wiggs's talent is reflected in her thoroughly believable characters as well as the way she recognizes the importance of family by blood or other ties."

—*Library Journal*

"Wiggs is one of our best observers of stories of the heart. She knows how to capture emotion on virtually every page of every book."

—*Salem Statesman Journal*

"Wiggs' prose is both compelling and moving... Each and every character is finely detailed, and finishing the book feels like saying goodbye to dear old friends."

—*RT Book Reviews* on *Summer at Willow Lake*

"*Just Breathe* is tender and heartbreaking... It's a beautiful novel."

—Luanne Rice

"Wiggs takes serious situations and weaves them into an emotionally wrought story that will have readers reaching for the Kleenex one moment and snickering out loud the next."

—*Publishers Weekly* on *Just Breathe*

Praise for the novels of Sheila Roberts

"Sheila Roberts makes me laugh. I read her books and come away inspired, hopeful and happy."
—Debbie Macomber, #1 *New York Times* bestselling author

"This is an engrossing story with strong characters and arcs similar to Debbie Macomber's Cedar Cove titles. The light romance, delicious descriptions of chocolate and recipes add to the flavor of Roberts's promising new series."
—*Booklist* on *Better Than Chocolate*

"Roberts does a terrific job of juggling her lively cast of characters...and readers who enjoy a-second-chance-at-love stories will especially appreciate this sweet romance."
—*Booklist* on *The Lodge on Holly Road*

"Heartwarming and full of second chances at love, Roberts's latest is...full of genuine, colorful characters. Roberts tells their story with a sweet, modern flair."
—*RT Book Reviews* on *The Lodge on Holly Road*

"Homing in on issues many readers can identify with, Roberts's women search for practical solutions to a common challenge with humor."
—*Publishers Weekly*

"Within minutes of cracking open the book, my mood was lifted.... The warm, glowing feeling it gave me lasted for days."
—*First for Women* on *The Snow Globe*

SUSAN WIGGS

SHEILA ROBERTS

The Summer it Begins

mira

mira

ISBN-13: 978-0-7783-0908-6

The Summer It Begins

Copyright © 2019 by Harlequin Books S.A.

The publisher acknowledges the copyright holders of the individual works as follows:

The Goodbye Quilt
Copyright © 2011 by Susan Wiggs

A Wedding on Primrose Street
Copyright © 2015 by Sheila Rabe

www.Harlequin.com

Printed in U.S.A.

Look for Sheila Roberts's next novel

CHRISTMAS FROM THE HEART

available soon from MIRA Books.

CONTENTS

THE GOODBYE QUILT

Susan Wiggs

To my curly-headed daughter, Elizabeth—
you are my sunshine.

DAY ONE

Odometer Reading 121,047

Wanted: a needle swift enough
to sew this poem into a blanket.

—Charles Simic,
Serbian-American poet

One

How do you say goodbye to a piece of your heart? If you're a quilter, you have a time-honored way to express yourself.

A quilt is an object of peculiar intimacy. By virtue of the way it is created, every inch of the fabric is touched. Each scrap absorbs the quilter's scent and the invisible oils of her skin, the smell of her household and, thanks to the constant pinning and stitching, her blood in the tiniest of quantities. And tears, though she might be loath to admit it.

My adult life has been a patchwork of projects, most of which were fleeting fancies of overreaching vision. I tend to seize on things, only to abandon them due to a lack of time, talent or inclination. There are a few things I'm truly good at—*Jeopardy!,* riding a bike, balancing a checkbook, orienteering, making balloon animals... and quilting.

I'm good at pulling together little bits and pieces of disparate objects. The process suits me. Each square captures my attention like a new landscape. Everything about quilting suits me, an occupation for hands and heart and imagination.

Other things didn't work out so well—Szechuan cooking, topiary gardening, video games and philately come to mind.

My main project, my ultimate work-in-progress, is Molly, of course. And today she's going away to college, clear across the country. Correction—I'm taking her away, delivering her like an insured parcel to a new life.

Hence the quilt. What better memento to give my daughter than a handmade quilt to keep in her dorm room, a comforter stitched with all the memories of her childhood? It'll be a tangible reminder of who she is, where she comes from…and maybe, if I'm lucky, it will offer a glimpse of her dreams.

All my quilting supplies come from a shop in town called Pins & Needles. The place occupies a vintage building on the main street. It's been in continuous operation for more than five decades. As a child, I passed its redbrick and figured concrete storefront on my way to school each day, and I still remember the kaleidoscope of fabrics in the window, flyers announcing classes and raffles, the rainbow array of rich-colored thread, the treasure trove of glittering notions. My first job as a teenager was at the shop, cutting fabric and ringing up purchases.

When Molly started school, I worked there part time, as much for the extra money as for the company of women who frequented Pins & Needles. Fall is wonderful at the fabric shop, a nesting time, when people are making Halloween costumes, Thanksgiving centerpieces and Christmas decorations. People are never in a hurry in a fabric shop. They browse. They talk about their projects, giving you a glimpse of their lives.

The shop is a natural gathering place for women. The people I've met there through the years have become my friends. Customers and staff members stand around the cutting tables to discuss projects, give demonstrations and workshops, offer advice on everything from quilting techniques to child rearing to marriage. The ladies there all know about my idea to make a quilt as a going-away gift for Molly. Some of them even created pieces for me to add, embroidered with messages of "Good Luck" and "Congratulations."

You can always tell what's going on in a woman's life based on the quilt she's working on. The new-baby quilts are always light and soft, the wedding quilts pure and clean, filled with tradition, as though a beautiful design might be an inoculation against future strife. Housewarming quilts tend to be artistic, suitable for hanging on an undecorated wall. The most lovingly created quilts of all are the memory quilts, often created as a group project to commemorate a significant event, help with healing or to celebrate a life.

I've always thought a quilt held together with a woman's tears to be the strongest of all.

Nonquilters have a hard time getting their heads around the time and trouble of a project like this. My friend Cherisse, who has three kids, said, "Linda, honey, I'm just glad to get them out of the house—up and running, with no criminal record." Another friend confessed, "My daughter would only ruin it. She's so careless with her things." My neighbor Erin, who started law school when her son entered first grade, now works long hours and makes a ton of money. "I wish I had the time," she said wistfully when I showed her my project.

What I've found is that you make time for the things that matter to you. Everyone *has* the time. It's just a question of deciding what to do with that time. For some people, it's providing for their family. For others, it's finding that precarious balance between taking care of business and the soul-work of being there for husband, children, friends and neighbors.

I'm supposed to be making the last-minute preparations before our departure on the epic road trip, but instead I find myself dithering over the quilt, contemplating sashing and borders and whether my color palette is strong and balanced. Although the top is pieced, the backing and batting in place, there is still much work to be done. Embellishments to add. It might not be proper quilting technique, but quilting is an art, not a science. My crafter's bag is filled with snippets of fabric culled from old, familiar clothes, fabric toys and textiles that have been outgrown, but were too dear or too damaged to take to the Goodwill bin. I'm a big believer in charity bins. Just because a garment is no longer suitable doesn't mean it couldn't be right for someone else. On the other hand, some things are not meant to be parted with.

I sift through the myriad moments of Molly's childhood, which I keep close to my heart, like flowers from a prized bouquet, carefully pressed between sheets of blotter paper. I fold the quilt and put it in the bag with all the bright bits and mementos—a tiny swatch of a babydoll's nightie, an official-looking Girl Scout badge, a precious button that is the only survivor of her first Christmas dress… So many memories lie mute within this long-handled bag, waiting for me to use them as the final embellishments on this work of art.

I'll never finish in time.

You can do this. I try to give myself a pep talk, but the words fall through my mind and trickle away. This is unexpected, this inability to focus. A panic I haven't been expecting rises up in me, grabbing invisibly at my chest. Breathe, I tell myself. Breathe.

The house already feels different; a heaviness hangs in the drapes over the old chintz sofa. Sounds echo on the wooden floors—a suitcase being rolled to the front porch, a set of keys dropped on the hall table. An air of change hovers over everything.

Dan has driven to the Chevron station to fill the Sub-urban's tank. He's not coming; this long drive without him will be a first for our family. Until now, every road trip has involved all three of us—Yellowstone, Bryce Canyon, Big Sur, speeding along endless highways with the music turned up loud. We did everything as a family. I can't even remember what Dan and I used to do before Molly. Those days seem like a life that happened to someone else. We were a couple, but Molly made us a family.

This time, Dan will stay home with Hoover, who is getting on in years and doesn't do well at the kennel anymore.

It's better this way. Dan was never fond of saying goodbye. Not that anybody enjoys it, but in our family, I'm always the stoic, the one who makes the emotional work look easy—on the outside, anyway. My solo drive back home will be another first for me. I hope I'll use the time well, getting to know myself again, maybe.

Scary thought—what if I get to know myself and I'm someone I don't want to be?

Now, as the heaviness of the impending departure presses down on me, I wonder if we should have planned things differently. Perhaps the three of us should have made this journey together, treating it as a family vacation, like a trip to Disney World or the Grand Canyon.

On the other hand, that's a bad idea. There can be no fooling ourselves into thinking this is something other than what it is—the willful ejection of Molly from our nest. It's too late for second thoughts, anyway. She has to be moved into her dorm in time for freshman orientation. It's been marked on the kitchen calendar for weeks—the expiration date on her childhood.

At the other end of the downstairs, a chord sounds on the piano. Molly tends to sit down and play when she has a lot on her mind. Maybe it's her way of sorting things out.

I'm grateful for the years of lessons she took, even when we could barely afford them. I wanted my daughter to have things I never had, and music lessons are one of them. She's turned into an expressive musician, transforming standard pieces into something heartfelt and mystical. Showy trills and glissandos sluice through the air, filling every empty space in the house. The piano will sit fallow and silent when she's away; neither Dan nor I play. He never had the time to learn; I never had the wherewithal or—I admit it—the patience. Ah, but Molly. She was fascinated with the instrument from the time she stretched up on toddler legs to reach the keys of the secondhand piano we bought at auction. She started lessons when she was only six.

All the hours of practice made up the soundtrack of

her growing years. "Bill Grogan's Goat" was an early favorite, leading to more challenging works, from "The Rainbow Connection" to "Für Elise," Bartok and beyond. Almost every evening for the past twelve years, Molly practiced while Dan and I cleaned up after dinner. This was her way of avoiding dishwashing duty, and we considered it a fair division of labor—I rinse, he loads, she serenades. She managed to make it to age eighteen without learning to properly load a dishwasher, yet she can play Rachmaninoff.

In the middle of a dramatic pause between chords, a car horn sounds.

The bag with the quilt falls, momentarily forgotten, to the floor. That innocent *yip* of the horn signals that summer has ended.

Molly stops playing, leaving a profound hollow of silence in the house. Seconds later, I can still feel the throb of the notes in the stillness. I go to the landing at the turn of the stairs in time to see her jump up, leaving the piano bench askew.

She runs outside, the screen door snapping shut behind her like a mousetrap. Watching through the window on the landing, I brace myself for another storm of emotion. She has been saying goodbye to Travis all summer long. Today, the farewell will be final.

Here is a picture of Molly: Curly hair wadded into a messy ponytail. Athletic shorts balanced on her hip bones, a T-shirt with a dead rock star on it. A body toned by youth, volleyball and weekend swims at the lake. A face that shows every emotion, even when she doesn't want it to.

Now she flings herself into her boyfriend's arms as a sob breaks from her, mingling with the sound of morning birdsong. Oh, that yearning, the piercing kind only love-dazed teenagers can feel. Hands holding for the last time. Grief written in their posture as their bodies melt together. Travis's arms encircle her with their ropy strength, and his long form bows protectively, walling her off from me.

This kid is both the best and worst kind of boyfriend a mother wants for her daughter. The best, because he's a safe driver and he respects her. The worst, because he incites a passion and loyalty in Molly that impairs her vision of the future.

Last spring, he won her heart like a carnival prize in a ring toss, and they've been inseparable ever since. He is impossibly, irresistibly good-looking, and there's no denying that he's been good to her. He makes no secret of the fact that he doesn't want her to go away. He wants her to feel as if *he* is her next step, not college.

All summer I've been trying to tell her that the right guy wouldn't stand in the way of her dreams. The right guy is going to look at her the way Dan once looked at me, as if he could see the whole world in my face. When Travis regards Molly, he's seeing… not the whole world. His next weekend, maybe.

Hoover lifts his leg and pees on the tire of Travis's Camaro, the guy's pride and joy. Travis and Molly don't notice.

I can't hear their conversation, but I can see his mouth shape the words: *Don't go.*

My heart echoes the sentiment. I want her to stay close, too. The difference is, I know she needs to leave.

Molly speaks; I hope she's telling him she has to go away, that this opportunity is too big to miss. She has won a scholarship to a world-class private university. She's getting a chance at a life most people in our small western Wyoming town never dream of. Here in a part of the state that appears roadless and sparse on travel maps, life moves slowly. Our town is filled with good people, harsh weather and a sense that big dreams seem to come true only when you leave. The main industry here is a plant that makes prefab log homes.

I turn away from the window, giving Molly her private farewell. She is far more upset about leaving Travis than about leaving Dan and me, a fact that is hard to swallow.

Dan comes back from the service station. He visits with Travis briefly. I compare the two of them as they stand together talking. Dan is solidly built, his shoulders and arms sculpted by his years at the plant before he made supervisor. He looks as grounded and dependable as the pickup truck he drives. By contrast, Travis is tall and lithe with youth, his slender body curving into a question mark as he gestures with pride at his cherry-red car.

The two of them shake hands; then Dan heads inside. Our eyes meet and skate away; we're not ready to talk yet. In the kitchen, the two of us make a few final preparations—bundling road maps together, adding ice to the cooler of drinks.

Summer glares against the screen door, its hot scent a reminder that the day is already a few hours old. I think of a thousand other summer days, whiled away without a care for the slow passing of time. We built a tree house, went on bike rides, hung a rope swing over a swimming hole, made sno-cones, watched ants on the march. We lay faceup in the grass and stared at clouds until our eyes watered. We fought about curfews, shopped for back-to-school supplies, sang along with songs on the radio. We laughed at nothing until our sides ached, and cried at movies with sad endings.

I sneak a glance at Dan. I can't picture him crying at the movies with me. That was always Molly's role, the exclusive domain of females. Without really planning to, she and I created rituals and traditions, and these things formed a powerful bond.

There is a vehemence to the thoughts tearing through my head, a sense of rebellion—How can I just let her go? I didn't sign up for this—for creating my greatest work only to have to shove her away from me.

When I pushed her out into the world, she was handed immediately into my arms. I never thought of letting her go, only of holding her next to my heart, under which she'd grown, already adored by the time she made her appearance. The idea of her leaving was an abstraction, a nonspecified Someday. Now it's all happening, exactly as we planned. Except I didn't plan for it to throttle me.

Dan seems easy about the process. He's always accepted—even welcomed—life's movements from one phase to the next, like birthdays or promotions at work. He is the sort of person who makes life look effortless, a trait I admire and sometimes envy in him.

As for me, I find myself unable to move. I'm not ready. This wrenching grief has blindsided me. I didn't expect it to be this intense. All kids leave home. That's the way it works. If you do your job of parenting correctly, this is the end result. They leave. When it *doesn't* work that way, that's when a mother should worry. If the kid sticks around, takes up permanent residence in her childhood bedroom, you're considered a failure.

Ah, but the price of succeeding is a piece of your

soul. I bite my lip to keep from trying to explain this to Dan. He would tell me I'm being overly dramatic. Maybe so, but everything about this process *feels* dramatic. This child has been the focus of every day of my life for the past eighteen years. After being a parent for so long, I am forced to surrender the role. Now, all of a sudden, a void has opened up.

Snap out of it, I tell myself. I have so much to be thankful for—this rich, full life. Health, husband and home. And lots to look forward to. It's wrong to mope and wallow in the tragedy of it all. What's the matter with me?

The matter is this—I'm facing a huge loss. The biggest part of my daughter's life is about to start, and it doesn't include me and Dan. Granted, we've had plenty of time to prepare, but now that the moment has arrived, it's as unexpectedly painful as a sudden accident.

Although greeting card companies have created themes around every possible life event, there's no ritual for this particular transition.

This is surprising, because when a child leaves for college, it is the end of something. Other than birth or death, leaving home for any reason is the most extreme of life transitions. One moment we're a family of three. The next, we've lost a vital member. It's a true loss, only people don't understand your grief. They don't send you sympathy cards or invite you to join a support group. They don't flock to comfort you. They don't come to your door bearing tuna casseroles and bottles of Cold Duck and platters of cookies on their good chintz china.

Instead, the journey to college is a rite of passage we mark as a joyous occasion, one we celebrate by buying luggage and books on how to build a fulfilling life. But really, if you ask any mother, she'll tell you that deep down, we want to mark it as a loss, a funeral of sorts. We never show our sorrow, though. Our sadness stays in the shadows like something slightly shameful.

Travis leaves, peeling himself away like a Band-Aid that's been stuck on too long. His union job at the plant keeps him on a strict schedule; he cannot linger. Molly stands on the front sidewalk and watches his Camaro growing smaller and smaller down the tree-lined street, flanked by timber frame houses from the 1920s, remnants of the days when this was a company town. Molly's face is stiff and pale, as if she's been shocked and disoriented by unexpected pain. Her arms are folded across her middle.

I hurry outside, wanting to comfort her. "I know it's hard," I say, giving her a hug.

She is stiff and unyielding, regarding me like an intruder. "You have no idea how this feels," she says. "You never had to leave Dad."

She's right. Dan and I met at a bar twenty-some years ago, and after our first dance together, we already knew we'd be a couple. If somebody had told me I had to leave him and head off to a world of strangers, would I have been willing to do that? Yes, shouts a seldom-heard voice inside me—oh, yes.

Molly waits for an answer.

"Aw, Moll. Your dad and I were in a much different place—"

"Nobody forced you two apart," she says, her voice rising.

"And nobody's forcing you and Travis apart."

"Then why am I leaving? Why am I going thousands of miles away?"

"Because it's what you've always wanted, Molly."

"Maybe I've changed my mind. Maybe I should stay and go to college in state."

"We need to finish loading the car," I tell her.

We argue. Loudly, in the driveway. About what won't fit in the car. About what is necessary, what Molly will not be able to do without. She flounces into the house and returns a few minutes later with a duffel bag and a green-shaded lamp.

"Sweetie, I don't think you need the lamp," I point out.

"I want to bring it. I've always liked this lamp." She crams the duffel bag in the back, using it to cushion the lamp.

It has shone over her desk while she worked diligently at connect-the-dots, a report on Edward Lear, a tear-stained journal, a labored-over college essay, a love letter to Travis Spellman. The lamp has been a silent sentinel through the years. Remembering this, I quickly surrender. I don't want to argue anymore, especially not today.

Like making the quilt, driving her to college seemed like a good idea at the time. She could have flown, and shipped her things separately, but I couldn't stand the thought of leaving her at the curb at the airport like a houseguest who's overstayed her welcome.

A road trip just seemed so appealing, a final adventure for the two of us to share. A farewell tour. All through the summer I've been picturing us in the old Suburban, stuffed to the top with things Molly will need in the freshman dorm, singing along with the radio and reminiscing about old times. Now as I face the sullen rebellion in Molly's face, the idyllic picture dissipates.

The trip is still a good idea, though. A long drive with no one but each other for company will give us a chance to talk about matters we've been avoiding all summer long, possibly her entire adolescence. When she was little, we discussed the great matters of her life at bedtime, lying together in the dark, watching the play of moon shadows on the ceiling. In high school, she stayed up later than I did, and our conversations shrank to sleepy utterances. Nighttime was punctuated by the creak of a floorboard under a furtive foot, the rasp of a toothbrush washing away the smell of a sneaked beer. Some days, we barely spoke a half-dozen words.

I want these long, empty hours with her on the road. I need them with an intensity that I hide from Molly, because I don't want her to worry that I'm getting desperate. She's a worrier, my Molly. A pleaser. She wants everyone to be happy, and if she had some inkling of how I'm feeling right now, she'd try to do something about it. I don't want her to feel as if she's responsible for my happiness. Good lord, who would wish that on a child?

We finish packing. Everything is in order, every checklist completed, our iPods organized with music and podcasts, every contact duly entered in our mobile phones. Finally, the moment has arrived.

"Well," says Dan. "I guess that's it."

What's it? I wonder. What? But I smile and say, "Yep. Ready, kiddo?"

"In a minute," she says, stooping and patting her leg to call the dog.

I am unprepared for the wrench as she says goodbye

to Hoover. We adopted the sweet-faced Lab mix as a pup when Molly was four. They grew up together—littermates, we used to call them, laughing at their rough-and-tumble antics. Since then, she has shared every important moment with the dog—holidays, neighborhood walks and summer campouts, fights with friends, Saturday morning cartoons, endless tosses of slimy tennis balls.

Through the years, Hoover has endured wearing doll clothes and sunglasses, being pushed in a stroller, taken to school for show-and-tell, and sneaked under the covers on cold winter nights. These days, he has slowed down, and is now as benign and endearing as a well-loved velveteen toy. None of us dares to acknowledge what we all know—that he will be gone by the time Molly finishes college.

She hunkers down in front of him, cradling his muzzle between her hands in the way I've seen her do ten thousand times before. She burrows her face into his neck and whispers something. Hoover gives a soft groan of contentment, loving the attention. When she draws away, he tries to reel her back in with a lifted front paw—*Shake, boy.* Molly rises slowly, grasps the paw for a moment, then gently sets it down.

Next, she turns to Dan. I notice the stiff set of his shoulders and the way he checks and rechecks everything—tires, cell phone batteries, wiper fluid. I can see him checking Molly, too, but she doesn't recognize the pain in his probing looks. He hides behind a mask of bravado, reassuring to his daughter but transparent to me.

Their goodbye mirrors their history together through the years—loving, a little awkward. He's never been one to show his emotions, but he was the one who taught her to swim, to laugh, to belch on command, to throw a baseball overhand, to pump up a bicycle tire, to eat smoked oysters straight out of the can, to flatten pennies on railroad tracks.

Their farewell is perfunctory, almost casual. They both seem to possess a quiet understanding that their lives are meant to intersect and diverge. "Call me tonight," he says. "Call me whenever you want."

"Sure, Dad. Love you."

They hug. He kisses her on the crown of her head. His hand lingers on her arm; she doesn't meet his eyes. Sunlight glances off the car window as she gets in.

Dan comes around to the other side and kisses me, his lips warm and familiar. "Take care, Linda," he says in a husky voice, the same thing he always says to me, but today the words carry extra weight.

"Of course," I say, holding him for an extra beat. Then I whisper in his ear, "How will I get through this?"

He pulls back, giving me a quizzical look. "Because you will," he says simply. "You can do anything, Lindy."

I smile to acknowledge the kind words, but I'm not certain I trust them.

The rearview mirror frames a view of our boxy, painted house, where we've lived since before Molly was born. Not for the first time, it hits me that I'll come home to an empty nest. People say this stage of life is a golden time, filled with possibility. Someone—probably a woman with too many kids and pets—once said the true definition of freedom is when the last child leaves home and the dog dies. At last, you get your life back. Your time is your own. The trouble is—and

I can't bear to admit this, even to Dan—I never said I wanted it back.

As we pull out onto the street, he stands and watches us go, the dog leaning against his leg. My husband braces an arm on the front gate and lowers his head. When I get back from this journey, he and I will be alone again, the way we were eighteen years ago, before the explosion of love that was Molly, before late-night feedings and bouts of the croup, before scary movies and argued-over curfews, before pranks and laughter, tempests and tears.

With Molly gone, we'll have all this extra space in our lives. I'll have to look him in the eye and ask, "Are you still the same person I married?" Or maybe the real question is, *Am I?*

I picture us seated across the dinner table from each other, night after night. What will we talk about? Do we know everything about each other, or is there still more to discover? I can't recall the last time I asked him about his dreams and desires, or the last time he asked me something more than "Did you feed the dog this morning?"

I invested so much more time in Molly over the years. When there's a daughter keeping us preoccupied, it's easy to slip away from each other.

With all my heart, I hope it's equally easy to reach across the divide. I suppose I'll find out soon enough.

Two

~~~᭓᭓᭓~~~

I don't even bother offering to drive. Molly insists on driving everywhere, and has done so ever since she turned sixteen. At the moment this is a convenient arrangement. I can use the time to work on the quilt. I'm picturing the completed piece at the other end of the journey—warm and soft, a tangible reminder of Molly's past. Each bit of fabric is a puzzle piece of her childhood, tessellating with the others around it. All that remains is to finish quilting the layers together, adding more embellishments along the way.

Working by hand rather than machine is soothing, and the pattern is free-form within the wooden hoop. On the solid pieces of fabric, words and messages can be embedded like secrets in code: *Courage. You're beautiful. Walk it off. Freud was wrong.* I should declare the thing finished by now but, like a nesting magpie, I keep adding bright trinkets—a button from a favorite sweater, a blue ribbon from a piano recital, a vintage handkerchief and a paste earring that belonged to her grandmother. There's some old, faded fabric from Molly's kindergarten apron, green with little laughing monkey heads. And a bow from her prom corsage, worn with shining pride just a few months ago.

Though it's impossible to be objective, I know this thing I have created is beautiful, even with all its flaws. Even though it's not finished. This is a record of her days with me, from the moment I realized I was pregnant—I was working in the garden, wearing a yellow dotted halter top, which is now part of the quilt—to today. Yes, even today I grabbed Hoover's favorite bandanna to incorporate.

Like so many projects I've tackled over the years—like parenting itself—the quilt is ambitious and unwieldy. But maybe the hours of enforced idleness in the car will be just what I need to add the final flourishes.

As we drive along the main street of our town, Molly looks out at the flower baskets on the streetlamp poles, the little coffee stands and cafés, the bank and bike shop and bookstore, the fashion boutiques and galleries advertising fall sales, the congregational church with its painted white spire. There's the stationery shop, advertising back-to-school specials, and of course, Pins & Needles, my favorite place in town. The charming old building stands shoulder-to-shoulder between a bakery and a boutique, sharing a concrete keystone that marks the year it was built—1902. Arched windows in the upper stories, which house an optometrist and a chiropractor, are decked with wrought-iron window boxes filled with asters and mums. On the street level is the abundant display window, replete with fabrics in the delicious colors of autumn—pumpkin and amber, flame red, magenta, shadowy purple.

A small, almost apologetic-looking sign in the window says, "Business For Sale." Minerva, the shop owner, is retiring and she's been looking for a buyer since the previous Christmas. She's told all her customers that if it's not sold by the new year, she'll simply close its doors. This option is looking more and more likely. It's hard to imagine someone with the kind of passion and energy it takes—not to mention the capital—to run a small shop. Once the store is cleared to the bare walls, it will look like a blight on our town's main street, a missing tooth in the middle of a smile. On top of Molly going away, it's another blow.

Across the street is a trendy clothing boutique where Molly has spent many an hour—and many a dollar—agonizing over just the right look. As she was trying on jeans the other day, a debate ensued. Do girls on the East Coast wear skinny jeans or boot cut? Do they even wear hoodies? As if I would know these things. When she began worrying about what to wear, I realized that everything was getting very real for Molly. For a girl who has never lived anywhere else, this is a huge step. Now that we're on the road, she is facing the reality that college is an actual place, not just a display of glossy pictures in a catalog. I want to tell her not to be afraid, but I suspect the advice wouldn't be welcome.

Navigating the ungainly Suburban up the ramp to the interstate, Molly fiddles with the radio, but it's all talk so she switches it off. We've got our iPods if we're desperate for music.

From the grim look on Molly's face as she cranes her neck to check the rearview mirror, it's clear that she knows I was right about the lamp taking up too much space. I can't help thinking what I won't allow myself to say: I told you so.

Agitated, I put on my discount-store reading glasses—

the ones that perch on my nose and make me look like a schoolmarm. Another visible rite of passage. For me, the moment occurred a few years back, when I turned thirty-nine-and-a-half. I was in a gift shop, trying to read a sale tag, and suddenly my arm wasn't quite long enough to make out the price.

A sales clerk offered me a pair of reading glasses, and the fine print came into focus. The fact that the glasses had cute faux-Burberry frames offered scant comfort. At first, I was a bit embarrassed to put them on around Dan and Molly, but when you love needlework and crossword puzzles as much as I do, you swallow your pride.

I open the canvas quilt bag and the project spills across my lap. The oval hoop frames a section made of a calico maternity blouse I wore while carrying Molly. I stab the needle in, telling myself it'll be finished soon enough, one stitch after another. The needle flashes in and out like a little silver dart.

"Bad intersection up here," I say, glancing up when we reach the crossroads leading to the interstate. "Be sure you signal."

"He*llo*. I've only been through this intersection a zillion times. And did you know that at eighteen, a person's vision is performing at its peak?"

I adjust my glasses. "So is her smart mouth." My needle starts writing the words "be sweet," adding a curlicue at the end.

"I'm just saying, don't worry about my driving. I learned from the best."

This is true. Dan's an excellent driver, alert and confident, traits he passed along to our daughter. Most of her friends learned through Driver's Ed, but money was tight that year due to a layoff, and Dan did the honors. I used to wonder what they talked about during all those hours of practice, but when I asked, they both offered blank looks. "We didn't talk about anything."

What she means is, Dan has a way of communicating without talk. He can speak volumes with a glance, a chuckle or a shrug. The two of them are comfortable in their silence in the way Molly and I are comfortable nattering away at each other.

Sure enough, there's a small tangle of traffic at the intersection, but I bite my tongue. Literally, I press my teeth into my tongue. I will not speak up. The time is past for correcting my daughter, giving directives. These final days together should be special, sacred almost, the last slender thread of a bond that has endured for eighteen years and is about to be willfully severed.

Molly expertly accelerates up the on-ramp and merges smoothly with the flow of traffic. She keeps her eyes on the road, her profile delicate and clean-lined, startlingly adult.

It's a bright September morning, and the lingering heat of late summer shimmers, turning the asphalt into a river of mercury. With a flick of her little finger, Molly signals and moves into the swift current of the middle lane. She is a competent driver, skilled, even. She's competent and skilled at many things—water polo, trigonometry, getting rid of phone solicitors, being a good friend.

Her spirit, her self-assurance and independence, are the sort of wonderful qualities a mother wants in her daughter. My goal was always to raise a child capable of making judgments on her own. Teaching her has been a joyous process, while actually seeing her go off in her own direction is intensely bittersweet. Adulthood, I suppose, is the final exam to see which lessons she absorbed.

"What do you suppose your father's doing?" I ask, picturing Dan alone in the house. For the next several days, his diet will consist only of things that can be made from tortilla chips, cheese and cold cuts.

Molly shrugs. Her shiny dark curls spring with the motion. "He's probably breaking out the cigars."

I think of him standing on the driveway this morning, giving his daughter an awkward hug before stepping back, stiff-faced, his eyes shining. I wonder if she looked in the rearview mirror as we pulled away, if she saw her father bow his head, then lean down to pet the dog.

"Oh, come on," I chide her. "Is that what you really think?"

"I don't know. I figure he's been looking forward to this day for a long time. Dad's good with change."

Meaning I'm not. And although he might be good with this particular change, there's a part of him that has come unmoored. Dan loves Molly with both a consuming flame and a heart-pounding fear. Their complicated relationship has always been full of contradictions. Dan was in the delivery room when Molly was born on a cold February morning eighteen years ago, and the moment the baby appeared in all her pulsing, slippery, newborn glory, he wept, the tears soaking into the paper surgical mask they'd made him wear. The first time Molly was placed in his arms, he held the tiny bundle with the shocked immobility of abject terror. He hadn't smiled down into the red, wrinkled face, not the way I did, instantly a mother, with a mother's serene confidence and a sense of accomplishment so intense I was floating. He hadn't cooed and swayed to that universal internal lullaby all mothers begin to hear the moment the baby is laid in their arms. He had simply stood and looked as though someone had handed him a vial of nitroglycerin.

Yet last night, I awakened to find him crying. He was absolutely silent, but the bed quivered with his fight to keep from making a sound. I said nothing, but lay perfectly still, helplessly drifting. Have I lost the ability to comfort him? Maybe I just didn't want to intrude. We are each dealing with the departure of our only child in our own way. When you're married, you don't get to be let in, not to everything.

"Trust me," I assure Molly. "He's going to miss you like crazy."

"He never said so."

"He wouldn't. But that doesn't mean he won't be missing you every single second."

"I guess."

Too often, there's a disconnect between Dan and Molly, despite the undeniable fact that they love each other. I pause, frowning at a knot that has formed in my thread. "That's just the way he is," I tell Molly. This is my role—the go-between, translating for the two of them.

I tease the knot loose and go back to my stitching. The border abuts a trapezoid-shaped swatch of neutral-colored lawn, snipped from the dress she wore to the eighth-grade banquet, the first grown-up dance of her life. At age thirteen she was impossible, taking drama to new heights and sullenness to new depths. I used to try to turn our dirgelike family dinners into something a little more upbeat. "What's the highlight of your day?" I used to ask my husband and daughter. "What's the one thing that makes it worth getting up in the morning?"

Dan had been grinding pepper on his salad in that deliberate way of his. Barely looking up, he said, "When Molly smiles at me."

He startled both Molly and me with that remark. And our sullen, teenage daughter had smiled at him.

Now Molly's phone rings with a familiar tone—an Eddie Vedder song called "The Face of Love." It's Travis's ringtone.

A heartbreaking softness suffuses her face as she picks up. "Hi," she says, her voice as intimate as a lover's. "I'm driving." She listens for a moment, then ends with a "Yeah, me, too," and closes the phone.

More silence. The needle darts. The day slides by the car windows. Prairie towns between endless grasslands. We make a pit stop, eat some junk food, talk about nothing. Same as we always do.

DAY TWO

Odometer Reading 121,633

...it may have been some unconsciously
craved compensation for the drab
monotony of their days that caused the
women...to evolve quilt patterns
so intricate. Only a soul in desperate
need of nervous outlet could have
conceived and executed, for instance,
the "Full Blown Tulip"...

—Ruth E. Finley,
Old Patchwork Quilts and the Women Who Made Them

Three

"Remember this one?" I ask, angling part of the quilt into Molly's line of vision.

"I guess."

"I bet you don't remember it."

"Then why did you ask? You always do that, Mom."

"Do I? I never noticed."

"You're always quizzing me about stuff you think should be important to me."

"Really? Yikes." I brush my hand over the piece of purple cotton, covered by lace.

"So what about that one?" She is instantly suspicious. All summer long, little "do-you-remembers" and "last times" have sneaked in—the last time we drove to the lake at the county line to set off fireworks, the last time Dan and I attended one of her piano recitals, the last time she went for a haircut at the Twirl & Curl.

"It's from a dress your father bought you," I say, needle pushing in and out, running a line of stitches to spell out *Daddy's girl*.

"Dad bought me a dress? No way."

"He did, at the Mexican Marketplace. I can't believe you forgot."

"Mom. What was I, three or four years old?"

"Four, I think."

"I rest my case."

In my mind's eye, I can still see her turning in front of the hall mirror, showing off the absurd confection of purple cotton and cheap lace. "It swirls," Molly had shouted, spinning madly. "It *swirls!*" I was less charmed when she insisted on wearing it to church for the next nine weeks. The dress fell apart years ago, but there was enough fabric left to work into the quilt.

Memories flow past in a swift smear of color, like the warehouses and billboards lining the interstate. When I shut my eyes, I can picture so many moments, frozen in time. So many details, sharp as a captured image— the wisp of my newborn baby's hair, the sweet curve of her cheek as she nurses. I can still imagine the drape of her christening gown, which is wrapped in tissue now, stored in the bottom of the painted cedar chest in the guestroom. I can clearly see myself poking a spoonful of white cereal into a round little birdlike mouth. I see Molly spring forward on chubby legs off the side of the pool, into my outstretched arms.

All those firsts. The first day of kindergarten: Molly wore her hair in two tight pigtails, her plaid jumper ironed in crisp pleats, her backpack filled with waxy-smelling new crayons, sharpened pencils, lined paper, a lunch I'd spent forty-five minutes preparing.

"Do you remember your first day of school?" I ask her now, flourishing the part of the quilt made of the uniform blouse.

"Sure. My teacher was Miss Robinson, and I carried

a Mulan lunch box." Molly changes lanes and eases past a poky hybrid car. "You put a note in my lunch. I always liked it when you did that."

I don't recall the teacher or the lunch box, but I definitely remember the note, the first of many I would tuck into Molly's lunch over the years. I always tried to write a few words on a paper napkin with a little smiling cartoon mommy, with squiggles to represent my hair, and the message "I <3 U. Love, Mommy."

I tried to upgrade my wardrobe for the occasion, wearing slacks, Weejuns and coral lip gloss from a department store counter. I felt important, compelled by mission and duty, as Molly chattered gleefully in the back of my station wagon.

Stopping at the tree-shaded curb of the school, I pretended to be calm and cheerful as I kissed Molly's cheek, stroked her head and then smilingly waved goodbye. She met up with her friends Amber and Rani. The girls went inside together, giggling and skipping the whole way, into the redbrick institution that suddenly looked huge and forbidding to me.

There was a New Mothers' coffee in the library. At the meeting, we moms worked out party plans and carpool arrangements with the sober attention of battle commanders. I felt secretly intimidated—not by the working moms in their power suits and high heels. On some level I understood they were as scared and uncertain as I was, even with their advanced degrees and job titles.

No, I was overawed by the stay-at-home moms. They were the gold standard we all aspired to. They seemed so organized and poised, in khakis with earth-tone sweaters looped negligently over their shoulders, datebooks open in front of them, monogrammed pens poised to make notes. Independent yet obviously supported by the unseen infrastructure of husbands and homeowners' associations, they were eminently comfortable in their own skin.

To this day, I don't remember driving home after handing my child over to a new phase of life. All I remember is bursting into the house, sitting down at the breakfast counter with the view of the jungle gym Dan had built in the backyard, and shaking with a sense of emptiness I hadn't expected to feel. Even Hoover, huddled in confusion at my feet, couldn't cheer me up. But back then, hope had glimmered at the end of the day. Molly would come home, she'd eat pecan sandies and drink a glass of milk while chattering on about kindergarten, and all would be well.

Although years have passed since that bright August morning, I never quite mastered the put-together look or the air of confidence I observed in my peers. I didn't really fit in with the stay-at-homes, but I wasn't a career woman, either. A scattershot woman, you might call me, aiming myself in different directions, my only true calling that of loving my family.

I kept meaning to find something—a vocation, a passion, a marketable way to spend my time. But after Molly was born, the quest simply didn't seem to matter so much. Unconcerned with a career trajectory, I bounced around to a few different jobs, never quite finding the right fit. This didn't bother me, because without really planning it, I had lucked into a life I loved so much I never wanted it to change. The quilt shop became my second home. I loved the creative energy of the shop, the dry smell of the fabric, the crisp metallic bite of my super-sharp scissors on the cutting table. Working at Minerva's shop became more than a part-time job during the school year. It was a place of refuge from the empty hours of the school day.

Molly glances over; I see her watching my busy hands.

"What?" I ask.

"Did you know Athena is the goddess of quilting?"

"She's the Warrior Woman," I correct her. "It's one of the few things I remember from mythology."

"Most people don't know she's also the goddess of arts and crafts," Molly says, full of authority, the way she gets sometimes. "Domestic crafts require planning and strategy, too. That's how the logic goes, anyway."

"Athena was superwoman, then. Waging war and weaving baskets." I settle back with the quilt draped over my lap and try to focus on feeling like a goddess. My stitches meander into overlapping spirals. These will be a reminder of the cyclical nature of families, the comings and goings of generations. They say a child leaves home in phases. She is weaned: Molly weaned herself as soon as she learned to walk, preferring a binky she could carry around in her pocket. Then she starts school. Goes on her first sleepover. To sleep-away camp. A field trip to the state capitol. She learns to drive, and each time she heads out the door, it takes her out of reach, on her own. This is simply the next step in the process. She'll be fine. I'll be fine.

I swear.

"I spotted an *A*," Molly says abruptly, bringing me back to the present. "The Aladdin Motel. And there's a *B*—Uncle Porky's Burger Barn…"

The hunt is on—an old alphabet game we used to play on long car trips. We quickly find our way through to the letter *J,* calling out names of towns and cafés, cribbed from highway signs, billboards and truck stops. The town of Jasper keeps the game moving. The *Q* is found on a hand-lettered roadside "Bar-B-Q," and we are grateful for colloquial spelling habits. We never get stuck on *X,* thanks to the freeway exit signs, and *Z* is found on a radio station billboard, KIZZ: Downhome Country for Uptown Folks.

In a Big Boy restaurant in Franklin, a young mother is trying to work the newspaper Sudoku puzzle while her toddler, strapped into a little wooden high chair, makes monkeyshines to get her attention. He leans as far sideways as the high chair permits, makes a sound like a cat, bangs his fork on the table, crams dry Cheerios into his mouth and uses a chicken nugget to smear ketchup on his tray like a baby Jackson Pollock. The young mother tucks her hair behind her ear and fills in another blank space on the puzzle.

I want to rush across the dining room and shake the woman. Can't you see he needs you to look at him? Play with him, will you, already? It'll be over before you know it.

It's easy to recognize a little of myself in the weary, distracted young mother. I used to be like her—preoccupied with matters of no importance, never seeing the secretive, invisible passage of time slip by until it was gone. Yet if someone had deigned to point this out, I would have been baffled, maybe even indignant. Disregard my child? What do you take me for?

However, when you're with a toddler who takes forty-five minutes to eat a chicken nugget, the moments drag. Or when your baby has the croup at 3:00 a.m. and you're sitting in the bathroom with the steam on full blast, crying right along with her because you're both so tired and miserable—those nights seem to have no end.

From my perspective at the other end of childhood, I want to tell the young mother what I know now—that when a child is little, the days roll by at a leaden pace, blurring together. You're like a cartoon character, blithely oblivious while crossing a precarious wooden bridge, never knowing it's on fire behind you, burning away as you go. Sure, everybody says to enjoy your kids while they're little, because they'll be grown before you know it, but nobody ever really believes it. The woman at the next table simply wouldn't see the bridge, see time eating up the moments like a fire-breathing dragon.

Fortunately for everyone involved, even I'm not crazy enough to intrude. For all I know, she's got a load of worries on her mind, or maybe she just needs ten minutes to dream her own dreams. Maybe she craves the neat, precise order of a Sudoku puzzle as a reminder that everything has a solution. By the time she finishes her puzzle, the kid has given up on her and finished his Cheerios and nugget. She wipes his face and hands, scoops him up and plants a perfunctory kiss on his head as she goes to the register.

Molly has missed the exchange entirely. She is absorbed in paging through the college's glossy catalog. The booklet depicts an idyllic world where the grass is preternaturally green and weedless, buildings stand the test of time and students are eternally young, sitting around in earnest groups or laughing together over lattes. Professors look appropriately smart, many of them cultivating a kind of bohemian quirkiness that, in our hometown, would probably cause them to fall under suspicion.

"See anything you like?" I ask as she pauses on a page of course descriptions.

"Everything," she states, her eyes dancing. "There's a whole course called 'Special Topics in Women's Suffrage Music.' And 'Transgender Native American Art.' 'The Progressive Pottery Experience: Ideas in Transition.'" She struggles to keep a straight face. "I want it all."

We have a laugh, and I can feel her excitement. The catalog is a treasure trove of possibilities, new things for her to learn, ways to think, ideas about life, maybe even a way to change the world.

Though I'm thrilled for her, I feel a silly twinge of envy. There are matters Dan and I can't begin to teach her, I remind myself. That's what college is for.

"I have no clue how I'm going to pick," she says, her hand smoothing the pages.

"I wouldn't know where to begin." The admission masks an old ambivalence. I had always meant to finish college and even had a plan. For many people, this didn't seem particularly bold, but in my family, it was a big step. Neither of my parents had gone to college; their own parents were immigrants and higher education was simply out of reach for them. My folks regarded college as an unnecessary frill, an expensive four-year procrastination before you get to the real part of life.

My dad worked as a shift supervisor at the tile plant. My mom stayed home with us and ironed. Really, she did. She took in ironing. We saw nothing unusual about this. There was never any shame, no judgment. It was who we were, and we were perfectly happy together.

The house often smelled of the dry warmth of a heated iron and spray starch. There was a little rate sheet posted behind the kitchen door. People would leave their stuff in a basket by the milk box on the back stoop in the morning; Mom would iron it and the next day, my big brother Jonas would deliver the items—crisply pressed dress shirts and knife-pleated slacks for the plant executives, party dresses and St. Cecilia's uniform blouses for their wives and kids.

I never really thought about what went through my mom's mind as she stood at the ironing board, perfecting the details of other people's clothing while Dire Straits played on the radio. Now I wonder if she was hot. Uncomfortable. Resigned. Or maybe she liked ironing and the work made her happy.

I wish I'd asked her. I wish she was still around, so I could ask her now.

Instead, eager for my independence, I planned my future. My dreams were nurtured by hours and hours in the library, reading books about women who created amazing lives for themselves, studying music and painting, science and business. I swore one day when I was a mother, I would instill these dreams in my children. I would be the mother I wanted my mother to be. And so I made a plan.

After high school, I would spend the summer working to save up money for tuition. Both my parents shook their heads, unable to fathom the idea of putting off work and life and independence for another four years, at the end of which there would be a massive debt and no guarantee of success. Besides, the closest university was nearly two hours away.

It was a powerful dream—maybe *too* powerful, because to someone raised the way I was, it seemed more like a fantasy. Particularly when I tallied up the cost of living without income for four years. Particularly when reality came crashing down on me, first semester. For monetary reasons, I had to live at home and quickly found the commute in my second-hand Gremlin to be almost unbearable. Later, I shared an apartment near campus with some friends, returning home each weekend with a sack of laundry. Worse, my classes were boring, keeping my grades decent was a struggle and dealing with a couple of bad professors nearly broke me.

Then Dan came along, Dan Davis with his incredible eyes, strong craftsman's hands, his sturdy work ethic and air of assuredness. In his arms, I realized the true meaning of happiness. My dreams of some nebulous *someday* stopped making sense in the face of such overwhelming happiness.

I once read in a book somewhere that the way you spend your day is the way you spend your life. Did I want a life of days filled with rushing back and forth on a commute, juggling coursework and having barely enough time for Dan? Or a life nurturing the love I'd found with him?

A no-brainer. We got married, Dan worked harder than ever so we could buy a house, and I got a job working retail. Don't ask me where. There are too many places to count. I put off returning to college; the plan kept being pushed back by the unending forward march of bills, and the sheer bliss of spending my time loving Dan, making a home, creating our life together.

After Dan and I married, I didn't exactly drop out of school, I just stopped going. There were a hundred rationalizations for this. Tuition was costly, and we wanted to save up for a house. The commute to campus took too much time and gas money. It seemed self-indulgent to spend our hard-earned money on classes like "Special Topics in Esoteric Cubism."

And then one day, after we'd been married a few years, the idea of getting a degree was taken off the table. We did use contraception, I swear we did, but mother nature and youthful zeal overrode the precautions. Along came Molly, the ultimate—and only truly valid—excuse for interrupting my education.

I always meant to go back. Early on, I told my friends and family I planned to finish my degree once Molly was in grade school. Of course, by then I knew what all mothers learn when their kids go to school. Those hours are spoken for, too. They're filled with everything else you put off when your child is young and at home, with that part-time job to give the bank account a much-needed boost. With Brownie projects and volunteer service. With taking care of that little female problem that's had you so worried for so long. With adding on an extra bathroom to the house—she's going to need that once she hits her teens, after all. Throwing in college-level courses simply seems impossible.

Nobody was surprised when I dropped the idea. My parents were simple, honest people who expected their kids to live a good life. I hope I didn't disappoint them.

My departure from the nest was not the dramatic, long-distance leap Molly is taking. My first home with Dan was only eight miles from my parents.

I wonder if they dreamed of a bigger life for me, if they wanted me to go further, do more. Probably not, I think, watching my needle flash through the fabric. I suspect they were perfectly content for their daughter to live close by.

My friend Erin wears her hard-earned law degree like a badge of pride. I used to envy her—the big career, the big house, the big car, the big *life*. It all came at a price, though. There was a divorce; though she's remarried now and loving her empty nest, there were hard years when she'd come over and cry from the sheer exhaustion of juggling everything. I came to understand that there is no such thing as a perfect life, just a constant shifting, like the wind on the lake. You adjust your sails to catch the wind, not the other way around.

I often wonder, if I'd stuck with my degree program, would I have found my passion? That first semester, I floundered, unable make up my mind. I had friends who were so clear-eyed, wanting to be a kindergarten teacher. Or a CPA. Or a landscape designer. Not me. I never quite found the right fit. Skipping college, setting aside the thought of a professional career, turned out well for me. Life is good enough. We wanted more kids, but because of that female problem, which turned out to be not so little, it was not to be.

As each mile brings Molly and me closer to goodbye, I realize how little I know about this rarefied world she is about to enter. I wonder if it will drive a wedge between us, turn her into a stranger to me, a sophisticated stranger with a big vocabulary and bigger dreams. There won't be any three o'clock bell to start my world turning again. No swing to push in the backyard, no cookies to bake.

What there *will* be is time. So much of it. All the time in the world to figure out what to do with my life, now that I can do anything I want. This should not feel so fraught with uncertainty. Parents have done this since time immemorial. Fretting about it is silly.

I'm not fretting, that's the thing. I'm *afraid*.

We argue about where to spend the night. Should we stop on the west side of Omaha, or try to make it to the east side by nightfall, thus avoiding tomorrow's morning rush of inbound traffic?

"I'd just as soon stop now," I declare, checking the dashboard clock. "We're making good enough time."

Molly wants to keep driving. She has an adolescent's inexhaustible supply of late-night energy combined with an eagerness to get there. "Forget it," she says. "I'm going past the city for sure. No need to cut the day short."

"Come on, Moll—"

"I'm driving, Mom. You said I could. That means I get to pick where we stop. Find a stopping place in the Triple-A guide and pick a motel."

For a moment, I feel disoriented. Who is this person in the driver's seat, telling me what to do? A small laugh erupts from me.

"What's funny?" asks Molly.

"You sound like your mother."

"And that surprises you?"

"Yes. A little. I guess." Bemused, I take out the Triple-A guide. It is something I recall from my own childhood. We used to go on grim road trips each summer, with me and my three siblings fighting in the backseat, our dad hunched doggedly over the steering wheel and our mom flipping pages in the triptych while reciting facts and figures from the guidebook.

"Grady, Nebraska. Population 4,500," I tell Molly

now. "There are four possible motels, two with two-diamond ratings and two with three."

"Go for the three."

Finally, something we agree on.

Four

◦◦◦

We make our way to the Star Lite Motor Court and Coffee Shop. I'm not sure what the three diamonds in the auto guide signify. There's a pool, but a suspicious-looking green tinge stains the tiles, so Molly and I decide against taking a swim. The coffee shop looks promising; it's open late, and features a grill hissing with frying burgers, and a revolving glass case displaying pies of mythic proportions.

We let ourselves into our room, wondering what three-diamond amenities we'll find there. The carpet smells faintly of mildew and ancient cigarettes, so we open a window to let in fresh air. Ugh, I think with a twinge of disappointment. Given the nature of this journey, I'd hoped for better accommodations. I'd pictured the two of us sharing a charming suite in a B&B, or working out in the fitness room of a modern hotel. As usual, there's a gap between expectation and reality.

Molly flings herself on one of the beds, bouncing happily. "I love road trips," she crows. "I love staying in motels."

And with that, the disappointment is gone, lifted

away by the grin on her face. I am forced to notice this small but significant shift. Molly's mood has the power to determine my own. This was never apparent when she was at home, but once she's gone, where will the happiness come from? I need to make sure I remember how to find it.

"What's this?" She indicates the metal Magic Fingers box on the nightstand.

"You've never heard of Magic Fingers?"

"What?"

"Move over." I dig some quarters out of my jeans pocket, drop them in the slot and lie down next to Molly. "Your education's not complete until you've experienced Magic Fingers."

Nothing happens. "I guess it's broken," I say. "The thing is probably thirty years old if it's a day."

"Just because it's old doesn't mean it's broken." Determined, Molly reaches across me and gives the box a shake. Still nothing. She messes with the cord. And then: "Whoa. Did you feel that?"

I lie very still. There is a mechanical hum, then a faint vibration buzzes upward, penetrating through me and increasing in strength. Molly relaxes next to me, supine.

"Okay," she says. "This is weird."

"It'll stop in a few minutes."

"Weird in a good way," she amends.

"I can't believe you never tried this before." Through the years, we've stayed in dozens of motels together but this is the first time we've found Magic Fingers. "I guess they're a thing of the past," I tell her.

"Good thing we decided to stop here, huh?" She sighs with contentment.

A kinder way of saying "I told you so." We lie side by side, the bed humming beneath us for long minutes. When the vibrations stop, I am startled to feel more relaxed, the rigors of the long driving day eased from my muscles.

"What are you thinking about?" Molly asks.

The question catches me off guard. "You, I suppose. I've always liked doing new things with you, even little things."

"Like Magic Fingers."

"Exactly. Everything was new with you. That's what was so much fun about raising a child. I'd be in the middle of doing something—whipping egg whites into meringue or riding my bike with no hands or graphing a parabola—and you'd think I was amazing. A magician or something."

"You *were* amazing," Molly says quietly, turning on her side and tucking her hand under her cheek.

I must be hearing things. I consider asking her to say that again, but I doubt she will repeat it. "Who will I amaze now that you're leaving?"

Molly laughs. "Excuse me?"

"I'm losing my audience."

"You should have had more kids," she observes.

I hesitate, caught off-guard by her words. Yet not off-guard at all. It's an opening to a difficult conversation. I know this before either of us speaks again.

"Mom?"

I turn to her. "I couldn't have any more babies after…"

Her eyes widen. "After you had me?"

I gaze into her face, seeing maturity and wisdom there, trusting the compassion in her expression. When I first conceived of this cross-country adventure, I knew things would come up between us, difficult matters. And I knew this matter was the most difficult of all. Through the years, I had protected Molly from the most painful episode of my life. It wasn't fair to reveal a wound she didn't cause and couldn't heal. What would be the point of that?

Things are different now. She's a young woman. Another person's pain won't confuse or destroy her. Isn't that, after all, the essence of maturity?

Deep breath, I tell myself, gazing into her doe-soft eyes. "I had a baby boy named Bruce." Even after so much time has passed, I still feel the piercing loss. I was bleeding, drugged half out of my mind, but I can feel him even now, his slight, unmoving weight in my arms. Weeks premature, he was as pale and beautiful and silent as a fallen angel, having never drawn breath in this world.

Molly's eyes instantly fill with tears. "Mom, really? What happened? When?"

Pulling in a deep breath, I explain in a shaky voice. "You were just two years old at the time. He came too early, and I was bleeding. There was a tear in my uterus."

"Oh, Mom. Why didn't you ever tell me?"

I feel a tear slide over the bridge of my nose. Such an old, old wound, made fresh again by indelible memories. When it happened, it changed me in ways I am still discovering, even now. That kind of loss has the power to stop the world. My baby boy's tiny, other-worldly face will always haunt me. He looked so very much like my other newborn, Molly. "It was just so sad, honey."

She reaches for me and we're quiet together for a long time, the moments slipping by, measured by our breathing.

"I don't know what to say," she whispers.

"You don't have to say anything." There are some things that simply can't be made better, not by talking or weeping or praying or pretending they didn't happen. Yet her reaction is exactly as I'd hoped it would be—compassionate without being pitying or obsessive.

"I wish…" Her voice trails off, but I understand exactly what she's saying.

"So do I."

More quiet moments. We turn on the Magic Fingers again to shake us out of the somber mood. "You're all the kid I need," I tell her. She's heard that from me before. Now she understands the hidden meaning behind the words.

"Well, I hope you know, I'm the one losing my audience," Molly insists. "When I'm away at college, who will *I* perform for?"

This surprises me. I know there are things she worries about, being so far from home in a strange world where no one knows her. Still, I thought her eagerness to go out and find her life had banished all her fears. Now I realize she's well aware of what she's leaving behind. And it's not just Travis Spellman. From her first smile to her last day of high school, and all the lost teeth, soccer trophies, piano recitals and Brownie badges in between, I've been there for her, cheering her on.

"I'll still be your number-one fan," I assure her.

"Sure, but it won't be the same." Then she smiles and bounces up off the bed.

I sit up and link my arms around my drawn-up knees. "You seem pretty okay with that."

"It's hard work, being your daughter."

"You're kidding, right?"

Now it's her turn to hesitate. "Right. Let's go check out the game room. I think I saw a ping-pong table."

Late at night, long after our dinner of iceberg lettuce salads and oyster crackers, Molly steals away to sit on the stoop in front of the motel room and call Travis on her cell phone. Although college beckons like a mysterious garden of rare delights, she has formed a deep bond with this boy, with his funny grin and Adam's apple, his appealing combination of cluelessness and charm.

A hometown boy at heart, he is causing her to have second thoughts about going to school so far away. For that, I could throttle him. At the same time, I feel an unexpected beat of empathy. I, too, would love to keep her close.

On their final night at home, Molly and Travis went out with a group of their friends, some college-bound, others already immersed in jobs and responsibilities. They stayed out late, visiting all the places they knew they'd miss after dispersing like seeds to the wind. There were stops at the rusty-screened drive-in movie theater, the empty stadium, the all-night diner, the parking lot at the spillway below the lake. I don't doubt there were other stops as well, which were not revealed to me.

I can't be certain, but I suspect that Molly surrendered her virginity at the spillway at some point during the summer, in the secret place known to revved-up teenagers everywhere, tucked into the shadows of the sloping man-made bank. She didn't tell me so, but there have been subtle signs. I've watched her and Travis grow closer, their bond tightened by a private and impenetrable intimacy that is both invisible and obvious.

Sexually active. It's a clinical-sounding term. It's nothing a mother wants to think about with regard to her own child, but at some point, you have to take the blinders off. Or not, I suppose, thinking of Dan. Whenever I try to bring the subject up with him, he says, "They're good kids. They won't do anything stupid."

Pointing out that good kids who are not stupid get in trouble all the time doesn't seem to advance the conversation. I have given up on discussing it with Dan. Now and then, I try to broach the topic with Molly.

"I'm *fine.* Don't worry," she said when I got up the nerve to ask her.

It doesn't matter what century we're in. Parents and children were not meant to talk together in detail about sex. Nor should we pretend to be all-knowing experts on love, even if we are. I understand exactly what love feels like in a young girl's heart because I was that girl once, long ago. That's why the Travis situation worries me, because I understand. It has a power like the pull of the moon on the tides, overwhelming and inevitable. There is no antidote for the passion and certainty a girl feels for the boy she loves, and no end to the fantasies she spins about their future together.

I can explain convincingly that the emotions engulfing her and Travis are not likely to last. I can tell her they'll both grow and change, heading off in different directions. But then I would have to talk about my own choices, my own regrets, the many times I spent wondering about the life I would have had if I'd taken a different path.

For a brief moment, I consider telling Molly about Preston Warner, my first and, as far as I was concerned at the time, my only, forever and ever. Senior prom was the kind of magic-filled night every girl dreams about and, in my case, the dream came true. I wore something blue and silky; Preston was slicked-down, tux-clad and nervous. Not only did we consummate our relationship that night, we pledged to stay true forever, even though Preston was going far away to college.

That night, I surrendered not just my virginity but all my hopes and dreams, handing them over to a boy who—though I didn't realize it at the time—had no idea what to do with them. So he did what guys his age generally do. Three months into his first semester at a trendy private school a day's drive away, he started dating other people. When I found out, I wanted to die. I walked around like a zombie, every bit of happiness having bled from my broken heart.

I still remember the drama of our final confrontation—he came in person to tell me it was over. To this day, I can still feel the horror of facing a future without him. I raged, I wept until I was weak and drained, I swore I could not go on. It caused a pain I couldn't share with anyone. My mother brought me a pint of Cherry Garcia, but I promised her I'd never eat again. She said with utter confidence that I'd get over him. Then she went downstairs and ironed clothes, filling the house with the scent of lavender water. I ate the Cherry Garcia. Watched *Seinfeld* reruns and learned to laugh again. Somehow, one day dragged into the next…and eventually I realized that I didn't miss him.

Hearing a heartbroken sniffle and the murmur of Molly's voice drifting through the window screen of the motel, I decide not to tell her any of that. She and Travis will grow apart because that's the way it works. She will have to find this out for herself. The end of love has to be experienced firsthand, not explained by your mother.

I turn on the radio to give her more privacy. Even so, I can guess what they're saying. There are whispered promises of love-you-forever and we'll-stay-together, and no one knows as well as I do that they mean it—every word. Preston and I certainly meant it, all those years ago. We were going to travel the world and live a charmed life together.

These days, Preston owns the hardware store in town and has a cushy paunch around his middle, a receding hairline and four kids. When I drop in to buy upholstery tacks or a can of paint, I always think about that last summer after high school, the passionate hours in the backseat of his car, the vows we made to each other. I can look past his bifocals and graying temples, and still see a boy who was as handsome and romantic as a fairy-tale prince. As Preston rings up my purchases and we make small talk, I wonder if he thinks about the way we were, too, if he remembers. Does he look at me in my pull-on slacks and gardening clogs and re-call the girl I used to be?

Running into him is, weirdly enough, not awkward in the least. He's someone who came into my life for a brief time, and then stayed in the past. I feel no wistful-ness for him, no regrets. I do envy him those four kids, though. When one goes away, he still has the others to keep him company.

Or maybe saying goodbye four times is harder than saying it once.

When Molly comes back into the room, her eyes red and her chin trembling, I offer a smile, but I don't say anything. This is a volatile issue, and I don't want to push it. Travis is a boy of good looks and small ambition, one who regards his union job at the plant as a ticket to independence as well as an opportunity to work on his Camaro at his uncle's garage on the weekends.

Travis has a peculiar sweetness about him, a quality Molly finds irresistible. She loves him, and her love is as real as her grade point average. She trusts that love to endure, no matter what.

Molly expects so much of herself and wants so much from the world. At the moment, she is tender and lonely, missing him, her heart sore as it can only be for one's first love.

I have to wonder: Did I teach my daughter to love this hard and feel this deeply? Was I wrong to do so? On the other hand, maybe I shielded her too much from pain, and she never learned to deal with it. As more men loom in the future, a whole campus full of them, it makes me wonder if I've done enough to equip her to deal with love and heartache. My own mother never seemed comfortable discussing matters of the heart with me. That's what I used to think, anyway. Now I wonder if she simply knew I'd discover it all for myself.

"Hungry?" I ask Molly, after she's lain on the bed, staring at the ceiling for a while. "The coffee shop's still open."

"No," she says softly. "You?"

"No." This is a lie. The dinner salad was a disappointment. But I don't need to eat. I don't need that big, messy cheeseburger I've been fantasizing about since spotting it on the coffee-shop menu. I don't need the coconut cream pie I noticed in the revolving refrigerated case. Something my mother never told me—when you hit forty, not only does your vision start to go. Your

body changes. Nowadays if I eat things like cheeseburgers and cream pie, the calories magically trans-
form themselves into saddlebags on my hips. I don't
feel any different than I did ten years ago, but boy, do
my jeans fit differently.

My mind drifts. Maybe when I get home, I'll join
the local gym, start a regular fitness routine. Running
around with Molly has kept me reasonably fit all these
years. Thanks to her, I've hiked miles with Brownie
and Girl Scout troops, led field-trip expeditions to mu-
seums or nature preserves, ridden for hours on family
bike trips. I suppose I could still hike and bike without
Molly around, but why would I? Motivating myself is
not going to be as easy as it used to be.

A quiet sniff brings me back to the present. I look
over at Molly to see that she is still staring at the ceiling. Tears track sideways down her temples.

I don't say anything, because I know everything will
come out sounding like empty platitudes. Instead, I
find another quarter, drop it in the slot and start up the
Magic Fingers once again.

DAY THREE

Odometer Reading 122,271

It is not wise to be didactic about
the nomenclature of quilt patterns.

—Florence Peto, *American Quilts and Coverlets*

...it is unwise to be didactic
because the facts are very elusive.
I now realize that not every
pattern has a name, that there is
no correct name for any design.

—Barbara Brackman, *Encyclopedia of Pieced Quilt Patterns*

Five

The roadside is littered with last night's carnage, a raccoon here, a possum there, occasionally someone's household pet reduced to an unrecognizable smear. Neither Molly nor I say a word. I hate the idea of creatures suffering while people sleep, oblivious.

This morning's breakfast—the Bright Eyes Surprise, which I'd ordered solely because I liked the name—churns in my stomach. From the driver's seat, Molly reaches over and turns up the radio. She glides into the passing lane to get around a semi with a tweeting cartoon robin on the side.

I refold the map to encompass the day's journey. We plan to make tracks today, covering at least four hundred miles. The few towns along the way are no more than pinpricks with quirky names, like Nickel Box and Mulehorn and Futch's Corner. Mostly, it appears we'll be crossing uninhabited terrain, much of it protected by the Department of Natural Resources, shaded in green.

"Do we have plenty of gas?" I ask.

"Three quarters of a tank. Same amount we had the last time you asked, ten minutes ago."

The biggest of the pinpricks, Futch's Corner, lies at the halfway point. We'll get gas there.

"I can't decide whether to quilt or read," I tell Molly.

"Why don't you listen to music and look at the scenery?"

"I already did that."

She laughs a little, shakes her head. "You always have to be busy doing something."

"Nothing wrong with that."

"Except you might miss something. Chill, Mom."

"All right. I'll look out the window." The most interesting thing I spot is a red-winged blackbird in a thicket of cattails.

If I'm being honest with myself, there's a reason for staying busy. Being preoccupied with other things means I don't have to be preoccupied with my own baggage. I'm sick of myself, of my indecisiveness and mental whining. My daughter's leaving the nest, as all daughters eventually do, and my job is to let her go and move on with my life. It should be a simple matter to set a goal for myself, one that doesn't involve Molly, even indirectly. Maybe I don't have a college degree, but I'm not stupid.

I know I have to figure out who I am again, now that I'm not Molly's mom. Well-meaning friends tell me to go back to being the person I was before Molly. Am I that twentysomething woman who used to sleep late and smoke Virginia Slims and never felt the need to look at a clock?

That's not me anymore. It can never be me again. I don't want to go back to being that person who lived each day so thoughtlessly, spending the moments like nickels in a slot machine, as though she had an unending supply of time and could squander it any way she pleased.

Other friends remind me that my marriage moves to the front burner now. Dan and I will have to figure out how to be a childless couple again. What were we before we became Molly's parents? What did we used to talk about, dream about, laugh and cry about? A better stereo system, a bigger house, an extra week's vacation from work? How could those things matter now?

It was Molly who showed us the things that matter most. They're the moments that sneak up on you unexpectedly, when you're barely paying attention. You're going out to see if the mail has come, and you discover that your child has learned to ride a two-wheeler and is as thrilled about it as if she's learned to fly. Or you uncrate the new refrigerator you scrimped and saved for, and she shows you that the best thing about the new appliance is the empty box.

Before Molly, what was it that mattered to Dan and me? When we were first married, he'd grab me the second he woke up each morning and say, "You're here!" as if I were the answer to his dreams. I can't remember when he stopped doing that. Granted, it would seem tedious and downright weird if he kept it up indefinitely, but there was a clear appeal in knowing exactly where I stood with him.

Inside the oval hoop is a swatch of my mother's favorite cotton blouse, the one with tiny umbrellas printed all over it. For some reason, I'm inspired to stitch a message: "Do the thing you fear."

Not the thing your mother fears. The thing *you* fear. I hope Molly will understand the difference.

Something extraordinary flashes past my line of sight. "Molly, slow down," I say. "Look over there."

It's a turnoff marked Leaning Tower of Pisa, Iowa.

"Let's check it out," I say.

Molly looks dubious. Her gaze flicks to the dashboard clock. I feel a twinge of annoyance at her eagerness to reach our ultimate destination. Can't she slow down, just a little?

"You're the one who wanted me to watch the scenery and chill," I remind her. "We're making good time," I point out.

"All right. Let's do it."

We go take a look at the leaning tower, and it is exactly that. A water tower that has listed to one side. In the next big wind it could topple, explains a placard in the field beside it. We take pictures to email to Dan. We've been calling him to check in each day. The conversation is predictable—we're to keep the tank full and check the oil and tire pressure at least once a day. We're to take care of ourselves.

"See?" I try not to act too smug as we return to the car. "You learn something new every day."

Molly decides to give me a turn at the wheel. She wants to phone Travis and she's not allowed to do it while she's driving.

"No freakin' signal," she says, scowling at the screen of her cell phone. "That's lame."

"You'll just have to watch the scenery and chill."

She rummages in her bag and pulls out the folder of information sent to her by the college. "Kayla Jackson from Philadelphia," she says, referring to her roommate. "I wonder what she'll be like."

"Lucky," I say. "She was matched up with you, wasn't she?"

"Her mother's probably saying the same thing. Oh, man, what if we can't stand each other?"

"You said she sounded great in her email."

"Sex predators sound great in email, Mom."

My head whips in her direction. "How do you know that?"

"Everybody knows that. Geez, don't get your panties in a twist. I don't talk to perverts on email. I don't talk to perverts at all."

"Suddenly I feel as if we haven't discussed this topic enough."

"What, perverts? I'll talk about perverts anytime you want, Mom."

"All joking aside, honey—"

"Mom. We went through this a long time ago, the stuff about respecting myself and using my head. That women's self-defense class went on for twelve weeks and yes, I read *The Gift of Fear*. I'm as safe as it's possible to be."

"You have all the answers, don't you, Missy?"

"I'll have even more once I'm in college."

We stop for lunch and a fill-up in Futch's Corner, a town with four stoplights, a defunct train depot and a bus station. A row of storage silos covered in graffiti lines the main road. The lone café has a pictorial menu, which makes it easy to avoid the chopped salad, which in these parts appears to be coleslaw.

In the booth next to us, an elderly couple sits across from each other, slowly and methodically eating their cups of beef barley soup with soda crackers on the side. They manage to get through the entire meal without uttering a single word. The wife puts cream in both cups of coffee. When they get up after finishing their meal, the husband keeps one hand on the small of the wife's back.

"Old people are so cute, aren't they?" Molly remarks.

Old people are a nightmare. It's too easy for me to see myself and Dan in a couple like that, silent and companionable, with nothing to say to each other. I want so much more for us, laughter and interesting conversation, the richness of shared moments. I used to think I knew what my life would look like after Molly, but now I'm not so sure.

Once she's away at school, Dan and I are going to have to face each other once again with nothing between us, no sports matches to attend, no carpools to drive, no curfews to enforce, no school calendar to dictate our lives. To me, it looks like a void, a yawning breach. Empty space. It's supposed to be a good thing, but I've never been the sort to tolerate empty space. Maybe that's why I like quilting. Each piece fits perfectly against the others to fill the grid completely.

On the highway heading east again, we come upon a breakdown pulled off to the side of the road. I slow down but don't stop. The hood of the car is raised and there's a woman standing beside it. She has a baby on her hip and there's no one else in sight. I go even slower, checking the rearview mirror, hoping to see that she's on a cell phone, getting help.

She isn't. She's jiggling the baby and taking a diaper bag out of the car.

Someone else will come along and help her, I figure. But this is a lonely stretch of highway and there's no one in sight in either direction.

"What are you doing?" Molly asks when I stop and make a U-turn.

"Making sure that woman back there is okay. Maybe she needs my cell phone."

"Mom. Aren't you the one with all the rules about not picking up strangers?"

"I didn't say anything about picking her up. But I'm not going to leave her stranded." I pass the breakdown, pull another U-turn and park on the shoulder in front of the woman's car, a dusty Chevy Vega with Nevada plates.

"Thanks for stopping," she says. "I blew a radiator hose." She doesn't appear to be much older than Molly. She's wearing a man's ribbed tank top under an open shirt, shorts and flip-flops. Her eyes are puffy and the baby is fussing.

"Have you called for help?"

"I don't have a phone and the last town's forty miles back."

"Let's try my cell phone," I offer, getting out of the car and handing it to her.

The baby glowers at me. It's a boy, maybe fourteen months, and he smells like ripe fruit. His nose is running green sludge, and he has a rattling cough. As his mother dials the phone, he pokes a grubby finger at the buttons.

"Nothing," she says after a moment. "No signal. Thanks anyway." She hands back the phone. I resist the urge to clean it off on my shirttail.

The baby barks out a cough. The woman looks around. A breeze shimmers through the silver maples and a few dry leaves fall off, scattering. There is a folded umbrella stroller and a car seat in the back of the car.

The silence stretches out. I take a deep breath, violating my own better judgment as I say, "We'll give you a ride."

"You don't have to do that." Despite her words, the woman looks as if she might melt with relief.

Molly gets out of the car, map in hand. The cranky baby glowers at her.

"Really, you don't," the woman persists.

"It's fine," I assure her. "Where are you headed?"

"Honeymoon," she says. "It's my hometown. I'm moving back there, but this piece of crap car doesn't want to cooperate."

Molly finds the town on the map. It's about fifty miles to the north on a road marked with a faint gray line, well out of our way. The smart thing to do would be to drive on until I get a cell phone signal and then call in the location of the breakdown.

Maybe I'm not so smart. I keep thinking if Molly were stranded, I'd want a nice woman to stop. "Molly, can you give me a hand with the baby's car seat?" I ask.

My daughter's eyebrows lift, but she instantly complies.

I introduce myself and learn that the woman's name is Eileen. Her baby is Josten. "His grandparents have never seen him," she says. "I sure appreciate this." Wrinkling her nose, she adds, "He needs a change." She lays him on the backseat of her car. The creases of the seat are filled with bits of broken cookies and dry cereal. "Last one," she says, extracting a diaper from the bag.

The little one yowls as she peels off his romper and

diaper. "Cut it out," she snaps as he kicks at her. "Josten—oh, Josten. What a mess." She digs in the diaper bag. "Shoot. I'm out of baby wipes."

Molly looks on in horror for a moment, then grabs something from the quilt bag. "Here, use this."

It's a piece of an old Christmas tree skirt from Dan's and my first Christmas together. You can't really tell it was ever a tree skirt; it just looks like a green tablecloth.

"Are you sure?" Eileen asks.

"No problem," I tell her.

"Thanks."

Molly's expression is priceless as she watches Eileen dry the kid's tears and wipe his nose, then clean his bottom. This is a better justification for birth control than any lecture from me, although it means a sad end for the old tree skirt. Eileen puts on a clean diaper, but the romper is soaked through. The baby starts wailing again.

"I don't have a change of clothes for him." Eileen looks like she's about to lose it, too.

I glance at the quilt bag, hesitating only a moment. At the bottom is a pair of Oshkosh overalls in candy pink. "This will probably work. It was Molly's when she was about his size. See if it fits." I answer the question in her expression. "I brought along a bag of old fabric scraps to add to the quilt I've been working on."

"Then I can't take this."

"Sure, go ahead. I've got plenty. I have enough."

She threads him into the overalls. The baby cries as she straps him into his car seat, the sobs punctuated with liquid coughs. Eileen gives him a plastic bottle of Gerber apple juice, but he flings it away. Molly is actively trying not to cringe; I can tell.

"Hush," Eileen says. "Please. Sorry about him."

"You don't need to apologize. Is he running a fever?"

"A little, I think. I gave him some Tylenol drops right before you stopped." She loads in the diaper bag and her purse, then locks her car, and we all take off.

Eventually, the storm of crying subsides as the monotony of the ride lulls the baby. The stretch of road that looked so innocent on the map is narrow and curving, with a posted speed limit of forty. It's too late to change our minds now, though. We're committed.

We learn that Eileen and her boyfriend went to Vegas together to get work. "My mother didn't want me to leave, but there was nothing for me in Honeymoon, except maybe some crap job at a fast-food place. Vegas was our best bet, especially since I wanted to be a dancer. I *was* a dancer, until I got pregnant."

"Onstage, in Vegas?" Molly turns to her in interest.

Eileen nods her head. "I was in the chorus line of a show at the Monte Carlo."

"That's so cool," Molly says.

"It was. But…harder than you'd think, especially with a kid and a lousy boyfriend. My mother danced, too, but never professionally. She always wanted to work onstage and didn't ever have the chance."

"Then it's great that you got the opportunity," I tell her, trying to say something positive.

Eileen gives a brief, humorless laugh. "I doubt my mother would think so. She was scared I might succeed at something she never got to do."

I have no idea what to say to this. I peek in the rearview mirror. Eileen is stroking the hair off Josten's forehead. "Mama tried like hell to talk me out of going, but I went anyway," she says. "Big mistake."

"What, leaving home?" Molly asks.

"Leaving with *him*. With my boyfriend, Mick. My ex, now."

There is no air of I-told-you-so when we stop at a modest clapboard house at the far side of a town called Honeymoon. Eileen's mother, who doesn't look a day over forty, gathers her into a hug that emanates relief and gratitude. She inspects the baby, now groggy and mellow from his nap, and holds him against her as if he's a missing piece of herself. "Look at this doll baby," she whispers, shutting her eyes and inhaling. "Just look at him."

Through the lines of fatigue around her mouth, Eileen beams. "It's good to be home," she says.

"I'm glad you're here," the mother replies. "No idea what I did without you." Then she turns and thanks me in a trembling voice. "Would you like to stay for supper?" she asks. "I got some sweet corn from a neighbor. And I just made some lemonade, fresh."

"Thanks, but we have to keep going," I tell her.

Molly surprises me by saying, "Maybe a glass of lemonade…"

The woman, whose name is Shelley, serves it in mismatched glasses and asks us about our trip.

"My mom's dropping me off at college," Molly says.

"Goodness, college. That's exciting."

The baby starts fussing himself awake and Eileen turns away to tend to him. I admire the patchwork quilt draped over the back of the sofa, and Shelley tells me it's a family heirloom.

"I'm working on one myself," I say. "It's my biggest project to date."

"I like sewing," she says. "I made all of Eileen's cos-

tumes for her dance routines. I don't sew much anymore. The local fabric store folded, and the nearest
superstore's thirty miles away. They got everything
you need there, but I miss the shop. All the women were
friends, you know?"

I think of the shop back home. Here in the middle
of nowhere, this woman had nailed it—a community
for women.

She gives us a local map that shows more detail than
my Triple-A triptych. She indicates a route back to the
highway that will put us a good eighty miles ahead of
where we were.

Molly takes over driving again. I pick up my quilting. She says, "Dad's going to freak when you tell him
we picked up a stranger."

"She needed a lift. We had no choice."

"I'm glad we helped her out. We're behind on our
schedule now, though."

"We don't need to be anywhere specific," I note. "It
was a goal, the four hundred miles."

We drive through a few towns fringed by strip malls
or trailer parks. There is an air of exhaustion that seeps
into the atmosphere of these places, and we're glad to
leave them behind.

By the time we reach the highway, dusk has fallen
and it's time to find food and a place to spend the night.
An eerie emptiness hovers over the open road and few
cars pass by.

"It's looking bleak," Molly says. "How far to the
next city?"

"Almost a hundred miles. You up for it?"

"Looks like we don't have a choice."

She plugs an adaptor into her iPod so we can listen

on the stereo speakers, and we get into a discussion about the stupidest lyrics ever written—"This Is Why I'm Hot" would be my pick. But Molly points out Van Morrison's "Ringworm" and then we dissect the lyrics of some old Yes songs.

"Anything sounds stupid if you listen too closely," I say.

Molly switches to a track that's in French. "Clearly, we've been in the car together too long."

A few minutes later, I spot a billboard rising from an alfalfa field, with a light shining on it. "Ramblers Rest, in Possum, Illinois. Want to check it out?"

She nods and drives another mile to the next sign. There's a red-neon light indicating Vacancy in the window of the office, which also contains a convenience store. The tires crackle over the gravel in the drive.

"What do you think?" Molly asks.

"It's worth a look. If it's horrible, we'll drive away."

It's not horrible, just a bit strange. Ramblers Rest consists of a group of small, self-contained wayfarers' cabins at the edge of a small trout pond. Our room is plain but clean, with walls of scrubbed pine, checkered curtains and an old-fashioned prayer posted above one of the beds.

The proprietor, a man in jeans and a plaid shirt, tells us there's a bonfire down by the pond where guests gather around to sing songs and toast marshmallows.

"Songs?" Molly mutters. "No way."

"We could harmonize 'You Are My Sunshine.'"

She cringes, and I send her a wicked grin. "Or 'Kumbaya'?"

The closest restaurant, our host says, is a place called Grumpy's, a few miles down the road.

"They're probably closed now," he warns.

Starving, we head up to the convenience shop adjacent to the office and buy hot dogs to roast over the fire, plus bright yellow mustard and squishy white buns—the kind of meal that is forbidden in a proper kitchen. On a whim, I buy the ingredients for a kind of dessert we haven't made since Molly's childhood camping trips. We hike down to the water's edge where a teepee-shaped bonfire roars at the night sky. There are at least three discrete groups here, but all share that sort of instant camaraderie that seems to crop up among strangers at campgrounds. They make room for us in the firelit circle and we roast hot dogs, sharing the extras.

It's amazingly tranquil around the pond, the sky intensely black in the absence of city lights. It's so dark you can make out the colors of the stars—red and violet, silver and the shimmering green of moss in shadow. Their reflections glow like coins on the surface of the water.

Molly and I sit shoulder-to-shoulder and make small talk with the other travelers. There's a young family from Cottage Grove, who just sold their house and are moving to Cleveland. A not-so-young family is there, too. The parents are about my age, but the kids are little, with Asian features, so I assume they're adopted. A retired couple, who seem self-contained and not as eager to mingle, tell us they're on a monthlong driving tour of the midwest. Molly, of course, gravitates toward two boys who seem to be about her age. They're juniors at Penn State, so leaving home is routine to them, and they're driving themselves.

She seems to have forgotten about dessert, but the younger kids eagerly gather around when I ask them if they want to help. I demonstrate how to put a little whipping cream and sugar into a small Ziploc bag. The sealed bag then goes into a larger plastic bag of ice and salt. This is the kids' favorite part—you shake until the cream and sugar in the sealed bag turns to ice cream.

"What a great trick," the young mother says to me, watching her little ones shiver and shake.

"I learned it from my mother." I look across at Molly, who is now explaining the process to the college boys, who are totally into it. Before long, everyone around the campfire is making ice cream in a bag, the kids turning it into a wild dance. Sparks land on someone's blanket, and a tiny flame ignites. Fortunately, it is spotted and beaten out. People tuck their loose blankets away from the fire, and we're more vigilant after that.

Everyone pronounces the ice cream delicious. In fact, it's a bit bland, but flavored by the fun we had making it. One of the college boys plays a harmonica. Then, possessed by the silliness of knowing we'll never see these people again, Molly and I sing "You Are My Sunshine" in perfect harmony, and our listeners are polite enough to clap. We stay by the fire way too late, until I feel the stiffness of the long day and the cold night at my back.

"I'm heading to bed," I tell Molly. I worry that she might want to linger here with the college boys. Her eyes glow when she talks to them. I battle the urge to remind her that these guys are strangers and we're in a strange place. Pretty soon, I won't be around to protect her at all, so I'd best get used to the churning nervousness in my gut.

She surprises me by getting up and helping collect the trash and leftovers. "I'm going to turn in, too. If we get an early start, we can make up for the time we lost today."

We didn't lose any time. I know exactly how and where we spent it, and I wouldn't change a thing.

As we walk together to our cabin, Molly says, "Those kids loved making the ice cream."

"Remember the first time I made it with you?"

"The Brownie campout at Lake Pegasus. I was— what—six years old? And I had the coolest mom."

What I remember about that campout was feeling inadequate. The professional moms, as I'd come to regard them, had remembered everything from bug spray to breakfast bars. They knew how to roast a whole meal in a foil packet, braid a lanyard into a friendship bracelet and name the constellations. My clever little ice cream trick didn't seem like much. Now I'm ridiculously pleased to know she thought I was the coolest.

Molly goes off to shower. I flip through the Triple-A book, wondering what tomorrow will bring. On the back cover is an ad I never noticed before, with a list of phone numbers—who to call in event of a breakdown.

DAY FOUR

Odometer Reading 122,639

As her father and brother constructed
the simple, sturdy shelter that might
house generations after her, a young
girl at her mother's knee would
work her own Log Cabin. It became
the quintessential American quilt.

—Sandi Fox,
Small Endearments: 19th Century Quilts for Children

Six

The next day we make tracks and we're curiously quiet with one another, both lost in our private worlds and lulled by the monotony of the road. We stop for the night at a far more conventional place, one with wireless internet and pay-per-view movies. We are not nearly as entertained by this as we were by last night's bunga-lows and campfire. The room smells of new carpet and cleaning solution. The beds are like two rectangular rafts, covered in beige spreads.

"Let's go out," I say, opening the door to the parking lot to scan the neon collage of signs along the main drag.

Molly looks at me as if I've sprouted horns. "What do you mean, out? We already had dinner."

"I mean out. To one of these clubs."

"And do what?"

I have to think for a minute. It's been a long time since I've gone to a club. "Get something to drink," I explain. "I'm sure bartenders still remember how to make a Shirley Temple. We can people-watch and lis-ten to music."

"What if I get carded?"

"It's legal for you to be in a bar in Ohio so long as you aren't served."

"You checked?"

"I always check."

She looks so dubious that I feel vaguely insulted. "What?"

"It's just weird going clubbing with your mom."

"We're not going clubbing. We're going to a club, just to get out a little bit. Nothing else seems to be open."

"That's weird."

"Fine. Let's stay here. You can watch *Simpsons* reruns and I'll work on the quilt and reminisce about the past."

Fifteen minutes later, we're headed out the door. Molly spent the entire preparation time in front of the mirror. I have to admit, she has a knack for primping. Her eyes are now smoky around the edges, her hair glossy and her lips slick and pink. She gives me the once-over and frowns again.

"I've seen that shirt before, Mom."

"I never realized you *noticed* this shirt before." I smooth my hands down the polished cotton. Except it's not so polished anymore. I think the polish wore off some time ago.

"Isn't it kind of...old?"

"It still fits. It's in perfectly good shape."

"But you've had it forever. Those jeans, too, and the shoes. And the purse. You carried that purse when you drove first-grade carpool."

"I take care of my belongings," I explain. "It's a virtue."

"Sure, but... Mom? You keep things too long."

She speaks kindly, yet I know what she's saying. Although I've always been quick to get something new for Molly, I never paid much attention to my wardrobe. Other than the occasional school event, I don't tend to need much in the way of clothes. I can sew like the wind, but I like doing costumes and crafts, not blouses and shifts. And I've never been much for shopping. I laugh at Molly as I grab a light jacket and my purse. "Trust me, the world is not interested in my lack of style sense. Especially not when I'm with a girl who's flaunting her midriff."

"I'm not flaunting." She checks out her cropped shirt in the mirror.

A year ago, she had begged us to let her get a tattoo and, of course, we refused. Once she turned eighteen, she didn't need our permission but, to my immense relief, she didn't run out to the tattoo parlor. Maybe she forgot it was the one thing that was going to make her life complete. I'm not about to remind her.

We walk out together into the twilight, and the breeze holds just the faintest hint of the coming fall. There's none of the coolness of autumn in it, but a nearly ineffable dry scent. The smell of something just past ripeness.

The main street is lined with mid-twentieth-century buildings of blond brick or cut stone. The shops and banks are closed, window shades pulled like half-lidded eyes, but in the center of the block, the sound of music and laughter streams from three different clubs.

One of them, called Grins, has a sandwich board out front boasting No Cover. Across the street is Tierra del Fuego, featuring unspecified live music, and two doors down is a place called Home Base. Twinkling lights surround a picture of Beulah Davis, and we choose that club because she has the same last name as us and because I like her picture. She's smiling, though there's a wistful look in her eyes. Her hands, draped over an acoustic guitar, look strong, capable of bearing the weight of a large talent.

We enter between sets. Canned music pulsates from hidden speakers. The place is crowded with people clustered around bar-height tables. The yeasty scent of beer hangs in the air. A group of guys is playing pool under a domed light with a Labatts insignia. In the corner, the musical set is dark and quiet, two guitars—acoustic and steel—poised in their holders like wallflowers waiting to be asked for a dance.

I pause, letting my eyes adjust to the dimness, and a wave of uncertainty hits me. I can feel Molly's hesitation, too, and unthinkingly I grab her hand, still the mom, leading her to a booth that has a view of the dance floor and stage. A good number of couples are swaying in the darkness, the women's bare, soft arms draped around men's shoulders.

I miss Dan. It hits me suddenly, a swell of nostalgia. He's not fond of dancing, but he's fond of me. Sometimes he has no choice but to sweep me into his arms and dance with me.

Molly orders a 7UP with lime, and I ask for a beer on tap.

"I'll need to see some ID," the waitress says.

"The beer's for me."

"ID, please," she says, bending toward me.

This is both startling and flattering. I readily show her my driver's license; she nods in satisfaction and heads for the bar. Molly samples the snack mix and scans the crowd. It's a diverse bunch, people of all ages relaxing and talking, some of them drinking too much and laughing too loudly. A couple in a booth across the room appears to be in an argument, leaning toward each other, their mouths twisted, ugly with overenunciated insults.

The music stops and the dancing couples fall still. The singer appears on the corner stage, accompanied by a drummer, a bass player and a woman on keyboard. Applause greets them and we set aside our drinks to listen. She picks up the steel guitar and smiles as they tune up, then places her lips close to the speakers. "Here's something by a guy I once knew, Doug Sahm, from Kilgore, Texas." A ringing, sweet melody slides from the speakers as she strokes the guitar.

It's the kind of song that sounds fresh, even though we've heard it a hundred times before. There's something about good live music that does that to a person. I feel a sense of happiness sprouting from within, and when I look across at Molly, I can tell that she feels it, too. There are very few people you can talk to without words. The fact that my daughter has always been one of those people for me is beyond price.

I grab and hang on to this moment, because I learned long ago that happiness is not one long, continuous state of being. Like life itself, happiness is made up of moments. Some are fleeting, lasting no longer than the length of a sweet song, yet the sum total of those moments can create a glow that sustains you. Watching Molly, I wonder if she knows that, and if she doesn't, if it's something I can teach her.

Sensing the question in my look, she tilts her head to one side and mouths, "Something wrong?"

The singer is joined by other band members, and the set segues into a lively swing tune. The volume increases tenfold. I lean across the table. "Nothing's wrong. I'm just wondering if we've talked about what happiness is."

She cups her hand around her ear and her mouth moves again.

"Happiness," I say, nearly shouting. "Do you know how it works?"

She shakes her head, at a loss, then meets me halfway across the table. "Are you happy?" I ask in her ear.

She sits back down, laughing, and mouths the words, "I'm fine."

Her words remind me that there are some things I'm not meant to teach her. She'll only learn them by finding out for herself. I can hope and pray that I've raised a young woman who knows how to be happy, but I can't hand it to her like my mother's button collection, sealed in a mason jar. Starting now, she will have to be the steward of her own life.

After four songs, greeted with enthusiastic applause, the band takes a quick break and we buy a copy of their CD. The singer smiles a little bashfully and we smile back, two strangers who like the sound of her voice. She signs the case with an indelible marker. "Y'all enjoy that, now," she says.

"We will," I say.

The waitress reappears, another beer and another 7UP on her tray, even though we didn't ask for a second round.

"The gentlemen over there sent them," she explains, indicating with her thumb and a wink.

"Oh, uh…" My cheeks catch fire. I can't bring myself to look.

The waitress sets down the drinks and leaves.

"Get out of town," Molly says. "Mom, those guys sent us drinks."

"Don't make eye contact. And for heaven's sake, don't drink—"

She takes a sip of her fresh 7UP. Watching her expertly made-up eyes over the rim of the glass, I see a whole world of things I haven't told her, matters that need to be explained to someone who, in so many ways, is still only a child. I've had eighteen years to teach her not to accept gifts from strange men. I never got around to doing it. So much of this thing called parenting is a matter of waiting for a situation to arise and then addressing it. Just when you think you have all your bases covered, you—

"They're coming over," she says in a scandalized whisper.

I want to slither under the table. I've never been good in social situations, not with men, anyway. For Molly's sake I need to get over the urge to slither. This is a teachable moment.

"Thank you for the drinks," I tell the older one. He's maybe thirty, and the way he's looking at me makes me glad I'm wearing the mom clothes. "We were just leaving, though."

"I bet you have time for one dance," he says, smiling beneath a well-groomed mustache. He looks like the guy in that old TV series *Magnum PI.* Magpie, Dan called it. I never did like that show.

His friend is clean-shaven, late twenties, checking out Molly with an expression that makes me want to call 911.

And here's the thing. I can't call 911. Nobody's doing anything illegal. It just feels that way to me.

"My mother and I really need to go," Molly says, polite but firm as she stands up. She tugs her shirt down, probably hoping they don't notice her midriff.

"Just trying to be friendly," the clean-shaven one said. His buddy seems to be having a delayed reaction to the word *mother*.

On the way out, I hand the waitress $20 and don't ask for change.

"Okay, that was weird," Molly says as we step out onto the street.

"Honey, when a guy approaches you—"

"I didn't mean it was weird that they approached me," she interrupts. "I'm just not too keen on guys hitting on my mom."

"Guys hit on women. It's what they do. They don't think about whether she's somebody's mother. Or daughter, or sister. And when we were in there, all I could think about was whether or not I've talked to you enough about staying safe around strange guys."

She laughs. "You're killing me, Mom."

"Oh, that's right. You know everything. Sorry, I forgot." She doesn't realize it now, but the older she gets, the wiser *I* get.

Something I probably won't share with her—the last time I met a man in a bar, I married him. Not right away, of course. But there are eerie similarities. The bar was dim, like the one we just left, and—in those days—smoky. Dan didn't send a waitress to do his work for him. He strode right over to me and said, "Let me buy you a drink."

I was too startled to say no. By the time the drink arrived, it was too late. I had noticed his lanky height and merry eyes, the heft of his biceps and the humor in his voice and his mouth, even when he wasn't smiling. I wouldn't go so far as to say it was love at first sight, but it was definitely something powerful and undeniable.

He was a guy with clear potential and big plans, and I was a mediocre student at the state college. Less than half a year later, we found ourselves standing face-to-face at the altar, with nothing between us but dreams and candlelight. I still remember our first lowly, undemanding jobs and the way the days melted into a rhythm of partying every weekend, making love before dinner, staying up late and watching edgy movies.

Then Molly came along, and nothing was ever the same. We thought, at first, that nothing would change. Our denial ran deep; we walked around with her in a Snugli or stroller, pretending she was a fashion accessory.

Of course, she was so much more than that. She had the power to turn us into different people. We were no better and no worse, but different. She was our happiest, most blessed accident.

All of which goes to show what can happen when you talk to strange men in bars.

In the middle of the night, I wake up and blink at my surroundings, my sleep-blurred gaze tracking the seam of the drapes, glowing amber from the lights of the motel parking lot. I hear Molly breathing evenly, sweetly, a sound that catches at my heart now as it did the first time I ever heard it and thought, My God.

Emotion and memory chase away sleep and I get up, shuffling over to the laptop computer. I touch the keyboard and it wakes up, too. Little boxes tile the screen;

Molly was IMing with Travis late into the night. I quickly close the IM windows without reading the text.

It's 3:00 a.m., and the internet is there, waiting for me. Following the stream of my own thoughts, I click to site after site, surfing from link to link as though pulling myself along some invisible, unending chain. Ultimately, it's unsatisfying, filling my head with too much information. Yet it's given me a huge idea.

Slipping on a light jacket, I step out into the parking lot with my cell phone. The whole world is asleep. There are no cars on the street, no critters rooting in the trash, no breeze stirring the tops of the trees. I punch in our home number on the cell phone.

"It's me," I say when Dan picks up on the second ring.

"What?" he asks, grogginess burgeoning to panic. "Where the hell are you? Are you and Molly all right?"

"We're fine. We're in…" I think for a moment. "Ohio. She's sleeping."

"So what's the matter?" In Dan's book, if everything is fine with Molly, everything is fine, period. I can hear the bed creak, can picture him rolling over, pulling up the covers. "What time is it?"

I'm not about to tell him. "Late," I admit. "Sorry I woke you. I couldn't wait. Dan, I just thought of something."

"What did you think of, Lindy?" He never gets mad when I wake him up out of a sound sleep. I wonder how that can be. Suddenly I wish I was there with him, rubbing his warm shoulders with gentle persistence.

"We need to get an orphan."

"A what?"

"An orphan. You know, adopt a child."

"Huh?" Another creak of the bed, or maybe it's the sound of Dan, scowling.

"From Haiti."

"Linda, for Chrissake—"

"No, listen, I found this site on the internet. There are thousands of them, waiting for families. We have so much, Dan. We're still young. We could give some poor child a chance.

"There's one I found named Gilbert. He's six. He lost his family in the earthquake."

"Go back to bed, Linda. It was hard enough raising our own healthy, well-adjusted child."

"It hasn't been hard at all."

"Speak for yourself."

His comment reminds me of their struggles. His frustration, Molly's tears, the long silences and the breakdowns I used to feel compelled to fix. "We did a great job."

"I'm not saying we didn't. But we're done. It's our time now, Linda."

"And I want to do something with it, something that matters. Think about it, Dan. These kids…they're not sick or abused. They didn't grow up in institutions. They're kids like Molly, except they had the bad luck to come home from school one day to find that their families were gone."

"I'll send a check to the Red Cross."

"They need *families*. We could—"

"We could do a lot of things, but adopting an orphan from Haiti isn't one of them." He must know how that sounds, because he takes a breath and adds, "Honey, you're in panic mode over Molly leaving. This is no time to be discussing such a huge undertaking."

I pull the jacket tighter around me. Panic mode. Am I panicking?

"I need a child who needs me," I blurt out.

"Lindy. Slow down. What you need is a life of your own."

The words fall like stones on my heart. He's right. *He's right.* "I'll work on that," I say, feeling a bleak sweep of exhaustion.

"Have fun on your trip," Dan says, a yawn in his voice. "I love you both."

"Love you, too." After we hang up, I sit for a while and look at the stars. It's so quiet I can hear a train whistle blow, miles away.

DAY FIVE

Odometer Reading 123,277

From the manner in which a woman
draws her thread at every stitch
of her needlework, any other woman
can surmise her thoughts.

—Honoré de Balzac

Seven

"I'm running out of thread," I tell Molly.

"We can stop somewhere in the next town," she says, unconcerned. She is more interested in finding a radio station. We have a rule. Driver gets to pick the music. We're already bored with our playlists and she's hungry for something new.

"This is mercerized thread spun from Sea Isle cotton," I explain. "It doesn't grow on trees, you know."

"I know how cotton is grown, Mom."

In quilting, the type and quality of thread you use matters greatly. Just think of all the stitches that go into a quilt. You need the kind of thread that pulls through smoothly, that is strong despite repeated tugging, that will never fray or pill.

To people who don't practice the craft of hand-sewing, thread is thread. Therefore, this is far less of a concern than the dearth of radio stations. The FM band yields too much static, and the AM stations are crammed with crop reports or the phony sentiment of country tunes.

"In pioneer days, mothers and daughters worked on their quilts together," I tell her.

"Good thing we're not pioneers." A soybean rust update comes on the radio, and she groans in exasperation.

I tried to get her interested in quilting a time or two, to no avail. She was impatient with the detail and repetition. Our few "lessons" ended with her pricking herself with a needle and sighing loudly with boredom. She usually wound up shooting baskets in the driveway with her dad.

She fiddles with the dial a bit more, and hits paydirt. The announcer's voice says, "Settle back and enjoy this local favorite, from Beulah Davis and the Strivers."

"Hey, isn't that the group we heard last night?" asks Molly. "Cool."

The melody and words are soothing and emotional, and I pause in the quilting to look out the window. It's a sea of grass, rolling out on both sides, and I imagine Molly and me as pioneers, setting off on a journey into the great, wide unknown.

I wonder what it was like for those women and their daughters, when their lives took them in different directions. They weren't able to pick up the phone or log onto the internet and get in touch. Separation meant the possibility of never seeing each other again. I should count my blessings.

The quilt section in my lap is made of cornflower-blue fabric sprigged with tiny daisies. It was a dress I made for Molly to wear to her very first piano recital, back when she was just eight years old. Her first public performance. What a nerve-wracking day that was. I recall her practicing Bach's "Minuet in G Major" over and over again until it drove Dan out into the yard with the weed-whacker. And I, of course, couldn't help tuning in on every note. I adjusted my breathing to the rhythm of her playing and when she hesitated—the long, agonizing pause in the fifth bar as she spread her tiny hand over the keys of a big chord—it made me hold my breath until she found the right notes. When she hit the wrong note I would wince and then remind myself not to do that at the recital.

The dress was meticulously put together, every stitch in place with hand-smocking across the bodice, the full skirt crisply ironed. She wore white ankle socks and Mary Janes, her hair held back in a blue band, and she looked like a dark-haired version of Alice in Wonderland.

"I'm not going in." I can still recall the exact sound of her little-girl voice as she balked at the door to the recital hall. It was an intimidating auditorium, filled with echoes. On the stage, the Steinway crouched like a slumbering black dragon.

"Okay," Dan said, immediately agreeable. "Let's go home." He had come under duress to begin with and was already chafing in his good shoes and starched shirt. He reached up to adjust the bill of the baseball cap that wasn't there. "Better yet, let's go for ice cream."

"We can't leave," I said, shooting daggers at him with my eyes. "Look, Moll, your name's already on the program." I showed her the printed sheet the piano teacher's son had given us at the door.

She refused to let go of Dan's hand. He was her ally and suddenly I was the enemy. We stood on either side of her, locked in a silent tug-of-war.

Not for the first time, it occurs to me that he was always quick to back off while I played the ogre, pushing her into new situations, sometimes against her will. I wonder if I'm doing that now, pushing her across the country to college. Dan, like Travis, would prefer for her to go to the state school.

Elsewhere on the quilt is a rosette of red stretchy fabric from the swimsuit she wore when I delivered her to her first swim lesson. At the YMCA pool, she had clung to me like a remora. Her howl of panic ricocheted around the pool deck, and her slippery, strong little body strained toward the locker room. Dan had rescued her that day, coming out on deck in his board shorts, looking like a hunk on *Baywatch* as he snatched her up. I was furious with him, but didn't want to make even more of a scene, so I bit my tongue. He took her by the hand and led her away from the noisy echo chamber of shrieks, punctuated by coaches' whistles.

An hour later, I found them both in the rec pool. "Watch me, Mommy, watch!" Molly yelled, and leaped off the side, disappearing under the surface. She sprang up and swam, struggling like a puppy, straight to her waiting father. "See?" she said, her wide eyes starred by wet lashes, "I don't need lessons."

This is different, I thought at the recital. He can't save her from the piano. He can only help her run away.

In the end, the decision was taken from all of us. "There you are," said Mrs. Dashwood, the piano teacher, bustling forward. "Let's go backstage and get some lipstick on." The teacher, who had an MFA and the face of a pageant winner, was idolized by her little-girl students. Mrs. Dashwood was wise, too, understanding the power of the promise of stage makeup to distract a kid from fear. She took Molly by the hand and walked her down the sloping aisle of the auditorium.

Molly glanced back once, her eyes filled with uncertainty, yet she was unresisting as Mrs. Dashwood led her away. I watched the teacher stop at the edge of the stage to point something out. By the time Molly disappeared behind the curtain, there was a discernible spring of excitement in her step.

I found myself clutching Dan's hand. I didn't even remember grabbing it, but I would never forget what he said. Leaning down to kiss my cheek, he said, "Relax. She's in good hands."

"Hey, if it were up to you, she'd be at the ice-cream parlor."

"And guess what—the world wouldn't come to an end."

As the youngest on the program, Molly went first. Mrs. Dashwood welcomed everyone, then introduced her. A smattering of applause and a few adoring "Awws" came from the audience, which consisted of carefully dressed parents, grandparents and the occasional doting aunt or restless sibling.

Molly walked slowly with a curious dignity, her full skirt tolling like a bell with each step she took. So tiny, I thought. A porcelain doll, all alone up there. She didn't look at the audience, didn't try to find me with her eyes. She stood still, and my heart skipped a beat. But Molly knew what she was doing. She jacked up the stool to its highest level so she could reach the keyboard.

We had practiced how to smooth the full skirt in order to sit down properly. She remembered every unhurried move. Her patent leather shoes glittered in the stage lights, dangling above the pedals. Mrs. Dashwood said she wouldn't use the pedals until she was tall enough to reach them.

She rested her little hands on the keyboard. This was

it, I thought. This was her moment. I took in a breath, ready to be dazzled.

It was a disaster from the first chord. Wrong notes, hesitation, whole measures forgotten. It was the longest ninety seconds of my life.

When it was over, I had aged a decade. Molly barely made it through the adorable curtsy we'd rehearsed. She fled into the wings and we found her in the stage hallway, a crushed flower surrounded by blue petals.

"This is the worst thing that ever happened to me," she sobbed, going limp against Dan when he picked her up. "This is worse than missing *larynx* in the spelling bee."

"I still can't spell *larynx*," I murmured.

"We should have gone for ice cream," Dan said.

In the passenger seat of the Suburban, I dart my needle into the heart of the fabric, quilting it with the words "Be audacious." The cornflower-blue fabric is like new. Molly never wore the dress again.

She didn't give up piano, though. Following the recital, she walked into the house, went straight to the piano and played the Bach flawlessly, every note ringing sweet and true through the empty rooms. "Just to make sure I could," she said.

Glancing over from the driver's seat now, Molly notices me working the blue piece. "What's that one?" she asked.

I angle it toward her. "Your first piano recital."

"I don't remember that dress."

"Bach's 'Minuet in G Major.'" The name of the piece usually jogged her memory.

"I'm blanking. Cute fabric, though."

Funny how the heart holds its memories, or lets them go. Each detail of that day is etched into me. I can even remember the flavor of ice cream we got afterward— maple walnut with chocolate sprinkles. Yet Molly has cast the nerves and trauma of that day from her mind. They are not important to her.

"Remember that red silk charmeuse you wore to your senior adjudication last January?" I ask her.

"Of course. I brought it along to keep you from cutting it up," she says, her urgency making me smile. "I love that dress."

"I know. I figured you'd want to wear it again." Unlike the flounces and sashes of her childhood, the red dress makes her look truly grown-up, slender and elegant. Maybe even sexy, with its clinging shape and single bare shoulder. In the same auditorium where she'd once stumbled through a minuet, she had performed last on the program. Supple as a ribbon of scarlet silk in a breeze, she had swayed through a grand, emotional rendition of Chopin's "Nocturne in C Minor," a piece he composed when he was seventeen, the same age Molly was.

Mrs. Dashwood, scarcely changed from the no-nonsense teacher we'd known for years, had handed her a tube of Chanel lipstick and declared her one of her most accomplished students ever.

The adjudicator gave Molly the highest possible marks and pronounced her the winner of the competition. Had she played better than the other students? It was hard to say. The adjudicator was Italian, a retired professor from the state college. All the other competitors were boys. It was hard not to miss the professor's enthusiasm for a pretty, talented girl in a red dress.

Still, I believed she had outdone the others in more than just looks. She had a gift. That nocturne sang with feeling. She knew how to take a heartfelt emotion and fling it wide for all to hear.

I'm kind of glad she doesn't remember the first disastrous recital. But I'm also glad I pushed her to do it. It occurs to me how much simpler it is to push your child in the right direction rather than yourself.

Molly flicks on the turn signal and drifts over to the right lane.

"What are you doing?" I ask.

"Thread, remember? You need thread."

The Suburban glides down the exit ramp and she takes a right, following a sign that points to "City Center."

Before too long, we find one of those chain craft and fabric stores. "They won't have the right kind," I lament.

"Then get another kind. No biggie." She catches the look on my face. "You should have brought more of the magical thread, if it's so important."

We step into the bright commercial glare of the craft shop. "You're right," I admit, "but Minerva's ran out and won't be getting in any more. She's closing the shop, you know."

"Nope, I didn't know. I thought it was for sale."

"It is. She's retiring and selling the place, but I doubt she'll find a buyer in this economy. I'll miss it. All her customers will. The idea of driving all the way to Rock Springs has no appeal to me at all."

"Bummer," Molly says, tucking her thumbs in her back pockets as she regards a display of notions.

As always, beautiful fabrics draw my eye. A few impossible-to-resist fat quarters make it into my shopping basket. The lure of a new project beckons. This happens a lot; I get close to the end of one thing and another pops into mind, seductive and infinitely more alluring than the project at hand.

At the end of a multitiered aisle, Molly fingers a green glass suncatcher marked Special of the Week. "Can I get this?"

My knee-jerk reaction is, *You don't need more junk.* But she takes after me, a magpie drawn to every glittering object that catches her eye. She's always been this way. Besides, it's in the shape of a music note, and it's only five bucks.

"One more pit stop," Molly says. Instead of going to the car, she heads into the shop across the way, a department store named Bradner's.

I happily follow her. It's fun shopping with someone who has her figure; everything looks good on her. But when I step into the store, I catch a whiff of White Shoulders perfume. This doesn't seem like Molly's kind of shop.

"What do you need, sweetie?"

"Come on," she says, her eyes sparkling. "We're going to pick out some new clothes for you."

"But…"

"But *what,* Mom?" Her excitement flashes to annoyance.

The usual litany of excuses piles up: I don't need new clothes. I don't have time. I don't want to spend the money. I want to lose some weight before I buy a bunch of things. *I'm not important enough.*

I look at Molly and grin. "Let's do it."

She did not inherit her fashion smarts from me. Must be all those style blogs and glossy magazines she loves to read. When she teams up with a salesgirl named Darcy, there is no stopping the two of them. I surrender to their superior savvy and wait in a big double dressing room in a bra and panties that have seen better days, bare feet in need of a pedicure.

The glaring fluorescent lights and full-length, three-way mirror have no mercy. I stare at myself in triplicate, the images growing smaller and smaller into infinity. Molly and Darcy bring in tops, slacks and jeans, silky cardigans and jackets nipped in at the waist, belts and low-heeled pumps. They can't resist accessorizing with statement jewelry, bright scarves, slender hoop earrings. The attention feels good—and the clothes look good on me.

Molly hands me a cream leather hobo bag. "You are so pretty, Mom. Wait until Dad sees you. Wait until everyone sees you."

In the end, I buy about half of what she wants me to get. Even that seems excessive to me, but with all the nice things to choose from, it was hard to narrow them down. We walk out of the store with a parcel as big as the quilt bag. It's filled with new jeans and shoes, a top and sweater and skirt, a wrap dress and hoop earrings, and a melon-colored paisley scarf I couldn't bear to leave behind. Molly and Darcy made me keep the new undergarments on, leaving my elastic-less ones in the trash. "When you start with a good foundation," Darcy pointed out, "everything looks better."

"Well," I say, setting the shopping bag on the backseat next to the quilt. "That was unexpected."

"That was fun," Molly said. "Way more fun than a fabric shop."

"A different kind of fun than the fabric shop."

She's not done, and her enthusiasm is infectious. On Darcy's recommendation, we go to a nearby salon for a shampoo and style. We have our toenails polished candy pink and emerge from the salon flipping our hair around and giggling.

"Look at us," Molly says, primping in the Suburban's visor mirror. "We're new women."

Eight

◆━⟨⟨◎⟨◎⟩⟩━◆

The next day, the sheen is off our hair. Molly urges me to wear something new but I decline, not wanting to wrinkle the clothes, sitting in the car all day. The bag with the beautiful new things stays on the backseat. The outfits are too nice for a car trip. I want to save them for something special.

According to the peeling roadside billboards, we have two choices for lunch—a Stuckey's that has ninety-nine-cent burgers, or Bubba's Beach Shack, on the scenic shores of Lake Ontario.

"It's a lake," Molly says. "How can it have a beach?"

"It's one of the Great Lakes." I am nearly cross-eyed from sewing. The end of our journey looms closer, an outcome I can see and practically touch. I stayed up late last night, working on the quilt. Working is, of course, an elastic concept. I can be staring out at the night sky and call it "working" if I'm planning the next quilt.

"I never thought about a lake having a beach. Back home it's just…a shore, I guess."

"We should have taken you to see the Great Lakes when you were little." And here it is again, that sense of things left undone, unfinished. What else have I forgotten to show her, to teach her?

She glances over at me. "You took me to Mount Rushmore and Yosemite and the Grand Canyon and the Everglades. You can't show me everything."

"I wish I had, though. We always had such fun on those summer driving trips, didn't we?"

There is a heartbeat of hesitation. And in that heartbeat, I hear a contradiction. Could be, she has memories of being hot, carsick, bored. Sometimes Dan and I were short-tempered and we were terrible at picking out places to stay. Bad motel karma became a family joke. Remembrances of summers past are marred by nonfunctioning swimming pools, moldy smells, shag carpets.

"Sure," Molly says. "We had a blast."

"But the Great Lakes—I remember going to Mackinac Island on my high school senior trip. I saved up for months in order to go. It was so beautiful, like stepping back in time. I wish we'd taken you there."

"You can't take me everywhere," she repeats.

New adventures lie ahead of her, a vast stretch of unexplored terrain. She'll be taking trips without me, seeing and experiencing things I'll never share. Which is as it should be, I remind myself.

Without further debate, she takes the next exit and wends her way through a threadbare town of redbrick buildings and convenience stores plastered with fading advertising posters. The route to Bubba's is well-marked, and within a few minutes we enter Tanaka State Park in western New York, a quiet oasis on a weekday afternoon. As we head toward the water, I notice that the colors of summer are fading here, the greens subtly shifting to yellow, the wildflowers casting their petals to the breeze.

The beach shack is adorable, and I'm instantly glad we've come. It has a huge deck with picnic tables covered in red-and-white checkered oilcloth, and a long dock reaching out to the deep, wind-crested waters of the lake. And it truly is a beach, fringed by sand and weathered by wave action. From this perspective, the lake looks as infinite as the sea itself. There are even herring gulls here, and I wonder if they lost their way and became landlocked, and if that would matter to a bird.

The waiter is the sort of gorgeous teenage boy who makes me feel like an urban cougar as I check him out. I can check him out as much as I want, because he has not even noticed me. He's eyeing Molly. Who wouldn't? Boys have always been drawn in by her pretty eyes, her smile that hints that she knows a secret.

We order the fish fry lunch, and it arrives in paper-lined baskets with French fries and coleslaw. It's beautiful here, and graceful boats skim across the water in the distance, the sails puffed out in the breeze.

"Check that out," Molly says, indicating a parasail kite flying from the back of a speedboat.

"Yikes, looks scary."

"Looks awesome." She dips a French fry in her coleslaw, a habit she acquired from Dan ages ago. She gazes dreamily at the sky, studying the little sailing man with stick legs, like a paratrooper GI Joe.

As we watch, the parasail is reeled into the back of the boat, and they tie up at the dock right below the restaurant.

"It's definitely awesome," the cute waiter says, coming to refill our iced tea glasses. From the pocket of his half apron, he hands her a card. "Here's a coupon for $5 off a ride."

I shake my head. "We won't be needing—"

"Thanks." Molly snatches the card. "Thanks a lot."

"We're not doing it." I dole out cash to cover our tab, leaving a generous tip even though I wish he hadn't put ideas in Molly's head.

"Come on, Mom. We've got time." Ignoring my protests, she heads down the stairs to the dock, her steps light with excitement. When I get to her side, she's already talking with the guys in the speedboat.

"It takes fifteen minutes," she says, "and we won't even get wet, except maybe our feet."

"We're not doing it."

"Ma'am, it's very safe. I've been doing this for years," the boat driver assures me.

I hate looking like a stick-in-the-mud. But I also hate the idea of dangling several hundred feet above the lake, tethered to the world by a rope no bigger than my finger.

Molly has that expression on her face. I don't see it often, but when I do, I know she means business. The stubborn jaw, the fire in her eye. A minute later, she's signing a faded pink form on a clipboard without reading it, and asking if I'll pay the fee. I haven't read the disclaimer, either, but I'm sure it absolves the boat guys of any liability if we happen to wind up at the bottom of Lake Ontario.

Studying the form over her shoulder, I point out one line. "It says here you need to weigh at least a hundred pounds. Last I knew, you were just under that."

She shrugs it off. "After this summer, I'm well over a hundred."

The boat guys seem to believe her. They put her in a high-tech life vest and helmet and she kicks off her shoes.

"A helmet?" I ask.

"Just a safety precaution," the man says.

I want to ask how a helmet is going to keep her safe if she plummets into the lake. I want to say that she's never tipped the scale past a hundred pounds, but I stop myself. It's my nature to cite the potential disaster in every situation. I recognize that. So, apparently, does Molly, because she learned to dismiss my fears years ago. She has gone mountain biking, horseback riding, scuba diving. A spirit of adventure is good, I remind myself. It's small and mean of me to dampen it.

Just the other day, I was thinking about what a pushy mother I've been. But the things I pushed her to do didn't place life and limb at risk. Especially pointless risk.

She's grinning ear-to-ear as they harness her to the sail. "'Bye, Mom," she says. "See you when I come back around."

"Be careful," I can't help saying, and now there's a fire in *my* eye as I send out warning signals to the boat driver and his helper.

Then there is nothing more to say as they head away from the dock, the big engine cutting a V-shaped wake behind the boat. My heart is in my throat as they reach open water, and the rainbow-colored sail fills with wind. Then, a moment later, Molly is aloft, a tiny doll tethered by a slender cord. She flies like a kite tail, higher and higher until they run out of rope. I shade my eyes and look at her, silhouetted by the sun.

Then my heart settles and I wave both arms wildly

over my head. "Go, Molly!" I shout, jumping up and down on the dock. "Go, Molly!"

Watching her fly is incredibly gratifying. I fumble with my mobile phone, try to get a picture to send to Dan. She'll probably look like no more than a speck against the sky, but he'll get the idea.

A gust of wind ripples across the water in a discernible path. I can actually see the gust filling the sail and then turning it sideways. Molly's stick figure legs swing to and fro like a pendulum.

"Omigod," I say. "Omigod, she's going to fall."

Apparently the boat driver knows something isn't right. His partner starts cranking in the cord, his movements fast, maybe frantic. I stand motionless on the dock, my feet riveted to the planks, my stomach a ball of ice. Here is the definition of hell—knowing something terrible is happening to your child and being completely powerless to stop it.

If she dies, I think with grim clarity, so will I.

The wind whips her like a rag doll. Her screams sound faint. I wonder if she's calling my name. I send up a prayer, pushing it out with every cell of my body and soul.

The screams grow louder, and then I realize she's not screaming at all. She's laughing.

Nine

"You should try it," Molly says, combing back her wind-tossed hair and pulling it into a bun. She is still shivering from the lake, her lips tinged a subtle blue. With her hair pulled back, she looks sophisticated, older. We return to the beach shack to get her something warm to drink. The hunky waiter hovers, bringing her hot tea in a small stainless steel pot.

"In my next life, maybe."

"Seriously, Mom, you'd love it."

"I'm too chicken to love something like that." Still, I feel a slight twinge. What would it be like, dangling in midair like the tail of a giant kite? But no. That is so far out of my comfort zone I can't even imagine myself doing it.

"What's that piece of fabric?" Molly asks, indicating the dotted Swiss. She's been enjoying my stories about the pieces in the quilt.

"This is from your grandmother's square-dancing skirt. There's plenty of fabric, yards and yards of it, so I used it for sashing. Do you remember how she and Grandpa used to go square dancing?"

"Sort of. Maybe just from looking at old pictures, though."

My parents were avid square dancers. They belonged to a club that held a dance the first Saturday of every month. I can still see them in my mind's eye, my dad trim and dapper in a Western-cut shirt, with mother-of-pearl snap buttons, and a string tie. My mother's dresses were outrageous confections. She made them herself, with yards of ruched calico or dotted Swiss draped over a pinwheel froth of crinolines. The dresses had puffy sleeves that sat like weightless balls on her shoulders, and she always wore these horrible little one-strap dancing shoes.

The sight of my folks in their square-dancing getup might have made me squirm, except that they were so damn happy to be going out to the dance hall together, to laugh with their friends and drink sticky fruit punch.

"They loved those dances so much," I tell Molly, drawing a stitch through the sashing. "Grandma more than Grandpa, but he was a good sport about it."

"I never saw them dance," Molly says.

"Every once in a while, they'd have family night and we'd go." Of course she wouldn't remember that; she was in a stroller at the time. Still, I could see her swinging her tiny feet and clapping, mesmerized by the noise and the movements.

When Molly was in the second grade, my mother suffered a massive stroke. She was just sixty-four; it shouldn't have happened. I took Molly to see her, praying my child wouldn't act frightened when she saw Mom's altered face, the left side slack and unresponsive, her neck encased in a cervical collar.

I needn't have worried. Molly had happily rolled an

ergonomic table in front of my mother and said, "Now you can play cards with me."

The funny, sewing, square-dancing mom I knew vanished that day, even though she lived for two more years. Her personality changed, and dark anger emerged from a place we never knew was inside her. It was as if the stroke awakened a slumbering dragon inside her. She raged at how hard she had worked, and how frustrated she was that she hadn't given her kids more. I constantly reassured her that what she'd given her family was enough. She always liked it when I brought Molly to visit her, though. Seeing her only granddaughter quieted the angry sadness.

She was supposed to get better with a long and rigorous course of physical and occupational therapy. She hated the therapy, though—squeezing a hard blue rubber ball, poking a thick shoelace through holes on a board to form the shape of a spider, walking back and forth between parallel bars. Most days, she refused to do any of it, preferring to let my dad tie her shoes and push her wheelchair. Her hands, which used to effortlessly knit Fair Isle sweaters and mittens and hats, closed around some invisible object and refused to open. Once or twice, she tried knitting again, but the yarn wound up in knots of frustration on the floor. The physical therapists told my father that in the long run, she'd be better off dressing herself and learning to walk on her own, but Dad didn't listen. It was more important to him to do what my mom wanted.

"I wish I could remember the square dancing," Molly says. "Not the assisted living place."

I wish that, too. Even though I know it's irrational, I feel irritated at Molly because she doesn't remember my mother the way I want her to. I want her to recall the funny singing voice, the strong hands with their faint smell of onion, the perfect bulb of hair held slick with Aqua-Net. I want Molly to miss *that* woman, even though I understand it's impossible.

"How did she die?" Molly asks. "You never talk about that."

"Ask me how she lived. After all, that's what she spent most of her life doing."

"You talk about that all the time," Molly notes. "And I do love hearing the stories, Mom. But you've made her into this Disney grandma who's barely real to me."

"She got pneumonia and was too weak to fight it." I smooth my hand over the fading calico. "She died early one morning when you were in fourth grade. I didn't tell you right away because you had a school party that day. I didn't want to ruin it for you. So I waited until you got home."

Molly is quiet for a minute, sipping her tea, staring out across the lake, where the wind whips up white tufts in the water. Wrapped in a blanket someone at the restaurant gave her, she looks little and lost. But there is a sharpness in her eyes. "You were always cushioning me, Mom."

"It's what mothers do." I wish my own mother could see this young woman now, vibrant and excited about her future. My dad, who has grown quiet and slow with age and loneliness, often tells me he wishes that, too.

"It didn't work," she says, not looking at me. "I knew, anyway. I could tell from the way you rushed me off to carpool. I was scared to say anything because I didn't want to see you cry."

This shocks me. Dan and I had been prepared;

Mom's doctors had let us know her death was immi-
nent, even offering signs and markers to watch for. For
me, the sense of loss was so overwhelming that I hadn't
been able to talk about it.

Even now, years later, it's still hard. There is something about losing your mother that is permanent and
inexpressible—a wound that will never quite heal.

"I had a rotten day at school that day," Molly explains. "Hated the party. There were these awful cupcakes, and the games were lame. So it's not like you
spared me anything."

"Moll, I never realized you knew what was going
on that day."

"Nope. You didn't. I didn't say anything because I
didn't want to upset you. We were both trying to protect each other, and it didn't work."

I draw the thread to the end and make a tiny, invisible
knot before cutting it free. "How did you get so smart?"

"Must've inherited it from my mother. We'd better
get going." She drinks the last of her tea, combs her
hair again. The breeze is reviving her curls. She stands
up and folds the blanket. She waves a thank-you to the
waiter and he hurries over to our table.

I put my things into the crafter's bag and head back
to the car while she lingers to talk to the waiter. Looking back, I feel a jab of annoyance. I don't like the way
he stands so close to her, checking her out. It's on the
tip of my tongue to call out, to remind them both that
I'm standing here. Then I think about what Molly said
about me always stepping in, trying to smooth things
over for her, to absorb the body blows life tends to deal
out from time to time.

The afternoon at the lake caused an almost imperceptible shift in our mood. We're more on edge. Our silences are longer, corresponding to the flat, boring stretches of highway.

How do long-haul truck drivers handle the tedium? How will I handle it, driving back alone, the Suburban emptied of Molly's things, devoid of her fruity-smelling hair products and her lively chatter?

What's really eating me is this. We're almost there.

DAY SIX

Odometer Reading 123,597

No other border was applied with
greater ingenuity and diversity
than the Sawtooth. It could be applied
in one of three methods to a perfect
turn and direction, but it is in its less
precise applications that it often assumed
its greatest charm.

—Sandi Fox,
Small Endearments: 19th Century Quilts for Children

Ten

There is a change in Molly's phone calls with Travis. Pacing back and forth, the tiny silver phone glued to her ear, she talks to him at every rest stop, it seems. The shift in tone and emphasis is subtle but palpable. She is both more animated and more intense.

I don't say anything, of course. What is there to say? They're eighteen, and in love.

Give it time, I remind myself. The drifting-apart is not going to happen overnight. I picture the two of them like the huge layers of ice we get on the lake back home. All winter long, the frozen surface is strong and impermeable; the skating goes on for weeks. Yet in spring, the ice cracks apart, and once that happens, the pieces never fit together properly again. Even if the temperature drops sufficiently at night to re-freeze the ice, it's not the same; it's rough and chunky, prone to breaking. The skaters all go home for the season.

Separation is rough on any relationship. On a pair who have barely dipped a toe into adulthood, it's usually a death knell. They just don't have the emotional hardware to sustain a love that depends on physical closeness. And I won't kid myself. Those two were close. They were physical.

I can't imagine Travis Spellman going dateless for movie nights or football games, not for long. Likewise, I don't want Molly to be like a war widow at college, holding back from the social scene because of her hometown boyfriend.

That lack of availability, physical and emotional, is undoubtedly what will cause them to go their separate ways, as they must. Molly has a future ahead of her filled with brand-new people, challenging studies, a city she's never seen before. Settling into college will take all her time and energy. Nurturing a long-distance relationship is simply not feasible.

Except, of course, that she believes it is. And here's the thing about my daughter. If she believes in something with her whole heart, no one can tell her otherwise.

At a rest stop where we park to stretch our legs and use the facilities, she is pacing back and forth on the sere, dun-colored grass that has gone dormant from drought. The phone is still glued to her ear and her flip-flops kick up dust in her wake.

I wander along the walkway of the rest stop. It's a pleasant spot, insulated from the noise of the interstate by a stand of thick trees, evergreens and sugar maples that are just getting ready to take on their fall colors.

The local historical society in this area has a craft booth set up at the rest stop, and I buy a bottle of amber maple syrup from a woman in a homespun apron and—I kid you not—a poke bonnet. The clear glass bottle is in the shape of a maple leaf, and when I hold it up to the sun, it sparkles like a jewel.

According to the information flyer that came with the syrup, the maple trees will put on a dazzling display of fall color. These country roads will soon be crowded with RVs and busloads of leaf-lookers, coming to enjoy the scenery so beautiful that it attracts tourists from the world over to view them each year. After the riot of color, the trees lose all their leaves and appear to die.

Yet it is then, in the dead of winter, that the maples are most productive. If you tap deep enough into the tree, sinking a metal tube into its most hidden heart, you'll discover a gush of life.

The sap is drained through the tube, collected in covered buckets and boiled in huge vats to make maple syrup.

Who the heck thought of that? I wonder. At some moment in the unremembered past, someone walked up to a leafless maple tree, hammered a tube into its center, harvested the sap and rendered it into sweet syrup. What a random thing to do.

One thing I'd guess—whoever thought it up wasn't a college graduate. She—I'm quite certain it was a *she*— was probably a mother. An ancient Algonquin desperate housewife. At the end of a long winter, her kids were probably bored and cranky from being cooped up in the longhouse, chasing each other and driving her crazy with their noise. They had no idea supplies had run low, that the men hadn't done too well on the latest hunt. Pretty soon, the kids' war whoops and giggles would turn to whining. Yelling at the older kids to keep the younger ones away from the fire, the woman strapped on snowshoes made of hide, with gut laces, and trudged out into the deadening cold to look for food.

How did she know about the secret inside the maple

tree? Maybe the deer clued her in. During the starving season, the hungry animals stripped the bark from the trees as high as they could reach. Maybe the woman, her vision sharpened by desperation, noticed the glistening ooze from the flesh of the trees. Maybe she touched a finger to the sticky dampness, tasted a faint sweetness on her tongue. And the rest was history. An industry was born. The hunting party came home with their limp, skinny rabbit to find the women and children feasting on boiled cornmeal, magically sweetened with an elixir from the sugar maples.

I reach the end of the walkway and wander back. The woman in the poke bonnet is standing behind her booth, furtively smoking a cigarette.

Still on the phone, Molly notices me watching her and wanders over to an information board covered with maps and tourist brochures. She tucks one hand into the back pocket of her shorts and keeps talking.

Her face is bright with love.

Seeing her like this conjures up mixed emotions. On the one hand, I am proud and gratified that my daughter has a great heart, that she can give it away with joy and sincerity. Yet on the other, I wish she understood the difference between the passionate heat of first love and the deep security of a lasting commitment.

But there is no difference, not in Molly's mind, and no amount of discussion—lecturing, she would call it—on my part will change her mind about that. Love is love, she'd tell me, and who am I to say she's wrong? I can't claim to be an expert. There is a part of me—and it's not even a small part—that keeps wondering what my marriage will be like when I get home and it's just Dan and me.

Agitated, I take a seat at an empty picnic table, which faces a lovely marsh fringed by cattails, the reeds clacking in the light breeze. The distant hiss of truck brakes joins the singing of frogs from the marsh.

I pull out the quilt, thinking I'll add a stitch or two. The feel of the age-softened fabrics is oddly soothing. Yet at the same time, I am nagged by the sense that I wish I'd never started this thing. What a crazy notion, to think I could actually put the final touches in place in time for the journey's end.

"That's a beautiful piece," someone says, and I look up to see a woman about my age, walking a scruffy little dog on a retractable leash. The dog ranges out to the end of the leash and then comes reeling back toward her, like a yo-yo on a string. The woman is checking out the quilt with a practiced eye.

"Thanks," I say, recognizing the expertise with which she studies the project. It's gratifying to realize quilters are everywhere. It's such a universal art, beloved by so many women. "I'm making this for my daughter's dorm room."

She nods appreciatively. "What a great idea. Wow, are you hand quilting?"

"More portable that way. More variety." This morning I stitched the word *Remember* across a piece made from my mom's square-dancing dress.

"I've always thought crazy quilting was much more challenging than a regular pattern," the stranger remarks.

"You might be right. At first, I thought it would make the work to go faster. Instead, I keep trying to force things together and changing my mind."

"I like going slowly when I quilt," she comments. "It keeps me in the moment, you know?"

I do know. And here's what happens when quilting women meet. When one quilter encounters another, there's always something to talk about. We go from being strangers to friends in about three seconds. I've seen this happen again and again, back home at the shop. It's like the fabric itself is common ground, the pattern a secret handshake. Quilting women already know so much about each other. We get to skip over the petty details.

Within moments, I am giving her a guided tour of Molly's quilt—the snippet of fabric from the tooth fairy pillow, upon which she placed her first lost tooth. The blue ribbon she won at the seventh-grade science fair, for her pond water display. A Girl Scout badge she earned delivering Christmas cookies to a nursing home. One square is decorated with pink loops of ribbon in honor of the time she raised a thousand dollars in a Race for the Cure.

Sometimes I wonder if I'm being fair with the milestones and memories I'm stitching into this quilt. It's easy to block out a square to celebrate her little victories and happy times. But what about a square to commemorate her detention notes for skipping school, or the time she pierced her own navel and it got infected, or the night the local police brought her home, reeking of peach-flavored wine cooler? Why not remember those times? They're part of her history, too.

"You're making a family heirloom," the woman remarks.

Ha, I think, vindicated. That's why I don't need those

reminders in the quilt. "It's not going to be finished in time."

The woman smiles, leans back against the picnic table. "In time for what?"

"Move-in day at the dorm."

"I have a rule. If it's not falling apart, it's finished." She is about my age, I surmise, yet she seems wiser, and I'm not sure why. Her posture is relaxed, and she appears to be in no hurry.

I tell her about the shop back home, how I'll miss it when it's gone, how it won't be the same, buying my fabric somewhere else.

"Maybe someone will take over," the woman suggests.

"I sure hope so. I'm not optimistic, though. Most of the women I know who'd be capable already have other jobs, or they're retired, or too busy with their families. It's a huge risk and a huge commitment."

"I hear you," the woman says. The dog has finished its business in the reeds, and she calls out to a little girl who is playing on the swing set. "Amanda, we'd better get going."

The dark-haired child runs over on chubby legs. "Five more minutes," she begs in a voice every woman within earshot recognizes.

"One more," my companion says, and we both know it will stretch out to five.

"Your daughter's adorable," I tell her.

"Thanks, but she's not my daughter." The woman glances over at Molly, her fleeting look filled with insight. "Amanda's my granddaughter."

Oh, man. She's a grandmother. I don't want to be a grandmother. I'm not finished being a mother.

Yet when she finally reels in her dog and calls to the dark-haired little girl, and Amanda runs into her arms, there is a magical joy in their bond. It's sweeter, somehow, than motherhood, probably because it's simpler.

"Drive safely," I tell them.

"You do the same," she says, "and good luck with the quilt."

Eleven

On the final leg of our journey, the landscape is a patchwork of forest, field, stream and village, stitched together at the seams by country roads and rock or whitewashed fences.

"God, do people actually live here?" Molly wonders aloud, taking it slow as she navigates the Suburban down a hill to an old-fashioned town, complete with white church spire and village green. "It looks like a movie set."

She's right. It's a strange and beautiful land, innocent and pristine, yet with a faint air of danger that comes with alien territory. As a girl, I dreamed of traveling far, but I never did. In my family, vacations were few and far between, and when we went somewhere, it was usually a car trip to a state park. For my parents, life at home was enough.

My mother had a favorite escape, and it was as simple as turning on the TV. She was fanatical about the TV soap *Dallas,* about a family like none we'd ever known. In my head, I hear the brassy theme song that heralded the start of the show. It's one of the most vivid memories of my childhood. The churning melody signaled my dad's bowling night and my mother's sacrosanct program. On Sunday nights, the routine never varied. She would shoo him out the door, then fix an Appian Way pizza out of the box, oiling her hands with Wesson and expertly spreading the dough in a thin circle on a round baking sheet. A splash of canned tomato sauce, a sprinkle of questionable-looking cheese, and heaven was only minutes away.

Unlike any other day of the week, we didn't have a proper, sit-down family dinner on Sundays. No salad or side dishes, no pretense of a token vegetable. Just slices of hot pizza and glasses of cold milk. Maybe a Little Debbie for dessert.

Then, despite my deeply resentful protests and martyrlike sighs, I was sent to bed. Even in the summer, when the light lingered for an extra hour, Mom made me decamp upstairs to my room, because Sunday nights were sacred. They were *Dallas* nights.

Mom wanted no interruptions. I suppose she would have taken the phone off the hook, but she didn't have to, because all her friends were doing the same thing— hastening their children off to bed, urging their husbands out the door—so they could spend an hour in that fabled living-color world of millionaire matrons and the scoundrels who loved them.

I wasn't allowed to watch and wouldn't have wanted to, anyway. To a kid, the endless adult conversations, high-stakes oil deals and secret affairs were deadly.

Sequestered in my room, I always knew when the show started. First, there would be the clink of a glass. On Sunday nights, Mom opened the wicker-clad bottle of jug wine we kept in the cupboard and poured herself exactly one round-bellied, stemmed glass, full to the brim. Next, a curl of cigarette smoke would snake its way upstairs, emanating from a Parliament 100 with recessed filter, whatever that meant. It was all part of Mom's curious ritual of self-indulgence. I wonder if she ever imagined Southfork Ranch as a real place, tucked into the green folds of the Texas countryside, with skyscrapers in the distance.

The high-octane music would swell, the sound boiling up the stairs to my resentful ears. Mom loved the theme from that show so much that she bought the sheet music. Even though we didn't have a piano, she learned to hum the notes. A few years ago, Molly found the music in the piano bench and picked it out while I was working in the kitchen. I felt the same curious shiver of resentment and intrigue I'd felt as a child.

Nowadays, women escape by running away to urban spas, yoga retreats or wild-woman weekends of paintball drills and primal screams. Others frequent male strip clubs or dress to the nines for high tea. Back then, women like my mom didn't have to go any farther than their living rooms.

We stop at a deli for a take-away lunch, and Molly is drawn to the counter girl's flat New England accent, which skips blithely over the "r" and elongates the vowels.

The sub sandwiches are called "grinders," and the milkshakes are "frappes." The word feels awkward and foreign in my mouth, and when we place our order, Molly and I don't look at each other because we'll start giggling.

We take our lunch to a roadside park with a scenic

overlook. There is a sign pointing the way to the Norman Rockwell home.

"I can see where he got his inspiration," I tell Molly, gesturing at the spill of rounded mountains below us.

"Who?"

"Norman Rockwell." I indicate the signpost.

"Who's that?"

Not again. This is crazy. Is it possible that she isn't familiar with the quintessential American artist of the twentieth century?

"You know, the one who did all the illustrations of kids fishing and families praying," I say. "He did the cover of the *Saturday Evening Post* for years. That was even before my time, but you saw those illustrations everywhere—calendars, greeting cards, posters, dentist's offices."

"I guess."

"Maybe we could drive over there, check out the place where he created his art."

"Let's not." She speaks quickly. Maybe there's an edge of urgency in her voice.

I let the topic go. "I've got one thing to say about grinders and frappes, or frapp-ays, however you say it."

"What's that?"

"They rock."

She nods in agreement. The homemade bread and exotic cold cuts—olive loaf, dry salami, maple-smoked ham—and tart dressing and relish are delicious. I tell myself I can start my diet when I get home.

It's too nice a day to hurry. Molly decides to take a walk, her euphemism for going somewhere private in order to call Travis. I doubt she'll get a cell phone signal here, but I don't say anything. Instead, I pull out the quilt and jab my needle into the fabric, piercing through all the layers. The quick silver flash travels fast, but not fast enough. Bit by bit, I am coming to realize that I have failed. By the time we get to the college, the quilt still won't be finished.

Feeling unsettled, I watch Molly walking down the road, hands in her back pockets. Suddenly she looks very small and alone to me, and the urge to protect her—from what? Who knows?—rises up strong in me. Soon I won't be around to protect her. But she has to go.

And as for me, I have to let her. After that, I have to figure out how to be my own person again.

"What's that look?" Molly asks, returning from her walk and sitting beside me at the picnic table.

"I don't have a look."

"Come on. Spill."

"Just thinking of this huge change. It feels so sudden."

"It's not like we didn't see it coming."

"I know. And this is what I wanted. I wanted to raise a child. And I did, I raised a wonderful child. But now you're leaving."

"Mom." She offers a sweet, ironic smile. "That's the whole point."

"Well, I just wish someone had told me how hard it is to let go."

"Did you think it would be easy?"

"Of course not." The needle darts again, in and out of the quilt.

"A little bird once told me you shouldn't avoid doing something just because it's hard."

My exact words, only I'd probably said them to her

in order to get her to go off the diving board or eat a portobello mushroom.

"If you go away and screw up," I blurt out, "how will I help you fix it?" I am instantly horrified. What a stupid thing to say. An apology rushes up through me. It came out all wrong. I shouldn't have said that.

Before I can babble out *I'm sorry, I didn't mean it*, Molly bursts out laughing. "News flash, Mom. It's not your job to fix it."

I laugh with her, but I can't help the next thought that pops into my head: Then what *is* my job?

We spend longer than we intended at the roadside park. It's so pretty and the air feels so good. When the breeze shifts just so, I can sense the forward march of the season, and I can see it in the crowns of the distant trees in the high elevations, which are starting to turn.

Molly seems preoccupied. I wonder if she's thinking about what lies ahead—or what she left behind. Her phone calls and text messaging with Travis have decreased in frequency, which I take to be a good sign. She is driving while I keep doggedly working on the quilt, and she is fixated on the posted distance to the city. "Only forty more miles," she says. "Hard to believe we're finally that close."

My needle slides through the fabric, paying homage to a swatch of old flannel from Dan's pajamas, something she probably doesn't even remember. But I do and suddenly I miss the feel of his arms around me, the sound of his breathing, calm and steady. I think about his warmth and his scent as he sleeps beside me. I miss him. If he were here, he'd make me say exactly what's on my mind. No use bottling it up.

"I suppose we could go all the way right now," I say, "instead of finding a place to stay way out in the suburbs." We had planned for a noon arrival on orientation day, so she would have time to organize her dorm room before heading into the maze of new student activities.

"No." Her reply is surprisingly swift and firm. "That's not the plan. We don't want to get to the city after dark. And I bet there won't be any vacancies near the school, anyway, and even if we found a place to stay, the hotels are massively overpriced and the residence halls don't open to new students until tomorrow at noon."

Her barrage of protests is a bit mystifying. She couldn't wait to get to college but now, the night before her new life is set to begin, she seems to have all the time in the world. I'm gratified that she wants to extend our time together.

"You're right," I agree, and I watch out the window for the exit sign to the town we'd picked out as our final stop. "We should stick to the plan."

She nods and glances at her cell phone, lying on the seat beside her. Travis hasn't called all day, which I suspect is the cause of the prolonged silences that stretch between us. I, with a terrible and dark sense of satisfaction, find myself hoping this is the beginning of the end for them, that his failure to call is not due to the lack of a signal, but to the lack of commitment.

My own thoughts make me feel horrible. She adores Travis, and he makes her happy. Isn't that what I want for her, to be happy? Still, I don't want my daughter's future to belong to him, a charming local boy who has spent the entire summer trying to convince her that there is no better life than the one our small Western town has to offer.

It was enough for me, I realize with a surge of guilt, and I swiftly glance at her. There in that same small town she's been forced to leave, I've found all of life's happiness. Suppose I'm robbing her of the chance to do the same?

And why do I hope her dreams are bigger than mine ever were? What is it that I want for her that I never wanted for myself?

The onslaught of second thoughts assaults me. Molly flips on the turn signal. "This will do."

We have a club card for Travelers Rest, a chain of midrange hotels, and so I nod in agreement. The room is predictable, clean and bland, a faint whiff of stale air blowing from the register vent. We are plenty early, with a large portion of the afternoon ahead of us. Maybe I'll finish Molly's quilt after all.

Instead, I am possessed by restlessness. I take the Suburban to a nearby station and fill it with gas, asking the attendant to check the oil, the tires, the wiper fluid. I use the squeegee to clear the squished bugs from the windshield and grill. It occurs to me that I performed this same routine the day I went into labor with Molly. In childbirth class, we'd been told that a woman on the brink of labor often experiences a burst of energy—the nesting instinct kicking in. I cleaned and scrubbed the house and car all day and was just settling down for a good night's sleep when my water broke.

So what is this, the *de*-nesting instinct? Simple common sense, I tell myself. Tomorrow, I don't want to be distracted by the menial tasks of checking gauges and tires. I want everything to go smoothly, with the Suburban as ready as a criminal's getaway car.

When I return to the motel, Molly is at the pool, a turquoise oval set in an apron of groomed grass. It's not exactly swimming weather, but this might be the last swim of the summer. So, despite the hint of a nip in the air, I decide to join her. I duck into the room, don my swimsuit, one of those figure-flattering jobs with hidden panels designed to suck everything in. Of course, it can't suck in what it doesn't cover, so I slip on the secret weapon of the forty-year-old woman—the cover-up.

My flip-flops slap against the sun-softened asphalt of the parking lot as I approach the pool. Molly is wearing the yellow-and-white bikini we picked out in the end-of-season sale at the mall back home, and her hair is slicked back, her skin dewy from swimming. She sits at the edge of the shallow end, watching two little kids, a boy and a girl who are maybe four and six.

I take in the sight of her, wondering when we'll travel together again, when we'll pick a motel because of its pool, when we'll eat junk food and watch TV together late into the night. Everything on this journey is more significant and intense because it's the last time.

The kids are laughing and splashing under the watchful eye of their mother, who turns occasionally to make conversation with Molly. As I watch, Molly wades in to help the little girl adjust her water wing, then holds her hand and turns her in a circle while making a motorboat sound. The little girl giggles and flails while I stand off to the side, watching. And suddenly I am seeing Molly and me, hearing our laughter echo across the water, feeling her tiny hand in mine as I lead the way.

I'm struck by how like me she is right now, angling

her arm just so, making certain she's not going too fast or too deep for the small, trusting child. Where did she learn her gentleness with children, her humor? I don't remember teaching it, yet here she is, replicating a moment I didn't recall until just now. Suddenly, the memory is as clear to me as if it had happened the day before yesterday. One long-ago summer day, we looked exactly like this, a young woman and a little girl, sharing a small moment together.

Except I am not in the picture. This is Molly's moment, one that has nothing to do with me. And it's weirdly okay with me. She is her own person and I don't feel the need to insert myself into any of this.

Her cell phone, which is lying on a metal poolside table, suddenly goes off. Travis's ring sounds like a fire alarm.

Molly rushes to hand the little girl off to her mother, then leaps out of the pool, swift as a trained dolphin. She dabs her hand on a towel, then snatches up the phone. At the same moment, she sees me coming toward her.

Her face lights up with a glow of pure joy, a clear echo of the look she used to give me when she was tiny and I'd say, "Let's go for a swim, Moll."

She's lighting up for someone else now. She acknowledges me with a wave, then says into the phone, "Omigod. Omigod, really? I don't believe you!" She is jumping up and down now, a young adult no longer but a child bouncing with excitement. "Where?" she asks, and then, *"Now?"*

The settled feeling that had enveloped me only moments ago now swirls away. I set my towel on the chaise next to Molly's, wondering what's got her so excited. Here I thought she was uncoupling herself from Travis, their calls growing fewer and shorter as our journey progressed. Now she is as excited as she was when he asked her to prom.

Watching her, listening to the sparkle in her voice, I realize that I miss this Molly. Throughout this journey, she has been pleasant but guarded. Even soaring over Lake Ontario or watching line dancers at a honky tonk, she has been entertained, but not exuberant. Not until now.

What's he saying to her that causes the air to slip under her feet and lift her up?

And then with a laugh of joy, she drops the phone onto the table. "I don't believe it," she keeps saying and then she scoops up her flip-flops and runs. I am slow, not really hooked into this reality, not really believing it, either.

In slow motion I stand up and walk to the chainlink safety fence that surrounds the pool. Her bikini flashing in the sunlight, Molly races across the parking lot, shooting straight up in the air when the asphalt burns her feet, then hopping up and down as she throws her flip-flops to the ground and jiggles into them. Then she resumes running but she doesn't have to go much farther, just across to the porte-cochère, straight and true as an arrow shot from a bow, into Travis's waiting arms.

Twelve

Travis catches her in his embrace, and my mind races with panic. What the hell is this kid doing, stalking her across the country?

With an effort of will, I restrain myself. For now. He's come all this way. The least I can do is give them a little privacy.

I offer Travis a greeting that is brief but not unkind. "I'm going for a swim," I tell Molly. "I'll see you in a little bit."

Yes, a swim in the pool. I need to cool off, calm down, clear my head. I don't want to go off halfcocked, say things in haste, jump to conclusions.

When it comes to pools, I'm usually a toe-dipper, getting wet gradually, inch by careful inch. Today I peel off my cover-up and dive off the edge in one swift motion, surrounding myself with a storm of bubbles, hands brushing the gunite bottom. The water is cold but I'm glad for that. Every nerve ending is wide awake, as I imagine a soldier's would be on the eve of battle.

For me, this is a nightmare—to bring my daughter to

the brink of a brand-new, exciting future, only to have the past reach out and pull her back.

Yet for Molly, it's a dream come true. What girl doesn't romanticize about a love so strong, it makes a guy fly across the country just to see her? And in my heart of hearts, I can understand this. We teach our daughters to dream of love. We read them stories of damsels in distress and the knights in shining armor who rescue them, laying happiness at their feet like a carpet of roses.

Of course, in this day and age, we also read about enlightened princesses who do just fine without a man, but those are not the stories that stick with our girls. For some deep-seated, primal reason, the politically correct tales lack appeal. The stories that stay with them always seem to involve a big-shouldered alpha male, sweeping them off their feet.

After a long, vigorous swim, I shower and dress, trying to compose myself. Flying off the handle, yelling, getting mad won't help the situation in the least. I try calling Dan but get voice mail, and hang up without leaving a message. If I try telling his voice mail what's going on I'll use up all our free minutes.

Instead, I head outside to find Molly. She and Travis have been in the shady garden of the motor court, talking and holding each other for a good half hour.

"What's going on?" I ask them. Molly's hair has dried stiff with chlorine, the curls out of control, her eyes red from crying.

"I had to see Molly," Travis says. His ears are scarlet. I can tell it's hard for him to talk to me.

I struggle to erase all anger and judgment from my

stance. "Travis, I understand it was hard to say goodbye. I know you guys miss each other a lot. But it's time—"

"Okay, don't freak out," Molly says. "I have a plan."

To screw up your life. I bite my lip to keep from saying it.

"I'm listening."

"I changed my mind about college," she says, in one short phrase bringing my most negative fantasies out into the open. "I mean, I'll still go. Just not so far away."

"Whoa, hang on. This is a big decision." Brilliant, I tell myself. You're a real rocket scientist.

"It's the right decision." She is instantly defensive. "What I realized this week is that it's too hard, being apart from Travis. I'll be happier at UW."

"Aw, Molly. I know you think that now, but remember, you always wanted—"

"This has never been about what I want," she says, each word slashing like an finely-honed blade. "It's about what you want for me."

"We want the same thing."

"Do we? When was the last time you checked, Mom? This train started out of the station as soon as I got the acceptance letter. It was never, *Do you want this?*"

"I didn't think I had to ask. Forgive me for assuming you wanted to study at one of the best schools in the country and see where it takes you. Forgive me for assuming you worked so hard in high school so you could explore a future beyond the boundaries of a small town."

"I've been thinking about it all week long. We never talked about other options, Mom. We never talked about the fact that one of those options is that I can say, 'Thanks very much, but I have other plans.'"

Travis, never a kid of many words, simply stands there, stalwart and—I can't deny it—impossibly handsome. He shuffles his feet, looks at the message window of his phone as though someone has sent him an answer through the digital ether.

"Tell me about these other plans, Moll. I really want to know."

"The state school makes perfect sense," she insists, her voice as intent and convincing as a trial lawyer's. "It's way cheaper."

"You have a scholarship. One you earned, I might add, all on your own. I didn't make you. This is something you went after because you wanted it."

"And now I want something else." She sends Travis an adoring look, but he's still studying his phone.

The state university is filled with commuter students juggling marriage, motherhood and work in addition to their courseload. No doubt they're gifted, hardworking people who are doing it all, succeeding, living happy and fulfilling lives. Of course the state school is a good option.

Still. It's not the same as the rarefied world of students hand-selected from a pool of the best and brightest, with an endowment big enough to give scholarships to kids like Molly. There will be none of the things we've heard about, no bonfires or late-night study sessions or elaborate pranks, no students from Ghana or visiting lecturers from the UN, no Nobel laureates, no dorm hall dramas or campus productions of the Vagina Monologues, no Parents' Weekend or commencement addresses in Latin.

"I'll get to have what you and I both want," Molly continued. "An education, and Travis."

"There's so much more for you to discover," I tell her, knowing she doesn't believe me.

"Trav and I will discover it together."

I grit my teeth, refusing to let myself explode. "Travis," I say to him, "could Molly and I have a minute?"

"He should stay," she says, clinging to his hand.

"Er, that's okay." He disengages his hand. "Go ahead and talk stuff over with your mom." He steps aside with a conciliatory smile, barely concealing his relief. I almost feel sorry for him, knowing the tension between Molly and me is stretched to its limit, and very palpable. He walks over by the pool and plugs some change into a vending machine.

"Oh, Molly." I pause, trying to find a way to persuade her. "Look how far you've come. Don't give up on something you've been dreaming of for years."

"It's my decision," she says, her eyes welling with tears. "I'm the one who has to go through the next four years. I can either spend them with strangers, struggling to keep up and trying to fit in, thousands of miles from home, or I can be near the people who love me, getting good grades and an education without sacrificing four years of my life."

This sudden streak of practicality is something new. But I can be practical, too. "Most people wouldn't regard a scholarship to a top university as a sacrifice."

"For me it would be. Even this week has been torture," she says. "I *love* him."

Her stark passion gives me pause. What if Travis *is* the one? What if he's the love of her life? It's not as if love comes along every day. Do I have the right to turn her away from him? Suppose she does it my way and tells him goodbye, and something terrible happens? How would I ever forgive myself?

If turning around and going home with Travis is a mistake, it's hers to make, not mine. If it's the right thing to do, then it's only right that she gets to choose.

I can't deny that this unexpected new plan has its appeal. The thought of Molly living in state, coming home with her laundry on weekends, having Sunday dinner with us, draws me in. Yes, I think, yes, that could work, after all.

Still…

Over at the vending machines, Travis has scored a Coke and a bag of Cheetos. He's chatting up the young mom with the two little kids.

Molly sees me rallying a defense. "A college degree… I can get that anytime—anywhere—I want."

"That's what I used to think."

"But Travis. There's only one of him. There are a lot of ways to get a college degree but there's only one Travis."

"And if he loves you, he'll love the dream you're going after."

"If he loves me, he can't stand to be without me. He spent a whole week's pay to fly out here, even."

I bite my tongue to keep from expressing my opinion of *that*. Long ago, I had rationalizations of my own that sounded eerily similar to Molly's. What if she makes the choice I made? "Sweetie, you're so young. Let yourself *be* young instead of closing all those doors."

"I can be young with Travis." As though reading my mind, she adds, "It's exactly what you did, Mom. You went for love and look how your life turned out. It's wonderful. You and Dad are wonderful. You focused on what's important."

This is what I've taught her. I've modeled it for her. Go for the love, every time. It's surprising—and admittedly gratifying—that she looks at Dan and me and thinks we're wonderful together. I hope like hell we are.

Yet her insistence on choosing this path still sits poorly with me. Travis is…just so damn young. He's a good enough kid, from a nice enough family, but he can be careless with Molly's feelings, though I've never pointed that out for fear of starting an argument.

Maybe Dan was that way, too, and I never noticed because I was crazy about him. Now, years later, I sometimes catch myself wondering, what could I have done, who could I have been, if I'd gone for the big life instead of the big love?

Am I making Molly live the life I missed out on? Is that fair to her?

I gather in a deep breath of courage. "I don't want to force you into a decision. If you stick to the original plan and it turns out badly, you'll never forgive me. I'll never forgive myself. You call the shots, Moll. I'll support you, no matter what."

"Really? You're not just saying that?"

Maybe. No, I mean it. Molly's life is her own now. "I mean it."

I feel her strength and determination. She goes to find Travis.

And just like that, that world shifts. The dream changes. Love has transformed her life. Love has a way of doing that.

I call Dan and give him the news. Travis has come for her. He has convinced her to change her mind about going to college so far away. The rundown of Molly's rationalizations spills from me—she claims she can still enroll in the honors program at UW. We won't really forfeit all that much, just this past roller coaster of a week and a percentage of the first tuition payment.

"Says something for the kid, traveling all that way to make his case," Dan tells me.

"What?" I ask, exasperated. "What does it say, Dan? That he's got nothing better to do? That he's ready to take responsibility for her, to hold her heart and her dreams and keep them safe? Or that the plant had a temporary layoff and he got bored hanging out with his friends?"

"Maybe he'll surprise you."

"This is not helping. We need to be on the same page."

"No, we don't. We're two completely different people, and Molly's her own person, too. She's old enough to understand we can have differing points of view."

As we talk, I move around the room, needing an outlet for my agitation. I seize on the bag of quilting supplies. There's a piece made from a pocket with a little embroidered dog on it. This was from the pedalpushers Molly had worn the day she learned to ride a two-wheeler.

By five years of age, she had worn her training wheels down to the rims and I insisted it was time to take them off. She had balked, arguing to the point of tears.

She agreed only when Dan promised he would run alongside her, holding her up.

"I won't let go until you say," he vowed.

I was certain she'd never get to the letting-go phase, so I went about my business. I was in the kitchen, trying a new recipe, when I heard shouting and the faint *brrring brrring* of the bell on Molly's bike. I went out to see her cruising on two wheels, Dan standing in the middle of the street and grinning from ear to ear.

"They're young," Dan is saying, "but they're still adults."

"If he was thinking of Molly, then he wouldn't take this opportunity away from her."

"The thing is, it's not up to us—not anymore. Back off, honey. Let Molly work on this herself."

Back off. I can hear Molly's voice—*Oh, like* that's *going to happen.*

I hang up the phone. Something has happened to me over the days of our journey, a subtle shift in the way I see my daughter. She is smart, genuine and more mature than I've given her credit for. Trying to bend her to my will won't work on her any more than it would have worked on me when I was her age. Dan tells me to back off. He has no idea how hard that is. With a heavy sigh, I pick up the quilt where I left off. My needle easily pierces through the layers of cloth and batting, soft beneath the pads of my thumbs. I work in a phrase my mother loved to quote: *To thine own self be true.*

There's a dot of blood on the white underside of the quilt. I didn't notice I'd pricked my finger. I grab an ice cube from the bucket I'd filled earlier and try to get the stain out. It dissolves to a faint rusty shadow but doesn't disappear completely. A bloodstain never does.

After blotting the stain, I set the quilt aside. I don't feel like quilting. I don't feel like anything.

I lie on the bed, staring up at the pockmarked tiles on the ceiling. It's getting late, but I'm not sleepy in the least. Is it my job as a mother to convince her to stay on track for college? No. It's not. It's my job to raise a daughter with an open heart and a good head on her shoulders.

It's a balancing act. Love and dreams and duty. I pick up the quilt again, filled with the softness of memories. All the wisdom in the world is in this quilt.

I stare at it for a long time, wondering if there's anything in it for me.

I wake up in the morning to discover a warm lump of girl curled up against me, under the quilt. She stirs and snuggles closer.

Other memories—all the mornings I awakened her, doing my best to soften the ordeal of getting up for school. I'd lie down next to her on the bed and rub her back until she surrendered to the day. Then I think about all the late nights lying awake, listening for the reassuring rumble of her car engine. We used to have long, whispered conversations when she came in moments after curfew, sitting on the side of the bed to tell me about her date.

Now I marvel at how tender I still feel toward this fully grown creature.

Oh, baby. I used to be responsible for drawing the boundaries around your world. Now you're on a path that leads you over the boundaries and away from me. I'll always cherish our time together. Always. But you'll never be my baby again.

She curls closer, a subtle natural movement, a drawing in. I tuck my arm around her. After a while, she pulls away as though preparing herself for her departure.

"Moll?"

She sighs herself awake. "Yes," she whispers, turning away from me. "This means what you think it means."

"Where's Travis?"

"Where do you think? He went standby on the next flight home."

I exhale a cautious breath of relief. It doesn't last long. Molly comes fully awake, crying with the kind of sobs that shake the whole bed. She's crying too hard to speak, so I just wrap myself around her and hold on for a while, silently willing her to stop. As an infant, she'd been fretful, and I spent many midnight hours walking the floor with her, making mindless shushing sounds, just as I do now.

Eventually, the storm subsides. She is still tearful, her voice shaky. "He was so mad at me, Mom. He was so mad. He might never speak to me again. I hurt him that bad."

"I'm sorry, Moll. I know you can't stand hurting anyone."

"Why couldn't you just let me go home? Why did you have to make a federal case out of it?"

"I left it up to you," I reminded her.

"But it was the *way* you did it. It made me feel like an idiot." Agitated now, she blots her tears with a corner of the quilt and sits up.

"I never meant to do that." But wow, is she right. I want her to have the life I passed up in order to be a wife and mom. She is my road not taken. And it's not fair to put that burden on her. "I'm sorry," I tell her. "If you want to turn around now, we'll do it. No hard feelings, no recriminations."

She's quiet for a long time. "I'd hate myself if I didn't go for this. But I need for you to listen, Mom. This is my choice. I'm not doing it because you never had the chance. I'm doing it because I want the chance for me."

DAY SEVEN

Odometer Reading 123,937

Take your needle, my child,
and work at your pattern;
it will come out a rose by and by.
Life is like that—one stitch at a
time taken patiently and the
pattern will come out all right
like the embroidery.

—Oliver Wendell Holmes

Thirteen

———◆◇◆———

I hold the map, with the route to the city highlighted. "I think our turn-off is coming up." We pass through suburbs filled with crackerbox houses, small businesses, big-box stores. I notice a fabric shop with a nice window display; maybe I'll stop in on my way back home. There's a charmless strip center with a beauty salon called the Crowning Glory and a charitable organization called New Beginnings, apparently dedicated to providing clothing and supplies for a local women's shelter. There's also a bakery that fills the air with a smell so delicious, it brings tears to my eyes.

We treat ourselves to butterhorns and insulated cups of strong coffee. Molly, always a compulsive reader of free literature, grabs a flyer with a hair salon coupon and a rundown of the women's shelter services: "Help someone make a New Beginning. Career clothes needed." We try to imagine what it might be like, running for shelter with nothing but the clothes on our backs. It puts our own issues into perspective, for sure, and I keep the flyer, vowing to send a check. We don't linger, though. The destination we've been driving toward for days now lies just a few miles ahead.

We haven't said much about yesterday. Finally, Molly says, "So Travis is home now. He just sent me a text."

I brace myself. She might still want to turn around. "I know you're hurting and I hate that. Everything that happens to you goes straight through my heart."

"Then you know how it feels."

In the beat of hesitation, I hold my breath and wait for her to speak again.

"I have to do this," she says. "I want it, I really do."

"I'm proud of you, Moll. You're going to do great."

We take the interstate to the multilane bridge. Like thick arteries, ramps delve down toward the heart of the city.

An official green-and-white sign marks the city limits. Elevation 40 Feet. Population 101,347.

Molly whips her head toward me. "Which way, left or right?"

"Left."

My thumb traces the route, inching forward as each side street flips past. This place has no grid, just densely aligned roads, some only a block long, others leading nowhere. It's like a web or a net. How will Molly get around in this strange, busy city? How is she going to find her way?

"You have to go left here. Can you make a left from this lane?"

A sense of change takes hold as the city rises around us; I am delivering my only child into uncharted territory. We're here. Our arrival seems abrupt, even though the drive lasted for days. We go from one world to another in a matter of steps. One moment, we're wending our way through a tangle of turnpikes and traffic jams, and the next, we find ourselves in a placid oasis of calm.

The quiet brick street looks like a movie set: trees gracefully shedding the first of their leaves, green rectangular yards crisscrossed by footpaths, colonial-style redbrick buildings with small-paned windows, their frames painted a fresh white. Gaslight fixtures line the sidewalks. The brick walkways bear generations of pockmarks and dents.

We stop and purchase a one-day parking permit. Cars and minivans and SUVs are parked along the curbs on both sides of the roadway. Shiny vehicles disgorge long-legged, laughing girls, slender boys staggering under boxes and cartons, mothers consulting lists, a father or two, standing around talking on cell phones or looking lost.

It's a good thing Dan's not here, after all. He hates feeling like a misfit.

Upperclassmen, facing their orientation groups and talking constantly, are showing the new students around. The tour guides walk backwards with impressive confidence, certain they won't stumble.

Molly maneuvers the rumbling old SUV into the narrow street. It's easily the largest noncommercial vehicle in sight. She pulls into a gap at the curbside, her mouth grim as she tries to align the big truck along the curb. "I won't miss parking this beast," she grumbles.

She switches off the engine. It dies with a shudder. I turn to find her looking at me, and for a moment, the two of us just sit, staring into each other's eyes, not smiling, not talking, just…looking.

It's amazing how much you can see in a face you love, all the layers of years, still visible in the present moment. The infant Molly, her eyes as blue now as they were then, round and open wide, staring upward at me. And my face, eighteen years ago, had filled the baby's whole world.

"Okay," Molly says suddenly, unbuckling her seat belt with a decisive click. "We're here." The car inhales the belt as she jumps out and slams the door.

A black Lexus trolls along the street, headed straight for Molly. *Watch out.* I nearly scream the warning, but the moment passes before I open my mouth. She steps up onto the curb, the car whizzes by and I sit alone in the passenger seat, my heartbeat a stampede of anxiety.

"Okay," I mutter, echoing Molly. "We're here." The breeze carries a subtle chill, a whiff of dry leaves, the tang of autumn. If we were back home, I'd be posting the high school football schedule on the fridge and paging through bulb catalogs.

Molly has the cargo doors open and is staring at the lopsided stacks and bundles. Uncertainty creases her brow.

I offer a suggestion. "Maybe you'd better—"

"—check in first," Molly finishes for me. "I was *so* going to do that."

"You want me to come in with you?"

"That's okay, Mom. It'll probably only take a few minutes."

"I'll wait out here, then."

The Suburban huddles in a rusty heap, disreputable, inferior compared to the gleaming, late-model cars with plates from Massachusetts, Connecticut, New York, Virginia. In contrast to the forest-green and burgundy imports, the old Chevy, with its flaking paint job, is as garish and ungainly as a parade float left out in the rain.

The Joads go to college, I'm thinking, certain everyone is staring at me. Glancing in the rearview mirror, I focus on the shopping bag filled with my brand-new, never-worn clothes. I should have worn something special for today, comes the belated thought.

Old worries surface. I still find myself feeling inferior, the misfit, the one who gets picked last. Oh God. Does Molly feel inferior, or did I teach her better? I check her out to see if she's self-conscious about the car. But no. Molly's oblivious as she makes her way inside. She couldn't care less what the car looks like, what state is on the license plate.

I call Dan. I've never been a big fan of mobile phones, but right now, I love my cell phone so much I would marry it. It's proof that someone wants to talk to you. It saves you from having to loiter in a strange place, trying to appear as though you belong.

Molly called him this morning to talk about Travis. He doesn't sound surprised. We backed off and she made her own choice.

"We're here," I tell Dan. "It's amazing."

"How's our girl doing?"

"She didn't have much to say about Travis. We're not talking about it yet. I'm hoping she'll just focus on getting settled here." My gaze skips over the quad, currently an anthill of activity as students move in en masse. "Looks like there's plenty to keep her busy." I take a breath. "Speaking of which, I had a thought."

"Lindy, not another orphan."

"No. Not now, anyway. Saying goodbye to Molly is making me crazy, I admit it. What I've been thinking about is that I need a new life when I get back."

"Something wrong with your old life?"

"Not at all, but without Molly there, I need a plan. So I thought… Don't freak out."

"I'm listening."

"I'm going to talk to Minerva about the shop."

"What do you mean, talk to her?"

"About taking over the shop. She's retiring, and I thought maybe… I could see if I can qualify for a small-business loan and…" I falter. Spoken aloud, it sounds silly. "Anyway, maybe it's a crazy idea, but I think I can make it work."

Silence.

"Dan?" I wait for him to tell me how foolish I'm being, especially now, with a kid in college.

"You can make anything work, Linda."

It's the last thing I expected to hear from him. "Really?"

"Hell, yeah. Don't sound so surprised."

"But…you never… I never knew you felt that way."

"Sweetheart, I've always felt that way about you. Just because I didn't say it every day doesn't mean the sentiment's not there."

"You were such a skeptic about my last idea—"

"Adopting an orphan? Come on, Linda. This is hardly the same. This is something you want for you, not to fill some void left by Molly."

I shut my eyes, catch my breath. When did I stop knowing this man? I never did; I just let the busy part of life get in the way. *"Thank you."*

"I miss you," he says. "I can't wait to see you."

His words ignite a rush of passion in me, an emotion as strong and fresh as the first time I felt it. "Same here," I say, smiling.

Carrying a thick manila envelope, Molly comes out of the dorm, talking to a woman with a clipboard. The woman is about my age, early forties, but she wears her hair in a sleekly careless ponytail and sports an ethnic-print skirt, a trendy blouse and a tooled silver thumb-ring. Molly looks enchanted with her.

Acutely aware of my lap-creased jeans and the mustard stain on my sweatshirt, I chastise myself again for not wearing a selection from my new clothes. Then I put on my best smile, walk over to the sandstone steps and introduce myself.

"Linda," the woman says. "I'm Ceci Gamble. The residential facilitator." She has a slightly nasal voice and a distinctive, East Coast boarding-school accent.

The theme music of the Wicked Witch of the West buzzes in my head. Who is this exotic new mentor, poised to supplant me? "Nice to meet you. So is Molly all set to move in?"

"Absolutely. Everything's in the information packet. Let me know if you need anything, anything at all."

I smile in gratitude, quashing the sudden resentment, but Ceci Gamble is already turning away, her glossy ponytail flying. She greets another mother who is busy unloading a Mercedes station wagon with a Choate sticker on the back. They crow at each other, embrace, old chums from prep school or the country club. Girls stream past in groups, all talking, the autumn sun strong on their silky, straight hair as they mount the stairs to the freshman dorm.

For a fraction of a second, Molly looks uncertain, her full lower lip soft and vulnerable. She scrunches a hand into her hair. The beautiful corkscrew curls have been the bane of her existence for years, no matter how much her friends claim to covet them. She wishes for straight hair. Prep school hair. East Coast hair.

She's the outsider here, after fitting in so comfortably

in high school, playing varsity sports, winning music competitions, laughing on the phone, never at a loss for a friend or a date. She looks lost in the moment now, uncertain. Hesitation is written in her stance, though I'm the only one who can see it. I see the tiny girl afraid to take off her training wheels, jump into a pool, recite a poem for the class, endure her first piano recital, taste an oyster for the first time.

I was always the one pushing her to get past the fear and do it anyway. Dan tended to want to whisk her away from it all. Now I wonder if she felt the constant push-pull of our warring need to protect and promote. Then I remember her confidence in sports, in music, in academics. The gift of her hard work is that self-confidence. She's going to be fine.

I can see her rally in the determined set of her chin. We head inside, to a building that once housed future scientists, jurists, artists and world leaders. Following the directions in the packet, we find a bare room, hung with the smell of Pine-Sol and airless summerlong neglect. Molly heads straight for the window and opens it wide.

The roommate hasn't arrived. Kayla from Philadelphia is nowhere in sight. The barren room contains two phone jacks and wireless modem setups, two desks, twin consoles of drawers and shelves and the requisite two beds. We climb up and down the worn concrete stairs, bringing stuff from the truck to the room. "Want some help unpacking?" I ask.

"That's all right. I'll do it myself. That way, I'll know where everything is." She is clear on not wanting me to linger, to tuck shirts away in drawers, stack office supplies, stand in registration lines with her.

She tackles the first box—towels and toiletries. Then she opens another. Her face looks tense.

"Did you remember your alarm clock?" I ask a mundane question to distract her, but it doesn't work. "Moll?" I ask, tentative, not pushing at all now. "What's up?"

She pulls out the green-shaded desk lamp. "It's broken. I wonder when it broke. Maybe when I slammed on the brakes to miss that deer."

"It can be fixed. We could find a store, look for a replacement for the shade."

"I don't need it."

"You're the one who insisted on bringing it."

"And I was wrong. So sue me. Geez, I can't believe you're still doing this," she snaps.

"Doing what?"

"This… I don't even know what to call it. You want me to be here, to have the whole college experience, but at the same time, you keep acting like I'll fall apart any second. You don't need to fix everything. You don't need to be my human shield anymore. I'm not that fragile. I won't break, I swear. Don't feel like you have to protect me."

"It's my job to protect you."

"Well, congrats. You're finished. Now you can do something else."

The breeze through the open window is reviving her curls.

"Why are you acting so annoyed?" I ask her. I'm getting annoyed, too.

"You always try to make everything easier for me. It's like I live inside this artificial bubble you created.

That's what's annoying. It's my time. My life. My turn to screw up and suffer the consequences."

"Your turn to succeed and be amazing."

"Whatever. The point is, it's my turn, Mom. What happened with Travis—just to remind you again, it was my decision. Not yours or Dad's or even Travis's. Mine, a hundred percent. Right or wrong, I own it, okay?"

"Of course."

"So quit worrying." She's close to tears, her expression taut with suppressed panic.

My Molly is terrified. She's afraid she'll be lonely. Afraid she'll fail. Afraid she won't measure up.

"Aw, Moll."

Her shoulders hunch. "What if I blow it? What if I disappoint you?"

Finally, I know what she needs. Maybe this is the whole point of the past week. She needs to be free of the weight of her parents' expectations. "That will never happen."

With a decisive air, she shoves the lamp into a trash can. She looks at me for a long time, her stare penetrating. I try to offer a reassuring smile. She doesn't smile back. Instead, she says, "I'm worried about you, Mom."

It's the last thing I expected to hear. "Worrying is my job."

"No, I mean it. We've had our moments, but you know I think you're great. The thing that worries me is what you're going to do now that I'm gone."

"Don't be silly. I'll do what I've always done."

"What you've always done is be my mom. You need to figure out something else now."

"There's nothing to figure," I say reassuringly. "I have a fulfilling life, great friends, a loving husband.

I never defined myself as a mother and nothing else. I have other roles to play."

"Really? Like what?"

"Lots of things. I just have to figure out which roles to pursue. I've been thinking of doing more volunteer work."

Molly clearly notices my lack of enthusiasm. "You should do something you love."

What I love is being your mom. I bite my tongue. I will not lay that on her. Setting my jaw until my back teeth ache, I take out her alarm clock and set it to local time.

Soon we'll be living in different time zones.

"Mom, didn't you used to say you wanted to finish your degree?"

"Yes, but I put it off when I—"

"You put it off," Molly prods.

"I was so busy with everything else, it just wasn't practical. Now it's not important."

"Are you sure? When was the last time you thought about it?"

"Say, I've got an idea—I could get my degree here, while you're here. We could even get an apart—"

"Very funny." Molly's face flashes panic—no doubt she senses I'm only half joking. "Anyway, what's stopping you now?"

"I'm not sure. Lack of ambition, maybe." But there is something I do want, something I have only begun to believe in. "Your dad liked the idea of me taking over Pins & Needles."

"Of course he liked it. It's a perfect idea, are you kidding? You can do anything, Mom. I love the thought of you running the fabric store. I totally love it. I hope you go for it."

Fear and uncertainty turn to something else—Hope. Excitement.

She takes out a small stack of framed pictures, gazes at a shot of her dad with Hoover.

"I know he wishes he could be here," I tell her.

"No, he doesn't. You think I don't know why Dad didn't come?" Molly is incredulous. "You think he stayed home because he doesn't care? He's my father. He didn't come for the same reason he didn't go to the vet with you last spring when Hoover was so sick. It's not weakness or that he doesn't care. It's that he cares too much."

"You know your father well."

"You don't need a college degree to figure Dad out." She sets the photograph on a shelf in her dorm room and her gaze lingers on it. "Look what you're going back to, Mom. How can you not be happy?"

The tension in my chest unfurls on a wave of lightness. I am married to a man with a great heart. My daughter and I both know it.

"Where are you going to eat tonight?" I page through the orientation booklet. "The freshman dining room's in Memorial Hall—"

"Don't worry, Mom. I won't starve. I'm still full from lunch. I might just settle for granola bars and juice."

"You should go to the dining hall, even if you're not hungry." I bite my tongue. I have to stop with the you-shoulds.

I take out the quilt, which I've carefully folded and tied with a ribbon in her high school's colors. "I want you to have this, a reminder of home. It's not really finished, though," I point out. "There's a lot more I wanted to do to it."

"It's great." She unties the ribbon and wafts the quilt over the bed. Sunlight falls across the crazy patchwork, the loopy quilting with its hidden messages.

"It's not finished," I say again, feeling a thrum of panic all out of proportion with the situation. "I thought I would finish it during the trip, and we're here and it's still not done."

"It's beautiful, Mom. I love it."

"I still have to—"

"No, you don't."

"Maybe you could bring it home at Christmas break and I'll work on it some more then."

"Mom, would you stop?" Her sharp tone brings me up short. Out in the hallway of the dorm, we hear a clatter. Then someone shouts, "We need a cleanup on aisle one! I just dropped a blue raspberry slushie." More noise and laughter ensue.

Very slowly and carefully, her hands brushing over the fabric, Molly folds the quilt in half, and half again. And again, revealing the soft, faded underside. She makes a perfect bow with the colored ribbon. "Listen, Mom, don't freak out, okay? But this doesn't belong here, in a dorm room."

"What?"

"I mean, I appreciate it and all, but this is a dorm room. And the quilt is a wonderful, one-of-a-kind work of art. I don't want it to get damaged. I don't want it being used to mop up spilled beer or whatever, not that I would do that but who knows about other kids?"

"You should have it, Moll. See, all the fabric comes

from things that are familiar to you, stuff I've saved over the years. It's a keepsake. A picture of your life so far."

"I know, Mom. Believe me, I know. And I love it for that reason," she says. "I love you for making it. That quilt is incredible." She takes a breath, regards me with a wisdom I never knew she possessed. "But it's not my story, Mom. It's yours."

The clarity and wisdom of her words fills me up completely. She's looked at the big picture and seen what I never could. I was so focused on each tiny stitch and detail that I didn't realize what I was creating. What a nutty idea, thinking I could stitch together some kind of patchwork picture of Molly's life so far. It's arrogant, too, to presume to tell her story. Because like she says— it's not a picture of her life. It's a picture of mine. The best part of mine.

"What do you want me to do with it?" I ask her.

"Just don't leave it here where it could get ruined or lost. Keep it for you and Dad… I don't know. Mom, it's so beautiful. It doesn't belong here. Seriously, you know I'm right." She holds the folded quilt out to me, handling it with reverence and respect. "You decide."

I hesitate, then take the quilt from her, holding it against me, knowing my heart is stitched into every square inch of the piece. Each bit of fabric comes from a vanished but fondly remembered moment in time. All along, I thought it was about Molly, but ultimately, it is about me—the mother I was, the moments I remember, the hopes and dreams in my heart.

But bring it home? What will I do with it then? It'll just end up in the old cedar chest, stale and forgotten. For me, the joy of the quilt was in its creation, not in *having* it. But that doesn't mean Molly's obligated to drag it around.

The last thing she needs is the smothering burden of this blanket I've patched together, covered with messages from the past. She wants to create her own story, in her own way, on her own blank canvas.

That's the daughter I raised.

Fourteen

"Then..." I shove my hands into the back pockets of my jeans. "I guess I'd better hit the road."

Alarm flashes in Molly's eyes. It's finally real to her. I'm leaving, and she'll soon be all by herself. But she visibly conquers her fear, squelching panic with steely resolve, evident in her posture and the set of her jaw. "Okay," she says. "I'll walk you downstairs."

I turn to conduct one last survey of the place that will be her home for the next year. The room isn't ready. The furniture arrangement isn't ideal. The bookcase is too close to the radiator, and there aren't enough outlets. With every fiber of my being, I want to stay here and fix things, make adjustments, improvements. I force myself to turn away.

The hallway smells of bleach and fresh paint. Someone is mopping up a spill on the floor. Other parents and kids are moving in, some in weighty silence, others with caffeinated chattiness, a few engaged in low-voiced arguments.

"You're not going to lose it, are you, Mom?" Molly asks.

"Yes," I say. "I might."

Molly looks startled. She's used to being protected, shielded, having troubles glossed over and smoothed out so they don't snag on her. But as she pointed out to me earlier, she is a young adult now, old enough to know her mother is not infallible. She swore she didn't need me running interference for her at every turn.

"Check it out," she says, bracing her hands on the windowsill. A cluster of students has gathered in the old yard below. "I think that's the meeting point for the orientation groups. It's geeky, but I kind of want to go."

We step out into the sunny afternoon. I feel a piercing sweetness deep in my heart. A barely dammed river of tears pushes against my chest.

"If you cry," Molly warns, "I'll cry, too."

"Then we'll both cry." And we do, but somehow we manage to stop, regaining control by focusing on the long line of departing cars.

"I've got that orientation meeting," she says, pressing her sleeve across her eyes.

"And I need to get going, too. Maybe miss the traffic heading out of the city."

"That information packet lists some local places to stay," Molly points out. "I mean, if you don't feel like a big drive today…"

"I'm kind of eager to head back to your dad and Hoover," I tell her. What I don't tell her is that I can't face a night at the Colonial Inn with its stupid plaster lamplighters in three-corner hats, knowing Molly is only a short walk away. The temptation to go check on her would be too great and prolong the pain of separation. I plan to drive a couple hundred miles, take a long soak in the hotel hot tub, then phone Molly from a safe distance.

The breeze that sweeps through the quadrangle smells of autumn. A few yellow leaves flutter down with lazy grace. Students and statues populate the ancient, broad lawns laid out centuries before by idealists who embraced order and harmony.

The grassy yard is crisscrossed by walkways littered with new-fallen leaves. Long-bodied boys lie with their heads cushioned on overstuffed backpacks, their noses poked into dog-eared novels. Girls with sweaters draped over their shoulders sit cross-legged in small groups, engaged in earnest debate.

All up and down the street, there is the sound of car doors slamming shut, farewells being called out.

Molly and I walk to the SUV, which is now as empty as an abandoned campsite. My lone suitcase lies in the back alongside the parcel filled with my new clothes. I place the quilt back in its bag and set it down next to the glossy sack from the department store. The thing is coming home with me after all, it seems. Maybe I'll finish it this fall.

"So, okay," Molly says uncertainly. Her eyes dart here and there; she does not look at me. "Thanks for driving with me, Mom. Thanks for everything."

"Sure, honey. Promise you'll call if you need anything, anything at all. I'll have my cell phone on, 24/7." I touch her arm, feeling its shape beneath my fingers. Then I give up pretending to be casual. No point trying to minimize the moment. "Oh, baby. I'm going to miss you so much."

"Me, too, Mom."

Everything I need to say crowds into my throat—eighteen years of advice, guidance, warning, teaching. And it overwhelms me. It is too much…and not enough. Have I forgotten something important? Have I taught her to do laundry and balance her checkbook? To write thank-you notes by hand? Turn off the coffee-maker when it's done? To fend off a horny guy and to contest an unfair grade? To look in the mirror and like what she sees?

There is so much to say. And so I say nothing. There was a time when eighteen years felt like forever, or at least more than enough time to cover every possible topic, but I was wrong about that. I can only hope Dan and I equipped her to make the right choices.

I am amazed to feel something new. I don't want to spout out any more advice or commentary. I want life to happen for Molly in all its pain and joy and richness, revealing itself moment by moment, unfiltered by a mother's intervention. An unexpected, settled feeling creeps in. There are things she knows that will hold and keep her, whether or not I am there. Finally, I'm start-ing to trust that.

I want her to be on her own. This is what she is sup-posed to do. It's the natural progression of things. Dan and I have given her everything we have. Now it is time for her to fly, seek new mentors, find her place in the world. I think about all the things that will happen to Molly. Things that will bring her joy and break her heart, make her laugh, cry, rage, exult. I wish I could protect her from the rough parts, but I know I can't. And really, I shouldn't.

The essence of life is the journey, unblunted by an overprotective parent. There is a richness Molly will find even in the deepest sadness. She has a beautiful future ahead of her. Sticking around, interfering and shielding her will rob her of something she needs to

figure out on her own. I don't want to stand in the way.
Life as it unfolds is just too incredible.

She knows we will always be here for her. Our lives
are forever entwined. And yes, she's going to suffer a
broken heart and face disappointment and make bad
decisions and do all those other things we humans do,
but she'll survive them. She's smart and big-hearted and
deeply resourceful, probably more than I know, though
on this trip I've seen glimpses.

"You're going to be incredible," I finally say. "I'm
so happy for you." I am, but I had no idea happiness
could hurt so much.

This is it. This is really it. This is goodbye. Suddenly
I don't care that there are people all over the place,
people who are going to be Molly's friends and neighbors for the next four years. I take my daughter's face
between my hands and stare into the eyes I know so
well, into a soul that is as bright and clear as the September sky.

She's going to soar, I'm certain of it. Higher than she
or I can ever imagine. "Goodbye, Molly," I say. "Goodbye, my precious girl."

Smiling mouth. Trembling chin. "'Bye, Mom."

I kiss her soft cheek, and we embrace, a long strong
hug, filled with the wistful scent of autumn and of
herbal shampoo. "You are golden," I whisper to my
daughter, quoting one of our favorite songs. "You are
sunshine." We pull back, smiling, eyes shining.

"I'll call you tonight, okay?" I tell her.

"That'd be great, Mom."

One more kiss. A squeeze of the hands. With slow
deliberation, I climb into the truck, roll down the window. We hold hands again while I start the engine. Then

I put the car in Drive and let go. Our fingers cling for a heartbeat, then slide apart.

In the rearview mirror I can see Molly standing on the sidewalk, as slender and graceful as the turning trees of the old college yard. Golden leaves fly upward on a gust of wind, swirling around her lone form. My daughter stands very still, and just as the truck turns the corner onto the busy avenue, she raises one hand, waving goodbye.

Tapping the horn to acknowledge the wave, I let out a breath I didn't realize I was holding.

I set the iPod to a mix of quiet songs. The first one is a classic, from my dating days with Dan. As the music plays, I head for the interstate, tears still escaping to soak into the neckline of my sweatshirt. I flex my hands on the steering wheel, set my jaw. So what if I'm crying. I'm the mother. I get to cry if I want to.

The traffic flows like a viscous liquid, undemanding, carrying me swiftly away from the city, the car a fallen leaf in a rushing stream.

As the city fades away behind me, I picture Molly in her freshly painted dorm room, unpacking her belongings, putting her new sheets on the narrow iron-frame bed, propping up snapshots of her friends and family, her dog and Travis, shelving books and supplies, plugging in the computer, organizing her things. Eventually she will come across the covered plastic box I filled with her favorite snacks— microwave popcorn, granola bars, Life Savers, pecan sandies, canned juices, cinnamon-flavored gum. Inside she will find a familiar note scribbled on a paper napkin: a little smiling cartoon mommy, with squiggles to represent the hair, and a message that will remind her of all the homemade lunches of her childhood: "I <3 U. Love, Mommy."

I think about giving Dan a call and I will, but not just yet. This moment is too raw, but it's mine to feel—the bittersweet triumph, the sadness, the hope. On this leg of the journey, there will be no detour or scenic route as I make my way home.

Home, to Dan, who said he can't wait to see me. Home, to a life that is open like the pages of an unread book. *Yes.*

I'm ready to live my life. Okay, maybe I'm a little scared, but in a good way. I want to discover who I am on my own, what I love beyond the obvious, and what I really want for the rest of my life.

At the west end of the city, I pass a suburban strip mall I remember from the day before, with the Crowning Glory Salon, the delicious-smelling Sweet Dreams bakery and the charity called New Beginnings. The charity is closed for the day but there's a big metal donation box in the front. Under the Web address for the charity is its slogan: "Comforting women and children in need."

On impulse, I turn into the parking lot, go around to the back of the Suburban and open the gate. Molly's observation drifts back to me: This is about *your* life, Mom.

I stand there for a minute, thinking about the woman I've been for the past eighteen years and wondering who I'll be for the next eighteen. It's a bit scary to contemplate, but exciting, too.

When I grab the parcel, my resolve wavers. Then I think, go for it. The true meaning of charity is to give freely, no strings attached. I have to let go, only trusting that my gift will be out there in the world somewhere, doing whatever it's bound to do.

And then I push the bag into the drop box, having to shove its soft bulk inch by inch through the narrow slot. At first I worry that it won't go down the chute, and I have to push hard. Then the last bit slips through easily and disappears.

Stenciled under the chute are the words, "Thank you for your donation."

I return to the still-running car. Something stirs inside me, a sensation as empty and light as the curling, cup-shaped leaves lifted by the autumn wind.

Stopping at the last red light before the on-ramp to the interstate, I catch the blinding beam of the late afternoon sun in my eye. The days of summer have grown shorter. The year is getting old already.

I flip down the sun visor, and a stray slip of paper drifts into my lap. Picking it up, I unfold it and see a little smiling cartoon face, corkscrew squiggles for hair, and a note that says, "I <3 U. Love, Molly."

Epilogue

The shop called Pins & Needles looks the way it always has, since its founding decades ago. Its brick and concrete façade glows in the evening light, the windows framed with swaths of fabric. The holidays are past and winter has settled in. The air is sweet and dry with the peculiar clarity that the winter cold brings. The shop is open late tonight, but there is no business to be done.

In the window is a hand-lettered sign: "Retirement Party. Come celebrate with us."

Standing behind the counter, I feel as if I'm glowing, too, with a sense of happiness and fulfillment. All around me are my customers, the women who frequent the shop, talking together and sharing all the events of their lives. They've brought platters of cookies and a crystal bowl filled with punch. Minerva, now in a wheelchair, beams at me. "It's a good time to move on, eh?"

"I can't believe it's been twenty-five years," says my best friend, Erin, as she gives me a hug. "Happy retirement, Linda."

I can't believe it either, sometimes. All those years

ago, when I struggled with myself after taking Molly to college, the answer was staring me in the face. I didn't need a bag full of gorgeous new clothes to find my new life. They did more good giving someone else a fresh start; donating the brand-new things to the women's shelter was the right thing to do. Dan loves me as I am. The women at Pins & Needles do, too. I just needed to be the person I've always been—a wife, a friend and neighbor, a needleworker, a dabbler.

The proof is here before me now, a warmhearted shop filled with women I've come to know like sisters through the years. Minerva, who celebrated her nine-tieth last year, has been my mentor. As the festivities go on, Molly and her husband arrive, their three kids in tow, and suddenly my arms are filled with grandchildren. The sweetness of this moment makes my heart expand with joy. Dan comes over, laughing about being outnumbered by females. He's as strong and handsome as the day I met him nearly fifty years ago, wearing his age like a fine patina. He raises a cup of punch to me. "I knew you could do it, but now I can't wait to have you all to myself." Still a man of few words, he retreats with our son-in-law to forage for snacks and to escape the chattering women.

After Molly left for college, I missed her terribly, but my life took a new turn and opened up in new ways. I found a dream of my own and went for it. Running the quilt shop didn't make me a rich woman, not in the financial sense. But it enriched my life beyond measure, and I can see that so clearly now, looking around at the faces of my family and friends, customers and well-wishers. The big changes can't be seen, only felt.

Molly gives me a hug and steps back, her eyes shining. "Happy retirement, Mom. I'm really proud of you."

Her words light me up like sunshine, as they always have. We turn together to the display wall behind the counter, regarding the quilt, the one I was making for Molly so long ago. She had it right all along—it *was* my story, and it wasn't finished.

Family. History. Love and loss. I've touched every inch of this fabric. It's absorbed my scent and the invisible oils of my skin, the smell of our household, the occasional drop of blood, and sometimes my tears. I've added to the piece through the years; it's an ever-expanding record of our days as a family. There's a swatch from Molly's graduation gown, and a ribbon from the table decorations on her wedding day. There's a piece from her husband's desert fatigues, and little precious bits from my grandchildren. A tiny silver bell marks our twenty-fifth wedding anniversary. I'm already wondering what little symbol will commemorate our golden anniversary. I try not to plan ahead. Why rob life of its surprises?

I plan to take the quilt home with me tonight, and no doubt more keepsakes will make their way into the design. Life has taught me not to be afraid of starting something new.

How do you say goodbye to a piece of your heart? You don't ever have to. There's always a way to keep the things we hold most dear.

* * * * *

Acknowledgments

I'm very fortunate to have a publisher that allows me to put my heart on paper. Many thanks to my editor and great friend, Margaret O'Neill Marbury, and to everyone at MIRA Books. As always, I'm indebted to Meg Ruley, Annelise Robey and their associates at the Jane Rotrosen Agency—your wisdom, patience and friendship mean the world to me.

To my fellow writers—Anjali Banerjee, Kate Breslin, Carol Cassella, Sheila Roberts and Suzanne Selfors—thank you so much for reading multiple drafts and helping me pull this patchwork of emotion together.

I'm grateful to master quilter Marybeth O'Halloran for the insights and expertise into her colorful world— any liberties and errors in the text are my own. A very special thank-you to my dear friend Joan Vassiliadis, for creating the original Goodbye Quilt and for sharing her talent in the pages of this book.

The Goodbye Quilt Pattern

by Joan Vassiliadis
www.joanofcards.blogspot.com

Finished size is approximately 45" x 56"
Instructions based on 42" wide fabric
All seams are ¼"

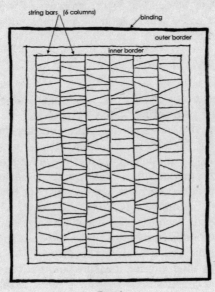

Figure 1

Fabric Requirements

Collect 100% cotton fabric scraps that have special meaning to you. Don't be afraid to cut into old things. You will be able to enjoy them much more in a quilt that will be seen and touched every day. Make sure your scraps are at least 7" wide and total approximately 2½ yards. Inner border: ½ yard solid color to frame the string bars. Outer border: 5/8 yard. Backing: 3¼ yards. Binding: ½ yard.

Cutting Instructions

Cut approximately 220 strings all 7" in length—cut uneven widths ranging between 1"and 3". Inner solid border: cut 4 strips crosswise (from selvage to selvage) 2½" wide. Outer border: Cut 4 strips crosswise 4" wide. Binding: Cut 2½" strips to total the perimeter of your finished quilt.

Sewing Instructions

Play music while you work, sing along and remember why each piece of fabric is special to you. Begin constructing the bars first into pairs and then into fours and so on. Put dark colors next to light if possible, but don't worry too much about it if you have more darks than lights or vice versa. Do be careful to pin and press. Whenever possible, press towards the dark fabric. Construct six bars at least 44" long. Your edges will be uneven so trim each bar to 6" wide (see Figure 2). Sew all six bars together and press. Trim the ends so they are all even and you're ready for borders.

For the inner border, measure your quilt lengthwise first, and construct two strips 2½" wide to this length Sew to the sides of the quilt and press. Next, measure the width of your quilt. Construct two strips 2 ½" wide to this measurement. Sew to the top and bottom of the quilt and press. Now for the outer border: Measure the sides of your quilt and construct two strips 4" wide to this length. Next, measure the width of your quilt. Construct two strips 4" side to this measurement. Sew to the top and bottom of the quilt and press. Your top is now complete! Think about all of the memories sewn into this quilt…remember the sweetest moments of life.

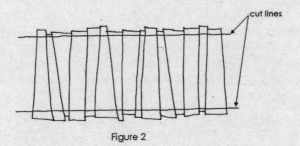
cut lines

Figure 2

Finishing the Quilt

Linda finished her quilt on the drive with Molly. You can finish yours in the car, in a comfy chair, with your quilting friends at the dining-room table…any way and anywhere you please! If tying your quilt you can embellish with more memories: buttons, ribbons, badges. Do think about how often your quilt will be washed and how your embellishments will endure. If you make your quilt an art piece, then you can incorporate almost anything. After quilting, measure the perimeter and sew binding strips together to total this measurement. Attach binding.

A WEDDING
ON PRIMROSE STREET

Sheila Roberts

For Karen

One

Anne, Wedding Planner and Mother of the Bride

"I don't care what my daughter thinks she wants. We are *not* having daisies at the wedding. They stink."

Anne Richardson pinched the bridge of her nose in an effort to stop the headache that was forming. She loved being a wedding planner…most days. But difficult clients did suck some of the joy out of her job. Everyone talked about Bridezillas, but in Anne's opinion Momzillas were ten times worse. And she was sure that Seattle had ten times more Momzillas per capita than any other city in the country.

"I mean, really," Laurel Browne continued. "Would you want daisies at your daughter's wedding?"

No, but if her daughter wanted daisies Anne would order them. Laurel was stepping over the line. Actually, she was stomping over the line.

Anne flashed on an image of Laurel as a giant mutant monster in a mother-of-the-bride dress, trampling a field of daisies. "Well," she began.

"I am *not* paying for daisies," Laurel said, her voice

rising to a level that had Anne moving her phone away from her ear. "In fact, I no longer want to go with that florist at all. I thought I made it clear yesterday when we were in your office how subpar I think these floral arrangements are."

Oh, yes, more than clear. And that had started Wedding War III with her daughter. (Wedding War I had been fought the very first week over the colors the bride had chosen. Laurel had lost that one. Wedding War II had been over the venue and she'd come out the victor. Now she was pushing to win more wedding territory.)

"Of course, I understand your feelings completely," Anne said. But not her behavior. She had her daughter's special day in a choke hold.

"I should hope so," Laurel said huffily. "I am *not* paying you all this money to organize a wedding where I have to sit in a pew and smell daisies while I watch my daughter take her wedding vows. In fact, I sometimes wonder what I *am* paying you for."

To be your verbal punching bag? Anne ignored the jab about money. A wedding planner had to be thick-skinned. She also had to be a diplomat. Anne succeeded at both, which was why Memory Makers Weddings and Events was still in business after eighteen years.

"We do want your daughter to be happy on her special day," she said. At least one of them did. "So I'm going to suggest a compromise."

"What kind of compromise?" Laurel asked suspiciously.

"We could have the florist add daisies to the brides-maids' flowers and the bridal bouquet, and that would make Chelsea very happy. Then the flowers for the church and the table settings could be totally different, say yellow and white roses." She'd wanted to suggest that the day before when Laurel and Chelsea were in her office but hadn't been able to wedge in the words with mother and daughter going at it so vociferously. They'd left, still fighting.

"Hmm," Laurel said thoughtfully. "That might work."

"And really, this florist will do a lovely job for you. She's always open to suggestions." Or, as in Laurel's case, commands.

"Well, all right. Let's see if she can do that. Tell her we want something unique. Roses aren't enough. I want something with flair."

Flair. Who knew what that meant? But Anne promised flair to the max—for a reasonable price, of course—so she and the florist would have to become mind readers and translate the vague request into specific arrangements. Maybe Laurel would like her to spin some straw into gold while she was at it.

"Lord help me," she said with a groan after ending the call. "What did I do to deserve Laurel Browne as a client?"

"Happy Friday the Thirteenth," teased her younger sister, Kendra, who was busy making a spreadsheet for a new client.

"That woman is out of control." But then, this sometimes happened with younger brides whose parents were footing the bill.

"Sounds like you've got it handled," Kendra said.

"Yet another wedding crisis averted."

Kendra smiled. "Laurel has no idea how lucky she is that she has you for her wedding planner."

Obviously. "I *am* good."

And she'd proved it time and time again, organizing every imaginable kind of wedding, from medieval fairs to events in which the bride and groom parachuted onto the site where their vows would be exchanged. She never tired of planning weddings.

"Compensating," her mother had said when she'd first started doing it at church for free twenty years ago. If she was indeed making up for her own less-than-stellar wedding, she was doing a great job of it. She didn't plan weddings for free anymore, and her mother passed out her business cards as if they were chocolates. Even with her sister's help she often had to turn away business.

Too bad she hadn't turned away the Brownes, she thought, looking out her office window at the dripping Seattle sky. If Laurel reminded her once more that she was paying a lot for this wedding, she was going to pull out her eyebrows. And Laurel's, too.

The phone rang again. It was Marla Polanski, another Momzilla, wanting to know if Anne could change her daughter's wedding venue. It would be the third time. "We found a place up in Icicle Falls," Momzilla Marla raved. "It's a beautiful Victorian house with the most elegant gardens and a fabulous staircase Gwyneth could come down. I'm sending you the link right now."

"Okay," Anne said, "but you may have to adjust the size of your guest list." A house wouldn't hold as many people as the Kiana Lodge, the current venue of choice. A big, spread-out place across Puget Sound from Seattle with lovely grounds, it was a popular choice for many of her clients.

There was a moment of silence. Then Marla said, "Oh. Yes, that is an issue. Well, Gwyneth will simply have to pare it down a little because this place is exactly what we want—much more intimate and with so much charm. Anyway, I think they can handle up to a hundred."

That meant cutting their guest list in half. Anne hoped Marla would do the math. "Why don't you talk it over with your daughter?" she suggested.

"I will, but meanwhile book this place. I see they have the second Saturday in August open, and I don't want someone else to get it. We can always change back to the lodge."

"I suppose so," Anne said dubiously. "Meanwhile, how about we keep the lodge booked until you're sure?" If they let go of their date they'd never get it back.

"I don't think we'll be needing it," Marla said in a confident voice. "I really want Gwyneth to be married up in Icicle Falls."

The customer was always right, even when she was wrong. "Of course," Anne said and hoped that was what Gwyneth wanted, too.

She'd barely ended the call when flowers from In Bloom arrived. "Cam's already begun the Valentine's Day spoiling," Kendra observed, looking at the huge vase crammed full of pink roses. "I wish he'd give lessons to Jimmy. All I'm going to get is my usual chocolate rose. Not even a box of chocolates."

"He's just trying to help you stay on your diet," Anne said.

Kendra frowned. "I don't want to stay on my diet on Valentine's Day." Or any other day, which was why she was still complaining about the extra twenty pounds that refused to fall off. "It's not fair that you got the skinny genes."

As if Anne didn't have to give those skinny genes a boost with regular visits to the gym. She decided now was not the time to mention that to her sister. Anyway, Kendra wasn't fat. She only thought she was.

"I bet Cam's taking you someplace fabulous for dinner tomorrow," Kendra said, her words tinged with sisterly envy.

"No, he's not. We're staying in and he's cooking."

Kendra heaved an exaggerated sigh. "Why did I pick such a Neanderthal?"

"Because he can fix a broken toilet?"

"There is that," Kendra admitted with a grin. "I guess I'll have to settle for ordering pizza since I'm sure Jimmy completely forgot about the big day." Her cell phone began to sing—"Born to Run," her husband's ringtone. "Hey, babe, what's up? Yeah? Are you serious?" Kendra gasped. "And here I was thinking you'd forgotten."

From the way her sister was smiling Anne could tell that Jimmy had managed to come through for Valentine's Day.

"Well, what do you know," Kendra said after she'd ended the call. "We're spending tomorrow night at the Four Seasons. I wonder which of the kids he had to sell to afford it."

"Probably both of them." Considering that the Four Seasons was one of Seattle's most luxurious hotels. "So I don't want to hear any more whining ever again about how your husband doesn't get it right on Valentine's Day," Anne said, pointing at her sister.

If she wasn't married to such a great guy herself she would've been jealous.

But she *was* married to a great guy, and come June

they'd be celebrating twenty-five years together. They still hadn't settled on what they wanted to do, but at the moment an Alaskan cruise looked tempting to Cam.

Speaking of tempting, she thought the following day as she stopped by Le Rêve bakery on her way home from running errands. Their chocolate mousse cake would make the perfect finish to the steak and baked potatoes Cam was serving up.

Actually, the perfect finish had more to do with the lacy red bra and panties she was wearing under her black blouse and jeans. Eye candy that Cam would enjoy unwrapping.

Back at their 1906 traditional on Queen Anne Hill she found him out in the remodeled kitchen, comfortable in jeans and a T-shirt, putting together a tossed salad. Salad, grilled meat and baked potatoes—that was the extent of his culinary skills.

But he had other, more valuable skills, and he gave her a sample of what was going to happen later when he pulled her against him and kissed her. Oh, he was a luscious thing. Six feet of beautiful muscle, dark hair with a few silver highlights sneaking in to make him look distinguished and a mouth that could melt a girl with one kiss. She'd been hot for him way back in high school, and nothing had changed.

"Did you resist the urge to go by your office?" he asked.

"Yes, smart guy. After yesterday I need a break. I swear, Laurel Browne is enough to make me want to set my hair on fire with a unity candle."

He snickered. "Well, I guess you can't blame the woman. It's a big thing when your kid gets married.

Speaking of kids, guess who called a couple of minutes ago."

"Laney." In spite of the fact that their daughter was ostensibly sharing an old house in the Fremont district with a girlfriend and no longer lived at home, she stopped by a couple of times a week and texted or called Anne every day. Sometimes to say hi but usually because she was experiencing a crisis or seeking advice or had news to share. She'd had a fight with her boyfriend, Drake. Or the tips at her barista job had been crummy. Or—and here was good news—she was going back to school next fall. Now she wanted to get a teaching degree so she could teach art as well as create it. Anne had smiled at that. Cam could finally quit worrying about whether Laney would ever be able to earn a decent living.

"Close but no cigar," he said. "It was Drake."

"And he was calling because?"

"To tell me he's going to propose tonight. Did you know they'd been looking at rings?"

"No." Anne felt the slightest bit hurt. Why hadn't Laney told her?

"He's taking her to the Space Needle to pop the question."

"He can afford that on an auto technician's salary?"

Cam shrugged. "Where there's a will there's a way. The guy is a saver. Anyway, don't be surprised if they show up here later."

Hmm. Maybe it was time for a plan B. Anne began to unbutton her blouse. "What if we had plans for later?"

Cam's gaze was riveted on her breasts, wrapped in red lace. His voice turned silky and he ran a hand up her arm. "Never put off till later what you can enjoy right now," he said, slipping off the blouse. "Red, my favorite color."

"I know," she said.

He tugged playfully on the waistband of her jeans. "What have we got under here? More red?"

She slithered out of her jeans and showed him.

"Oh, yeah. That's what I'm talkin' about." He pulled her close once again and nibbled her ear. "How do you do it, babe?"

"Do what?"

"Stay as beautiful as you were back in high school?"

"You're so full of it," she murmured, sliding her fingers through his hair.

"No, it's true. You're still the most beautiful woman I've ever seen."

Then he hadn't looked around much. Her nose was too thin and her feet were too long. Gray hairs were invading the brown ones at such a rapid rate she was having to increase her visits to her favorite salon on The Ave, and she had a colony of cellulite growing on her thighs. Those flaws didn't seem to bother him, though.

They sure weren't bothering him at the moment. He picked her up and hoisted her onto the kitchen counter. "Let's start with dessert tonight."

"You mean the cake?" she teased.

"I'm not dignifying that with an answer," he said and kissed her.

Oh, yes. Happy Valentine's Day.

Later, as they ate steaks off the grill and toasted each other with champagne, she was still feeling the glow from their lovemaking. Her husband had magic hands, and he sure knew how to make Valentine's Day memorable.

This one was going to be extraspecial. Cam was right; Laney would either call or come by to show off her new ring. What a perfect ending to the day, celebrating love with the next generation of family.

Her baby, her only child, was getting married, and to her high school sweetheart, just as Anne had done. Technically it was more a case of marrying a post–high school sweetheart, although the two had been friends for years. Anne and Cam had watched Drake change from a skinny, pimple-faced boy with tats and crazy-colored hair to a responsible young man who was ready to settle down. She could hardly wait to help Laney plan their wedding.

Of course, they'd talked a lot about weddings over the years. How could they not, considering what Anne did for a living? It had started when Laney used to play bride as a small child, dressed up with a pillowcase for a veil and a bouquet of some silk flowers Anne used for crafting. When Laney was in high school, she used to joke about wearing sneakers under her wedding dress like the bride in the old Steve Martin movie *Father of the Bride*. (Naturally, they'd watched that, along with *My Best Friend's Wedding*, *Runaway Bride*, *Made of Honor*, *27 Dresses*, *My Big Fat Greek Wedding* and any other wedding movie that came down the pike.) Hopefully, Laney had forgotten the tennis-shoe idea.

Anne could already envision Cam escorting their daughter down the aisle at Queen Anne Presbyterian, surrounded by flowers, Laney wearing a beautiful wedding gown, her long, chestnut hair falling to her shoulders in gentle waves. Anne's vision conveniently ignored the tattooed artwork running up Laney's neck and covering her right arm.

"There is such a thing as overkill," she'd said when her daughter went for her second tattoo, but Laney had just laughed and kissed her and skipped off to the tattoo parlor to commemorate her twenty-first birthday with more body art. Why, oh, why did her daughter have to take everything to extremes?

Because she was Laney. She'd always pushed the boundaries, staying out past curfews, cutting classes her freshman year in high school (thank God they'd broken her of *that* habit), dyeing her hair every color of the rainbow, adorning her ears with piercings. She'd gotten her nose pierced, too, but Anne had persuaded her to get a little diamond rather than the big stake she'd talked about, so at least that looked classy.

She's another generation, Anne constantly reminded herself, *and they have their own style.* Except style was such a subjective thing, and it wasn't only Laney's generation getting tattoos. Women Anne's age did it, too. One of her friends had a discreet rose on her ankle. It just seemed that the younger women, especially her daughter, never knew when to stop. It was enough to make a mother crazy. But then, she told herself, it was the duty of every generation to drive their parents nuts. Heaven knew, she'd done it to her own mother. Still…

"What are you thinking about?" Cam asked as he cut off a piece of steak.

She smiled at him. "Our baby's getting married." And that eclipsed fashion frustration. Fashion issues could be dealt with later.

"Yeah, I can't believe it. Seems like only yesterday that she had colic and I was walking the floor with her." He shook his head. "They're so young."

"So were we," Anne pointed out.

He nodded. "Our parents probably had this same conversation."

Anne was thankful she'd been spared hearing her parents' conversation. The one she'd had with her mother had been unpleasant enough.

"Drake's a good kid, though," Cam said. "They'll be happy."

"If they're half as happy as we are, they'll have a great marriage," Anne said and took a bite of her baked potato, which she'd slathered in butter and sour cream. Sour cream, butter, chocolate cake. She'd have to eat nothing but salad for the next week.

They were watching a romantic comedy and eating their cake when Laney called. "Mom, can Drake and I come over? We've got something to show you."

"Sure," Anne said, playing dumb. "Come on by."

"Okay. See you in a few."

Twenty minutes later, her daughter was walking through the door, dressed for Valentine's Day in black leggings and a short denim skirt she'd probably scored at her favorite consignment store. Her curls peeped out from under a black tam and she wore red platform shoes and a matching red top under her black leather jacket. She'd accented the outfit with a long, red scarf.

She was followed by her boyfriend, a tall, skinny, tattooed drink of water wearing jeans and a black T-shirt under a black leather bomber jacket. Unlike Laney, he didn't have an ear full of hoops and cute earrings. Instead, he wore gauges that had stretched holes in his earlobes. Anne had to admit that if she'd gone boyfriend shopping for her daughter she would've passed him over in favor of a preppy-looking boy in law school. But what would Laney have had in common with that kind of boy? She and Drake loved each other and that was what counted. Just as Cam said, he was a good kid. Tonight he wore a smile that reached from ear to ear.

And Laney sported a ring with a diamond best viewed under a magnifying glass. "See what I got for Valentine's Day?" she crowed.

Anne took her daughter's hand and gave her ring the attention it demanded as Cam clapped Drake on the back and welcomed him to the family. "It's gorgeous," she said. Then she hugged both her daughter and her future son-in-law. "We're so happy for you two. Come on in and let's have some chocolate cake to celebrate."

"You'll never guess where we went to dinner," Laney said, following Anne into the kitchen. "The Space Needle."

"Pretty impressive. Did Drake rob a bank?"

"He's been saving for this since Christmas."

At least someone in their marriage would be good with money. "Well, how was it?"

"Oh, wow," Laney said. "The view from up there, you can see everything. Puget Sound, the city, the mountains. And the food was sooo yummy."

"Maybe you don't have room for cake," Anne teased.

"I always have room for cake. You know that."

Anne cut pieces and put them on plates, and Laney took them to where Drake and Cam sat in the living room. Meanwhile, Anne grabbed two more glasses and another bottle of champagne.

Once the glasses were filled, Cam raised his in salute to the happy couple squeezed together in an oversize armchair. "To Laney and Drake. May you both be as happy as we are."

"Thanks, Dad," Laney said, and she and Drake kissed each other.

"Have you set a date?" Cam asked.

"We're thinking June," Laney said.

The same month Anne and Cam had gotten married. "An excellent month," he said, winking at Anne.

But it didn't give them much time to pull together a wedding.

"We thought it would be really cool to go to Vegas," Drake added.

The two exchanged besotted smiles.

Anne hardly saw them. Instead, she was seeing her daughter in some tiny chapel, all dressed up like a showgirl with a big, feathery headdress. And there was Drake, wearing a sparkly, white Elvis jumpsuit. To Laney's "I do," he responded, "Thank you. Thank you very much."

Vegas. Aaack!

Two

Roberta, Wedding Maven of Icicle Falls

Roberta Gilbert smiled as she surveyed the wedding guests dressed in their finery. This wedding had a Valentine theme, and Roberta had placed little heart-shaped boxes filled with chocolates on the linen-clad tables, along with the pink carnations and red roses the bride had requested.

It was the second time around for both bride and groom, who'd each been badly hurt by their exes. But that was behind them now, and the couple was clearly delighted with their new beginning as they swayed together in the center of the reception room.

It had once been two separate rooms, but Roberta had combined them years ago, making more space for guests. Every time she entered it she could feel the positive energy stored up from so many happy events. Tonight the chandeliers glowed in the antique gilded mirrors, reflecting the image of two beaming people, surrounded by forty well-wishers.

Roberta's eyes misted, partly from sentiment and

partly because, darn it all, her bunions were killing her. Much as she loved these touching moments, she'd be very happy when midnight came and the party ended. Her daughter kept telling her she was getting too old for this, but what did Daphne know? Seventy-one wasn't that old. Anyway, Roberta couldn't imagine living anywhere other than her pretty, pink Victorian with the white trim here on Primrose Street. She did love weddings, and after thirty years of hosting as well as planning them, it was a hard addiction to break. So here she would stay until she keeled over and they carried her out, bunions first.

All right, maybe she could be tempted to pack in her business if some handsome older man who enjoyed Caribbean cruises and watching old doo-wop groups on PBS arrived on the scene.

The odds of that happening were about as good as the odds of Roberta winning the lottery…which she never played. Besides, she had several wedding years left in her.

"How are you doing?" asked a voice at her elbow, and she turned to see her assistant, Lila Kurtz, looking festive in a red dress and white apron decorated with red hearts.

In charge of the caterers, Lila always saw to it that everything ran smoothly. And tonight's food was especially elegant. It had been prepared by Bailey Sterling, who owned Tea Time Tea Shop and Tearoom on Lavender Lane, and the guests had raved about the three-cheese stuffed chicken, the pasta and tossed salads and the lavender cake. Roberta would definitely use Bailey again.

"Just fine," Roberta lied. Even though she had Lila

and her crew, Roberta worked on the table settings, plated some of the food and did whatever else needed to be done. And no matter how much help she had, there was always plenty to do when a woman offered a full-service venue. Her bunions would attest to that.

"You could duck out now," Lila suggested.

She could. Once she was in her bedroom, she'd be oblivious to any noise coming from below or from the second-floor changing room at the front of the house reserved for the bride and her bridesmaids. Lila would see the revelers on their way and then lock up. But for heaven's sake, it was barely past nine o'clock. Only little old ladies went to bed at nine o'clock.

Still, she had her Vanessa Valentine romance novel waiting for her. "You know, maybe I will." She used to love watching the bride toss her bouquet but tonight her nice, soft mattress and a looming love scene were winning out over sentiment. "If you don't mind."

"Of course not," Lila said. Lila was a single mom with two grown children and she liked to stay up late.

"Well, then, I'll go upstairs. I have a few things to do," Roberta added in case Lila thought she was pooping out.

Lila nodded approvingly. "Take it easy tomorrow. Leave the mess for the cleaning crew on Monday."

"I will," Roberta promised. She had no desire to work any harder than she had to.

"And don't forget you've got Muriel Sterling coming over to do that interview for the paper on Monday afternoon," Lila reminded her.

Ah, yes. The interview. Roberta hoped Muriel didn't ask any nosy questions that would be awkward to answer, but if she did, Roberta knew how to dodge them. She'd been doing it for years.

The DJ was now spinning an upbeat song and the room pulsed with dancers. Roberta made her way around the edge of the crowd, ready to put her feet up and read her book. With her comfy flannel jammies on, she'd be free to let the story carry her away.

Suddenly it looked as if there wasn't going to be any carrying away—not considering who'd just arrived at the party. Roberta blinked, wondering if her eyes were playing tricks on her. But no, Daphne was still there, hovering in the doorway, her lovely face contorted with a scowl. What on earth was her daughter doing here?

She hurried over to where Daphne stood, wearing dark jeans and a leather jacket thrown over a plain, black sweater, a carry-on suitcase parked next to her. Her big blue eyes were bloodshot and her nose was red, probably from too many close encounters with a tissue.

"Daphne, darling, what are you doing here?" *On a weekend, looking like the bad wedding fairy. And with a suitcase?* Oh, wedding bell blues. Roberta could already guess what was wrong.

Daphne took in the crowd of happy revelers. "All that money wasted on champagne and cake. It never works out."

Sure enough. "Come upstairs," Roberta said, steering her daughter toward the staircase. "We'll get you settled and you can tell me what's going on."

Daphne didn't wait until she was settled. She started in right away, towing her suitcase up the stairs. "I knew something was wrong." *Thump.* "I've suspected for months." *Thump.* "I kept asking him and he denied it." *Thump, thump.*

Roberta sighed. Men were beasts. "So Mitchell's been cheating on you."

"You were right—he's slime," Daphne said, her voice trembling. "How could he do this to me?" she wailed. "Is it that hard to be faithful to someone?"

In Mitchell's case, obviously, yes. Poor Daphne. She was so pretty, so trusting. She was like a man magnet. Sadly, she didn't seem able to attract anything better than the man equivalent of paper clips.

"I'm so sorry," Roberta said.

They'd reached the top floor now, and Roberta led her daughter to the back of the house, to the room opposite hers, the same room that had been Daphne's growing up. Here they were, together again, mother and daughter. And daughter was going through yet another romantic crisis.

Daphne was an underachiever when it came to relationships. Her first husband had been a lazy bum who spent as much time collecting unemployment as he did working. He drank too much and helped Daphne around the house too little. The only good thing to come out of that marriage had been Roberta's granddaughter, Marnie. (Unlike her mother, Marnie knew how to pick a man who had his act together and was now busy setting the world on fire, working in New York as an editor.) Husband number two had bailed on Daphne when Marnie hit her teen years. As for number three, Roberta had never liked him. She'd seen the way Mitchell ogled other women when Daphne wasn't looking. You couldn't trust oglers. She'd told Daphne as much but would she listen? Of course not.

Where was the ogler now? Back home, in Daphne's

bed with another woman? "Did you kick him out?" Roberta demanded. Sometimes her daughter was too soft.

Daphne draped her coat over the bedpost and got busy unpacking her suitcase.

"Daphne," Roberta said sharply.

"I told him he had until next week to get his stuff out." Her face turned red and she pulled off her sweater. She opened the window and stuck her head outside.

A very convenient time for a hot flash, Roberta thought cynically. "So you left him in your house? Why?" She grabbed the coat and hung it in the closet.

Daphne pulled her head back in and scowled. "I didn't want to look at him. Honestly, Mother. Did you expect me to stay there after what I found out?"

"Yes," Roberta cried, exasperated. "That house belongs to you. He should be the one to leave, not you. When you go home, you call a locksmith first thing. Even if you have to take Monday off."

Daphne bit her lip, a sure sign that she was hiding something.

Oh, heavens, what now? "Daphne?"

Daphne pushed aside a lock of long, blond hair. "I'm not going home, not for a while."

"But you have to. Your job."

Not that it was a high-powered job. Daphne had used her college degree from the University of Washington to land a position as a receptionist for a seafood distribution company in Seattle, where she'd remained ever since as an underpaid fixture. In spite of her talents and her mother's high hopes, she had never felt the need to reach for the stars.

She could've been a fashion model or started her own interior decorating business or…something. Roberta had given her any number of suggestions over the years, but Daphne had preferred to stay on the bottom rung of the ladder of success. If Roberta hadn't been there for the birth she'd have sworn her daughter was some other woman's.

"I quit," Daphne said, breaking into Roberta's thoughts like a wrecking ball.

"You what?"

"I quit."

Roberta fell onto the bed. "Oh, Daphne."

"I can't stay in Seattle anymore," Daphne said, her lips trembling. "I just… I need a change."

"No," Roberta said firmly. "You need a job." Daphne couldn't jump off the high dive and assume there'd be water in the pool.

She couldn't, but she had.

"I'll find a job, but first I have to take some time off, get myself sorted out. Anyway, I have some money saved up."

"So do I, if you need it. But, oh, Daphne, what were you thinking?" Clearly she wasn't. Had Mitchell tipped her over the edge?

"I was thinking I need to make a new start," Daphne said in a small voice.

"You're fifty-three!" Who did she suppose was going to hire a fifty-three-year-old woman? It wasn't right, but age discrimination was a very real thing.

"Haven't you ever wanted to walk away from your life, start all over again?" Daphne pleaded.

Yes, and she had. So how could she discourage Daphne from doing the same? Now tears were leaking out of her daughter's eyes. "I thought I could stay with you for a while. Just till I get on my feet," she added, probably because she'd seen the consternation on her mother's face.

It wasn't that Roberta didn't love her daughter. It wasn't that she didn't want to see her. But living together? They were so different. They'd drive each other insane. Daphne herself had said so on more than one occasion.

Roberta always kept her house neat as the proverbial pin. Daphne's often looked as if it had been caught up in a tornado and then set down far from any store with cleaning supplies. On a good day you could find decorating magazines strewn on the couch and shoes scattered everywhere, coats hanging from the handle of the closet door rather than inside it. She had a flair for decorating, but what was the use of painting and purchasing expensive sofa pillows if you never dusted and your toilet was dirty? Roberta had never understood how her daughter could be so efficient at work and such a slob at home. Of course, to be fair, not one of the bums she'd married had ever helped her. Not that she'd ever asked them. She'd been far too easy on the men in her life.

And too easy on herself. Why she'd never wanted to improve in the areas where she was lacking baffled Roberta. But she didn't. She hated it when Roberta commented on her bad housekeeping habits or tried to offer advice. In fact, it seemed as if every time Roberta tried to help Daphne improve her life they wound up squabbling.

Still, she'd never turn Daphne away. She put an arm around her daughter's shoulders and gave her an encouraging squeeze. "Of course you can stay." She needed a plan, though. She needed to be proactive. "But, darling, you can't hide up here indefinitely and mope."

"I'm not going to mope. I told you, I'll find a job."

"In Icicle Falls?"

"There are businesses in Icicle Falls," Daphne said stiffly.

"Yes, of course, but you're not going to find anything with the salary or benefits you had at your job in the city." Not that her job in the city had paid *that* well.

"I don't need much to live on," Daphne said, raising her chin.

Roberta wasn't so sure. Her daughter had always had a husband to supplement her salary (although some were more reliable than others). She had no idea how difficult it could be to live on one small income.

"I'll have money when I sell the house."

"You're used to city life. You'll be bored," Roberta predicted.

"I can find plenty to do here in Icicle Falls. I could help you."

"With weddings?" Not only would they be living together, they'd be working together? Now Roberta's bunions weren't all that hurt. She felt as though her forehead was about to crack open. She rubbed her temples in an effort to stop the crack from spreading.

"Why not?" Daphne demanded, correctly interpreting her mother's body language. "In case you've forgotten, I helped with Marnie's wedding."

Roberta remembered. Daphne had forgotten to order the invitations and they'd gone out three weeks late. Giving her daughter a chance to regroup was one thing, but weddings...

"We'll see," she said, making Daphne frown. "For

now, let's get some rest. Everything will look better in the morning." That was total baloney and they both knew it, but at least with a good night's sleep they'd be more able to cope.

Meanwhile, Roberta was going to bed with her romance novel. When she kissed her daughter good-night and wished her pleasant dreams, Daphne teared up and nodded bravely.

Roberta skedaddled across the hall to her own bedroom, where she fell on the bed. She should have been more supportive, listened more and said less. Daphne was in no mood for advice right now.

Her poor daughter wouldn't get a wink of sleep tonight. Roberta suspected she wouldn't, either. Not that she ever slept all that well anyway. Getting up two or three times during the night to go to the bathroom always interfered. Oh, how Mother Nature turned on her sisters after a certain age.

Well, there was nothing she could do now. And there likely wasn't anything she could do tomorrow. It was hard having grown children. A woman had so little control over her daughter's choices once that daughter was grown.

She got into her pajamas, picked up her romance novel and cuddled under the covers, ready—*finally*—to let the story carry her away. But she got carried only as far as the first kiss in the seduction scene before her mind wandered.

Kisses, seduction, Mitchell the ogler... Roberta frowned. If only Daphne had met a decent man, someone who'd treat her with respect and kindness. She was a good woman, tenderhearted and giving. She didn't deserve to have her heart broken. This was what came of being a poor judge of character.

Worrying about her daughter was exhausting. She set aside her book and went in search of sleep, but she didn't find it. Finally, she gave up, turned her bedside lamp back on and opened her romance novel again. At least there she could be assured that life would work out perfectly.

On Monday afternoon Muriel Sterling, Icicle Falls's resident writing celebrity, was knocking on the front door of Primrose Haus promptly at two. Just in time for tea.

"It's really kind of you to see me," she said to Roberta as she stepped inside, a gust of brisk mountain air following her in. "I hope it's not too much trouble after the wedding you had this weekend."

Muriel Sterling knew how to be gracious. "No trouble at all," Roberta told her. "I'm happy to see you. It's been ages since we've had a chance to chat."

"My life has gotten a little busy."

That wasn't a bad thing. Muriel had pulled away from her friends after the loss of her second husband. When she finally came out of mourning, she did so with a vengeance, helping her daughters run Sweet Dreams Chocolates and enjoying a blossoming writing career.

"Your mother would've been proud of all your success," Roberta said.

"You've been pretty successful, too."

She'd done all right. "I'm still not sure why you wanted to interview me, though."

"The editor at the *Gazette* approached me with the idea that it would be nice to feature some of our time-honored businesses run by local women, so of course we immediately thought of your wedding house."

"Come on into the parlor," Roberta said. "I have some lavender sugar cookies from your daughter's tea shop, along with a pot of Lady Grey."

"Those sugar cookies are impossible to resist," Muriel said and followed Roberta to the formal parlor at the front of the house. The room offered a fireplace and pretty antique chairs, some of which were even comfortable. Granted, the fireplace didn't put out a lot of heat, but on a cold February afternoon having a fire in it warmed the heart. Today the crackling logs enhanced the cozy feeling of the room.

She settled Muriel in front of the coffee table where Daphne had left a half-full coffee cup and a copy of *Better Homes and Gardens*. Roberta scooped them up and fetched tea and cookies. There were considerably fewer in the box than there'd been when Roberta brought it home that morning, which meant her daughter had gone on a cookie raid. Shades of her divorce from husband number two.

She returned to find that Muriel had taken a steno pad from her purse and flipped it open. "I was trying to remember. How many years have you been in business?"

"Thirty years." Had it really been thirty? Where had the time gone? "You may remember our first wedding in the house was my daughter's," Roberta added. "Daphne was the one who actually gave me the idea of opening it up to other people." Cleverness, one of her daughter's underused gifts.

And speaking of Daphne, here she came, wearing jeans, a sweater and a woebegone expression—a shining testimonial to the joys of wedded bliss. Roberta noticed the little watering can in her daughter's hand. Much as Daphne loved to decorate, she wasn't all that good with houseplants. Roberta guessed her sudden interest sprang more from a desire to search out some company than to water the plants. She couldn't blame Daphne. The pain of rejection was one that cut soul-deep and it was hard to be alone with that kind of hurt.

Although God knew Roberta had done it.

"Daphne, how wonderful to see you," Muriel said politely.

"Oh, hi," Daphne said, feigning surprise.

"Are you in town for a visit?" Muriel asked.

Daphne shook her head and got busy watering Roberta's ficus plant. "I'm up here to make a new start. I'm getting divorced." She studied the ficus, then moved it to the other side of the room, setting it next to the philodendron.

Muriel looked properly sympathetic. "I'm sorry to hear that."

Daphne shrugged. "It's for the best."

Which was more than Roberta could say for the new location of her houseplant. "Daphne, dear, what are you doing?"

"Hmm? Oh, I just thought this plant would look better over here beside the other one, in a group."

"That's a charming idea, but the ficus needs full sunlight," Roberta said.

Daphne's cheeks grew pink. "Oh." She picked it up and returned it to its original spot.

"Do you know what you want to do?" Muriel asked her.

"I figured I could help my mother with weddings."

"What a good plan," Muriel said, beaming with approval.

Yes, wasn't it? The very thought had Roberta reaching for a cookie.

"I'm sure your mother's delighted to have you home," Muriel said and helped herself to some cookies, as well.

"Oh, yes," Roberta lied.

"So, your daughter's was the first wedding held here, wasn't it?" Muriel asked, bringing them back to the interview.

Daphne gave a snort of disgust.

Roberta ignored her. "Yes, and then, a generation later, my granddaughter was married here."

"That was a beautiful wedding," Daphne said, her voice wistful.

"And you've had many in between," Muriel said to Roberta. "I still remember the lovely reception we had here when I married Waldo," she added.

"It was lovely. And who knows? Maybe someday you'll get married again," Roberta suggested. Muriel's longtime admirer, Arnie Amundsen, would marry her in a minute if she ever gave him any encouragement. So far, though, she hadn't.

"I suspect not. After Waldo..." Muriel's smile faded.

"He was a sweet man," Roberta said.

"He was," Muriel agreed. "And you know how rare a good man is."

"You can say that again." Daphne tipped her watering can over Roberta's spider plant. The water spattered onto the antique music cabinet beneath it and Roberta tried not to grind her teeth.

Daphne frowned and mopped up the spill with the sleeve of her sweater.

"You never remarried," Muriel said to Roberta. "In fact, I remember when you first moved to Icicle Falls. You were a widow."

"I lost my husband in a car crash." Oh, how easily the lie slipped out after all these years.

Muriel looked at her with compassion. "I remember that. You never found another man to measure up."

Roberta was suddenly aware of her daughter's gaze burning into her. How many times growing up had Daphne wanted to know about her father, wondered why they didn't have any pictures of Daddy?

"Daddy's dead," Roberta had replied. Learning the truth when she was older hadn't sat well with Daphne, not until she heard the whole story. But even after that, she'd longed for more, tried to find a way to make what she had into more. Of course, it hadn't worked.

There were so many times Roberta had wished she could give her daughter a happy Ward and June Cleaver experience. Instead, Daphne'd had to settle for just June. But they'd done all right, the two of them. Anyway, family wasn't always what you were born into; it was the people in your life who cared about you, and in Icicle Falls they'd found plenty of people to care.

As for a man… "There wasn't exactly an abundance of single men in Icicle Falls back in those days," she said. "All the good ones were taken. Anyway, I've been happy on my own."

"Well, you've been an inspiration to a lot of women," Muriel said. "And your beautiful house is always in demand. What's the most memorable wedding you've ever had here?"

"Not mine," Daphne said bitterly.

Her daughter was not helping with the Primrose Haus image of happy brides and perfect occasions.

"It was a lovely wedding, though," Muriel said, clearly trying to be diplomatic. She'd attended that wedding. And Daphne's second one, as well. Fortunately, by the third try Daphne had narrowed her guest list considerably, so all their Icicle Falls friends were off the hook for wedding presents. "Is there any one that stands out?" Muriel asked Roberta.

"Oh, we've had so many it's hard to narrow down." Roberta waved a hand airily.

Now Daphne jumped in. "How about the one where when the minister said, 'If anyone can show just cause why this couple cannot lawfully be joined together, let him speak now or forever hold his peace,' and the best man spoke up? It turned out he and the bride had been sleeping together," she explained to Muriel.

That would make an inspiring story for the paper, Roberta thought, and frowned at her daughter, who became very engrossed in watering plants.

Muriel blinked in shock.

"They weren't from around here," Roberta assured her.

Muriel nodded and scribbled away in her steno pad. "What did you do after that happened?"

Roberta shrugged. "They'd paid for a party, so we served the food." Muriel's expression was disapproving, whether of Roberta's callous the-show-must-go-on attitude or the behavior of the unfaithful bride, Roberta couldn't tell. Maybe it was a little of both. "The only thing you can be sure of about people," she continued, "is that they'll surprise you."

"And not in a good way," Daphne muttered.

"I'm sure you had some weddings that *did* surprise you in a good way," Muriel prompted.

"Yes, of course," Roberta said. "Only last fall we hosted an impromptu reception for a couple who'd been sweethearts when they were young and found each other again on Facebook. They'd both lost their spouses and were so lonely. They started talking on the phone every night, and when he learned she was coming to Icicle Falls to celebrate Oktoberfest with friends, he came, too. They hadn't seen each other in almost forty years but they picked up right where they'd left off. They were married the very next weekend."

Daphne let out an unladylike snort. "I bet they're not together now."

Muriel smiled. "Oh, I bet they are. That's a beautiful story, Roberta."

"Sounds more like fairy tale to me," Daphne said.

Roberta sent her daughter another reprimanding look and Muriel feigned deafness.

She asked a few more questions, then wrapped up the interview.

Having known Muriel since she was a girl, Roberta asked about her daughters and was quick to tell her what an impressive job her youngest one, Bailey, had done with the food for the recent wedding reception. "We'll definitely use her again," she promised, and Muriel beamed like the proud mother she was.

She had a right to be proud. All three of her girls were lovely and accomplished young women who were doing interesting things with their lives.

Meanwhile, in another corner of the room, Daphne had managed to knock over a houseplant. It landed on the hardwood floor with a crunch as the pot broke and potting soil scattered in all directions.

"Sorry," she said and disappeared, hopefully to get a broom and dustpan.

"I hope everything works out for Daphne," Muriel said.

"I do, too," Roberta said with a sigh.

Her daughter had come home in Humpty Dumpty condition. What was it going to take to put her back together again? And would they be able to keep from killing each other in the process?

Three

Anne, Mother of a Bride in Need of Guidance

When the kids came over for dinner on Sunday it was plain to Anne that they didn't know what they wanted. Ideas had flown around the table faster than bats out of a cave.

And some of the ideas had been just as scary to Anne. They could get married at the coffee shop. Cute, but how many people could you fit in a coffee shop? Or on a ferryboat. If any guests were a few minutes late they'd miss the boat *and* the ceremony. Ferries ran on time. Wedding guests, not necessarily. Of course, they could always charter an Argosy cruise ship.

Before Anne could even bring it up, they were on to a new idea—a pirate ship. Apparently, you could do that at the Treasure Island Hotel in Vegas. (Back to Vegas again—nooo!) Or they could have a zombie theme. This was another suggestion from Drake. He was just full of ideas. (Who asked him, anyway?)

By the time they left, Anne was on her third glass of white wine and on the phone to her mother. "This is insane," she'd finished after delivering the bad news of her daughter's sudden poor taste in weddings.

"Frustrating, isn't it?"

She'd received the message in her mother's tone of voice loud and clear. *Yeah. How does it feel?*

Okay, so she hadn't let Mom throw her the super wedding she'd wanted. "That was different," she'd reminded her. And at least her mother'd had Kendra, who'd come through with the traditional wedding. Anne had only Laney.

"All you can do is make suggestions," Julia had said. "And if you think she's going to take any of them, you've been eating too much wedding cake."

"Ha-ha. I'm sure glad I called you."

"I am, too," Julia had said, ignoring the sarcasm. "This is happy news, and I know whatever kind of wedding Laney wants, you'll give it to her."

Of course she would. There was nothing she wouldn't do, no length to which she wouldn't go, to give her daughter the wonderful wedding she deserved.

"In the end, you want her to have the day she wants."

"Well, yes," Anne had agreed.

And she knew what Laney wanted. It was the same thing she'd wanted since she was a little girl. Anne could still remember, when Laney was seven, watching the wedding scene in *The Sound of Music* with her— the first movie wedding they ever watched together. Laney sat transfixed at the sight of Maria coming down the aisle to the nuns' chorus. "I want a wedding like that someday, Mommy," she'd breathed, and Anne had vowed then and there to make sure she got it. She was no less determined now.

Laney needed guidance. "I don't want her to wind

up having any regrets." Wasn't it a mother's job to save her daughter from that? So far there'd been very little saving and a whole lot of running just to keep up.

Come Monday it was time to focus on other brides. In the morning Anne met with a bride-to-be, pinning down the details of her upcoming wedding.

"I love the idea of the treasure box," the bride gushed. "It would be great to fill that as part of the ceremony. What should we put in it?"

"Well, it can be anything you want. A copy of your wedding vows, for one thing. And didn't you say your bridesmaids were going to make tissue flowers to decorate the lodge? You could put in one of those, as well as your engagement picture. Also, a lot of couples put in something like a bottle of whiskey so they can toast each other on their one-year anniversary. You open the box again in another five years and another five and so on. Each time you can reread your vows. You'll have the flower as a keepsake and the picture to remind you how happy you are in this moment."

"And the whiskey to help us forget if we aren't," joked the bride-to-be.

"Or to congratulate each other on doing such a good job of building a life together."

Her client nodded vigorously, typing notes in her iPad. "We are so doing this."

Anne smiled. Happy brides were what made her world spin.

After lunch she spent two hours in the studio attached to her office with another bride-to-be, showing her table-setting options. Now it was time to book that venue Marla Polanski had requested.

Anne brought up the website for Primrose Haus in Icicle Falls and it was love at first sight. "Oh, this is beautiful," she said, and Kendra came to look over her shoulder.

The place was like something out of a fairy tale, with turrets and dormer windows and a front porch dripping with gingerbread trim. It was pale pink, the color of clouds at the end of a sunset, and the trim was white. The landscaping was just as charming, with lush lawns, a profusion of flowers, brick walkways and stone benches. And, of course, a fountain in the back. There was also a charming rose arbor where a bride and groom could exchange vows during a summer wedding.

"Wow," Anne breathed. She could so easily envision Laney and Drake standing under that arbor.

"Wow is right," Kendra said.

The inside of the house was as beautiful as the outside, all graceful furniture and chandeliers, and in the front hall a staircase with an elegantly carved banister that was perfect for a bride to come down. Gilded mirrors, vases filled with flowers—the owners knew what they were doing.

Anne clicked on the About Us button.

Roberta Gilbert has been hosting weddings at Primrose Haus for thirty years, but she never gets tired of opening her home to couples embarking on life's greatest adventure. Let her and her talented staff make your special day one to remember.

"I can see why my client wanted to use this place," Anne said.

"It makes me want to get married all over again," Kendra said with a sigh.

"Me, too. Want to go to Icicle Falls with me and check it out?"

"You bet. But only if we can stop at Sweet Dreams Chocolates while we're up there. I mean, you can't visit Icicle Falls and not go to the chocolate factory."

"Gee, twist my arm," Anne said as she punched the number for Primrose Haus into her phone. A town with its own source of chocolate... What was not to like about that?

The little town had more going for it than chocolate. She and Cam had gone there years ago for the Christmas tree-lighting ceremony and been swept away by the Bavarian charm of the place. Everything from the European facades on the buildings to the overflowing flower boxes hanging from their windows said quaint Alpine village. They'd gone a couple of times when Laney was small, had even talked about taking up cross-country skiing, but then life got busy and weekends got full. Anne's business took off and Cam started coaching basketball and football. So the Bavarian-style town remained a pleasant memory rather than a destination. As for this wedding venue, somehow she'd missed it completely. Probably because her clients hovered around the greater Seattle area.

She could hardly wait to tour the house. If it was even half as spectacular as it looked in the pictures on the website, it could be a wonderful place for her daughter to get married.

A cheerful voice answered, "Good morning. Primrose Haus. This is Roberta."

Anne introduced herself and explained why she was calling.

"We often have people come over from Seattle," Roberta said. "And yes, I'd love to meet you if you'd care to visit on a weekday. I'm afraid our weekends are pretty busy around here."

Anne could imagine. The place was almost completely booked, except that she'd seen an opening for the last Saturday in June.

She and Roberta chatted a little longer, then set a date for the following Tuesday.

"Let's spend the night," Kendra suggested. "I just found a website for the Icicle Creek Lodge and it looks gorgeous."

"Great idea," Anne said. Girl-time with her sister, chocolate, a pretty place to stay... After the week she had ahead of her, a getaway sounded good.

It turned out to be the week from hell. One bride was unhappy with the job the photographer had done on her wedding and wanted a refund. Another decided she couldn't afford Anne and fired her. A mother of the bride called to scold Anne for not checking out all possible options for a florist. Momzilla Dearest had found one that was half the price of the florist Anne was recommending. Anne knew the florist in question and had rejected her because she wouldn't be a fit for the bride's vision. Still, Anne apologized and promised to get an estimate. The next day she learned that the vendor she rented linens from had gone out of business, leaving her scrambling for table linens for Saturday's wedding.

Saturday was the final stressor. Two dozen extra guests showed up, which meant she and the caterer needed to reportion the food. She was busy helping with this when Cressa, one of the caterer's assistants, came running up to her. "There's a table on fire!"

Sure enough. On the lower level of the tour boat where the wedding was being held, amid a sea of tables covered with white linen and set with candles and peach-colored floral arrangements, one table was a floating flambé. A very large flambé, shooting up flames three feet high. With visions of the entire boat catching fire, Anne grabbed the fire extinguisher she always brought along and dashed from the galley to the burning table, Cressa following behind.

Cheers from the upper deck where the ceremony was taking place told her the bride and groom were about to come down the aisle. All the bride needed was to see her reception area looking like a giant hot-dog roast.

At the table Anne fumbled with the extinguisher, misaimed and got a window, making Cressa squeal as if she'd just caught fire. "You missed," she informed Anne.

"I noticed." Anne tried again and this time hit her target, spraying goo all over the table.

"Yuck," Cressa said, frowning at the mess.

"What happened here?" Anne asked, setting down the extinguisher.

Cressa shrugged. "I dunno."

Anne surveyed the scene, getting in touch with her inner fire marshal. Her best guess was that a rose petal had fallen into the flame and then ignited one of the place cards.

She could hear people visiting up above. Any minute the guests would be wandering down in search of food. *(Please let there be enough.)*

She began pulling off plates, stacking them in her arms, covering her blouse with goo. Thank God she always brought along a change of clothes.

"Let's get this table cleared," she said to Cressa, who was still standing there, staring at the mess.

"What about the flowers?" Cressa asked, gathering up silverware.

The flowers were now decorated with fire-extinguisher glop. "I'll find something," Anne said and hoped she was right.

Five minutes later the table had a new cloth, and a few roses, stolen from the vases on other tables, were artfully laid around a fresh candle. Anne was sweating like a pig and her heart rate was through the roof. Oh, that was fun.

The guests never knew. With the bar open, everyone was happy. Meanwhile, Anne continued to run around behind the scenes, making sure the evening went smoothly, that the DJ didn't start the music until the plates had been cleared and that the photographer (who, it turned out, had a problem with motion sickness) was on hand to catch the bride and groom eating their cake.

This was worth all the headaches, all the stress, she thought as she watched the happy couple feed each other cupcakes. A wedding was more than a party. It was an event, a lifetime memory in the making, an important marker for the beginning of a new adventure.

Did her daughter understand that? Sometimes Anne wasn't so sure.

She said as much to her sister as they made their way up the mountains to Icicle Falls on Tuesday.

"It'll work out," Kendra assured her, "whatever Laney decides to do. And hey, I've seen the pictures on the Treasure Island website. Those wedding chapels are really elegant, and I think the ship sounds like fun."

"Oh, yeah," Anne said in disgust. "Maybe we can get Captain Jack Sparrow to officiate." She realized she had the SUV's steering wheel in a stranglehold and forced herself to loosen her grip.

"It beats being a zombie."

"Barely."

"What would you do if someone came to us and wanted a zombie wedding?"

Anne shot an appalled glance in her sister's direction before returning her attention to the snow-trimmed mountain road. "You have to ask? I'd tell them I'm not the wedding planner for them."

"I don't know. Planning a zombie wedding could be interesting."

"Good. Then when Coral and Amy are old enough you guys can have one."

"The zombie apocalypse will be over by then," Kendra said. "Anyway, you've done a lot of unusual weddings."

"Unusual, yes. Gross and tacky, no."

"One woman's gross and tacky is another one's fun and clever. Remember the wedding at Wild Waves?"

"That was a picnic, and the wedding itself was cute." Well, until the bride got sick on the roller coaster.

"Zombies can be cute," Kendra teased.

Anne groaned. "If Laney does that I'm going to disown her."

"I doubt it'll come to that, but you'd better resign yourself. Your daughter is an artiste and she's going to want to do something different."

"I can live with different," Anne insisted. "I just want her to think this through, that's all."

"She will. Everything's going to be fine."

Anne sighed. "I hope so."

The road leveled out and twenty minutes later the sisters were pulling into the town of Icicle Falls. There was a fresh dusting of snow on the main street and all the shops were thickly frosted. The mountains rose up behind, studded with evergreens. There was something restful and calming about this view, Anne thought. Now that they were empty nesters, she and Cam needed to invest in some cross-country ski equipment and come up here.

"It looks like the inside of a snow globe," Kendra said. "Oh, there's a place that sells lace. And one that sells antiques. We have to get in some serious shopping this afternoon."

"Agreed," said Anne. "When can we check into the lodge?"

"Not until three."

"Well, we'll just have to kill time buying chocolate."

"Gee, what a shame."

But first they had an appointment with Roberta Gilbert at Primrose Haus.

Their GPS took them from the downtown area to a small street lined with older homes, all beautifully maintained. "This is it." Kendra pointed at the sign. "Primrose Street."

"I wonder if everyone has primroses in their flower beds," Anne said. It was hard to tell what anyone had right now, since the lawns were buried under a couple of feet of snow. She knew Primrose Haus had them because she'd seen them in the flower beds in one of the pictures on the website.

"There's the house," Kendra said.

Even under a blanket of snow, it was charming, and

Anne felt herself overcome with house lust. "What would it be like to live here?" A quaint house in a charming little town...

"It would be work. Old houses always are," said her sister, the happy new-construction owner. "Remember all the money you guys poured into your place?"

"Think of the value," Anne retorted.

Kendra acknowledged that with a nod. "You lucked out. Finding a house on Queen Anne for under a million these days is next to impossible. If you ever sell it you'll make a fortune."

"We'll probably be there until we're old and gray," Anne said, getting out of the SUV. That was fine with her. She loved their Queen Anne house, enjoyed the neighbors, liked being near her family.

But then Roberta Gilbert opened the front door and they stepped inside and the house lust was back. This place was so...romantic.

"Your house is lovely," Anne gushed once Roberta had settled them in a front parlor where a fire blazed in a marble-trimmed fireplace.

"I'm fond of it," Roberta said. She was an attractive older woman, slender with short, gray hair and pretty brown eyes. Like her house, Roberta was a class act, dressed in black slacks and a pale blue cashmere sweater accessorized with a pearl necklace and matching earrings. She'd brought in a tray with teacups and a pot of tea and the proper accoutrements, as well as a small plate of cookies.

Kendra picked one up and took a bite. "Oh, my gosh. This is absolute bliss."

"Lavender cookies," Roberta said. "They come from the tearoom here in town and I must confess I have a weakness for them. We also have a bakery that specializes in gingerbread cookies. Cass, the owner, makes lovely wedding cakes."

"Do you have a florist in town, too?" Anne asked. They probably did. She'd seen some of the wedding pictures on the Primrose Haus website, and the floral arrangements were exquisite.

"Oh, yes. Lupine Floral does a wonderful job," Roberta said and then went on to tell them about the various vendors she used for weddings. The women discussed prices and exchanged wedding tales, and after an hour Anne felt she'd made a new friend.

"Would you like to tour the house?" Roberta asked.

"Absolutely," Anne replied. Looking at all the beautifully furnished rooms took her from lust to love. "This is such a great venue," she told Roberta as they walked back to the parlor.

"Thank you," Roberta said. "I enjoy hosting weddings here, although I have to admit it's beginning to feel more like work than it did ten years ago."

"I can imagine," said Kendra. "Keeping this place up looks like a lot of work."

"We manage."

"Do you ever do other events, like birthdays or anniversaries?" Kendra asked.

Roberta shook her head. "Rarely. We're too busy with weddings."

"I'd like to book this for my bride and bring her and her mother up to check it out next week if that's possible," Anne said to Roberta.

"Of course."

"And I see you have the last Saturday in June open. I wonder if I could give you a deposit to hold that for me. My daughter just got engaged. I really want her to see this place."

"Beats a pirate ship," Kendra joked.

Roberta was obviously too polite to comment, but she did cock an eyebrow.

"Right now we're exploring a number of ideas," Anne explained.

Roberta nodded. "Brides these days have some unique ones."

True, but if you asked Anne, unique wasn't always good.

"That could be the perfect place for Laney to get married," she told her sister as they drove away.

"It *is* great," Kendra agreed. She brought up TripAdvisor on her cell phone and pulled up the information on Icicle Falls. "Looks like there's lots to do there."

"Let's go by the chamber of commerce and pick up some brochures to take back," Anne suggested.

Maybe they could find some *unique* experience for Laney, like getting married in a mountain meadow. Then they could have the reception at the pretty house on Primrose Street.

Compromise. Life was all about compromise. So were weddings, and Anne was sure that here in Icicle Falls she and her daughter would come up with just the right one.

Four

Laney, the Bride-to-Be

She and Drake were getting married! Sometimes Laney could hardly believe it, even though they'd known each other, like, forever. They'd shared the same circle of friends since middle school, been in the same church youth group, taken the same classes. Funny how she'd thought he was such a goofball and no one she'd ever end up with. She was always crushing on guys who played in rock bands or high school sports heroes with their beefed-up muscles who swaggered down the hall on their way to class.

In middle school Drake had been skinny with a colony of zits on his face, and his highest ambition was to beat the video game "Halo." In high school his ambitions changed and he'd turned out for football. He was still skinny and spent most of his time warming the bench, and Laney had teased him about that. (Gosh, she'd been mean!) But he'd persisted, and as high school went on, he began to change from a scrawny goof to something a lot more interesting. She found herself stealing glances at him in English class; he was usually tapping his pencil or sneaking looks at his cell phone, bored out of his mind.

"I don't care about Shakespeare," he'd complained once when a bunch of them had gone to Dairy Queen for Blizzards. "I'd rather work a math problem or do stuff on my car."

"Everybody should read Shakespeare," Laney had argued.

"Why? Who understands that shit? It isn't even English."

"It is, too," she'd said, rolling her eyes. "It's early modern English."

"Well, they need to update it."

"Mrs. Krepps says you shouldn't try to update Shakespeare," Laney had told him. "You lose the beauty of the language."

"Bullshit," Drake had said, showing what he thought of their high school English teacher's opinion. "They have modern translations of the Bible. Shakespeare's not more important than the Bible."

Laney hadn't been able to find a good comeback for that. She'd had to settle for "You're such a loser."

That Christmas she'd given him an edition of *Romeo and Juliet* that put Shakespeare's language side by side with a translation into modern English. She'd given it to him as a joke, but to her surprise he'd actually read it.

"Not bad" had been his assessment. Then he went back to Dean Koontz and Stephen King on audiobooks when he tinkered with the old muscle car he'd found on Craigslist.

She couldn't give him too hard a time about that because, when it came right down to it, she wasn't that crazy about Shakespeare herself.

Come senior year, he finally made first string on the football team and became one of the guys who swaggered down the hall on his way to class. He barely passed English, but he aced his math and science classes.

He'd been happy when Laney was accepted at the University of Washington but equally happy that he was going to train to be an auto technician. "I don't want to sit in an office all day or make kids read Shakespeare. I want to do something hands-on," he'd said.

That had triggered a vision of him doing something hands-on with her. Yes, things had changed since middle school. The more Drake talked about what he wanted to do with his life, the more she wanted to share that life with him. Traveling, mountain climbing, kayaking in Puget Sound, visiting cities like San Antonio and New York and LA. He'd been to Disneyland when he was little. Now he wanted to go back and get his picture taken with Donald Duck. He wanted to go to Vegas and play craps and see Criss Angel. He wanted to volunteer with Habitat for Humanity, maybe go to Mexico and build houses for the poor. With his goofy smile, big heart and sense of adventure, Drake was special and Laney didn't want to see him fall for another girl. She wanted him to fall for *her*.

When he started talking about taking some new girl he'd met at the beach to the Fourth of July fireworks at Green Lake, Laney had gotten pissy, told him he had no taste in women.

"I don't know. She's pretty hot," he'd said.

"So am I. Why don't you take me to watch the fireworks?"

He'd looked at her oddly and said, "Yeah, why don't I?"

They had their first kiss on the Fourth of July as the fireworks exploded over the lake, and that was it. She knew, she just knew.

And now they were getting married. Squeee!

She'd been dreaming about her wedding day since she was a little girl. In fact, growing up, she'd been sort of a wedding addict. Her mom had hooked her the first time she brought Laney home a slice of wedding cake. She could still picture that piece of cake with its pink-frosting rose and small silver dragées, could still remember licking the frosting off her fingers. Mom subscribed to *Brides* magazine, and Laney had never gotten tired of looking at the pictures of all those models showing off gorgeous gowns. Every wedding movie she'd watched had sold her on the big "I do." She used to imagine herself getting married in some old English castle with glittering chandeliers, saying "I do" to a guy who looked like Prince Charming. As she got older, Prince Charming began to look suspiciously like Zac Efron or Orlando Bloom. Now, of course, Prince Charming looked exactly like Drake.

She had to celebrate. So on Wednesday, Drake's night for gaming with the guys, she invited her friends over for a girl party.

The revelers consisted of her longtime bestie, Autumn, who was actually always "over" since she and Laney shared a funky house in Fremont; Laney's friend from college, Ella; and Drake's younger sister, Darcy.

She'd just put out the fondue when Darcy arrived,

bearing a gigantic bag of corn chips. "I'm so excited," she squealed, hugging Laney. "I finally get a sister."

"Me, too," Laney said, hugging her back. Her life growing up as an only child had been great, but she'd always wanted a sister. Now she had one.

Her friend Ella was next. "I'm so jealous," she said. "At the rate we're going, I won't be engaged until I'm fifty."

"I'm not getting married till I'm thirty. I've still got things I want to do on my own," Autumn said as she took the salsa out of the fridge.

"What do you want to do on your own that you can't do with Ben?" Ella scoffed.

"Live in Paris for a year, study fashion design."

"You could do that with Ben," Ella pointed out.

"I can't flirt with Frenchmen when I'm with Ben," Autumn said with a grin.

Ella rolled her eyes and flopped down on the fake-leather couch Laney had bought at a garage sale. "So spill," she said to Laney. "How did Drake propose?"

"He took me to the Space Needle. I had a feeling he was going to propose."

"How'd you know?" asked Darcy. "He didn't even tell *me*."

"'Cause he was acting all nervous. He was checking his pocket every five minutes, like there was something in there he didn't want to lose, and when we were at our table he kept fooling with the silverware and drinking water."

"That's so cute," Ella said dreamily. "So did he get down on one knee and everything?"

Laney nodded. "Yep, just before dessert."

"And you said yes right away," Darcy prompted.

"You should've made him sweat," Autumn said and took a sip of her pop.

Darcy frowned at her. "That's mean."

"No, that's psychology," Autumn argued. "Make 'em sweat. That way they really appreciate it when you say yes."

"I still think it's mean," Darcy muttered.

"Have you set a date?" Ella asked Laney.

"We don't have the exact date yet, but we're talking about June."

Ella's eyebrows shot up. "Wow, that doesn't give you much time to plan the wedding."

"It's plenty of time, especially if we go to Vegas."

"Ooh, baby," said Autumn. "Slots and shopping and glitzy pools and big, huge fancy drinks."

"And hookers." Ella wrinkled her nose.

"Don't worry. Nobody's gonna proposition your man," Autumn said, and Ella stuck her tongue out at her.

"It's not for sure yet," Laney told them. "We might get married here."

Her mom had made a good case for that—a big guest list, catered dinner, getting married by Pastor Ostrom, who had watched her grow up. He was going to retire at the end of the year. She'd probably be the sweet old guy's last wedding.

But Vegas sounded like fun, too. She and Drake had already looked at the Treasure Island website. The packages weren't cheap, but were definitely cheaper than what they'd pay if they stuck around Seattle to get married. And she loved the idea of being down there in the center of all that excitement.

"Let's check out Vegas," Autumn said, grabbing her phone.

The images for Vegas weddings were all impressive. Her mother had thought a Vegas chapel would be tacky. Mom must have been thinking about the old days, because what Laney and her friends were seeing was totally glam.

"Drake thinks Vegas would be really cool," said Darcy. She frowned. "But I'm not twenty-one yet. I can't drink. At least if you end up getting married here, somebody will let me have a glass of champagne."

"Well, *there's* a reason not to go to Vegas," Autumn cracked. "What do you want to do most?" she asked Laney.

A series of images flashed across Laney's mind—the royal wedding with all its pomp and splendor, the church weddings she'd attended growing up, images from the many websites she'd peered at over her mother's shoulder when Mom was working. Everything felt so wide-open she almost didn't know what to choose. But then she looked at those pictures on the Treasure Island site and smiled. "I want to go to Vegas."

Except Mom had called the other day to tell her about a place she'd found that would be perfect for the wedding. How the heck was she going to get out of that?

Five

Anne, Woman with a Plan

On Thursday Laurel Browne dropped by the office with her Pekingese, Rufus, cuddled in her arms. Anne had heard it said that owners and their dogs often resembled each other. Looking at Laurel and Rufus, she could believe it. Both had snub noses and blond highlights. And both wore a permanent scowl.

"Rufus and I were on our way to the groomer and thought we'd stop by," Laurel explained. "Didn't we, Rufus baby?"

Oh, goody. "Isn't he a handsome dog," Anne lied. "Hi, Rufus."

"Grrr," Rufus replied, showing her his teeth, and not in a sweet *Look, Mom, I floss every day* kind of way.

"I found some pictures on the internet of yellow floral arrangements," Laurel went on, holding up her finds.

Some? The sheaf of papers was the size of *War and Peace.* "Uh, thank you," Anne said. She could just imagine what Kate over at In Bloom would say when she saw this.

Anne reached to take it and Rufus snarled and snapped at her. She yanked back her hand. Yikes! Were all her fingers still attached?

"Rufus, behave," scolded Laurel. "I'm afraid he doesn't like going to the groomer."

Or else, like his mommy, Rufus didn't like wedding planners.

"I'll put them here on the desk," Laurel said.

"Thank you." Anne hoped her smile looked sincere. She thought they'd settled the flower issue. Obviously, they hadn't. "I'll pass these on to Kate. And maybe next week you and Chelsea could come and see a few table settings," she said, raising her voice to be heard over Rufus, who was conveying his displeasure at being deprived of a finger sandwich by barking at her.

"Rufus baby, stop now," Laurel cooed. "That will be fine." No cooing for Anne. "We need to get this settled."

"Great," Anne said, pretending she and Laurel and Rufus were all BFFs. "I know we'll find something you and Chelsea are both going to love."

"With what I'm paying you, I hope so."

That again. "It's not nearly enough to cover the pain and suffering," Anne said as soon as the door shut behind Laurel. "And what's with that dog?"

"Little dogs can get aggressive when they feel cornered," said Kendra, who owned a Norwich terrier.

"Cornered? I'm the one who nearly lost a finger."

"She should've put the dog on the floor."

"So he could bite my ankle?"

"So he wouldn't feel threatened." Kendra shook her head. "You're such an animal-hater. The dog probably sensed it."

"I am not an animal-hater," Anne insisted. "Just because I prefer cats."

"You haven't had a cat in years."

It was true. After Pansy died she'd been too brokenhearted to even think about getting another pet. "I already have Cam, and one animal is enough," Anne said, making her sister snicker. "I need a caffeine fix. Want a mocha?"

"Sure, if you're buying."

"It's your turn but okay," Anne said, playing the martyr.

It didn't work. Her sister grinned and said, "Great. I'll take a large."

So off Anne went to the coffee shop on Queen Anne Avenue, where her daughter worked as a barista. It was midmorning and the place was humming with caffeinated drinkers and people waiting to get their hit. The smell of roasted coffee practically made Anne's taste buds spring a leak.

"Hi, Mrs. Richardson," her daughter's friend and roommate said.

"Hi, Autumn. I'll have my usual white chocolate latte and a large…"

"Coconut mocha," supplied Autumn with a grin.

"You guessed it," Anne said and dropped a dollar in the tip jar.

"Hi, Mom," her daughter called from her station at the espresso maker.

Under her bright red apron she wore a short-sleeved shirt to show off the mermaid swimming up her arm past seashells and starfish. Anne preferred it when her daughter wore long-sleeved tops. That way she didn't have to be reminded of the mermaid's existence. Laney loved mermaids and had designed the tattoo herself. Anne loved mermaids, too, as long as they stayed in movies, where they belonged.

It's her life, Anne had told herself when Laney got her second tattoo, this one on her neck. A climbing rose. Like Laney herself, her tattoos were all about motion.

"It's your favorite flower," Laney had said. "Your favorite flower and your favorite daughter all rolled into one." Daughters—they were such a blessing. And such a source of irritation.

In spite of the tattoo irritation, Anne was proud of Laney. She had a nice guy, a college degree (something Anne had never gotten) and would soon be working on her teaching certificate so she could become an art teacher while she honed her silversmithing skills. She didn't do drugs or post naughty pictures of herself on the internet, and she was gainfully employed. She was creative and beautiful, and Anne loved her like crazy. She'd probably never love the tattoos, though.

Laney set out two to-go cups. "One small Americano and one double tall soy latte, no whip."

The two women who'd been waiting snagged their drinks and moved to a corner table.

Anne was next in line. She leaned over the counter. "So what did you decide about going up to Icicle Falls this weekend and checking out that place I told you about?"

Laney concentrated on putting a stainless-steel pitcher of milk under the steam wand, and for a moment all Anne heard was *whoosh*. Someone at a nearby table laughed.

"Hello?" Anne prompted.

"I've got that craft fair coming up. I've still got to make stuff for that."

"The fair isn't until Memorial Day weekend," Anne pointed out. "We need to get this venue nailed down. We don't have much time to plan your wedding."

"I know, but I think we want to go to Vegas. That won't take long to plan."

"You shouldn't make a snap decision until you've considered a bit more," Anne advised.

Laney shrugged and said, "I guess," a sure sign that she was underwhelmed by the idea of getting married in Icicle Falls.

"We can go up for a girls' weekend with Aunt Kendra and Grammy. What happens in Icicle Falls stays in Icicle Falls."

That made Laney giggle. "Mom, you crack me up."

"We can be wild."

"Where? There?" Laney set out the drinks.

"Let's at least go see it." They hadn't been to Icicle Falls since Laney was a little girl and she'd obviously forgotten what a special town it was. Once she saw the place, Anne knew she'd be on board. Laney and Drake liked to do outdoor things, and according to the brochure she'd picked up, there was plenty of that—hiking, river rafting, rock climbing. Laney just had to catch the vision. Then she'd be all over this.

"Okay."

It wasn't the most enthusiastic *okay* Anne had ever heard, but she'd take it. "I'll make reservations. It'll be fun. And this will give you another option to explore. Remember, your wedding's a big deal and you don't want to do something you'll regret later."

Laney gave her a you-might-be-right kind of nod,

and since more customers were waiting for their drinks, that was the end of the lecture. Anne left the shop, feeling that they were getting somewhere.

"I don't know why you're trying so hard," her husband said over dinner that night.

Of course he didn't. She'd rarely complained about their wedding. But even though she'd been a sport about it, she'd always wished she'd been able to have the wedding of her dreams, something that reflected the beauty of their love and the seriousness of their commitment. Not that what they'd opted for was bad; it was just… less. Could it have played out differently at the time?

No, she reminded herself as she relived that pivotal conversation and what followed.

1990

Anne and Cam sat in his souped-up truck outside her house in the late summer night with Michael Bolton on the radio asking, "How Am I Supposed to Live Without You?" Good question.

"I wish you'd never joined the army," Anne said, her voice as bitter as her tears.

"Come on, babe. You know we had a plan. This will pay for my college."

"If you live to go to college. If you come back." How was she supposed to tell him her news in light of this?

He reached out a hand and played with her hair. "Of course I'll come back, and then we'll get married just like we planned."

And by then… "I'm pregnant," she blurted.

His hand froze. "You're…pregnant? How could that be? We used protection."

"Well, I guess it wasn't very good protection," she snapped. "And now you're leaving for the Middle East."

"That wasn't exactly my idea," he said. "But…hey, a kid. This is cool."

"This is *not* cool," she informed him. He was going away. She'd be left on her own to deal with everything. They'd planned to have a big church wedding when he got out of the army. She'd work while he went back to school, and after he got his degree, she'd finish up hers. Then they'd have their two kids and a dog and a little house somewhere in the burbs and life would be perfect. Now nothing was perfect. "We should've waited."

"Are you serious? Babe, I've been taking cold showers since I was seventeen."

If she'd known this was going to happen, she would've kept sending him to the shower. Now look at the mess they were in. What would her youth pastor say? Never mind him. What would her mother say?

"We'd better get married."

"I don't have time to plan a wedding before you get shipped off to the Gulf." Everyone knew it took months to plan a wedding. She didn't even have a ring yet. Why did he have to go away? Why did this stupid war have to break out?

He stared out the window. There was nothing much to see on Tenth Avenue except tree-lined street and modest Queen Anne houses with their porch lights on. Then he began to tap his fingers on the steering wheel.

"We can go to the courthouse," he finally said.

"The courthouse?" Get married at the courthouse? That would be her big wedding?

He turned to look at her again, his face earnest. "I love you, Annie, and I want to spend the rest of my life with you. Let's make it official before I ship out. It doesn't matter where we get married just as long as we do. Right?"

Well, of course, that was the most important thing. But ever since she was seventeen, writing *Mrs. Cameron Richardson* in her high school notebooks, she'd dreamed of a traditional wedding with all the trimmings: the gown, the flowers, the church, the big reception afterward. Now reality was closing the door on that vision. She was pregnant; he was going off to the deserts of the Middle East, where who knew what would happen to him. They had to be practical.

She nodded but she couldn't talk. There was suddenly a boulder stuck in her throat.

Cam pulled her close and touched his forehead to hers. "Hey, I know this isn't what you wanted," he said softly.

She swallowed hard, forcing the boulder down. "I want to be with you," she told him. "That's what I want." If he didn't come back—horrible thought!—the only time they'd have together was right now. Was she really willing to give that up for a flower-filled church and a bunch of bridesmaids? Anyway, she wanted to start motherhood with a husband in the picture, even if that picture was of Daddy somewhere in a desert.

"Let's do it, then," he said. "Let's go downtown first thing Monday and get the license. Then we can get married next Friday."

She'd be with Cam. She'd be Mrs. Cameron Richardson. They wouldn't have much time before he left but it would be better than nothing.

"What do you say, Annie?" he prompted.

"I say yes!" She'd be crazy to say anything else.

"All right!" he crowed. And then he gave her a kiss that made her toes curl in her jelly shoes. Who needed a fancy wedding, anyway?

Not me, Anne told herself.

Not me, she reminded herself on Friday afternoon at four thirty as she entered the big, impersonal Seattle municipal courthouse wearing a white satin sheath and a small diamond ring, carrying a bouquet of red roses. She was flanked by her parents, her father smiling gamely, her mother smiling, too, although her smile didn't quite reach her eyes. Kendra trailed behind, the clueless younger sister, excited by the whole adventure.

And there, waiting for her, was Cam with his parents. His eyes lit up at the sight of her and he hurried over and kissed her. "You look incredible."

"You look beautiful, dear," his mother added and kissed her on the cheek before greeting Anne's mother. If she wasn't happy about the rush-job wedding, she didn't betray it.

"Well," said Dad, "let's get this show on the road, shall we?"

"Good idea," Cam said, smiling at Anne. He offered her his arm. She took it and they started down the hallway.

They made their way to the room reserved for weddings, passing lawyers busy conferring with their clients—sketchy guys in dirty jeans or angry women with naked ring fingers, probably in the process of getting divorced. This was her wedding march. No church filled with well-wishers, no big wedding reception after the ceremony, just a dinner at her parents' house with the two families and the small cake her neighbor Mrs. Hornsby had insisted on making for them. It was the world's ugliest cake, slightly lopsided ("I had a little trouble assembling it," Mrs. H. had confessed) with neon pink rosebuds that you needed sunglasses to look at and bride and groom toppers that must've been around since the fifties. But hey, it was a wedding cake.

An angry guy gave a man in a suit the finger and slouched away, knocking into Anne as he passed and telling her to watch where the hell she was going. It was all so different from what she'd dreamed of. *You're marrying Cam. That's what matters.* So why were tears springing to her eyes?

He looked at her with concern. "Are you okay?"

She nodded. "I'm just so happy."

And she had been all these years. Still, she'd always regretted the fact that she and Cam had taken their vows in such a sterile environment.

Laney could afford to wait and do things right, and somehow, Anne had to get through to her. When it came to her wedding, a woman shouldn't settle, even if her groom wanted to be a pirate.

Laney was going to have no regrets. Anne would see to it.

Six

Roberta, Woman of Mystery

"Nice write-up in the paper," Dot Morrison said when she stopped by Roberta and Daphne's table at Pancake Haus to say hi.

"Thank you," Roberta said, lining up the salt and pepper shakers. It *had* been a nice write-up, and sweet of Muriel to think of her.

"When are they going to do one on you?" Daphne asked.

"Next week," Dot said. "Looks like they're writing up all us old-timers first."

Old-timer. Sometimes it seemed like only yesterday that Roberta had arrived in town. Back then, Icicle Falls had been transforming itself from a struggling town on the verge of extinction to an Alpine village. The place was so full of hope you could almost taste it. Roberta had, and that was why she'd decided to settle here. She'd needed a good dose of hope. And a job.

She'd gone into this very restaurant when she hit town. Back then, before Dot had come to Icicle Falls and taken over the place, it had been nothing more than a greasy spoon catering to truckers and travelers crossing the pass, but to her it had felt like an oasis.

1961

Roberta got off the bus in front of the café and went inside. Summer was coming early to the mountain town of Icicle Falls and it was a relief to get inside and escape the heat. She ordered a cup of coffee that tasted like battery acid and a fried egg that upset her stomach, still delicate so early in her pregnancy. The toast that came with it, once she'd scraped off the burned part, helped with the queasiness.

"Honey, you look done in," said her waitress. The woman appeared to be the same age as Roberta's mother. Her hair was what Mother would have labeled "bottle blond," and the wrinkles around her mouth, along with the faint whiff of smoke coming off her, proclaimed her a smoker.

"I'm a little tired," Roberta admitted.

"We got a motel on the other side of town," said the waitress. "Nothing to write home about but it's clean."

Roberta couldn't afford a motel. She nodded and thanked the woman anyway.

"Course, pretty soon we'll have more going up, fancy ones like you'd see in Switzerland or Germany. This town is making some big changes. This time next year, it'll really look like something." She proceeded to tell Roberta all the plans in the works for putting Icicle Falls on the map. "My husband, Fred, and me, we're saving up to build ourselves a hamburger place. To pass on to the kids, you know?"

Roberta had nothing to pass on to her child.

No, she corrected herself. She had love. This baby would be well loved and well cared for.

If she could find a job.

And a place to stay. But her money supply was dwindling and she couldn't spend it on motel rooms. "Is there anyone in town who takes in boarders?" she asked.

Before the waitress could answer, someone new walked in, a pretty woman with brown hair wearing a white blouse and pedal pushers. She had an equally pretty little daughter with chestnut curls. The daughter stared at Roberta curiously as they approached the table.

She supposed she'd stare at herself, too, and wonder what someone her age was doing, traveling all alone. Soon she'd be showing, and with no wedding ring people would really stare. They'd do more than stare if they knew she was only seventeen. Well, she'd be eighteen in two months. Then she'd be an adult and no one could force her to do anything. She tried not to think about what a lonely birthday it would be.

"Hi, Flo," said the woman.

"Hi, Betty," the waitress said. "How's the cleanup going?"

"Great. The men have hauled those dead cars and car parts off for old Billy. And that's the last eyesore gone."

The waitress nodded approvingly. Then, remembering Roberta, said, "This young lady's looking for a place to stay. Do you know of anything?"

"Sarah Shepherd's taking in boarders," the newcomer named Betty replied. She turned to Roberta and introduced herself. "And this is my daughter, Muriel."

"Hi, Muriel." Roberta smiled and Muriel said a polite hello in return.

"So you're new in town?" Betty asked.

Roberta nodded.

"Where you from, dear?" asked Flo the waitress.

"California," Roberta lied.

Flo let out a low whistle. "You're a ways from home."

"I needed to make a new start," Roberta said. That was no lie. "I'm a widow."

"A widow," echoed Flo. "And you so young!"

"My husband was killed in a car accident."

"Oh, how sad," Betty said. "I'm very sorry."

Roberta murmured her thanks. "This seems to be a nice town," she ventured.

"You could do a lot worse than settle here," Flo told her.

"Hey, Flo," called a husky man seated a couple of tables down. "Are you gonna take my order or leave me here to starve?"

"You could live off that fat belly of yours for days, Hal," Flo retorted. She rolled her eyes. "Guess I'd better go take his order," she said and left.

"Mind if I join you?" Betty asked. Before Roberta could answer, she slid into the bench on the other side of the booth, her daughter following suit. "When did you lose your husband?"

"It's been…a while." Roberta could feel her cheeks warming. How many questions was this woman going to ask?

"I can't imagine losing a husband at such a young age," Betty said, shaking her head. "I hope he left you well provided for?"

"I'm afraid not," Roberta said. "We hadn't been married very long," she improvised. They hadn't been married at all, but that wasn't something she was going to share with a stranger. It wasn't something she was going to share with *anyone*. Ever.

"Do you know if anyone in town is hiring?" she hurried on. If no one was, there was no point in staying. She'd have to keep moving on. Where, she wasn't sure. When she'd first hit the road, all she'd wanted to do was put as much distance between herself and Seattle as she could. Now she realized she should have planned more carefully.

Except there hadn't been time to plan.

Across the table from her Betty was looking sympathetic. "I hear they need a teller over at the bank. My husband and the manager are friends. I'd be happy to put in a word for you."

"But you don't know me." For all this woman knew, Roberta could be a con artist. In a way she was.

"I'm pretty good at sizing people up. You seem like an honest young woman."

She was anything but.

"What do you think, Muriel?" Betty asked, smiling at the girl.

"I think she's pretty," Muriel said, then blushed.

"Thank you," Roberta murmured. Being pretty wasn't always an advantage. Sometimes it got a girl in trouble. "I'm a hard worker," she said to Betty. Not that she'd ever had any job besides babysitting. But she'd work hard for whoever hired her.

"I'm sure you are," Betty said kindly. "I tell you what. How about after breakfast I take you down to the bank and introduce you to Howard Mangle, the manager? Then I can show you where the Shepherds live."

The woman's generosity was almost too much. Roberta felt tears flooding her eyes. "You're very kind."

Betty cocked her head and studied Roberta in a way that had her cheeks heating again. "I suspect you're a woman in need of a little kindness right now."

If Betty had guessed Roberta's real story, she never let on. Instead, she'd taken Roberta under her wing and helped her get settled in town. Roberta had spent many a Sunday at Betty's house, enjoying dinner with her family. Betty and her husband, Joe, had helped Roberta move when, a few years later, she'd found her Victorian. Roberta had watched Muriel grow up and had been a regular customer of Sweet Dreams Chocolates ever since the day she got her job at the bank and splurged on a box of chocolate-covered cherries. She'd met new friends and made something of herself. Staying in Icicle Falls had turned out to be a good decision.

Maybe it would be for Daphne, too. Maybe here Daphne would finally get inspired to do more with her life. Open a shop, live up to her name and become a writer like Daphne du Maurier. Or Muriel. Something. Anything. So far all she'd been inspired to do was mope around the house.

"I hear you're back to stay," Dot said to Daphne.

"I've sure had enough of Seattle," Daphne replied.

"Well, I'm sorry your marriage didn't work out, kiddo," Dot said. "But sometimes a woman is better off on her own. Look how well your mom and I have done."

Daphne heaved a huge sigh. "You're probably right. I don't seem to do very well at picking men."

"It's hard to pick a good one when so many of the ones hanging on the branch are rotten," Dot said.

Daphne pushed back a lock of blond hair. "I suppose

there are still some good men out there. I've just never been able to find one."

My poor daughter, Roberta thought. *Where did I go wrong?* Daphne should have been happily married. And successful. But here she was, rejected, dejected and living with her mother.

"Muriel sure knows how to find the good ones," Dot said. "In fact, you should talk to her daughter. Cecily used to be a matchmaker. Maybe she'll have some ideas for you."

"Like how to murder my husband?"

Roberta frowned at her, but Dot chuckled. "Things'll work out. They always do."

"Daphne!" Roberta scolded as Dot moved on to greet her other customers.

"Sorry," Daphne said in an unrepentant voice, "but I really could murder him. Stake him out in the sun covered with honey and let the ants have at him."

"There's an appetizing image," Roberta said in disgust. "Although I must admit, even that's better than he deserves." She'd never say it publicly, but she wouldn't mind getting a chance to put her hands around Mitchell's throat.

"Every time I think of him and that woman I want to…" Daphne crumpled her paper napkin.

Roberta reached across the table and patted her arm. "He didn't deserve you, dear. You're well rid of him."

Daphne's eyes filled with tears. "How could he do this to me?"

Quite easily, it seemed. But since that was obviously a rhetorical question, Roberta kept her answer to herself. She gave her daughter's arm another encouraging pat. "We're not going to waste any more energy talking about him. Instead, we'll focus on you. We need to come up with a plan for what you're going to do next. You can't just mope around the house all day."

"I don't want to mope. Let me help with the next wedding."

"There's really nothing left to do," Roberta said. "Everything's under control."

Daphne looked at her, reproach in her eyes. "You don't want me to help."

Yes, that was part of it.

"You should let me," Daphne urged. "You may as well plug me in now. You've got bunion surgery coming up in May. You'll need the extra help."

She probably would. She'd planned to delegate more work to Lila. "Darling, you're going to be busy with your divorce."

"Not that busy."

"Well, then, you should be busy job-hunting. You don't want to work on weddings, not in your present state of mind."

"I want to help you. I want to be useful."

"You're being useful." Daphne had cleaned the whole house the day before, even transferred her dirty breakfast dishes from the sink to the dishwasher without being nagged.

"I could do more if you'd let me. If you'd believe in me," Daphne added softly.

Was that what Daphne thought? That she didn't believe in her? If she hadn't believed in her daughter, why would she have wasted her breath all these years suggesting things Daphne could do to improve her life?

"I'm fifty-three and you still don't see me as anything but a failure," Daphne said.

"That's not true." Except it was. Oh, dear.

The waitress arrived to take their orders, ending the conversation for the moment. Roberta found she didn't have much of an appetite. "Coffee, please," she said.

Why did everything have to be so difficult between mothers and daughters? Or was it just her and Daphne?

Maybe it *was* just her. She was always encouraging Daphne to try more, do more, be more, but whenever Daphne offered to help with the business, Roberta put her off.

Daphne wanted Roberta to be proud of her, possibly even more than Roberta did. She needed to give her daughter a chance to earn that pride, something Roberta's mother had never done for her.

"Would you like to assist with setup for the next wedding?" she asked after their waitress left. There was a task Daphne could manage just fine.

"I'd be happy to," Daphne said and smiled.

Roberta smiled, too. It wasn't too late to make some changes. Daphne needed to feel useful, and Roberta could use the extra help. Really, she was a lucky woman to have such a sweet daughter who wanted to be part of her life. This could be a win-win situation.

Or a disaster.

Seven

Laney, on the Bridal Trail

"What do you want to do this weekend?" Drake asked as he dragged a French fry through his ketchup.

Laney stared out the car window at the row of customers standing in front of Dick's Drive-in in the University district, waiting to order burgers and shakes. "Uh, I have to go to Icicle Falls this weekend."

"Huh?" The look he gave her was both surprised and accusatory.

Suddenly the hamburger she'd been eating didn't taste so good. She should've told him. She'd had all week to tell him. They always hung out on the weekend.

"I'm sorry," she said. "I should've told you."

"Yeah, that would've been nice."

Now he was frowning and she felt like a rotten girlfriend. People who were in love should spend their weekends together. "My mom wants me to go see a house up there that she thinks would be great for us to get married in."

He stuffed a handful of French fries in his mouth and digested that information.

"It can't hurt to look," she went on. "Since we haven't actually decided what we want to do."

"Well, I know what I want to do, and I thought you did, too."

"I do. I did. I don't know." Eloping to Vegas had sounded like fun. She'd never been and was dying to see the fountain at the Bellagio, eat in one of those fancy restaurants and play the slot machines. But then her mom had talked about how important her wedding was and how Laney didn't want to do anything she'd regret and she'd had second thoughts. And Mom kept talking about that place in Icicle Falls, as though it was so special. "I just want to go up there and see. Okay?"

"Sure, but..." He frowned.

"But what?"

"If you're going up to look at a place where we might get married, I should go, too."

He should, but nobody had invited him. Oh, that hamburger really wasn't sitting well. "It's a girls' trip. My aunt and grandma are going, too." As if that was supposed to make him *not* feel left out? "You'd be so bored," Laney added.

Now he was looking out the window and frowning.

"Don't be mad," she said, laying a pleading hand on his thigh. She hated it when he wasn't happy.

"I'm not mad. I'm..." The frown got bigger. "Well, okay, I'm kind of mad."

"I probably won't like the place anyway." But maybe she would. If Mom thought it was such a wonderful place, she needed to at least check it out. After all, Mom was the wedding expert.

He took a deep breath and expelled it, then reached over and gave her the little one-handed neck massage that always made her melt. "It's okay if you do. I want you to be happy."

"Hey, I'm marrying you. How can I not be happy?"

That took away the last of his frown. And the kiss she gave him put a smile back on his face. "We could go to Vegas for our honeymoon," he said. "We were gonna hang around there after we got married anyway."

It seemed like a good compromise. Laney set aside the vision of herself standing on the deck of the wedding ship in Siren's Cove at Treasure Island. If they had a more traditional wedding, they could have a big party with a ton of guests. That would be way better. Not very unusual or interesting, though. Kind of...boring.

She realized she was the one frowning now. A more traditional wedding didn't have to be boring, she told herself. She could give it flair, add her own personal touch. Besides, a wedding with lots of family and friends would be fun and would make her parents happy, especially her mom. Everyone would be happy.

Well, maybe not Drake. Oh, man.

"Would you really mind if we had a more—" *Oops, almost said "boring"* "—traditional wedding?" she asked.

He shrugged. "Hey, it's all about the bride, right?"

But he was disappointed; she could tell. His smile wasn't lighting up his eyes. "It's all about *both* of us."

"I'm cool with whatever you decide," he said.

"No, you're not."

He drew her to him and touched his forehead to hers. "Yeah, I am. So go up to Icicle Falls with your mom and have fun. And send me pics."

Okay, that settled it. Sort of. For now. Part of her still wasn't sure. She reminded herself that she didn't have to say yes to the house in Icicle Falls if she didn't like it.

Although if she didn't, Mom would be disappointed. Grammy, too.

Aunt Kendra, on the other hand, would say, "Do what you want." Only problem was, Laney wasn't sure what she wanted anymore.

That was both atypical and unsettling. Laney always knew what she wanted, and it was often very different from what her mom wanted for her. She still remembered the first time she and her mother had disagreed. She'd wanted to wear her princess jammies to kindergarten, and Mom had insisted on play clothes. She'd whined, cried and finally thrown herself on the floor, refusing to get up. And she'd won a major battle. Sort of. She'd gotten to wear her princess jammies, but she'd done it at home because Mom refused to take her to school. Even in kindergarten her mother hadn't approved of her sense of style.

Some things never changed. First princess jammies, then piercings, then tats. Mom thought she was with it, but she was really kind of a conformist. She didn't like coloring outside the lines. Literally. "Inside the lines, sweetie, like this," she'd said whenever she colored in Laney's coloring book with her. "That's right. A purple cow? Now, how about we make the next one brown?"

Like Dad, she'd worried when Laney decided to major in art that she'd never be able to support herself and had quit worrying only when Laney decided to go back to school in the fall and get a teaching degree. She thought Laney's place in Seattle's free-spirit Fremont district was dumpy and hated the way Laney and Autumn had decorated it. Not that she'd come right out and said so, but Laney could read her mother as easily as a graphic novel. Mom didn't do well with extremes. She had one piercing in each ear and wore the same small diamond earrings almost every day. She dressed conservatively and drove a Volvo because it was supposed to be the safest car on the road.

All of that was okay. For Mom. But Laney was different from her mother, and much as she loved Mom, she had to be true to herself. She'd look at the place in Icicle Falls but she wasn't making any promises.

A good thing she hadn't, she thought when they pulled into town. *This is so not Vegas.* Still, she had to admit it was cute. It was almost as though she'd stepped into another country, with the frescoes painted on the buildings and all the flower boxes under shop windows. Then there was the river running alongside the town. She could see herself and Drake rafting on it. She took a picture with her phone and sent it to him.

Let's go on it, he texted back.

"The river would be perfect for your wedding party to go inner tubing on before the rehearsal," Mom said.

Inspiration hit. "We could even get married on the river, on a raft." She texted Drake. Want to get married on it?

Sure, came the reply.

"It might be hard to get on a river raft in a wedding gown," Grammy said from the backseat.

Did she want a traditional wedding gown? Maybe not. "I could wear shorts and a bikini top. And a bridal veil," Laney added, picturing herself in white shorts and a white bikini top.

"Shorts?" Mom said weakly.

Okay, maybe that wouldn't work, either. "It was a thought." Suddenly she was remembering the princess jammies. "But if we get married on the river..." She needed to keep her options open.

"Let's get checked in and then go buy some chocolate," Aunt Kendra said, pulling them back from the river's edge.

"Great idea," Grammy said.

"I'm all for that," Mom agreed. "How about a trip to Sweet Dreams before we see the house?" she asked Laney.

"Great idea," Laney repeated. They might not see eye to eye on fashion trends; they might not see eye to eye on wedding venues, either. But there was one thing they always agreed on, and that was chocolate.

They all checked into the Icicle Creek Lodge, which, according to Mom, was the best place in town. "They've got a honeymoon suite," Mom said.

If you asked Laney, it looked like a place her grandmother would stay in with its old-fashioned carpeting and the ornate, old European-style furniture. But the beds in the room she was sharing with her mom were comfy with their crisp, white comforters, and the view out the window was killer awesome.

Mom joined her at the window. "It's gorgeous up here, isn't it?"

"Oh, yeah," Laney said.

"And there's a lot to do. Hiking, rock climbing, shopping, inner tubing."

She could get into all of that. Laney nodded.

Mom turned from the view to look at her. "What do you think of the town?"

"It's cute."

"If you don't like it, we can have the wedding in Seattle," Mom said. "But the house really is beautiful."

Laney nodded. It probably was.

"Well," Mom said, "let's go get some chocolate."

They went to the room next door and collected Aunt Kendra and Grammy, then went to the Sweet Dreams gift shop. Oh, yeah. It was worth coming up here just for the salted caramels. Laney bought some to take home to Drake.

Then they were off to check out Primrose Haus.

"This is charming," Grammy said as they parked in front of the pink Victorian.

Yeah, Laney would give it that. She snapped a picture and sent it to Drake.

Once inside, they met the owner, Roberta Gilbert, and her daughter, Daphne, who gave them a tour of the place. Laney could see why her mother had fallen in love with this house. With its fancy mirrors and decorations, it was impressive, almost like a museum.

Could she see herself in here in a long, lacy gown? Not sure, she texted Drake.

Your call, he texted back.

The outdoor space was impressive. It looked like the set of some PBS movie. And the mountains rising in the background were impressive. Maybe they could get married on the river and have the reception here. Laney took a picture with her phone and sent it to Drake with the subject heading This is cool.

Mtns, he texted back. Rock climbing?

Sure, she replied. They could find enough to do here.

Meanwhile, Mom, Grammy and Aunt Kendra were all firing questions at Mrs. Gilbert and her daughter.

"As I mentioned when I talked to you, we have a

wonderful florist in town," Mrs. Gilbert was saying to Mom.

"But we can also think outside the box when it comes to decorations," her daughter said. "Like balloons."

Laney smiled. "That sounds fun."

"Weddings *should* be fun," Daphne said with a smile. The smile soured. "Considering what you have to deal with after the wedding's over."

Mrs. Gilbert cleared her throat. "We also have a caterer here in town and an excellent baker."

"Can she make cakes like the ones you see on *Cake Boss*?" Laney asked.

"She can make anything you want."

"Including cakes made of donuts," added Daphne. "That's a new trend we've been seeing."

"I like that." The image of a big tower of donuts made Laney smile. "I'm thinking of actually getting married on the river."

"We have a lovely park there," Mrs. Gilbert said diplomatically.

"And having the reception here," Mom put in.

"We cater to whatever the bride wants," Mrs. Gilbert said. "We'll show you the reception room."

It was certainly bigger than the deck of a pirate ship. Laney looked around, picturing herself dancing there with Drake and their friends. Okay, a wedding on the river, followed by a reception here. They could do that.

"So, what did you think?" Mom asked as they drove away.

"It could work," Laney said.

"I can see you getting married under that rose arbor," Mom said.

There was something in her voice, as though she

was talking about what she'd do if she won the lottery. It left Laney biting her lip and looking out the window.

"Or coming down that staircase in a long, white gown," Grammy added dreamily.

"Or princess jammies," teased Aunt Kendra.

"You'll be such a beautiful bride," Mom said, smiling at Laney as if they'd already settled everything.

"I haven't decided on anything yet," Laney said, determined not to get pushed into a snap decision.

"Of course, you need time to think," Mom said.

Yes, she did. Still, Laney felt outnumbered and outgunned, as if no matter what she said, she was going to end up at the house on Primrose Street in an old-fashioned, lacy gown.

Maybe that was what she wanted, deep down, to look like Kate Middleton. Mom had been glued to the TV, watching the whole royal extravaganza and drooling over it. But it was hard to shake the excitement in Drake's voice out of her memory or the little thrill she'd felt when he said, "Let's get married in Vegas."

"What did you think of the house?" Aunt Kendra asked her as they stood in line at Herman's Hamburgers, waiting to order cheeseburgers and garlic fries for everyone.

Laney shrugged. "It's fancy."

"Yeah, it is. Is it you?"

Laney chewed her bottom lip. That was the problem. The house was beautiful. Any wedding held there would be like a storybook wedding. But *was* it her? She'd always thought she wanted to look like a Disney princess at her wedding, but she wasn't sure she was really princess material. So far no Disney princess had tattoos. Would it be the wedding of a lifetime or the mistake of a lifetime? Having a wedding reception in a house seemed so... *No, don't use the B word.* Anyway, her reception didn't have to be boring. A house that old, maybe it was haunted. Maybe they'd see a ghost. Maybe they could have the guests come as ghosts.

Maybe that was a dumb idea.

"If it isn't calling to you, don't do it," Aunt Kendra cautioned just as Mom joined them.

Mom's brows drew together. She looked like the bad fairy Maleficent in *Sleeping Beauty* right before she changed into a dragon. "What are you telling her?"

Oh, boy. Laney braced herself.

"Only that she needs to be sure she really wants to get married at Primrose Haus," Aunt Kendra replied calmly.

Okay, here it comes. Mom was going to breathe fire now and turn every chocolate shake in the place into hot chocolate. "Well, of course she does," Mom snapped. She smiled at Laney. "You do like it, don't you?"

"Yeah. It's nice." If they had the reception there that would make everyone happy.

Mom nodded. "I knew you'd love it."

It could work. She and Drake could make this wedding fun. Somehow...

Ten minutes later they were all seated at a booth, working their way through gigantic burgers, fries and shakes and throwing out wedding ideas. Neither Grammy nor Mom seemed very excited about Laney getting married on a raft on the river.

"What if you fall in?" Grammy worried, dabbing at her mouth with a napkin. She wore her gray hair in the same oversprayed helmet she'd worn in her own wedding pictures. There'd been no getting married on a raft for Grammy.

Or Mom.

But it appealed to Laney. "If I did, it would be something to remember," she joked.

"Not in a good way," Mom said.

"Oh, she wouldn't fall in," said Aunt Kendra. "That only happens in movies."

"And on *America's Funniest Home Videos*," Mom said with a frown. "You don't want your wedding to be a joke."

No, she didn't. And her mom was the wedding organizer, the specialist. Of course Mom would work with her to make sure she had a perfect wedding.

But would it be hers?

Eight

Daphne, the Warrior Princess

Daphne was back in Seattle, in her old house, on special assignment. Her job was to gather tax returns, financial statements and pay stubs.

"Don't worry," her new lawyer, Shirley Schneck, assured Daphne when they met. "We'll see that both of you get exactly what's coming to you." And the glint in her eye didn't bode well for Mitchell.

"She's a barracuda," Dot Morrison had told Daphne. "Thanks to her, I lost my best waitress. The girl got such a good settlement she was able to quit. Went back to school and became a dental hygienist. Shirley's divorced herself. She thinks all men are spawn of Satan. The woman will make sure your cheating husband gets pounded into the ground."

Looking at Shirley, it was hard to imagine her pounding anyone into the ground. She was around Daphne's age with a plump, motherly face and figure to match. When they'd met, she'd been dressed in black slacks and a pale pink sweater accented with a fringed scarf—

hardly the kind of apparel lawyers on TV wore. Her office was like something Martha Stewart would have designed with mint-green walls and antique (no leather!) furniture and paintings of flowers hanging on the wall.

But the sweet face had suddenly turned menacing. It had made Daphne glad that Shirley was working *for* her and not against her, and she'd left Shirley's office fired up and ready for battle.

Returning home to the scene of the crime had doused the fire. Mitchell's time to pack up his things was long gone and so was he. No more husband.

She stood in the living room, looking around at the house she'd worked so hard to turn into a home. She'd redone the living room only last fall, using a soothing tan palette. She'd paid a fortune for that deep chocolate mohair couch. And she and Mitchell had repainted the kitchen this past summer. "Yellow's such a happy color," she'd said, and he'd smiled and agreed. It had been so cozy, the two of them in the kitchen, painting.

He'd actually seemed to enjoy that project, even though he hadn't been very excited about it when she'd first brought up the idea. Mitchell, obviously, had been very good at faking it.

But he couldn't have been faking *every* happy moment they had together. He sure hadn't faked enjoying the sex; that much she knew.

And he'd sounded so sincere when he insisted, "I love you, Daph. That thing with Stella meant nothing."

Men said that in movies all the time. Apparently, they said it in real life, too. "How long have you been with her, Mitchell? How long has she meant nothing?" she'd demanded. Probably as long as he'd been "having to" work late, which made it about three months.

For three months her husband had been pretending to love her while he hooked up with another woman. For three months she hadn't been enough. Or maybe longer. Maybe there'd been other women, too.

She ran a hand along the back of the couch. They'd made love on that couch on New Year's Eve.

She'd sell the thing. Or set it on fire. With Mitchell strapped to it.

She sighed and moved into the office, where she spent the first part of the afternoon pulling together the information requested by her lawyer. Then she packed up the rest of her clothes. That done, she went to the garage to get her golf clubs. She could spend some time at the Mountain Meadows Golf Course.

The sight of them and her golf shoes brought tears to her eyes. She and Mitchell had taken lessons together. She'd envisioned them wintering in Arizona when they retired, playing golf, relaxing at the club and drinking iced tea. *Oh, Mitchell. Why did you have to be such a weasel?*

She grabbed the bag. She'd sell the stupid clubs on eBay. She really wasn't very good in spite of the lessons.

And there were his clubs, sitting right next to hers. She'd told him to get his stuff out of here. Maybe she'd sell his clubs, too. In fact, looking around, she saw quite a lot of stuff that should've been gone by now. Well, then, she'd make a little run to Goodwill. *You snooze, you lose, Mitchell.*

Into her car trunk went not only her cheating husband's golf clubs but his drill and toolbox. Oh, and his tennis racket. He was much too busy banging Stella to play tennis these days. He'd be furious when he found that stuff missing but, oh, well. He'd had more than enough time to get it gone. Anyway, what was he going to do, sue her? Ha-ha.

She was finished by five. A good day's work, she thought, pleased with herself. She was shocked to see that he still had a few clothes in the closet. Perhaps he'd moved in with Stella and was running around her place naked.

The idea of Mitchell running around some other woman's house naked sent a tear streaking down Daphne's cheek. *No, no, no*, she told herself. There would be no more crying over Mitchell.

She showered, put on fresh makeup and then went to meet some of her old friends from work for dinner at Anthony's Home Port in Shilshole. There she treated herself to a Dungeness crab salad and some chowder and plenty of bread, and washed it all down with white wine and encouragement from the girls.

"You're well rid of him," said her friend Ellie Meyers. "What a creep."

"He's lucky you don't Bobbitt him," put in Carrie Anne Hodges, the office manager.

"Bobbitt him? What does that mean?" asked one of the younger women.

"Look up Lorena Bobbitt on Google and you'll see," one of the older women said.

"You cut off his troublemaker," Carrie Anne explained. "I would."

"Whoa," Ellie said, "does Terrence know this side of you?"

"You bet," Carrie Anne said and stabbed her salmon fillet.

Carrie Anne had been married for twenty-nine years. No doubt fear and intimidation was how she kept her man.

Susan the bookkeeper shook her head. "You're so full of it. I've seen you two together. You're, like, soul mates."

Daphne sighed. She'd thought Mitchell was her soul mate. He loved romantic comedies as much as she did. And fine wines and travel. Although they hadn't done much traveling—mostly weekend trips to San Diego or Vegas. Mitchell had an ex-wife and he had child support to pay. Now Daphne couldn't help wondering about that ex. He'd said she was a real witch, insecure and possessive. Jealous. Had he given her reason to be? And what had he told Stella about Daphne? She didn't want to know.

From appetizers to dessert, dinner was a pep rally for Daphne. "You can do it."…"Divorce him."…"You'll be so much happier."

That was hard to believe, she thought when she came back to her house for a good night's sleep before returning to Icicle Falls. The place felt so…empty. Just like she did. She sighed and flopped onto the couch, staring at the lifeless TV. No sense turning it on since she'd discontinued the cable. She was in no mood to watch TV anyway. She much preferred to sit there and mope, remembering the good years she'd had with Mitchell. Like that time a friend lent him his sailboat and they went out on Lake Washington. It had been a perfect day, even though there'd been no wind. They'd motored around the lake, eating Brie cheese and crackers and drinking white wine. Then there'd been that weekend trip to Astoria last summer. They'd had so much fun walking along the waterfront, dining in that cute seaside restaurant. And that night…

She grabbed a sofa pillow and hugged it. How could a man make love so sweetly and not love a woman? Maybe the thing with Stella really didn't mean anything. Everyone made mistakes, right? He'd been so sorry, so upset, when she confronted him. Perhaps she should give him a second chance. She'd sleep on it.

She climbed the stairs to the master bedroom, changed into an old nightgown and went to bed. A hot flash hit her and suddenly the covers were too much. She kicked them off.

Even the simple act of kicking off the covers triggered a memory—Mitchell fetching an ice cube from the freezer and rubbing it all over her, the feel of the ice melting on her skin, then the touch of his lips as they followed its wet trail. She hated being in bed all by herself, hated being in this house all by herself. She'd never liked being alone. There was something so forlorn and unsettling about it. And she never felt safe. Every little noise set her nerves on edge.

She wished she'd gone ahead and driven back to Icicle Falls after her evening with the girls. She wouldn't have gotten in until late, but at least she wouldn't have been all alone in a big bed in a small house.

Don't be silly, she told herself. Her Ballard neighborhood was perfectly safe. *Think about something else.*

Well, that was a dumb idea. She lay there, staring at the ceiling, thinking about something else—her third divorce. Third time's the charm, right? Wrong. With her and Mitchell it had been more a case of three's company. She scowled. She shouldn't give him a second chance. That was just crazy.

But what they'd had together was good...

Until it wasn't. She punched her pillow and rolled over onto her side. She probably wouldn't sleep a wink.

At midnight Daphne was jerked out of a sound sleep by a noise. Downstairs. Someone was in the house.

Here in her safe neighborhood in Ballard. She scooped up her cell phone and dashed to the bedroom door to lock it. And when it wouldn't lock, she remembered that the lock was broken. Why, oh, why hadn't she gotten it fixed? She could hear the soft rumble of a male voice downstairs. Was it getting closer? Was the intruder coming upstairs?

Her heart was banging against her chest, crying, "Let me out!" She dashed into the bathroom. Maybe she could jump out the bathroom window. She shut and locked the bathroom door. Then she called 9-1-1. "There's a burglar in my house," she whimpered as she slid open the window. She gave the woman on the other end of the call her address and added, "I'm alone." *Again. For the third time. And now I'm going to get burgled. Alone.* This was so unfair! So sick and wrong. Mitchell should be here getting burgled along with her.

"The police will be there right away," said the nice lady. "I'll stay on the line with you until they arrive."

A lot of help a voice on the phone would be. *Go away, burglar, or the lady on the phone will yell at you.* Daphne stuck her head out the window and looked down. A second story didn't sound that far up until you contemplated jumping from one. She'd break a leg. Or her back.

"Meanwhile, have you got a safe room, someplace where you can go and lock the door?"

"I'm in the bathroom." *Thinking about jumping.*

"Good. Lock the door and stay there until the police come."

A flimsy lock on a bathroom door probably wouldn't stop a burglar. But maybe the burglar wouldn't care about the bathroom. Well, unless he had to go potty.

Daphne looked around for a weapon she could use in case the intruder had a weak bladder. Snapping him with a towel wouldn't help much. Too bad the mirror was screwed into the wall. She could've broken it over his head. The toilet plunger! She grabbed it and braced herself against the wall.

The voice was in the bedroom now. Aaaaah! Daphne's heart was going to explode. She was going to pass out right here on the bathroom floor.

She heard another voice. The burglar had an accomplice. A female.

Wait a minute.

She tiptoed to the door and pressed her ear to it.

"Baby, you make me so hot."

The burglar was having sex in her bedroom? Of all the nerve!

"There's no one like you, baby. Oh, yeah, that's what Daddy likes."

Daphne's eyes narrowed. She knew that voice and that pathetic no-one-like-you line. "Never mind," she told the woman on the phone. "The burglar is my husband. I'll take care of this on my own."

Now Stella was saying, "Mitchell. The bed's unmade. Has someone been here?"

Daphne unlocked the door and threw it open. "As a matter of fact, someone has."

"Daph," he gasped in shock. There he stood with his pants pooled around his ankles. His partner in infidelity already had her blouse off, her boobs wrapped in a black lace bra. They weren't even that big. Mitchell had left her for...that?

Daphne was across the room before you could say "dirty, rotten cheater." She gave Mitchell a whack with the toilet plunger. She'd been aiming for his head but missed, catching him instead on the shoulder. Still, the yelp of pain it produced was hugely satisfying.

It was like playing Whack-a-Mole. Only better. Whack-a-Rat. She took another swing, this time catching his arms, which were raised in self-defense.

"Daphne, cut it out," he protested, trying to both protect himself and get his pants back up.

"You were supposed to be out of the house," she growled and took another swing. He ducked and she missed. *Strike one.*

"I came back to get some things," he explained, hopping away and yanking his pants up.

"I can see what you came back to get. You came back to get laid." Daphne swung again as Mitchell jumped onto the bed. *Strike two.* Next time she was going to connect and hit a home run...with his head. "In our house, Mitchell. Our bed!"

"Daph, stop," he begged, struggling to dodge the toilet plunger and zip up his pants.

Stop? Not until his head was flatter than a pancake.

Meanwhile, his partner in romantic crime had her hands in her fake red hair and was screaming like a character in a horror movie. Daphne turned on her. "And you," she said in disgust. "You must be Stella."

"No!" the woman cried. "I'm Lydia."

"Lydia?" He'd moved on to yet another woman? Lydia, Stella, Rumpelstiltskin—Daphne didn't care who the woman was. She was toast. "Whoever you are, that's my husband."

"We're separated," Mitchell protested as Daphne raised the toilet plunger.

Lydia didn't stick around for any more details. She fled the room, screeching all the way.

Before Daphne could pursue her, Mitchell jerked the plunger out of her hands. *Strike three. Go back to the dugout.* Three was *not* her lucky number.

"Daph, calm down," he commanded.

"Calm down? Are you serious?" He'd scared her half to death and then humiliated her. Again. She was ready to expire from adrenaline overload and he was telling her to calm down? "Why are you here?" she demanded. "And give me back my toilet plunger."

"*Our* toilet plunger," he corrected her. "Not a chance."

"Fine. You want it, you can have it. And you can have that…that bitty-boobed fake redhead, too. You deserve each other. And the toilet plunger." Tears were spilling from her eyes now and she took an angry swipe at her cheeks. "I trusted you, Mitchell. I gave you my heart."

He hung his head. "I know. I'm sorry."

"You are. You're a sorry excuse for a man." To think she'd been stupid enough to entertain, even for one moment, the thought of taking him back. "Get out."

"Daph, I haven't found a place to live yet."

She couldn't believe her ears. "What, you want to stay here? With her? Not on your life. I told you to leave and I meant it. Go live at what's-her-name's place."

"Her place is too small," he protested, then had the grace to look chagrined.

"Small, just like you," Daphne snapped.

"Daph, I'm sorry. I made a mistake."

A mistake. So that was what you called cheating on your wife. Daphne shook her head. "Were you always such a waste of love and I didn't see it?"

His cheeks flushed russet. "I'm sorry. I really am. I never meant to hurt you."

"Oh, really? So you didn't think having another woman on the side would hurt me? Oh, Mitchell, I'm well rid of you."

"Mitchell?" the new Stella called from downstairs. "Are you all right?"

"I'm fine," he called back.

"As fine a rat as I've ever seen," Daphne snarled. With his George Clooney face he was almost prettier than she was. People had often remarked on what a beautiful couple they were. "Just like Ken and Barbie all grown up," someone once said. And, as it turned out, what they had was about as real as those plastic dolls.

The rat slipped by her and out the bedroom, taking the toilet plunger with him. She stood there in the middle of the bedroom and listened to the murmur of their voices while her heart settled back down. Then the front door slammed shut and she was alone again.

Nine

Anne at Work

Pulling together a wedding could be like going out to sea. You planned for it as best you could and then hoped for good weather. When you started, the sea could look calm, but there was always a chance that a typhoon would hit. Pirates might find you. Anything could lurk beneath the waters. Sometimes people didn't bring the right clothes for stormy weather or thought they'd packed enough food and then ran out. Or brought along someone who should've been pushed off the dock before they set sail.

Such was the case with the wedding Anne was co-ordinating this particular weekend. Teddy, the bride's nephew, should have been, if not pushed off the dock, at least left on it. Teddy was four and a bundle of energy. He had the attention span of a gnat and was as spoiled as a child could get. This did not make him a good candidate for ring bearer.

But Teddy was the only child, the only grandchild, the only nephew, the only...everything, and the bride was on board with having him in the wedding party, along with his mother, who seemed completely incapable of controlling him. At the rehearsal he ran up the aisle with the ring pillow, the ribbons with the rings swinging wildly. Positioned on one of the carpeted steps leading up to the podium, he soon became bored with the adult conversation and began to hop up and down the stairs. When he wasn't doing that, he was trying to look under the bridesmaids' skirts or making faces at Anne, who was getting things ready for the big day. He finally wore himself out and collapsed on the lowest stair for an impromptu nap, allowing the minister to finish walking the bride and groom through their vows.

"Maybe we can drug him," muttered his grandfather.

Anne suspected it would take more than drugs to tame Teddy.

The afternoon of the wedding it looked as if someone had, indeed, drugged Teddy...with speed. Or too much sugar. He bounced around the foyer like a kangaroo looking forward to an extra helping of Marmite until his exasperated grandfather finally took him by the arm and growled at him to stand still.

"You walk down the aisle like a gentleman," Grandpa cautioned just before Teddy's big moment.

The dose of sternness seemed to work. Or maybe it was stage fright. Whatever the case, Teddy did an admirable job of getting the rings down the aisle.

All right, Anne thought, taking in the scene. So far everything was going according to plan.

The bridesmaids did their stately walk, sophisticated in navy blue dresses accented with red shoes. Then it was time for the father to walk his daughter down the aisle. Anne gave them the cue and sent them on their way, daughter smiling and father teary-eyed.

Anne felt misty-eyed herself, watching them go. There was something about this moment in the wedding ceremony that always got to her. It was such a sweet tradition, the man who had raised the young woman, who'd been there to hear her nighttime prayers and sample her first baking efforts, who had fretted every time she was late coming home from a date, who had, in short, taken care of her and guarded her, now publicly declaring that he was willing to share her love with a new man, to let her start a new chapter in her life.

Anne stayed long enough to see the father kiss his daughter and join her hands with the hands of her groom. Then she went to the fancy old historical home in Seattle where the couple was having their reception to make sure all was in readiness.

She knew it would be. Everything had made it there safely. The cake was standing in place, a lacy tower of elegance, surrounded by tiered plates of cookies shaped like tuxedo-clad hearts; the tables were all set, draped in navy tablecloths and topped with green vases filled with gerbera daisies and ferns, while a giant swan sculpted in ice presided over the buffet table. The caterer was busy setting out the food—appetizer trays with everything from brûléed goat cheese to asparagus wrapped in prosciutto, Caesar salad and pasta salad, crab legs, crusty rolls, teriyaki chicken and rice pilaf. Soon the elegant room would be filled with a new Mr. and Mrs. and all their friends, ready to help them celebrate.

Soon happened in twenty minutes, with families starting to trickle in. Then came some of the younger couples, the women all lovely in heels and party dresses, their guys equally dressed up, their suits a traditional contrast to their piercings, gauges and tats. Two couples were talking and snickering, a sure clue that Teddy had put on a show at the wedding.

Next came the bride's parents. "Everything looks beautiful," Greta, the mother of the bride, said to Anne.

Anne murmured her thanks and asked Greta how the ceremony had gone.

"It was lovely," Greta said, tears in her eyes.

"It would've been better if Teddy hadn't been in it," her husband muttered.

Greta shrugged. "Little boys."

Her husband shook his head.

"Teddy went under one of the pews with the rings and my son had to get him out," Greta explained. "It'll make a funny wedding story someday."

"Yes, and it'll make a funny story when I tie him up and stick him in a corner," her husband said darkly.

"Now, Theodore," his wife scolded.

Obviously, Theodore wasn't happy with his name-sake.

"These things do happen," Anne said. Especially when the Teddys of the world weren't left on the dock.

"Well, that better be all that happens," said the bride's father.

But it wasn't. Teddy was on a roll. As the guests milled about or found seats at the tables, he darted in and out of the crowd, chasing a little girl with red ringlets. In the process he managed to run into a tall, willowy woman whose height was accentuated by six-inch heels, knocking her off balance. She grabbed for the nearest person, who happened to be another woman in equally high heels, and that woman, too, lost her balance. Down they both went, taking a bowl of Caesar salad with them and sending a tray of teriyaki chicken flying.

This was the final straw for Grandpa, who took off after Teddy. In an effort to escape, the child dived under the elegantly clothed table with the cake and cookies on it. Several people gasped, "Oh, no," and one of the groomsmen jumped to save the cake, which, thanks to the movement of the tablecloth, was in danger of sliding off the edge. He caught it in time, setting it back in place, and everyone heaved a sigh of relief...until the redheaded girl decided to join the mischief-maker under the table, taking the tablecloth with her, bringing down the cake and sending cookies flying just as Grandpa reached under the table and grabbed Teddy.

There was much howling as Grandpa took the young man to another room for a stern talking-to and the bride saw what had become of her cake.

"Not to worry," Anne told her. "We'll fix this."

"But my cake," the bride protested.

"I can't duplicate the cake, but I can make sure you have something."

And while the caterers cleaned up the mess and Teddy probably got tied up and stuck in a corner, Anne raced to the neighboring chain grocery stores, buying the prettiest layer cake she could find as well as all manner of cupcakes. Forty minutes later, a slightly less elaborate cake sat on the table, surrounded by tiered plates with a selection of cupcakes. Some strategically repositioned candles and flowers added elegance. The rest of the reception went off without a hitch, and after drinking champagne and dancing with her new husband and her doting father, the bride was smiling once more.

"You saved the day," Greta said to Anne later that evening.

Anne smiled modestly and shook her head. "Even when things don't go the way you plan, a wedding is always a happy event."

Laney's wedding would go perfectly, though. She was going to make sure of that. Thank God they didn't have a Teddy to mess everything up.

They still had a lot to do to see that everything went smoothly on Laney's big day, so Anne called her daughter on Monday when she had a few minutes between clients. The call went straight to voice mail and Anne sighed. It was after lunch. Laney would be off work now, and since the sun was out, she was probably running around Green Lake. Anne settled for a text. *We need 2 talk. Call me.*

She'd just finished conferring with her favorite caterer about food for an upcoming wedding—pulled-pork sliders, savory cupcakes, sushi and a dessert buffet—when Laney checked in. "What's up, Mom?"

Was it Anne's imagination or did her daughter sound wary? Maybe Anne's text had seemed a little…imperious. "Oh, nothing," she said airily. "I was thinking we should lock in Primrose Haus for your wedding reception, that's all," she rushed on and then held her breath. *Please, God, don't let Drake have talked Laney into Vegas.*

There was a moment of silence on the phone that shot Anne's heart rate up. Finally Laney said, "Okay, let's do it."

She seemed hesitant. Suddenly the buzzard of guilt perched on Anne's shoulders. *Way to go*, it said. *Pressure the poor kid.*

Oh, crud. The buzzard was right. She was forcing her daughter to do something she wasn't excited about.

But Laney had always wanted a fancy wedding, ever since she was a little girl. Deep down, she really did want this and if she settled for something else she'd regret it later.

Still, Anne had to ask, "Are you sure?"

"Yeah, I'm sure," Laney said.

"You don't sound sure."

"Mom. I'm sure. It'll be great for the reception. I still want to get married on the river, though."

"Okay." *Hopefully, in a wedding gown. No shorts and bikini top.* "Great. Tell you what. Why don't you come by the office and we can talk about your vision for the wedding."

"I need to get a shower first. I just finished running."

Laney loved to run. She'd been on the swim team in high school and had added running to her regimen in college.

She'd tried to convince Anne to take it up, but Anne preferred a brisk walk on the treadmill at the gym or a walk in the snow on a wintry day. She would just have to live without experiencing that mystical runner's high, because she'd never be caught running unless she was being chased by a bear. And since she didn't do camping, either, there was no danger of that.

Her daughter loved to tease her about her poor excuse for a sense of adventure. So she didn't like rock climbing or sleeping in leaky tents. If she was going to enjoy nature, she wanted to do it from the comfort of a cozy, little cabin.

"That's fine," she said. "See you whenever you get here."

Funny how a mother and daughter could have so much in common—a love of parties and romantic comedies and card games—and yet be so different. That wasn't a bad thing, she reminded herself as she ended the call. Her daughter was her own woman. And that was how it should be. Still, when it came to weddings...

"You're frowning," her sister said.

Anne blinked. "What?"

"You're frowning." Kendra studied her. "She's not even here and you're already worried."

"No, I'm not," Anne lied.

"You know, it *is* her wedding."

"I know that."

Kendra raised an eyebrow. "Do you? Really?"

Anne made a face. "Of course I do. The bride always gets the last say."

She punched in the number for Primrose Haus in Icicle Falls. She'd tell Roberta Gilbert they were definitely a go for that Saturday in June before her daughter could change her mind. This was the right decision, she knew it. Laney would have no regrets.

"We'll be looking forward to helping you create a wonderful memory," Roberta said when she and Anne had finished talking business.

A wonderful memory, Anne thought. Yes, that was what this was all about, a wonderful memory for her daughter.

Not just for her daughter, but for everyone who loved her, as well.

"I can hardly wait to see our Laney get married," her mother had said after the family dinner on Sunday, when it had been the two of them lingering over one

last cup of coffee once everyone else had left. "Drake
is such a nice boy."

"Yes, he is," Anne had agreed.

"It's the first wedding we've had in the family in a long
time. And who knows? Maybe there'll be a baby soon."

"I don't think they're in a hurry for that, Mom. Anyway, they're young. They've got time." The words had
barely left her mouth when Anne realized how false that
statement could be. She and Cam had thought they'd had
plenty of time to have another. How wrong they'd been.

Laney had ended up being their only child. Fortunately, she was a wonderful kid, but Anne would've
liked a couple more.

As if reading her mind, her mother had veered away
from that verbal path. "Well, we'll enjoy the wedding.
You know," she'd added, toying with her mug, "we all
assume weddings are just about the bride and groom,
but so many people get so much out of them. I'm sure
you've seen that over the years. A wedding gives those
of us who are older a chance to share in the couple's
happiness and to relive that special time when we found
the person we wanted to spend our lives with. Of course,
for the kids it's a party, but don't you think it's also an
example?"

"Of what?"

"Of commitment. A wedding, no matter where it
is—" Julia had reached out to cover her daughter's hand
with hers "—is a sign of loyalty, of responsibility." She
bit her lip, as if hesitating to continue.

"What?" Anne had prompted.

"I don't think you understood at the time why I was
so upset about your hurried affair. I wonder if you can
see now, after having planned so many weddings for

so many brides. It's an important event for the whole community."

Anne could only nod in agreement. Of course, given the options she'd had at the time, she'd do the same thing all over again. Still, if the situation had been different, if she hadn't gotten pregnant...

Some things in life you couldn't redo. But her mother had a point. You could relive. With Laney's wedding she and Cam could celebrate both their daughter's union and their own. They'd celebrate love, family and friendship. Yes, her mother was right. A wedding was a big deal for a lot of people.

But mostly for the bride. She could hardly wait until Laney arrived and they could start planning the details of the momentous occasion that lay ahead for all of them.

An hour later Laney was in the office, comfy in jeans and a long, black sweater, accented with one of her necklaces, a silver creation featuring her signature mermaid carrying a silver heart. She and Anne sat at the computer, discussing color themes and decorations, with Kendra tossing in the occasional comment.

"What's wrong with purple?" Laney asked with a frown.

"Nothing," Anne said quickly. "It can make for striking decorations." It also made Anne think of the red-hat ladies and the popular poem about a woman wearing purple when she was old. Of course, there was nothing wrong with being old *or* wearing purple, but it didn't seem like the right color for Laney's wedding.

"Purple might be kind of cool," Kendra put in.

Who asked her? "If that's what you want, that's what we'll go with," Anne said, reminding herself that her daughter got to make the final decision. Still, she wanted to make sure Laney would be happy with it. "Let's look at some other colors, too, though."

"Okay, fine," Laney said irritably. Her phone dinged and she checked it, then spent a moment thumbing a text.

"Who was that?" Anne asked. They were trying to get this wedding planned. Did Laney really need to stop in the middle of their meeting and text someone?

"Autumn. I told her I was coming over here to pick out colors. She's gonna be my maid of honor."

Not surprising, considering that they'd been friends since high school.

The phone dinged again.

Oh, great. "Honey, at this rate we're not going to get anything done," Anne chided.

"Autumn thinks purple would be ugly."

Well, then. That decides it.

"We should look at other colors," Laney said.

Obviously, Autumn's opinion did decide it. Anne wasn't sure whether she should be grateful or annoyed. "Tell her we'll keep her posted," she said and hoped Autumn would get the message and go have a latte.

They checked every imaginable color theme and style from red to pink polka dots. Finally, Laney said she wanted green and brown. All right. Progress. Ten minutes later, they found something new to disagree on. "Why can't I have balloons?" Laney demanded.

"I didn't say you couldn't have balloons," Anne insisted. "But in all different colors? That'll look odd." It made her think of circuses and clowns or state fairs. Might as well throw in some pigs and a Ferris wheel. And what was the point of using different-colored balloons if Laney had picked a specific color scheme? "Anyway, I thought you were going with green and brown."

"They don't make balloons in green and brown," Laney pointed out.

"Somebody must," Anne said and brought up yet another image on the internet.

"Eew," said Laney, frowning. "Lime green. That's gross."

Yes, lime green wouldn't work. They'd been talking about forest green. But Anne had an alternative suggestion. "You could have ferns and chocolate mint, and crystal votives on the tables would be gorgeous."

"But what about the balloons?"

"Honey, we can't find any in the color you want. You're going to have to bag the balloons."

Laney frowned, obviously unhappy with the idea of giving up on balloons.

"The ferns and mint will be pretty. And both you and Drake enjoy the outdoors, so it would be bringing something you love into the wedding theme."

Her argument produced a thoughtful nod.

"Let's look at cakes," Anne said and moved them on to new territory before Laney could argue for a rainbow of balloons again.

They found one on Pinterest—a beautiful green fondant with tasteful brown swirls. "Wow," Anne breathed.

"That's pretty," Laney conceded. "But I want a donut cake."

Okay, donut cake. That took them to a different set of images. The donut cakes were cute, Anne had to admit, but they weren't very elegant. She remembered feeding Cam some of the tacky cake their neighbor had made, telling herself how wonderful it was that they had a cake at all, yet wishing for one with a froth of white frosting and pastel-colored flowers from the bakery. She hadn't had time to budget for a cake, and she hadn't wanted to ask her mother to pay for one. Her parents had paid for her gown and bouquet, and under the circumstances that had felt like plenty. Looking back now, she realized Mom would happily have sprung for a cake and anything else she wanted if she'd only asked.

"Hey," she said, pointing to one image. "You could have a donut bar. What about a donut bar and a traditional cake? Something for everyone."

"Including Mom," Kendra added snidely.

Anne ignored her.

"A donut bar isn't the same as a donut cake," Laney said stubbornly.

"Not all of your guests are going to want to eat donuts," Anne pointed out. "If you do the donut bar *and* the cake, then everyone's happy."

Everyone except the bride. Laney's mouth slipped into a half frown.

"Don't you think that's a good compromise?" Anne nudged.

"Yeah, I guess it is."

One more thing settled. They were moving right along.

Next they chose invitations. This, too, involved much discussion. The save-the-date cards Laney finally picked were cute. They'd be trimmed with Laney's colors and feature a picture of her and Drake with conversation bubbles over their heads saying "I do" and "Me, too!" Underneath, block printing would say "How about you? Save the date to celebrate." It was a little unconventional, a perfect fit for her daughter.

"We'll need to go up to Icicle Falls to visit the florist next," Anne said. "When can you get away?"

"I'm not sure," Laney hedged. "I'll let you know."

Not sure? Let her know? They needed to get this planned. "Honey, we can't drag our feet. June's not that far away. There's still so much to do."

"I get that, Mom." Laney checked the time on her cell phone. "Oh, wow. I've gotta go."

"But we still have to talk about napkins and what kind of food you want and..."

"I know, but I've got company coming for dinner tonight and I haven't even shopped yet."

Anne felt deflated. They were just starting to have fun and her daughter had to leave? "Oh. Well, okay."

Laney gave her a quick kiss, hugged her aunt Kendra and then was out the door before Anne could suggest another day to get together.

"That went well," Kendra said after she left.

"It did." Anne ignored both her sister's sarcasm and the feeling that things could have gone better.

"Right. That's why she left at three thirty in the afternoon to get ready for dinner."

"She had to shop."

"Uh-huh. And you believe that? Hey, I've got an oil well in New York City for sale. Wanna buy it?"

Anne frowned and swiveled her desk chair to face her sister. "Okay, what exactly are you saying?"

Kendra swiveled her chair, too. "I can put it in one word. *Momzilla.*"

"I am not a Momzilla!" Anne protested.

"True," her sister agreed. "Not a full-grown one yet, anyway. Right now you're just a baby one."

"Oh, very funny," Anne snapped.

"I thought so," Kendra said and turned back to her computer.

They worked in silence for twenty minutes before Anne asked, "How was I being a Momzilla?"

"Well, let's see. You want to start with the great debate on the invitations or go back to the battle of the colors?"

"There was no battle over colors. I was simply making suggestions."

"Mmm-hmm. Like you did with the balloons. And how about the donut cake?"

"She's getting donuts," Anne said, choosing the most solid ground to stand on.

"She's getting a donut bar. And you're getting the cake."

"This isn't for me!"

"Are you sure?"

"Of course. I'm trying to make sure Laney has the perfect wedding she deserves."

"Everyone has a different definition of *perfect*," Kendra said.

Anne couldn't argue with that. So she decided not to. Instead, she got busy researching party favors for a client who was getting married at West Seattle's Golden Gardens, a favorite beach of many Seattleites. Can coolers would be just the thing for a beach wedding. And baseball caps. Yes, her bride-to-be would love those. Darn, but she was good.

And since she *was* good and had been doing this for years, there was nothing wrong with guiding her daughter. So there.

Still, the thought that maybe she was taking too much control moved into her brain and set up a broadcast tower. So that night over dinner with Cam, she re-capped her session with Laney, hoping for a different verdict. "Do you think I was being a Momzilla?"

He took a last bite of ice cream and pushed aside his bowl. "Nah. You were giving her advice. That's what you do, right?"

"It is. And I just want her to have a lovely wedding, something memorable."

"Understandable," he said with a nod. "Don't worry about it. She gets the final say."

"True." Laney did want a donut bar, didn't she? And there was nothing wrong with having cake, as well. She could have her cake and eat it, too. Ha-ha. Any-way, Anne and Cam were paying for the wedding, so if they wanted to throw in a cake as a bonus, why should Laney care?

Except Anne had talked her into having a donut bar instead of a donut cake. She'd talked her into a lot of things. She flashed on a sudden image of Laurel Browne insisting, "We are not having daisies at the wedding."

No, no. She wasn't anything like Laurel Browne. Laney was the one who'd settled on green and brown for her colors, and Anne wasn't about to rock that boat. And the balloons, well, they simply weren't the right color. That was hardly Anne's fault.

But the cake? Okay, they'd go with the donut cake. She grabbed her cell phone from the kitchen counter.

"Who are you calling?" Cam asked.

"Laney. I'm going to tell her we'll do a donut cake *and* a regular cake."

Cam made a face that plainly said "I'm a long-suffering husband" and got up to take their bowls into the kitchen.

Dinner was their time and they didn't take calls then. But they were done with dinner now. Anyway, this was important. Her call went to voice mail, and she remembered that Laney was having company tonight. Still, that never stopped her from answering her phone. She was one with her phone. Was she mad about the cake thing?

"Hi, honey," Anne said as soon as voice mail gave her the all clear to speak. "So, I'm thinking if you really want a donut cake, there's no reason you can't have one. Pick the one you like and email it to me and then I'll send it on to the baker. Hope you're having fun at your dinner party. I love you," she added.

There. No one could accuse her of being a Momzilla now, not even a baby one.

"Feel better?" her husband asked.

She nodded. "The donut cake will be cute. It's going to be a lovely wedding."

"They all are," he said. "Hey, and speaking of special events, we should talk about what we want to do for our anniversary."

An excellent idea. But after her busy workday and sorting out the issue of the cake, Anne was suddenly out of steam. "Could we do that tomorrow?"

"Yeah, sure."

He sounded the slightest bit disappointed.

"I'm too tired to think," she said. Anyway, they had plenty of time to plan their anniversary.

He came back to the table, bent over and wrapped his arms around her. She could still smell a hint of the woodsy cologne he favored. He put his face next to hers and she felt the brush of five o'clock shadow. "What do you want to do instead?"

Bury the baby Momzilla and cuddle on the couch. "Let's see what we've got in our Netflix queue."

"Okay," he said, and they moved to the living room.

Cam preferred action flicks, but he found a romantic comedy for her. "We don't have to watch this," she told him as they settled on the couch.

"Sure we do," he said, kissing the top of her head. "Tonight it's all about you."

It's all about you. Had that been the case this afternoon?

Of course not, she assured herself. Laney got to make the final decisions. Anne was there only to help her make the right ones.

She smiled and snuggled up against her husband. No Momzillas here.

Ten

Daphne, Starting Over

Daphne changed the locks on her house, but not before making sure Mitchell got the last of his clothes. She piled them all on the front lawn. "Feel free to come by and get them whenever you want," she said to his voice mail. Maybe, if he was lucky, there'd still be some left by the time he got to the house. Hee hee.

She merged onto I-90 eastbound and watched as Seattle got increasingly smaller in her rearview mirror. "Goodbye and good riddance," she muttered.

Not the city, just the last two men she'd found in it. What was wrong with her that she couldn't seem to get this love thing figured out? She was nice. And attractive—men had been telling her that all her life. She was responsible, didn't nag too much, and she never ate crackers in bed or complained when her man wanted to watch football, although she detested the sport. Surely that deserved better than she'd gotten so far. Why did she attract so many losers?

Oh, who cared? She was going to start a new life in

Icicle Falls, help her mother run weddings and laugh behind the backs of all those delusional brides who paraded through Primrose Haus in their overpriced gowns on their way to happily-ever-after. Ha! There was no such thing. Sooner or later that Cinderella castle always crumbled. Disney should be sued.

On and on the bitter thoughts went as she drove up the mountain highway to Icicle Falls. It took seeing the Willkommen in Icicle Falls sign to pull her out of her funk. The town looked like something out of a movie back lot with its charming Bavarian shops, its town center with the gazebo and skating rink, which during summer would get used for everything from outdoor art fairs to folk dance festivals. Church spires pointed heavenward, reminding the faithful that there was a God who cared about their troubles. And above it all, the mountains in their snowy majesty stood guard over the residents of the little burg. Here was a welcoming place where she could start over with people she'd known all her life, people who'd be genuinely interested in her, who wouldn't just pretend. So she'd be celibate forever. By the time a woman was in her fifties did she really need sex?

Except fifty was the new forty. And that put her at forty-three. A forty-three-year-old woman still needed sex. She frowned. She wasn't sure she wanted to go the rest of her life without physical intimacy.

You can do it, she told herself. Her mother had managed fine on her own.

She wasn't her mother.

Okay, she'd be like Mitchell and have sex whenever she wanted with whomever she wanted. There were probably plenty of single men her age in Icicle Falls. Plenty of men, anyway, but her age? Hmm.

Well, then she'd find a boy toy. Or a lonely old geezer. Her frown deepened. She didn't want to be like Mitchell and break hearts. That wasn't kind, and she wouldn't wish a romantic heart attack on anyone. With a sigh she concluded that she'd have to rise above her circumstances, look for the silver lining, cast her fortunes to the wind…know when to hold 'em, know when to fold 'em. Whatever. In short, she'd build a new and better life. She still had a lot of years left to carve out some happiness for herself and find fulfillment.

Without a man. She'd do it all without a man. And she'd never watch another romantic comedy again. Pandora selected a new song for her car radio and Barry Manilow began to croon, *"When will I see you again?"* She shut off the radio and shut Barry up. The next time she saw Mitchell it would be in divorce court.

Oh, how she wanted someone to love.

She *had* someone to love, she reminded herself when she walked into the Victorian on Primrose Street, carrying the surprise she'd picked up on her way home. She'd stopped at the local art gallery that also did framing. There was her mother, asleep in an armchair, one of her romance novels open on her lap. She looked… old. When had that happened?

Daphne had always thought of her mother as invincible, tireless. When she wasn't working she'd been at church, tending to the flower beds, at a committee meeting or seated at the portable sewing machine she'd bought when Daphne was in first grade, putting together an elaborate Halloween costume for Daphne or making her a dress. Saturdays had been cleaning day and Mother had worked herself into a fever sweeping, dusting and scrubbing. She'd made sure Daphne did the same. Long after Daphne had had enough, her mother would still be going at it. Even on Sundays there was little rest. Starting in spring, Sunday afternoons were for weeding. Once the yard was in shape, it was time for Sunday dinner, which often meant company. And more work, because after the company left the dishes had to be done. Finally, when it was only the two of them and *Bonanza* on TV, the embroidery would come out.

Once, when Daphne was in high school, she'd asked her mother, "Don't you ever want to just sit back and do nothing?"

Mother had been disgusted by the very suggestion. "I have too much to do. I'll rest when I'm old."

Today she looked like a woman who was losing the race against Father Time, the wrinkles carving deeper into her face, her hands small and heavily veined. She looked vulnerable and the sight pulled at Daphne's heartstrings.

Daphne leaned the present against the wall, then tiptoed over to where her mother slept. She was in the process of replacing the book with an afghan when Mother woke with a start.

"Daphne, you're home."

"Sorry I woke you."

"I wasn't sleeping. I was just resting my eyes."

Of course, a woman always snored when she was resting her eyes. "You look tired," Daphne said. *And old. When did you grow old on me?*

"I'm not," Mother insisted. "What time is it?" She squinted in the direction of the cuckoo clock in the kitchen.

"A little after one." Daphne walked toward the kitchen. "Have you had lunch?"

"Not yet." Her mother began to get up.

"Stay put. I'll make it."

Of course Mother didn't stay put. She joined Daphne in the kitchen and started taking bowls out of the cupboard. "We have chicken soup left over from the other night. Why don't you heat that up?"

Sounded good to Daphne. Soup was perfect for a blustery day and she'd loved her mother's homemade soup. Once Daphne became a teenager, Mother taught her to make it. *Cut the carrots smaller, darling. Big carrots in soup are the sign of a lazy cook. You don't need a lot of salt. A pinch of garlic. Basil. Well, let's try it. Hmm. Very nice. I think you might have a flair for cooking. Who knows? Maybe you'll have your own restaurant someday.*

Daphne had not gone on to have her own restaurant. She'd preferred working in an office where she could have regular hours and get evenings and weekends off. Cooking was a hobby she'd enjoyed. She hadn't wanted to take the fun out of it by doing it for a living.

Mother had been disappointed that she'd opted for such an ordinary life, but the life she'd chosen had suited her. She liked being an employee, liked being part of a team. She wasn't sure where she got that—certainly not from her mother—but she was wired to be a helper.

Seeing her mother asleep in her chair had driven home to Daphne how much she wanted to help out here. Roberta Gilbert would never admit she was slowing down, even a little, and yet obviously she was. She needed her daughter.

"How did things go in Seattle?" Mother asked.

No way was Daphne telling anyone about this latest Mitchell escapade. Ever. Especially not Mother. She'd go into I-told-you-so mode, and Daphne wanted that about as much as she wanted adult acne. (Although adult acne might be preferable to hot flashes.) "I got what I needed out of the house and changed the locks." Everything else she'd sell or give away. Or burn, she mentally added, thinking of the living room couch.

Mother nodded approvingly. "Good." She leaned against the kitchen counter and studied Daphne. "You didn't see him, did you?"

Define "see." Daphne decided her mother meant in the sense of doing something dumb like going out with Mitchell. "No." At least she hadn't succumbed to that stupidity. She supposed she should be grateful for the episode in the bedroom.

The studying grew more intense. Daphne could feel her mother's gaze on her as she heated the soup. "Are you all right?" Mother asked.

"I am now." Daphne dug out a package of crackers and stuffed one in her mouth. Ah, carbs, a girl's best friend.

"Daphne. What happened in Seattle?"

"Nothing," Daphne lied even as her cheeks burned. Why was it that every time she and her mother discussed her love life, she felt fourteen? She loaded another cracker into her mouth and turned up the heat under the soup.

"What kind of nothing?"

Daphne's tender feelings began to toughen up. Mother would've made a successful attorney. *I'm not letting you off the stand until you crack.* "No kind of nothing. Honestly, Mother. I'm a grown woman." Who was back where she'd started, once again living at home. She set aside that humiliating fact. "Do we really need the third degree?" she demanded, infusing her words with as much wounded dignity as possible.

Roberta shook her head. "No. Not at all. It just seems…" She clamped her lips together, killing the sentence. "I only want to make sure you're okay."

"I am," Daphne assured both of them as she poured their soup. "I will be."

It seemed as though all the men she'd chosen had done nothing but make her feel bad about herself. She was through with that. She was through with men. Period. Even if fifty was the new forty, which meant she was only forty-three. She could go the rest of her life without sex, and if she wanted someone to love she could get a dog. She flashed on a sudden image of a big, woofy dog wandering around Primrose Haus, jumping on the guests. Okay, maybe a cat.

Her mother smiled faintly. "Well, good for you."

Yes, good for her. Meanwhile… "I have something for you," she said. She hurried to where she'd left her gift, then brought it back to the kitchen and presented it to her mother.

"Now what's this?" Roberta asked, taking the wrapped picture-shaped package.

"Open it and see."

She pulled off the wrapping and her eyes lit up in delight at the framed article from the *Gazette*. "Oh, Daphne, how thoughtful."

"Do you like it?" Of course she did, but it was so nice to hear the pleasure in her mother's voice, Daphne couldn't help wanting to prolong the moment.

"I love it, darling. Let's hang it here in the kitchen, where we can see it every day."

As if Roberta Gilbert needed to be reminded of her success? But Daphne was happy to comply.

"Don't worry about the dishes. I'll do them," Mother said after Daphne had hung the picture and was disposing of the wrapping paper.

Actually, she hadn't been worried about the dishes at all. Naughty her.

Later that day her daughter, Marnie, called to check in.

"I'm sorry you're going through this, Mom. You deserve better."

Evidently not, but she appreciated her daughter's support. "Thanks, honeybee."

"I love that nickname," Marnie said, a smile in her voice. "And I love you. I wish you'd come out for a visit."

"I will soon," Daphne promised. "I need to get my feet under me first, though."

"Um, how's that going, staying with Grandma?"

"It's going fine." *Sort of.*

"You can always move out here, you know."

She knew. Marnie would have liked nothing more than to have her nearby. "You don't need me underfoot. You're busy with your own life." And dealing with her father, who liked to invite himself to New York for a visit whenever he was drying out (which was rare) or wanted a cheap vacation (which was less rare).

"I'd never be too busy for you."

"Thanks, honeybee. I appreciate that." She wasn't interested in moving to the East Coast. She liked it fine here on the western side of the States. But it was good to be wanted by someone, especially when that someone was her daughter.

* * *

"I brought everything you need," Daphne said to her lawyer the next day.

Shirley Schneck nodded as she took the fat sheaf of papers. "Thanks. How are you doing, by the way?"

"I hate men," Daphne informed her. "I'm going to become a lesbian."

"You have no idea how many women have told me that," Shirley said with a smile. "You'll change your mind at some point, though, and be ready for another man."

"I doubt it." Daphne scowled. "I'm going to get a kitten."

"Good idea," Shirley said. "Keep the anger going for now. You'll need it for the battle ahead."

A battle. She was going to be battling her former best friend and lover. She could feel a little spring of tears bubbling up. Then she thought of Mitchell and his latest Stella and the spring went dry.

"You'll get through this," Shirley told her and proceeded to get down to business. The business of war.

War was exhausting. By the time Daphne left the office, she felt like a dish towel after a round with the washing machine agitator. Divorce was awful. After her second divorce she'd vowed to be careful, pick more wisely, never find herself in this position again. Yet here she was.

Okay, she needed chocolate. It was almost lunchtime anyway. Chocolate for lunch, maybe not the most nutritious choice, but, oh, well. Right now her soul was more in need than her body.

Five minutes later she walked into the gift shop of Sweet Dreams Chocolates, a veritable cornucopia of treats. Display racks and tables offered everything from various-size boxes of chocolates to snack items such as chocolate-dipped potato chips and caramel corn drizzled with white and dark chocolate. Lovely smells drifted over from the adjoining factory, making her mouth water.

Heidi Schwartz was working the counter as usual. She greeted Daphne with a friendly hello. "Anything special you're in the mood for today?"

Sex. "What do you have that's new?" Daphne asked.

"Our big seller is the dark chocolate–chipotle truffles. I can put some in a box for you."

Daphne nodded. "Put in some of those white chocolate bonbons with the rose-flavored filling, too. And a couple of salted caramels."

Heidi got to work. "I hear you're back in town to stay. Are you going to help your mom with weddings?"

"That's the plan." Daphne supposed Heidi had also heard that she was getting divorced. News traveled fast in a small town. If Heidi saw the irony of a divorcée helping with weddings, she kindly didn't say anything.

Daphne was getting out her charge card when Samantha and Cecily Sterling made an appearance, probably on their way to lunch. "Hi, Daphne," Cecily said. "How are you doing?"

There was no need to ask what Cecily meant by that. "I'm fine, glad to be home."

"Have you found a job yet?" Samantha asked.

Good grief. Was there anything anyone didn't know about her? Oh, yes. One thing. No one knew she'd discovered her husband with yet another woman and attacked him with a toilet plunger. No one was ever going to know about that.

"Not yet," Daphne said. "I only need something part-time. I'm going to be helping my mother with weddings."

"Our mom's been talking about hiring an assistant," Cecily said. "I think you two would work well together."

"Yeah?" Daphne liked Muriel Sterling. Well, who didn't? Muriel was eternally sweet, perpetually positive. She'd make a great boss.

"You ought to go see her," Samantha urged.

Maybe she would.

She stopped by Herman's Hamburgers and treated herself to a fat Herman's burger loaded with fried onions. Then she decided to swing by Muriel Sterling's rented cottage and convince her that hiring an assistant would be an excellent idea.

She went there by way of Johnson's Drugs, where she picked up some mints to disguise her onion breath. Not that Muriel would care. She'd known Daphne all her life. Still, if a woman was going to talk jobs, even with an old friend, she needed to be professional.

Hildy Johnson was on the cash register. She was as tall and homely as Daphne remembered, only she'd put on some weight. Her breasts now stood out like cannons.

"I'm sorry your third marriage didn't work out," she said as she rang up Daphne's purchase.

Hildy, the soul of tact.

"It's hard to find a good man, especially once you get older."

Fifty is the new forty. "It's hard to find a good man, period," Daphne said and handed over a five-dollar bill.

Hildy nodded. "Yes, it is. But you're still a beautiful woman."

"Thank you." Much good it did her.

"I'm sure you'll have men lining up at your door. Or rather, your mother's door. You're living with your mother now, aren't you?"

Hildy made it sound like the hallmark of failure. Okay, Daphne wasn't exactly a success story so far, but her story wasn't over yet.

"I'm helping her run Primrose Haus," she said.

Hildy's eyebrows went up at that.

"I may be getting divorced but I can still plan a wedding reception," Daphne said, her Miss Congeniality smile disappearing.

"Oh, well, yes. Of course you can. It's not like you've never had your own reception before."

Three of them, but who's counting?

Hildy must have realized what that implied because her cheeks suddenly flushed red. "Your mother must be happy to have you back. And everything will work out fine," she added, handing over Daphne's change along with her breath mints.

"Thank you," Daphne murmured.

She left the drugstore, the memory of her romantic failures keeping her company. That was enough to depress even the most optimistic of women.

It was starting to drizzle and she drew her coat tight against the cold March air. Instead of popping a breath mint, she pulled out a dark chocolate–chipotle truffle from her Sweet Dreams candy box and gave her taste buds a treat. There. Life wasn't all bad. It was darkest just before the storm and every cloud had a chocolate lining. And she was taking her new life one day at a time, one step at a time. And the next step was to convince Muriel that she needed an assistant.

Maybe, while she was helping Muriel, Muriel could help her.

Situated next to a vineyard, Muriel's cottage was a Thomas Kinkade painting come to life. White with green shutters, the cottage was hugged by azaleas and rhododendrons. A dried-flower wreath hung on the front door in anticipation of spring.

Daphne's heart rate picked up as she knocked on the door. The very thought of trying to convince a potential future employer that she was worthy of being hired stressed her out. Which was probably one reason she'd stayed at the same job all those years. That hadn't gotten her very far, but when it came to moving up the ladder of success, she was afraid of heights. And all her mother's nagging had only increased her fear. Performance anxiety, she supposed.

This was an old family friend, though; she didn't need to be nervous.

Muriel opened the door and, at the sight of Daphne, broke into a delighted smile. "Daphne, what a nice surprise!"

Her delight was a balm to Daphne's wounded spirit. "I should have called. Are you busy?"

"Just editing some pages. I'm happy for the distraction," Muriel said. "Come in. How about a cup of chocolate mint tea?" she asked as she ushered Daphne into the small living room.

Mint…breath mints. She should've taken one before she got out of the car. Did her breath smell? "That would be great," she said, taking care not to stand too close to Muriel.

"Have a seat. I'll be back in a minute," Muriel said and disappeared into the kitchen.

Daphne settled on a floral love seat and dug out a mint. She popped it in her mouth as she looked around. The place was half the size of Muriel's old house, but it was homey. In addition to the love seat, it held two matching chairs and an ornately carved coffee table. In the far corner, off the kitchen, sat a small mahogany dining table and four chairs. A vase filled with green carnations brought spring into the house and served as a reminder that Saint Patrick's Day was right around the corner. A buffet stood against one wall, topped with a mantel clock. One large painting of a garden entrance blooming with wisteria hung over the love seat, and framed photographs of mountain scenes—her daughter Samantha's work—occupied space on other walls. The house smelled faintly of lavender.

Now Muriel was back bearing a tray with a chintz teapot, cream and sugar and two china mugs, plus a small plate with finger sandwiches and one with some of her daughter Bailey's famous lavender sugar cookies.

Daphne smelled something new, the enticing combination of chocolate and mint. "That tea smells delicious."

"It is," Muriel said with a smile. "Just the thing for a cold afternoon."

"It's sweet of you to feed me," Daphne said, helping herself to a cookie.

"I was getting hungry. I thought you might be, too." Muriel poured tea into a china mug and handed it to Daphne. "How are you settling in?"

"Pretty well. I'm glad to be back." Even if the whole town did know she'd failed at love. Again.

Muriel nodded. "This is a good place to come and heal a broken heart."

"I'm hoping it's a good place to build a new life," Daphne said.

"It is."

It was now or never. Daphne took a sip of tea for courage. "As I'm sure you've heard, I'll be working with Mother at Primrose Haus, but I'm also looking for something I can do part-time to bring in a little extra money. Cecily said you might need an assistant. I have a lot of experience in that area."

"I could certainly use the help," Muriel said. "It seems that these days an author has to do so much more than simply write a book, and I do find mailings and organizing blog tours to be very taxing."

Daphne knew what a blog was, but what on earth was a blog tour? Whatever it was, she was sure she could handle it. "I'm good with a computer and I'm very good at organizing."

Muriel looked at her eagerly. "Even paperwork?"

"Especially paperwork." She might not have inherited her mother's cleaning gene but she could certainly file.

"Let me show you my office."

Daphne followed her into a tiny bedroom that was serving as her office. It had a filing cabinet, several bookshelves crammed with books and a huge desk... piled high with papers. There was barely room for the computer. The filing cabinet was covered with more papers and so was the printer that sat on a little table next to the desk. A stack of books lay on the floor next to the desk, and in another corner a wicker basket overflowed with still more paperwork and magazines. Muriel Sterling definitely needed help. She'd written a book on simplifying your life. It obviously hadn't included a chapter on simplifying your office space.

"Between my personal life and my writing life, I'm afraid it's all kind of…overwhelming," Muriel confessed as if reading Daphne's mind. "I got rid of a lot when I moved, but managing my business is becoming too much for me. I think hiring an assistant would really bring some order to that part of my life."

"I think you're right," Daphne agreed. "I'd love to help you," she said. "And you'd be helping me, too."

"It's hard starting over, isn't it?" Muriel said kindly.

Daphne's eyes suddenly prickled with tears. "Yes, it is."

"But it can be done." Muriel opened the closet, revealing more clutter—shelving filled with everything from printer paper to sachets and soaps, candles and gift baskets. And more books. "When I do author events I always bring a basket full of goodies as a door prize," she explained. "I love giving things away. And speaking of giving things away…" She selected a book from one of the many stacks. "You might find this helpful. I like to think it helped Bailey when she came home to make a new start."

Daphne took in the book cover. It was simple and striking, with a single long-stemmed red rose against a blurred black-and-white garden. The title was gold embossed. "'Starting Over,'" she read. "That's me. Thank you."

"No, thank *you*. You're going to make my life so much easier."

Now, if Daphne could just find someone to make *her* life easier. Maybe a genie. Or a fairy godmother. Or a Jiminy Cricket to warn her every time she was about to make a dumb decision. No, never mind. She made dumb decisions only when it came to men, and since she was done with men she didn't need old Jiminy.

She left Muriel's place feeling far more positive about her life and her future. She could hardly wait to earn a paycheck again. She and Muriel had agreed on a fair salary for three mornings a week, and Daphne was going to start on Friday. That was fine with her. Cash flow was a good thing, and working only three days a week, she'd still have time to get her affairs in order, as well as take some of the load off her mother's shoulders. And prove she was capable of doing so.

Daphne sighed. Maybe that would never happen. Her mother was a perfectionist and an overachiever. Not content with her job at the bank and having a pretty house, she'd started her own business and turned herself into one of the grande dames of Icicle Falls. In the past, Roberta Gilbert had chaired any number of committees, seeing to everything from town beautification to organizing the Oktoberfest parade. She still rode in it every year on the Primrose Haus float, along with any of the local brides who'd gotten married or held their receptions at the house that year. Oh, yes, she was a hard act to follow. Not to mention an exhausting one.

But Daphne was determined to do it.

This job was a hopeful beginning. Her mother might not have thought highly of her skills but Muriel Sterling obviously did, enough to hire her. Who knew where she might go from here? Today Muriel Sterling's loyal assistant, tomorrow the organizer of some new Icicle Falls festival. She wouldn't always be a loser.

She smiled. Once she was free of Mitchell and had money from the sale of the house, she'd be sitting pretty. Heck, she was sitting pretty now.

She was so busy thinking about how her life was going to improve, she almost didn't see the dog darting into the street in front of her. She stomped on the brakes and just about throttled herself with her seat belt. The animal dodged out of the way, then romped back to the side of the road to give a huckleberry bush the sniff test.

"You are not going to last long if you do that," she muttered.

The dog, some sort of yellow Lab mix, still seemed to be a puppy. She got out of the car and called, "Here, boy," and the dog came bounding over, tail wagging.

The animal had on a flea collar but appeared to have slipped its dog collar. It looked well fed and happy, and she suspected, judging from the muddy paws and legs, it had dug out of someone's yard. "We'd better take you to the animal shelter," she said. She opened the back door of her car. "Wanna go for a ride?"

The dog happily jumped into the backseat. Her mother would have had a heart attack over the mess, but Daphne liked dogs, and she'd rather have a little mess to clean up than see this animal get hurt.

Dr. Wolfe, the town vet, was volunteering at the shelter. Although she hadn't met him, she'd heard about him and knew he'd recently married one of the local women.

"Hello, there," he greeted her as she came in with her new friend prancing by her side.

"I found this dog wandering loose. I think he got out of someone's backyard."

"That looks like Bandit."

The dog confirmed the vet's deduction with a tail wag.

"Well, Bandit, you little sneak," Dr. Wolfe said, squatting down to pet the animal. "I see you've made the great escape again." He smiled up at Daphne. "I'll make sure he gets back to Mrs. Little. She's probably out searching for him."

"Thanks," Daphne said.

"No problem. Maybe this will finally convince Mrs. L. to get an invisible fence. By the way, I'm Ken Wolfe," he said and smiled at her.

He seemed like a nice man. Too bad he was taken.

You're not looking anymore, ever again, she reminded herself. Mitchell had seemed like a nice man when she first met him, too. She wasn't going to waste any more time looking for nice men. If she wanted something to love, an animal was the best bet…the four-legged kind.

"I'm Daphne Gilbert," she said, reverting to her maiden name.

"Roberta Gilbert's daughter?" Daphne nodded and he said, "She's great. My wife and I got married at Primrose Haus. It's pretty impressive."

"Yes, it is." Daphne gave the dog a goodbye scratch behind the ears. How she'd love to have a dog, but she knew better than to even suggest it. She'd just turned to leave when, from out of nowhere, a small black cat trotted over to her and began rubbing against her legs. "Well, who's this?" she asked, bending down to stroke its soft fur. She hadn't had a cat since her sweet tabby died. And that was shortly before she'd married Mitchell. Mitchell had been allergic to cat dander, so no cats for Daphne. But Mitchell was gone now and Daphne wasn't allergic to cat dander.

"That's Milo. We got him a couple of days ago. His owners are getting divorced and neither one wanted him."

Poor guy, she thought. *I know how you feel, little fella. It's awful not to be wanted.* "He looks young."

"He is, under a year, so he's got energy to burn. But he's been neutered and he's had all his shots."

Daphne picked up the cat and he began to chew on her hair. It made her giggle. She couldn't remember the last time she'd laughed.

She'd love to take Milo home with her. A cat wouldn't be any bother. He'd probably run and hide when they had wedding guests. And if he wasn't prone to hiding, she could always shut him in her room for a few hours. She had a comfy bed with a homemade quilt (another of her mother's many talents), perfect for catnaps.

Except…she couldn't simply bring a cat home any more than she could a dog. The house on Primrose Street had been her home growing up but it wasn't now. In fact, it was more a business than a house—her mother's business. It would be selfish and inconsiderate of Daphne to do such a thing, especially considering the fact that her mother wasn't particularly fond of animals.

She sighed. "He's awfully cute. I hope you find a home for him quickly." Somewhere from the back of the building she heard a dog howl. Leaving without an animal…it felt wrong.

Never mind, she told herself as she drove away from the shelter. *You won't always be living with your mother.* Down the road she'd get a little place of her own here in town, a place like Muriel Sterling's that she could doll up with rustic furniture and gingham curtains. Then she'd get a pet. Or two.

She found her mother seated at the kitchen table, going over bills. "Where were you all this time?" Roberta asked.

"I had some errands to run." Daphne set a box of the chocolates she'd bought on the kitchen table.

Her mother cocked an eyebrow. "Should you be spending money on chocolate?"

Daphne sat down opposite her and nudged the box in her direction. She couldn't help smiling as Mother, unable to resist, selected a white chocolate truffle. "I think I can afford it. I got a job."

Her announcement produced a smile of approval. "You did?"

Daphne nodded. "Starting Friday, I'm going to be working for Muriel Sterling three mornings a week. I'm going to get her organized."

"That's a great beginning. But it surely won't be enough to live on."

Daphne's own smile curdled. Leave it to her mother to see the dark clouds instead of the rainbow. "If I'm working part-time I'll still be able to help you here," she pointed out.

Her mother's expression changed from approving to...wary. Hard to believe only a few days ago she'd suggested Daphne help her. Now it looked as if she was having second thoughts. What a surprise.

"Something else might come up," she said. "You don't want to be tied down here."

"Or you don't want me to be."

"I didn't say that," her mother said stiffly.

She didn't have to. Daphne had never had an aptitude for foreign languages, but she had no problem with body language, especially her mother's. "I really am capable of helping you."

"I know. Let's not talk about that right now, though. Let's talk about what you did with the rest of your day. Or have you been at Muriel's all this time?"

"No. I also went by the animal shelter."

Daphne got no further. "You brought home a dog?" Her mother's horrified gaze roamed the room as if she was looking for a Saint Bernard to suddenly dash out from around the corner or behind the curtains.

"No. I didn't think you'd want one here."

"Certainly not. They make huge messes and they smell."

Which was why, growing up, the only pets Daphne had were parakeets and goldfish. "Dogs are high maintenance. Cats not so much," she ventured.

Mother didn't seem any happier about the prospect of a cat. "Don't tell me you got one."

"I was strongly tempted. They had the cutest black cat there."

"Cats may be cute, but they scratch furniture."

"Not if you get a scratching post."

"I suppose," her mother said, and Daphne could almost hear her thinking, *And where, among my antiques, would that go?*

It was just as well she hadn't adopted Milo. Daphne sighed. "Don't worry. I won't bring one here. I wouldn't do that to you." She loved her mother dearly, but sometimes she wished the woman would loosen up a little.

"Darling, it's not that I wouldn't love you to have a cat. However, this place doesn't really work for pets, not with all the receptions we host. Some people are allergic."

"Of course," Daphne agreed. "There's something about pets, though. Animals love you unconditionally." Sometimes she wasn't sure she could say that about her mother.

"Down the road, when you get your own place…"

It was the same thing she'd told herself, but hearing

her mother say it stung. "And I know you're in a hurry for that to happen."

Mother frowned. "I didn't say that, and I wish you wouldn't put words in my mouth."

She didn't have to say it. Daphne was nothing but a big inconvenience. What kind of mother wouldn't be happy to have her daughter back with her? Everywhere Daphne turned these days, she found rejection.

That's not true, said her brain. *Your mother's not rejecting you. She's rejecting having a cat. And she's probably assuming you'll want your own place.* Of course she was being oversensitive and unreasonable. Still, her wounded heart wouldn't listen. She felt that prickle in her eyes again, signaling the arrival of tears. She pushed away from the table. "I'm going up to my room for a while. I need to check my email."

"Daphne." Her mother's voice softened, taking on that pleading don't-be-a-pill tone Daphne was all too familiar with.

"I'll be down later," she said, striving to keep the hurt from seeping into her words. She went upstairs to her old room and shut the door behind her, putting distance between them. Not too different from her teen years when they quarreled. Except she'd outgrown door slamming.

She settled on the bed with her old laptop and brought up her email. One of her neighbors in Seattle was inviting her to a party. Actually, she was on more of a fishing expedition. Are you two still together? I haven't seen you around much. Or Mitchell. And what was with the sacks of clothes on the front lawn?

Daphne gave a snort of disgust. "You'll figure it out soon enough."

A friend had forwarded a collection of cute animal

pictures with clever captions. Oh, she thought again, how she'd love to have a pet. She did need to get her own place. It was ridiculous living with her mother at her age.

Maybe it wouldn't be if her mother could ever admit she needed her, if they could work together and help each other. But her mother didn't want her help. Roberta Gilbert didn't need anyone's help.

Daphne shut the computer and looked out the window at Sleeping Lady Mountain. The view had always inspired her. Today it didn't.

She reached for Muriel's book and began to read. It was almost as good as actually being with Muriel, having a heart-to-heart talk.

Wherever you are right now, you're there for a reason.

Daphne frowned. *Yes, because I'm a failure at love.*

And whatever choices or mistakes brought you to where you are, know that you're in this place at this moment to learn something, to go somewhere new or to encourage someone else. The door is open. All you have to do is step out.

Easy for Muriel to say. She didn't have Roberta Gilbert for a mother.

Eleven

Roberta, the Expert on Love

Roberta suddenly had a headache. It happened a lot when dealing with her daughter. This time she couldn't lay the blame at Daphne's door, though. It belonged solely to her. In the space of a few short minutes, she'd managed to devalue Daphne's new job and insinuate that she wanted her gone.

Truth be told, she did. Not far away, of course, but far enough so she wasn't in such close proximity, constantly worrying and aggravating Roberta. Someplace like Seattle. Or even Wenatchee. Daphne had her own life to live, and she could make her own decisions, but when she made poor ones, Roberta had to grind her molars. Actually, if that was all she did, things would go so much better between them. But she never could settle for simple molar-grinding. She always had to say something.

Honestly, though, wasn't it a mother's job to give her daughter advice? And Daphne needed advice. On a regular basis. She did such impetuous things, and this job working for Muriel was the latest example. Roberta didn't see how a part-time job was going to be of any benefit to Daphne's bank account. Of course, at this point Primrose Haus could support both of them, particularly since Roberta owned the house free and clear. Not that Daphne had ever hinted at getting a paycheck from her. Roberta knew her daughter just wanted to help. But at the rate they were going, Roberta would be buying aspirin by the case.

She took one of the chocolates from the box Daphne had left behind. It was too bad Daphne's marriage hadn't worked out. Roberta had known it wouldn't and tried to warn her. But would she listen? No. When it came to men, she was entirely too trusting. Well, the apple didn't fall far from the tree, did it?

Ancient past, she told herself. Yet she could remember it all as though it was yesterday.

1961

Gerard was the best-looking boy in school. Everyone said so. He arrived the summer before their junior year and made an instant impression on the football coach. And from the very first day of school, he also made an impression on every girl in school, including Roberta. He dated enough of them, skimming the cream from the top of the social tier. That meant she didn't have a chance. She was a straight-A student and on the debate team, but that didn't carry the clout that being a cheerleader did. Come senior year, he was captain of the football team, which should have put him even more out of reach.

Remarkably, it hadn't. He'd fallen for her after she'd

tutored him in English. He thought she was wonderful. She was the only girl for him. He told her so every time they parked in some dark, deserted spot, his hands trying to sneak places they didn't belong.

He was the only boy for her, more addictive than a hot-fudge sundae, more exciting than any of the boys she'd gone steady with her sophomore and junior years. All two of them. It wasn't that she was homely. She was pretty, she knew that; the problem was that she was also smart, and that scared off a lot of boys. So, when it came to boyfriends, she'd been happy to take what she could get.

Andy the math genius had been shy—so shy, in fact, that he'd needed half a dozen dates to work up the nerve to kiss her. And that first kiss had been chaste and disappointing. The ones that followed weren't much better. They were always tentative, just enough to stir up her teen-girl hormones, certainly not the kind of kisses she'd seen on the movie screen when she went to the matinee with her girlfriends. She'd seen a few of those scenes at the drive-in with Andy, too, but somehow they never seemed to inspire him to greatness. She wasn't too upset when his father got a job transfer and the family moved to Maine.

Leonard wasn't any more interesting. He preferred making model airplanes and going to comic book conventions to movies or dances, and they parted by mutual consent. She decided to spend the rest of her junior year concentrating on her studies. And loving Gerard Jones from afar.

What a thrill it was when she entered her English class September of her senior year and found him in it. And how perfect that the teacher stipulated on alphabetical seating. Gilbert before Jones. She wound up in the desk in front of him, which finally put her on his radar. He wasn't intimidated by her smarts, probably because he had so much confidence in himself, and he loved playing with her long, dark hair when the teacher wasn't looking. Then came the tutoring sessions at the library. He'd say things like "You smell so good I can't concentrate" (this was thanks to Roberta getting into her mother's Chanel No. 5) and "Has anyone told you that you have beautiful eyes?" (She did, actually, and it was about time he noticed.) Then one day, as they were leaving the library, he said, "There's a new movie at the drive-in. Want to go?"

Of course she did.

At the drive-in he didn't give her an insecure, short-lived kiss. Oh, no. It had been a full-on force-of-nature attack, an assault with his lips. And tongue.

"What are you doing?" she demanded, pushing him away.

He gaped at her. "You don't know how to French-kiss?"

Obviously not. She felt like a fool.

"Never mind," he said, pulling her back toward him. "I'll teach you."

And what a teacher he was. His kisses left her breathless, and as they became increasingly more intimate with each date, she had difficulty remembering her mother's words of caution. *Never let a boy take liberties. He won't respect you.* But Gerard seemed to respect her just fine. He always opened doors for her, and the corsage he bought her for the Christmas Ball was the most beautiful one she'd ever had.

Still, she did what all good girls did. She kept her

legs crossed. After a while he got frustrated with her
crossed-leg syndrome and broke up with her. He started
seeing a cheerleader, and to show him she couldn't care
less, she started dating a boy on the debate team. But he
was no Gerard, and by spring they were back together.

One evening, as the windows of his daddy's Buick
became more and more foggy, she let him take off her
bra. When he unclasped those little hooks he pretty
much undid the last of her resolution. The thrill of what
he was doing with his mouth and hands was unlike anything she'd ever known. But what would her mother say
if she saw Roberta with her skirt up to her waist and
her top missing?

"Bobbi, I want you so bad," he murmured against
her neck.

"I can't," she moaned, but she didn't remove his hand
from her breast.

"I love you—you know that. That's why I couldn't
stay away."

She conveniently forgot that she'd been the one who'd
gone crawling to him, hinting that she'd give him what
he wanted.

"You love me, too, don't you?"

Now his hand was someplace it had absolutely no
business being. She tried to find her willpower. "My
mother would kill me."

"Who cares about your mother? She's old. What does
she know?"

He had a point.

"We've been going together all year."

Except for that short time they'd been seeing other
people. That had been a mistake. There was no one like
Gerard and she didn't want to lose him again.

"You've got my letterman's jacket. I wouldn't give that to just any girl."

The cheerleader had worn it for three weeks.

But it was hers again now. Ooh, she was melting.

"If you loved me you'd let me."

Of course she loved him. "I can't," she said, trying to squirm out of his arms. He knew good girls didn't go all the way. Oh, but she wanted to.

He pulled back his hand and moved to the other side of the seat, leaving her feeling rejected and unsatisfied. "Fine. I guess you don't love me, after all. I don't know why I'm bothering to be with you if you don't love me."

His words were like some horrible magic wand, bringing tears to her eyes. "I do love you."

"No, you don't. You haven't proved it."

She knew what she had to do to prove it.

You shouldn't do this. The thought wasn't strong enough to overcome her desire and the need to show Gerard that she did indeed love him. She slipped out of her panties and closed the distance between them. "Don't stop, Gerard. Let's not stop."

So they didn't. And from that night on, every date ended with a sexual encounter. They took precautions. Gerard got her some spermicide he said was guaranteed to prevent pregnancy and she believed him. It wasn't until almost the end of the school year that she missed her period.

"I'm late," she told him as they sat in a booth at the Dairy Queen with their burgers and shakes.

He looked momentarily confused. "What do you mean late?"

"My period," she said, blushing.

His face turned as white as his vanilla shake. "Are you sure?"

Her periods had been as regular as clockwork since seventh grade. "I'm sure."

Now his brows drew together and his mouth dipped in an angry scowl. "You'll have to do something about it."

What, exactly, did he want her to do? "What do you mean?"

"Get rid of it, Bobbi. I can't get married. I have a scholarship to Stanford. Remember?"

"You can still go to school. I'll work," she offered.

"While you're preggers? Use your head."

This wasn't the reaction she'd hoped for. She'd dreamed of him hugging her, telling her not to worry, it would be all right. He'd take care of her. She'd even hoped he'd say that he'd marry her, postpone school and get a job. Instead, look what he was asking her to do! She had no idea how to get rid of a baby and no desire to learn.

"Well, I can't get rid of it. I won't."

He pushed away his shake. "Suit yourself." Then he was scooting out of the booth. "Come on. I'm taking you home."

The ride back to her house was a silent one. "Are you mad?" she finally asked in a small voice.

"Yeah, I'm mad," he snarled. "And I'm done. I want my letterman's jacket back."

"You're breaking up with me?" No, this couldn't be happening.

"What do you think?"

"I think you're a jerk," she shot at him, hot tears stinging her cheeks.

"And I think you're a slut."

A slut. He'd called her a slut when he was the only boy she'd slept with? She hadn't even known how to French-kiss when she first met him. "I'll teach you," he'd said. Oh, yes, he'd taught her a lot. But just about sex. He hadn't taught her anything about love.

Of course, her mother hadn't taught her much about love, either. Her grandma had been the only one who really cared about her, but Grandma had been helpless to turn Roberta's mother from her plan once Roberta's secret was out. "You can't keep it. This is for the best," she'd insisted. Whose best, she hadn't specified.

No one could accuse Roberta of being like her mother. If anyone here had known the woman, which, thankfully, no one had. Roberta had actually cared. She'd loved Daphne with a passion, had wanted her beautiful little girl to have a successful and satisfying life. She'd done everything in her power to make that happen. Growing up, Daphne had it all—Girl Scouts, art lessons from a local artist, piano lessons, a lovely wedding, the kind Roberta herself had dreamed of. And then another. And another.

Through it all, Roberta had stoically stood by her daughter, watching her stumble from one romantic failure to the next, reminding herself that it was Daphne's life and she was free to choose her own destiny…if you could call such a bumbling mess a destiny.

Where had she gone wrong? Unlike her mother, she'd been supportive, constantly trying to bring Daphne up to her full potential.

Roberta sighed. Mothers always wanted their daughters to be perfect, and their daughters always disappointed them. It never changed from one generation to the next. The only thing that changed was the expectations.

Enough wandering around in the unpleasant past, she told herself. She had a darned good present and that was what mattered. She put the teakettle on the stove to freshen her tea, and as she waited for the water to heat, she gazed out the kitchen window at the grounds.

The grass was getting shaggy. She needed to have Hank Hawkins come over and start getting the yard in shape for spring. She picked up the phone and punched in the number for Hawkins Lawn Service. Not surprisingly, it went to voice mail. Hank and his boys were already busy.

Hank had moved to Icicle Falls seven years ago, which meant he was still considered a newcomer. His arrival had coincided with Roberta's knees getting tired of all the weeding she had to do. She'd hired him and been pleased, and he'd been working for her ever since. She'd recommended him to Pat York and Janice Lind and several other people, and now he was always in demand. Lucky for her she was a highly valued client.

"Hank, I think it's time to start cleaning up for spring around here. When can you fit me in?"

It turned out that he couldn't help her right away, even though she was a valued customer. "Sorry, Roberta, I can't make it until Friday afternoon," he said when he called her back.

She didn't like having Hank or his men there on Fridays. She often had clients coming in on Friday afternoons or evenings, or events to set up for.

This weekend was clear, though. "I'll take it," she

decided. Then, after that, they could get back on schedule and do midweek maintenance.

An unwelcome thought entered her mind after she ended the call. Daphne would be home Friday afternoon. This would not have been a problem if Daphne was happily married. But now...

Hank was a good-looking man, tall and broad-shouldered, but divorced and a bad risk. Daphne was a beautiful woman, a *vulnerable* beautiful woman, with poor taste in men. Roberta could envision her daughter and her gardener encountering each other by the azaleas and falling madly, stupidly, in love.

She'd have to make sure she found some time-consuming errands for her daughter to run after work; that was all there was to it. Daphne fell in love as regularly as some people ordered coffee at Bavarian Brews.

There would be no ordering up of a certain tall drink of water here. No, sir. Not on Roberta's watch.

Twelve

Anne, Wedding Planner and Shrink

"We want to get married at the beach, and we'd like our dogs, Cutie Pie and Commodore, to be in the wedding, too," said the excited bride. Rika Washington had hired Anne two weeks ago and called her every day since with a new question, concern or inspiration. Today was inspiration day.

The customer was always right, Anne reminded herself. Still, she couldn't help remembering some of the doggy disasters she'd seen over the years when brides included their pets. There'd been the irritable pooch who'd bitten the groom's hand when he went to put the ring on his bride's finger, and the happy mutt who'd done a mating dance with the leg of the bride's father as he stood waiting to give his daughter away.

The worst one was Bismark, the German shepherd who ran away with the flower girl. The bride had thought it would be adorable to have Bismark tow a flower-bedecked wagon holding the flower girl down the aisle during her garden wedding at Seattle's Washington Park Arboretum. Her father happily complied and got busy in his wood shop, producing an adorable little wagon.

Bismark seemed more than willing to do his part at the rehearsal the evening before. The day of the wedding, however, he spotted another dog at the far end of the park, and instead of walking sedately down the aisle with five-year-old Olivia, he took off at a gallop, the little girl clutching the wagon rails and screeching at the top of her lungs.

"No, Bismark!" yelled his mommy and took off after the dog, her veil flying behind her. Of course, the groom and the groomsmen went after the dog, too, who had a head start since he'd bolted before he'd barely begun to go down the aisle. Half the guests joined in the pursuit as Olivia and Bismark hurtled across the lush lawn, Bismark barking and Olivia screeching.

The wagon tipped, spilling Olivia onto the grass, flowers and all, but Bismark kept going. The owner of the other dog, a highly energetic mixed breed, pulled on his leash, keeping him tightly reined in, while the woman with him made shooing motions and yelled at Bismark to scram.

Bismark had no intention of scramming, and doggy mayhem broke out. After much growling and swearing and threatened lawsuits, not to mention a torn tuxedo, the groom got him and hauled him back.

Other than a grass-stained dress and a missing hair wreath, Olivia was none the worse for wear, but she was still shrieking even after her mother picked her up and carried her back.

The child was eventually calmed and the dog was, well, in the doghouse, on his leash and made to sit with the groom's father. It didn't seem to bother Bismark, though, because he spent the remainder of the wedding barking at the other dog, who'd long since departed.

Anne recounted the story of Bismark and Olivia and cautioned Rika that while animals could add a lot to a wedding, they could also be unpredictable.

Rika was unfazed. "Cutie Pie and Commodore will be well behaved. They're basset hounds. They don't have the energy to be bad."

Anne's family had owned a basset hound when she was growing up, and she knew exactly what the woman meant. "You're probably right."

"We're going to get Commodore a tux and a bouton-niere and Cutie Pie a little veil."

Anne could see the wedding pictures now. They'd be cute...or ridiculous. Anne leaned toward ridiculous, but she wasn't the one getting married.

"I'm so excited," gushed the bride-to-be. "This is going to be a beautiful wedding."

Every wedding was. Even ones that involved flower girls getting unexpected wild rides.

She'd just had time to share Rika's latest idea with Kendra when her next client arrived for their lunch meeting.

Lisbeth Holmes appeared to be somewhere in her thirties. She worked as a buyer for Nordstrom, and with her cashmere sweater, black pencil skirt and expen-sive shoes (not to mention the high-end costume jew-elry and that Coach purse), she looked like a walking advertisement for the store. She was a tall, svelte bru-nette, the kind of woman who would make a gunny-sack look good. Put her in a bridal gown and she'd be breathtaking.

Her groom was six inches taller, with a football player's build. He was dressed casually in jeans and a sweater (not cashmere). Maybe he worked for some company that wrote computer software or games and had a more casual work code. Or maybe he was an escaped Seattle Seahawk. But no. It turned out the future groom wrote murder mysteries for a living.

His name was Tad, and he and Lisbeth had been together for the past two years. He'd finally popped the question, and now Lisbeth was ready to start planning the wedding of her dreams. Judging by the modest diamond in her engagement ring, murder didn't pay all that well. Anne hoped the woman wasn't dreaming too big.

"We're talking about February, Valentine's Day," Lisbeth said.

They'd have a terrible time getting a table when they went out to celebrate their anniversary, but at least they'd have no trouble remembering it.

"That sounds lovely," Anne said. "What's your vision for the wedding?"

Sometimes a bride-to-be would seem a little confused by this question. Not Lisbeth. "I want a traditional church wedding," she said. "Red and white for my colors. And I'd like to have the reception somewhere with a pretty view."

Anne nodded, taking notes as Lisbeth talked. And now, before they went any further, she had to ask. "What's your budget?"

"I've been saving for this for the past two years," Lisbeth said, beaming, and named a figure that pleasantly surprised Anne.

"She's really good with money," Tad bragged, helping himself to one of the tea sandwiches Kendra had set out on the desk. "Considering what I make, it's a good thing."

"You'll make more," Lisbeth assured him. "He's going to be the next Stephen King," she predicted.

"But I don't write horror. And speaking of horror, my parents as well as Lisbeth's are divorced, and we've got a lot of exes and steps, and some of them aren't talking to one another. How do you work around that?"

"We'll find a way," Anne told him. She usually did, although sometimes it was a challenge.

She could see her sister, over at her desk, trying to hide a smirk and tried to forget the time she'd pulled aside an ornery grandma who hated her grandson's bride and was making a ruckus. Anne had threatened to lock her in the church broom closet if she didn't behave. Elder abuse, not one of her finer moments. The bride was grateful, though.

"Let's talk a little more about the big picture," Anne said, ignoring Kendra.

An hour later they'd made a good start. The bride had given Anne a clear idea of what she wanted. She'd also given her a check.

"When you have a chance, go to the website and download our timetable and checklist. You'll find them both very helpful," Anne said. "I'll get some ideas together and email you a few helpful links."

"Great," said Lisbeth. She smiled at her future husband, and he grinned back and took her hand.

"Man, I can't believe we're actually doing this," he said.

"It took both of us a while to decide," she confided in Anne. "We don't want to end up…"

"Like our parents," he finished. "I don't want to

spend a bunch of money on a wedding just to end up in divorce court."

"You're not spending anything," his bride said, her voice slightly condescending.

His cheeks flushed. "Well, I'm paying for the honeymoon."

She rolled her eyes. "I can hardly wait to see where that'll be. Tukwila probably."

The flush deepened. "Hey, I've been saving, too."

Oh, boy, here was a chink in the armor. Financial inequality could be a recipe for disaster. Anne hoped they'd also been saving for premarriage counseling.

"It's okay," said his bride. "Someday, when you're really successful, you can take me to Italy."

If they lasted long enough.

But what happened after the wedding wasn't her responsibility. She couldn't promise a couple a perfect marriage. Her job was to create the perfect wedding. And that she could do.

She was feeling happy about her calling in life until Laurel Browne walked into her office. And Laurel wasn't smiling. Which meant that soon Anne wouldn't be, either. Mothers of brides should be caged until after the wedding. Well, okay, not all of them, just some of them. Laurel in particular. Why was she here? She didn't owe Anne money, and any question she or her daughter had at this point they could ask via phone or email.

Anne forced her lips to turn up at the corners. "Hi, Laurel. What brings you here?" *I wish I didn't have to ask.*

"My daughter has a new idea. She saw it online. Or read it in a book. Or something."

"Oh, boy," said Kendra under her breath.

"Sit down." Anne took a seat behind her shabby-chic desk and motioned Laurel to one of the chintz chairs across from it.

"I think I've been more than reasonable," Laurel began as she sank into the chair.

Compared to what? Anne schooled her face into a supportive expression.

"But I draw the line at goldfish swimming in vases on the tables at the reception. What am I supposed to do with all those goldfish afterward? And what if one of them dies and…floats? That'll be appetizing for our guests."

"I do see your point," said Anne. This happened sometimes. Brides spent too much time on Pinterest and pretty soon they wanted to incorporate every idea they saw into their weddings.

"Well, I put my foot down. I had to. But…" That was as far as Laurel got. Her face crumpled and her eyes were suddenly awash in tears. "We're not speaking. My daughter and I are not speaking," she repeated on a sob.

Oh, dear. Now Anne knew the real reason Laurel had come to the office. She didn't need a wedding planner. She needed a shrink. Or just a sympathetic ear.

Anne reached across her desk and laid a comforting hand on Laurel's arm. Kendra, thinking in practical terms, placed a box of tissues in front of Laurel and murmured, "I'll get some coffee." And with that she disappeared, leaving Laurel in Anne's capable hands.

Capable as she was, seeing Laurel's meltdown unnerved Anne. Her own mother-of-the-bride mantle was still new, with no rips or tears, but here was Laurel, liv-

ing proof that anything, even something as small as a
goldfish, could rip that mantle to shreds.

Everyone had mother-daughter disagreements, as she
well knew. She and Laney certainly had when Laney
was growing up. There'd even been a time when they
weren't speaking. The fact that it was short-lived hadn't
made it any less horrible.

Anne had said no to Laney staying out all night after
her senior prom. Of course she'd been accused of being
the meanest mother on the planet, the only mother un-
feeling enough to ruin her daughter's big night. Anne
had insisted Laney come home after the post-prom
cruise, threatening dire circumstances if she didn't.
Voices rose to the point that Anne was sure someone
in the neighborhood was going to call the police. Anne
had the last word. Literally, because then the stony silence fell.

It turned out that Laney's life wasn't ruined, but an
entire week of Anne's was when Laney stopped talking to her. Cam convinced her to cave and Laney to
apologize and life finally settled back down. But now,
listening to Laurel, Anne could still remember that sick
feeling in the pit of her stomach, the irrational fear that
she and her daughter would never speak again, all over
a prom-night curfew.

Mother-daughter relationships were a complicated
mixture of love, loyalty, irritation and resentment, and
there was nothing like a wedding to stir that pot. Seeing Laurel sitting here in her office weeping gave Anne
the uneasy feeling that she was looking at the Ghost of
Wedding Future. No, she told herself. She and Laney
might have had their differences over the years—what
mother and daughter didn't?—but she was no Laurel.

"We never fight," Laurel was saying. "This is not like my daughter." She looked at Anne with tear-drenched eyes and a trembling lower lip. "What should I do?"

Anne sighed. "Let her have the fish."

Laurel dabbed at her eyes with a tissue. "Chelsea's out of control, Anne. I can't keep giving in to every crazy thing she wants."

"Sure you can," Anne said gently. "I know it all seems a little silly to you, but it's something she really wants. And honestly, a few fish won't cost much. We'll handle it so you won't have to worry about what to do with them after the reception." Anne had a couple of friends with ponds. They'd love more goldfish.

Laurel blew her nose. "Fish, Anne. It was…the final straw."

"I know," Anne said. "But think of all the presents you've given your daughter over the years, all the birthday presents, the Christmas presents, graduation gifts."

Laurel sniffed.

"This is the most important gift, maybe the last big one, you'll give your daughter. You want it to be special, to be what she really wants."

Laurel bit her lip and nodded.

Kendra returned bearing coffee in a ceramic cup with the company's logo on it—two entwined hearts dusted with confetti. Laurel took it and stared into it as if contemplating whether to drink the coffee or try to drown herself in it. "You're right, of course." She frowned at the cup and set it on the desk. "This is all becoming so…stressful."

"Don't worry. We're here to make it as easy as possible for you," Anne said.

Now Laurel did something she hadn't done since

she'd first walked into Anne's office with her daughter. She smiled at Anne. "Thank you. Thank you for being so understanding."

"I have a daughter, too," Anne said, "and we're planning her wedding right now."

"Good luck with that," Laurel said cynically. She sighed. "I just want Chelsea to be happy."

"That's what we all want for our children."

"She doesn't always know what's best."

"They don't," Anne agreed. "But they have to live their own lives, and after a certain point, all a mother can do is guide her daughter."

Laurel nodded sadly.

"The fish will be lovely."

"Yes, I suppose they will." Laurel frowned. "What if they die?"

Worse things had happened at weddings. Anne decided to keep that bit of information to herself. "Trust me," she said. "It'll be fine."

Laurel took a deep breath. "All right. The fish stay." She rose, once more in control of her emotions, in control of the wedding. Or so she thought. "I'll be in touch," she said and sailed out of the office.

"Well, that was exciting," Kendra muttered after she left.

"Never a dull day in the wedding business. You know that," Anne said.

"I bet she's on the phone to her daughter as we speak."

"I bet you're right. I would be."

"Me, too," Kendra said. "Kids turn us into such softies. By the way, Coral wants to start wearing makeup."

"What did you say to that?"

"I said, 'Heck, no. We'll talk when you turn fifteen.'"

"I'm sure that went over well." Anne could envision her nine-year-old niece flouncing out of the room, hurling threats that ranged from running away to hunger strikes as she went.

"Oh, yeah. She told me I was a heartless monster. Then she went straight to her father and asked him."

Anne grinned. "And what did *he* say?"

Kendra grinned back. "'Ask your mother.'"

"He's either the smartest man alive or he's a big chicken."

"Yeah. Which do you think?"

Anne chuckled and went back to her computer.

But even as she looked at the screen she couldn't get the image of a tearful Laurel out of her mind. Would that be her a week or a month from now? No, of course not. Laney was a grown woman now, not a temperamental teenager, and they had a great relationship.

And Laney knew that anything Anne suggested would be in her best interests. After all, Anne did this for a living. And she could be diplomatic; she could steer her daughter in the right direction.

Couldn't she?

Thirteen

***

Daphne, Wedding Hostess in Training

Daphne's first morning working for Muriel Sterling went faster than a plate of chocolate chip cookies at a family picnic. She got overheated organizing Muriel's messy supply closet (thank you, hot flash) and then, since she still had time left, dealt with a backlog of emails from readers who'd been inspired by Muriel's latest book.

"I hate not replying personally," Muriel had said, "but I tend to get bogged down when I'm writing back, and then I don't get any work done on my new book."

So she'd delegated, giving Daphne a series of stock phrases she could use. "Thank you for taking time to write me."…"So glad you found the book helpful."… "Remember, new beginnings can be difficult but they can be made."

Daphne caught herself reciting that last line whenever an image of Mitchell's handsome, smiling face came to mind. She'd thought they'd be together for the rest of their lives. The rest of their lives had lasted only six years.

It was oddly comforting to read the emails from readers who one moment had been riding high and the next found themselves in life's recycle bin, having to create something new out of what had become garbage.

I lost my job, but after reading your book I know another door is going to open, wrote one reader. My husband died. Reading about how you coped after losing yours was so comforting, wrote another.

Still another emailed, I thought life couldn't get any worse when I got breast cancer, but then my husband couldn't deal with it and left me halfway through my chemotherapy. That was when I didn't want to live anymore. Thank God a good friend gave me your book. After reading it, I decided no way was I going to let all the bad stuff define who I am as a woman. I got a wig and I've been taking piano lessons. I already feel better about my life and hopeful for my future.

Wow, and I thought I had it bad, Daphne mused. She began her reply using one of Muriel's stock phrases, but then her fingers insisted on typing more. Your hair will come back lovelier than ever, I'm sure of it. Congratulations on all the positive things you're doing.

She was suddenly aware of Muriel reading over her shoulder and she gave a start. "Sorry. I got carried away."

"Don't be sorry. That's exactly what I would've told her," Muriel said. "I knew you were the right woman to work for me."

The right woman, Daphne thought with a smile as she walked home from Muriel's cottage. Yes, things were looking up. From now on, her life would be better. Manless and better.

She went to the bank and opened a new account, then picked up the groceries her mother had requested. And because it was past lunchtime and, after all, a girl had to eat, she went by Gingerbread Haus to treat herself to a latte and a gingerbread boy.

Cass Wilkes, an old-time acquaintance, was still there and happy to wait on Daphne.

"Is business as good as usual?" Daphne asked as Cass rang up her order.

"Sure is. But I'm putting in fewer hours these days, hiring more help. Life's too short to work yourself to death. The kids are growing up fast, and I want to be able to spend more time with them. Did your mom tell you Dani's expecting her first in September?"

"No. Congratulations." Daphne would love to become a grandma, but that was waiting in the future, since her daughter was currently too busy with her career to think about babies.

"How about you? I hear you're about to join the ranks of the single. Are you doing okay?"

"I am. Who needs men, anyway, right?"

"These guys are your safest bet," Cass joked, handing over a gingerbread boy.

Daphne pretended he was Mitchell and bit off his head. Very satisfying.

"If you ever want to go to Zelda's for a huckleberry martini, let me know," Cass suggested.

Daphne was both touched and encouraged by her kindness. Who said you couldn't go home again? "Thanks. I will."

She returned to Primrose Haus to find a metallic-blue truck filled with lawn care equipment parked outside, the words Hawkins Landscaping Service emblazoned on the side of the cab. Mother's lawn guy was here. Daphne had seen him only once, when she'd come up to visit the year before, but she remembered him as a brawny man with a great smile. Not that she was interested. She didn't care how brawny he was.

Anyway, who had time for a man? She was going to be much too busy rebuilding her life to bother with the opposite sex. Tonight she'd read more of Muriel's book.

But first she had to make dinner. Like her mother, Daphne enjoyed cooking. She loved trying new recipes, experimenting with different herbs and food combinations and seeing what she could come up with. Mostly, she liked the fact that she could control what happened in the kitchen, and these days, that was more than she could say for the rest of her life. Her mother wasn't always easy to cook for, especially as she got older. Daphne had heard everything from "It's a little too salty for my taste" to "I can't eat garlic anymore. It gives me heartburn." For the most part, though, Mother actually liked what she made and complimented her on it. And cooking was one way she could do her share in the household and not feel like a burden.

Mother had complained about her bunions hurting that morning, so Daphne had offered to make tonight's dinner. Three-cheese stuffed chicken (light on the garlic) was on the menu, along with fresh asparagus and rosemary bread.

Mother was taking a break with a cup of tea and a book by Vanessa Valentine, her favorite author. She looked up from the book when Daphne entered the parlor, grocery bag in hand, and seemed almost startled to see her. "You're home earlier than I expected."

"Oh?" She was working only part-time. Had Mother been hoping she'd stay away until five?

Before she could ask what, exactly, that meant, her mother had moved on. "How was work?"

The job Daphne wasn't going to be able to earn a living at? *Okay, let it go.* Things had been a little strained the past couple of days. They didn't need to continue in that vein. She certainly didn't want them to.

"Great," she said and gave her mother a kiss on the cheek. "I like working for Muriel." Muriel was positive and encouraging. She probably never found fault with any of her daughters.

"I'm glad. She's lucky to have you."

In light of her earlier reaction to Daphne's new job, it was the proverbial olive branch. Daphne had no problem taking it. "Thanks."

She went to the kitchen and put away the groceries, then started out the back door to get some rosemary.

"Where are you going?" Mother called. She sounded almost panicked. What was that about?

"Just getting some rosemary for my bread. I'll be right back."

"You don't need to bother with that. Plain bread will be fine."

"No bother," Daphne said and slipped out the door. Her mother loved rosemary bread. What had gotten into her?

Daphne stepped onto the back porch just as Hank Hawkins came around the corner. In addition to his oh-so-manly build, he had brown, curly hair with a few wisps of gray hanging over a craggy brow, deep-set

brown eyes and a superhero-size chin, square and...
manly. His arms were like mini tree trunks. If he'd been
a firefighter he would surely have been chosen to pose
for a calendar. *Mr. July Hot.* Whew. She could feel the
waves of testosterone coming at her.

"Hi," he said. "Daphne, right?"

She nodded. Gosh, he was...manly.

"Don't know if you remember me. I'm Hank." He
pulled off a leather garden glove and held out a huge
hand.

"I remember." She held out her own hand and his
swallowed it. His hand was warm and slightly rough,
and she was suddenly sizzling in spite of the chill in
the air.

Great. Of all the times to have a hot flash. That was
all this was, she informed herself. Nothing more. Except she was hot where she didn't normally get hot...

Cooling down would've been a lot easier if he wasn't
looking at Daphne as if she was a bottle of cold beer
waiting for him in the desert. She knew that look. She'd
gotten it often enough over the years.

And right now he looked to her like the last chocolate chip cookie on earth. *Stop that! You are done with
men.* Even if she wasn't, she wouldn't take up with this
specimen. He was probably still in his forties. And if
fifty was the new forty, then forty was the new thirty,
and that made him too young for her. *Boy toy, boy toy,*
chanted her hormones. She told them to shut up.

"How long are you here?" he asked.

"I'm here to stay. I'm getting divorced." Now the
heat on her face was pure embarrassment.

"I'm sorry."

She shrugged. "It happens." *To me. A lot.*

"So, what are you going to do?"

"I've started working for Muriel Sterling, and I plan to help out with my mother's business."

That sounded good, and at least her mother was willing to give it a try, but Daphne knew Roberta still didn't trust her not to screw up. Daphne supposed she had reason. While she'd been perfectly competent at her job in Seattle, there was something about being under her mother's watchful eye that made her performance level sink like the *Titanic*.

Hank, ignorant of the mother-daughter dynamic, nodded. "She could use it. Roberta's a firecracker, but she's starting to slow down. Even so, she can still run circles around most of us." He'd probably said that to be polite. Big and strong as he looked, Daphne suspected Hank had plenty of staying power. Staying power...sex. *Don't go there!* Too late. She'd gone. With Hank. *Well, just pull yourself back, fool.*

"Are you settling in okay?" he asked.

"Yes. This is an easy town to settle into."

"It is. I imagine you know everyone here."

"I know a lot of people," Daphne agreed.

"So, how full is your calendar?"

Oh, boy. He wasn't wasting any time. The hot flash got hotter and she peeled off her jacket. "Pretty full."

"Too soon, huh?"

"You could say that. Or you could say I'm through with men," Daphne added. *Might as well stop this plane before it takes off.* And parts of her were ready for take-off.

He nodded, absorbing that information. "Guess I can't blame you. I've got an ex. I understand the feeling."

"I've got two. This will make number three."

His eyes popped wide. "Whoa."

"Yeah, whoa." How pathetic. She bent over to break some needles off the gigantic rosemary bush by the back porch, hoping he hadn't noticed the five-alarm fire on her face.

"Sometimes it takes a while to find the right person," he said in a chivalrous effort to put an optimistic spin on her failures.

"And sometimes you never do." She stripped a small branch and stood up. "I've decided to become a lesbian."

Now his eyes were as big as golf balls.

"Nice talking to you, Hank," she said and went back inside the kitchen. She almost ran into her mother, who was hovering by the door.

"Were you talking to Hank just now?"

It was the same tone of voice Mother had used when she was a little girl. *"Were you in the cookies?"* Come to think of it, she'd used that tone of voice plenty of times when Daphne was an adult. *"Are you seriously thinking of marrying that man?"*

"Just visiting," Daphne said, depositing the rosemary on the kitchen counter.

"He's divorced, you know."

It was hard to imagine any woman wanting to get rid of a man like that. Uh-oh. Here came the heat again, fast as a gas-stove burner. Daphne blotted her forehead and got busy digging around in the cupboard for yeast.

"The last thing you need is another man in your life," Mother said. "You don't have good luck with men."

As if she needed it pointed out to her? "I'm aware of that," Daphne said stiffly.

"I just don't want you to make another mistake." Mother ran a hand over Daphne's hair, pulling it away from her face, the same motherly gesture Daphne had often used on her own daughter when they were having a serious conversation.

"I know," Daphne said, trying to erase the irritation from her voice. "I'm not planning on it."

"Sometimes things happen that a woman doesn't plan on," Mother said. "You're better off not even talking to him."

"I'm not going to be rude." What was she supposed to do, hide in the house when he came over? *If you had any sense you would.*

"Daphne," Mother said sternly.

"Mother, I think I can decide for myself who I will and won't speak to."

"I'm just cautioning you," Mother snapped.

"Thank you. Now I've been cautioned." Daphne took out a pan to scald her milk and slammed it on the stove. That put an end to the conversation.

There wasn't much conversation at dinner, either. A compliment on the bread, which was obviously supposed to mollify her. A prediction that they might get some rain tomorrow. The chicken could use some salt—this from the woman who was trying to cut down on her salt intake. Oh, and Daphne wasn't going to leave the kitchen in a mess, was she?

After they'd finished eating and Daphne had cleaned every pot and pan, Mother announced that she intended to watch a rerun of *The Rockford Files* on her favorite classic-TV channel and invited Daphne to join her.

She passed on the invitation. Cozy mother-daughter evenings were highly overrated. She went for an evening walk instead and found herself at Zelda's. Maybe she'd visit with Charley Masters, the owner, ask her how her relationship with *her* mother was. Heck, maybe she'd go around the restaurant, take a survey, get some tips on how to be the ideal daughter.

Daphne settled in a booth and ordered a piece of huckleberry pie and a Chocolate Kiss martini. She drank the martini and pushed the pie around her plate.

She was playing with a chunk of crust when Charley stopped by to say hello. "Daphne, I heard you were in town."

"Is there anyone who hasn't?" Daphne frowned and pushed away her plate.

"Small town."

Where everyone knew everyone else's business. Daphne had heard Charley's story, as well, and realized she'd been down the same hurt-strewn road. Her first husband had cheated on her with one of their restaurant employees. If anyone could empathize, it was her.

Charley slipped into the booth opposite her. "I'm sorry. It sucks being betrayed like that, even when it's by a loser."

"Thanks," Daphne murmured. "My mother thinks I'm a failure." Oh, no. Had she said that out loud? One Chocolate Kiss and she had the loosest lips in town.

Her horror must have registered on her face because Charley smiled and said, "Moms always expect more from you. It's in the job description."

Daphne moved her empty glass away. "I can't believe I just said that."

"You probably needed to. And you know what else you probably need? Another Chocolate Kiss. I'll get you one."

True to her word, Charley fetched it herself and gave Daphne a free shrink session. "You didn't do anything wrong," she concluded. "You trusted the guy. You believed in him. That's what we're supposed to do. It's what we all *want* to do. Nothing wrong with that. And, you know, things have a way of working out. I'm living proof. I've got the best guy in the world now."

"Well, if you've got the best, there's no point in my looking," Daphne said, managing a smile. "Anyway, I'm done with men." She could hardly count the number of times she'd said that—to herself and others.

Charley rolled her eyes. "I've heard those words before. Hey, I said them." She slid out of the booth. "Stay for an hour or two. It's karaoke night in the bar, always good for a laugh."

"I could use a laugh."

She could also use a life, so she hung around the bar for a while, watching the locals warble to their favorite pop songs. Then, when she knew her mother would be asleep, she returned to the house and took Muriel's book to bed.

One of the best things about starting over is that the possibilities are endless. Don't worry about where you've been. It's where you're going that counts. The slate is clean. What gets written on it is up to you.

Daphne smiled. Her future wasn't dark and hopeless. It was filled with possibilities. And she was going to take advantage of every one of them. She was going to write a new story on that clean slate.

Muriel's inspiring words and Daphne's determination to do well combined to give her a very good week.

The days she worked with Muriel, she came home energized and pleased with herself. She cooked dinner every night and her mother not only complimented her, but had second helpings of everything from mushroom lasagna to salmon loaf, an old classic Roberta had taught her to make when she was a teenager.

"I swear, Daphne, I've gained five pounds," she said and took another bite of caramel cream pie. "This is incredible. Darling, you could have your own restaurant."

"Not here," Daphne said. "Too much competition."

Mother frowned at her pie. "Really, Daphne, sometimes you give up before you even start."

"I didn't know I was starting anything," Daphne retorted. It was more a case of her mother, as usual, concocting some grand scheme for her and then expecting her to follow through. Rather ironic, considering that Daphne practically had to beg to be allowed to help with weddings. Owning a restaurant would be twice as challenging as assisting with receptions.

Her response produced a long-suffering sigh. "I worry about you, Daphne. I don't know what you're going to do with the rest of your life."

Obviously not partner with her mother in the wedding business. "I don't, either," Daphne said, "but I'm going to figure it out. Let me get my ducks in a row first."

Mother sighed again and nodded, and they left the discussion there, with the ducks swimming about, trying to line up.

A wedding was scheduled for Saturday, and Daphne was on hand to assist with the setup. She'd enjoyed doing this for her daughter's wedding five years earlier. It had been such a lovely affair, and she'd had so much fun helping. Granted, she'd messed up on the invitations, but in addition to work, she'd been taking a neighbor to chemo and preparing meals for the woman's family. Plus Mitchell had been starting a new job and that had put them under a lot of stress. Still, the invitations had finally gone out and the wedding had been well attended.

Now she was ready to shoulder part of her mother's load and, yes, enjoy the vicarious thrill of a happy event.

"Thank you, dear," Mother said after everything was arranged and ready to go. "You've been a huge help."

Music to Daphne's ears.

"Would you like to serve during the reception? It's only appetizers."

This was like getting invited to sit at King Arthur's Round Table. "Sure," Daphne said.

And so she did, passing through the crowd of wedding revelers with a platter of hot wings the bride was particularly fond of. Why on earth anyone would pick something with barbecue sauce for a wedding was beyond her. It was so messy, and the guests were going through napkins as though there was no tomorrow.

Daphne wished Lila had given her the shrimp platter instead as she nervously made her way between revelers. She gave the mother of the bride an especially wide berth, since the woman was wearing a pale blue dress that would not go well with barbecue sauce.

The father of the bride waylaid her and helped himself to several. *Eat 'em all*, she felt like saying. *Then I can get rid of this ticking time bomb.* She'd barely finished that thought when two kids darted at her from out of nowhere. They were on a collision course and

Daphne took a step away to avoid them, which had her backing into the bride's grandmother.

"Pardon me," Daphne murmured and turned to avoid getting her with the deadly wings. Sadly, just as she turned, the bride passed by in all her wedding-gown glory. This might not have been a problem except that the bride had been indulging in a lot of champagne and was now weaving like a passenger on the deck of a storm-tossed ship.

Daphne tried to dodge her, but then an equally tipsy bridesmaid laughed at something one of the groomsmen was telling her and took a step back, bumping into Daphne, nudging her right into the bride. There was an "Oomph" and an "Eek," followed by a wail and a "Look what you've done!" and an "I'm so sorry." And then there were tears. Loud, copious tears. And then… there was Mother.

"Oh, dear," she said.

"My dress is ruined!" screeched the bride.

"Let's go to the powder room and see if we can fix this little spot," Mother suggested.

"Spot" was an understatement. It was more like a stream. No, make that a river, a river of sauce wending its way down the bride's front.

"I'm so sorry," Daphne repeated.

"You should be!" spat the bride.

And now here was Mom's assistant, Lila, with a rag and a small plastic bin, silently cleaning up the mess that had fallen on the floor. Lovely. How many women did it take to clean up a Daphne mess?

"We can fix this," Mother said again. "We have a wonderful dry cleaner here in town, and of course we'll pay for the cleaning."

"That won't help me now." The bride looked down at her stained dress and burst into a fresh chorus of wails.

"No, but baking soda will," Mother said, taking the hysterical bride by the elbow. "Daphne, fetch the bottle of white vinegar and the baking soda," she commanded and led the bride to the powder room.

Daphne hurried to the kitchen, trying not to cry, Muriel Sterling's words mocking her with every step. *The slate is clean. What gets written on it is up to you.* She was a disaster, the backward mirror image of King Midas. Nothing she touched turned to gold. It all turned to poop.

She got the baking soda and the vinegar and a dishcloth and dashed out of the kitchen, nearly colliding with Lila, who was coming in.

"That wasn't your fault," Lila said.

"Yeah, well, tell that to my mother."

"I will," Lila said firmly.

As if it would do any good.

The bride was still hysterical and threatening to sue when Daphne arrived at the powder room. The mother of the bride was hovering outside, begging her daughter to calm down. Too late for that.

Daphne squeezed inside (three was definitely a crowd in a powder room, especially when one of them was wearing a voluminous gown) and then stood by like a surgical nurse assisting in a delicate operation, handing over cleaning supplies. All the while the patient kept up a tipsy tirade, but Mother had nerves of steel and continued to work.

Finally she said, "I think we've got it." The operation was a success. "Daphne, run upstairs and fetch me the hair dryer."

Daphne dutifully fetched the hair dryer and watched as her mother blew away most of the stain.

"You did it," the mother of the bride gushed happily when her daughter finally emerged, and all the guests who'd been hovering nearby applauded.

Roberta Gilbert to the rescue. How embarrassing that the mess had been caused by her very own daughter.

"It could happen to anyone," she said to Daphne later that night as she and Daphne and Lila unloaded trays of champagne glasses onto the kitchen counter.

"It wasn't Daphne's fault," Lila put in. "The woman ran right into her."

"I know," Mother said, patting Daphne's shoulder. "I saw."

Vindicated. She wasn't done writing on that slate, after all.

There was another wedding scheduled for the following weekend, and her mother was actually giving her a second chance and allowing her to help with it. Maybe they *could* work together. Then someday, when Mother was tired of all this, Daphne could take over. Weddings could become a family tradition. Perhaps that would make up for the fact that a successful marriage didn't seem to be.

No, she corrected herself, Marnie was breaking that pattern. She was happily married. Marnie was, simply, Daphne's magnum opus.

The next Saturday dawned bright and sunny, with blue skies and fat, fleecy clouds floating over the snow-tipped Cascades. A perfect day for a wedding. And this was going to be quite the affair. Not as big a deal as the upcoming wedding for the mayor's daughter, which would take place in May, but a big one nonetheless. In addition to a cake worthy of a Food Network TV show, the bride had ordered swan-shaped cream puffs from Gingerbread Haus and a full-course dinner that was to be catered by Schwangau, the priciest restaurant in town. She'd spent a fortune on flowers at Lupine Floral and had ordered enough wine and champagne to get the entire town of Icicle Falls snockered. Not content with a DJ, she'd hired a five-piece band. Guests were all receiving small gift boxes of Sweet Dreams chocolates. Everyone was setting up when Cass Wilkes from the bakery arrived with the cake still in layers.

"We don't have the table quite ready yet," Daphne told her.

Cass checked the time on her cell phone. "I've got to get back to the bakery pretty quick. We're short-handed today."

"Tell you what. Let's unload it in the kitchen, and Lila and I can put it together," Daphne said.

Cass looked frankly worried by this suggestion. "I'd better wait."

"We can manage," Daphne assured her. She'd seen enough cakes put together in her time, and she'd seen the picture of this particular model. Very traditional, with layers held up by vintage champagne flutes. She and Lila could handle it.

Cass gnawed a corner of her lip. "I don't know."

"It'll be okay," Daphne promised her. "Anyway, it's our fault things aren't ready for you."

Cass yielded. "All right. Thanks, Daphne."

"No problem." And it wouldn't have been a problem if the lace on Daphne's tennis shoe hadn't come undone. Or if she'd even seen that it had come undone. Or if Lila

had seen it. But the sneaky lace worked its way loose
and dangled under her feet as she bore the top layer
of the cake, walking behind Lila, who had the middle
layer. They'd already set up the bottom one on the cake
table. When they were done, it would rise like a fondant
tower from a bower of roses and orchids. It was going
to be lovely. They were almost at the table when the
wicked shoelace played its joke, tripping Daphne, making her lurch forward. She tried desperately to keep the
cake from going down with her, but only succeeded in
bumping into Lila. For a moment they did a little dance,
both balancing their cakes in the air. The Dance of the
Wedding Cake, tra-la, tra-la. And then the dance was
over, and the dancers were down on the floor, one of
them with her face in the frosting. Filled with horror,
Daphne sat up, parting the sea of frosting on her face.
The sea parted and there came her mother.

    And that blank slate had fresh writing on it. It said
You're toast.

Fourteen

Anne in Charge

Some weddings came off like well-rehearsed plays. Most weddings, though, like the humans who participated in them, had flaws. Some of those flaws were small—maybe not quite enough food, the bride and groom trying a fancy dance move and collapsing on the floor, the flower girl sitting down and taking off her shoes in the middle of the ceremony. Some of the flaws were a little bigger—the best man losing the ring or getting drunk and making a completely inappropriate toast at the reception. Some flaws were huge, like the bride or groom not showing up.

That last flaw had marred only one of Anne's weddings and it had happened the year before. The groom failed to show. The bride had been in tears and her father had gotten into a shouting match with the groom's father and finally punched him in the nose, maybe figuring that was as close as he was going to get to the errant groom-*not*-to-be. The church was emptied, the caterers were sent home and the parents of the bride wound up paying for food nobody ate. Anne had waived her fee. She learned that, later on, the groom returned, begging for a second chance, and he and the bride had a quiet ceremony and then got out of town before his father-in-law could take a swing at him. Someday, hopefully, they'd all look back on the wedding disaster and laugh. Or at least not come to blows.

At today's wedding, nobody was going to take a swing at anyone, unless it was one of the caterers, slapping an amorous grandpa.

"He pinched me," an outraged Cressa told Anne. "I was walking past with a platter of cheese cubes and the geezer pinched me!"

"Let Renaldo go to him from now on and stay on the other side of the room," Anne advised.

Cressa frowned. "The old guy moves around a lot. I think he's following me."

Her and every other girl in the room. Anne watched as he put an arm around one of the bridesmaids and gave her a decidedly ungrandfatherly squeeze while attempting to look down her dress, then proceeded to hit on the mother of the groom.

There were other problems besides Grandpa. One twelve-year-old boy was systematically emptying every nut and candy bowl in the reception hall, gobbling the contents without restraint. Anne had already seen several adults chase him away, to no effect. His older brother, who was obviously too young to drink, was enjoying himself equally, sneaking into the champagne punch when no one was watching (not an easy feat, considering how many people were dipping into the punch bowl).

The male members of the party weren't the only ones

out of control. Two of the bridesmaids were already tipsy, and one of them was cozying up to the groom.

At the rate this gathering was going, there would be much to remember, and not in a good way. Anne always tried to caution her brides to think carefully about their guest lists. There was a direct correlation between the kind of people a bride invited and the kind of wedding she had.

Anne couldn't do anything about the tipsy bridesmaids or the lecherous grandpa. She did, however, diplomatically point out a potential problem with the underage tippler to the mother of the bride, and a few minutes later she saw the young man being hauled away by his father for a chat.

The gluttonous twelve-year-old was making for the nut bowl again and Anne decided to stop the little squirrel before any more nuts or candy were put out. She suspected nature was eventually going to take its course and he would pay. But by the time retribution arrived there'd be nothing left for the guests.

She got to the cake table just as he was scooping out another handful. "They're good, aren't they?"

The boy gave a start and looked over his shoulder, the picture of guilt. "Uh, yeah."

"I love nuts, too," Anne said and chose a couple of pecans, making them partners in nut thievery. "But, you know, you've got to be careful with nuts."

He looked at her suspiciously.

"Yeah. Too many of them give you—" she lowered her voice "—the runs. And it comes on really suddenly." She looked furtively around and hunched down, a woman about to share a secret. "I went to a wedding once where a boy ate too many and he…" She bit her lip. "All over everything, in front of all the wedding guests."

She had the squirrel's attention now.

"Everybody laughed," she added for emphasis.

The boy dropped the nuts back in the bowl. Lovely. But it looked as though a cure for gluttony had been found. "Aren't you going to have any more?" Anne asked innocently.

He shook his head. "I've had enough."

She watched as he slipped through the crowd, heading in the direction of the restrooms. Ah, the power of suggestion, she thought, and went to fetch more nuts.

The rest of the reception went well. The tipsy bridesmaid stopped hitting on the groom after she threw up in the rhododendron bushes and then passed out, the punch and nut thieves settled down and Cressa got a marriage proposal from Grandpa.

All in a night's work.

Watching the bride and groom, strolling from guest to guest with their arms around each other, left Anne feeling that same sense of accomplishment she always felt upon seeing another couple happily wed. Soon she'd be experiencing the thrill of her own daughter's reception…

It was a long and busy night, but that didn't stop her from getting together with her family the next day. Anne's family liked to gather once a month at her mother's house for Sunday dinner. Julia usually cooked a roast of some kind, with plenty of vegetables, and her daughters brought the rolls, salad and dessert. This Sunday the whole gang was there—Kendra and her husband, Jimmy, and their two daughters, Coral and Amy;

Anne and Cam; and Laney and Drake, family member in training.

When it was football season the men often drifted off after dinner to watch the game on TV, while the women either visited or played cards. The same thing happened during baseball season if a Mariners game was being aired. But since none of the men were big basketball fans, during basketball season they joined the women for conversation or some sort of game.

This afternoon it was Trivial Pursuit, and the women were behind, struggling to answer the sports-and-leisure questions.

"This is hard, Mommy," said Coral, Kendra's oldest.

"It sure is," Kendra agreed. "Who knows this stuff?" she protested, throwing up her hands.

"Men," Jimmy said.

"They should have cooking questions in here," Kendra grumbled.

"Talk about a sexist remark," Cam teased her. "What makes you think men don't know anything about cooking?"

"The greatest chefs in the world are men," put in Dad.

"Not anymore," Kendra said. "And there certainly aren't any at *this* table."

"That's because our women are such great cooks." Dad grinned at their mother. "Why try to compete with perfection?"

"I wouldn't object if you tried," Julia said, grabbing a handful of bridge mix.

"Aw, Julia, you know you love to cook," he said.

"Not all the time."

"All you have to do is say the word," Dad told her.

"Fine. Tomorrow night *you* make dinner."

He frowned. "You can't just spring that on a man."

"Sam Wellington, I've been trying to spring that on you for years."

Anne doubted her mother had tried very hard. Her parents had always had a traditional relationship, with her father working and her mother staying home and running the house. Still, she knew that after forty-five years in the kitchen, her mom was getting tired of KP.

"Daddy, tomorrow night's the perfect night to cook," Anne said. "All you have to do is put the leftovers in foil and stick them in the oven."

"Maybe we'll have sandwiches tomorrow night." Julia waggled a finger back and forth from Laney to Drake. "Make him cook some of the meals when you two get married. If you don't train them right from the beginning, they never learn."

"Don't worry, Mrs. W.," Drake said. "I know how to cook."

"He already makes dinner for us on Fridays and Sundays," Laney said proudly.

Her grandfather shook his head. "Young men today, they're all henpecked."

"Is that so?" asked his wife, cocking a disapproving eyebrow.

"Hey, I say do whatever works." Cam clapped Drake on the back. Then he looked at Kendra. "So, are you girls going to answer the question or not?"

"Not," Kendra muttered. "Who hit the most home runs for the Yankees? Who knows?"

"I do," Jimmy said with a smirk.

"Oh, go ahead and answer and then shut up," Kendra told him, turning his smirk into a grin.

The men won, and after much good-natured grumbling, it was time for pie and ice cream and more visiting.

"Have you two figured out where you're going to live after you're married?" Julia asked Laney.

"At Drake's place," Laney said, smiling at him. "His roommate's already moved out and I'm going to use the spare bedroom as a studio."

Julia smiled. "That sounds like an excellent idea. And how are the wedding plans coming?"

"Good," Laney replied.

Slower than a dying slug, Anne felt like saying. "We still have so much to do."

"At least you have your venue," Julia said. "That house is lovely."

Drake frowned. "I thought we were getting married on the river."

"We are," Laney assured him and leaned over to kiss his cheek.

"The house is for the reception," Anne reminded her mother.

Julia's eyebrows took a disapproving dip downward. "I thought you decided against the raft."

If Anne had her way, her daughter would be getting married under the rose bower in the garden at Primrose Haus. It would be in full bloom by June and so lovely. But she hadn't convinced Laney yet.

"That's still up for discussion," she said hopefully.

"No, it's not." Her daughter glared at her.

Drake looked from mother to daughter, and he wasn't smiling, either. "If we're gonna stick around here, we should at least do something cool like get married on the river."

"I thought you guys were going to Vegas," Jimmy said. Obviously, Kendra hadn't been keeping him in the loop.

Laney and Drake exchanged a look that was—what? Regretful? Oh, no. Anne had to be misreading that. "This will be better," she said quickly. "More people can come."

"I don't know. Vegas sounded like fun," Jimmy said. This was followed by a pained expression and an "Ouch" as his wife kicked him under the table.

"Anyone for more pie?" Anne asked with brisk cheerfulness.

Seconds on pie was a good distraction, and the conversation drifted into new avenues, but Anne felt discontent coming from her daughter and future son-in-law's corner of the table like a miasma. Surely they weren't changing their minds. No, they couldn't be. She was just imagining it.

"Drake doesn't seem all that excited about the new wedding plans," Cam observed as they drove home. "Are you sure they're both okay with this?"

"Of course I am," Anne said. "Primrose Haus will be great for the reception and they'll love getting married on the river." At least she'd talked her daughter out of wearing a bikini top—she hoped. "This will be something she can remember proudly all her life."

Cam shot a quick look in her direction. "As opposed to?"

"Well, having regrets."

He nodded and kept his eye on the road. "Like her mother."

She'd never complained, never said anything. "I don't have regrets."

He grunted.

"What's that supposed to mean?" she demanded.

"I know you wanted a big, fancy church wedding."

"I wanted you more," Anne said, and that was the truth. "Anyway, we're not talking about me."

He shrugged, ready to drop the subject.

Anne wasn't. "If Drake was in charge we'd all be wearing eye patches, walking around with parrots on our shoulders and saying, 'Aargh.'"

"I'd be fine with that," Cam said, smiling. "Just as long as nobody asked me to walk the plank."

"Who knows what they'd ask you to do." No, the direction they were taking now was the right way to go. Her daughter would thank her for this.

Planning a wedding was such a special time for a mother and daughter. That was another thing they'd be cheated out of if Laney just went off to Vegas. It was one last mother-daughter adventure to enjoy before Laney embarked on her new life. They would look back on this with such fond memories.

The next day, Laney's day off, they hit the road for Icicle Falls for some of that special mother-daughter time, armed with lattes Laney had made for them and a to-do list. Blue sky and sunshine promised an early spring.

"We've got appointments with the florist and the baker," Anne said. "The caterer couldn't meet with us today, but she's going to email some sample menus to look over. Oh, and I heard there's a local guy who DJs for weddings."

"We already have a band," Laney said as they exited I-5 for I-90 eastbound.

"You do?"

"Drake's friend Anders has a band. The Flesh Eaters."

"The Flesh Eaters," Anne repeated weakly. "Um, what kind of music do they do?"

"Some grunge, some progressive, some new wave. They're versatile."

That was versatility? Anne tried to picture her parents dancing to the earsplitting wall of sound produced by the Flesh Eaters and failed. "Sweetie, are you sure that's a good idea?"

"What do you mean?" Laney's voice was defensive now.

"I'm just wondering if that's really the best choice for your wedding music."

"I think it is."

"Well, yes, of course. But you'll have other generations at your wedding. You want them to enjoy themselves, too. If you have a DJ he can play a variety of music, something for everyone."

Laney chewed her lip. "But he's Drake's friend. We already told him he could play."

Ah, here was the crux of the matter. Laney didn't want to disappoint a friend. "Just tell him it didn't work out." Heartless, maybe, but that was the wedding biz.

"Yeah, like everything else so far," Laney grumbled.

Okay, that hurt. "That's not true," Anne said. "You're getting married on the river."

Laney frowned at the stand of evergreens they were passing. "I can tell how much you guys approve of that."

"It's your wedding," Anne said.

"Glad you remembered."

Ah, mother-daughter bonding. Nothing like it.

Once they got to Icicle Falls, Anne let her daughter have free rein. Laney picked out the biggest, boldest wedding cake possible at Gingerbread Haus and ordered a donut cake as high as the Trump Tower. By the time they added the groom's cake, a chocolate mountain complete with a rock climber to celebrate Drake's favorite hobby, they were over the cake budget by five hundred dollars. Anne didn't blink.

"The donut cake will be an excellent addition," said Cass, the bakery owner, which brought a big grin from Laney.

"Whatever my daughter wants," Anne said. As long as it didn't involve a pirate ship or zombie musicians.

"Thanks, Mom." Laney threaded her arm through Anne's as they walked away. "I love our cakes."

"You're welcome," Anne said and patted her hand. Her daughter's gratitude was worth an extra five hundred dollars.

Then it was on to Lupine Floral, where they met with Heinrich Blum, the shop's creative genius. He greeted them warmly and predicted that Laney would be the most beautiful bride Icicle Falls had ever seen. Anne suspected he said that to every bride who came through his doors, but Laney ate it up.

"And what's our budget?" he asked.

Anne told him and he nodded appreciatively. "We can give you something very nice for that. What are your colors?"

"Brown and forest green," Laney replied.

"Very tasteful," he said, and it was all Anne could do not to remind her daughter who had suggested those colors.

"We thought perhaps you might be able to do something with brown roses, ferns and some chocolate mints," Anne couldn't help adding.

"Chocolate mints. Love it!" Heinrich said, confirming Anne's good taste.

He showed Laney several pictures of past Lupine Floral creations and then they spent some time surfing the net and discussing ideas. Finally it looked as though they had a plan. "How does that sound?" he asked.

Laney shrugged. "Pretty good."

He held a hand to his chest in mock horror. "Only pretty good? I'm crushed."

Laney quickly corrected herself. "I mean, it's beautiful."

It just wasn't a pirate ship. Anne didn't want her daughter to be disappointed with the flowers at her wedding. She didn't want Laney to be disappointed with anything. "Maybe we could throw in a little more," she said.

"A little more...pizzazz?" Heinrich guessed.

"Well, yes."

"Of course. But you do want to stay in your budget, right?"

"Well, let's expand the budget."

"Okay, then," he said with a smile. "We'll see what we can do." What he could do was incredible. He put together a plan that would turn the beautiful Primrose Haus into an enchanted castle, employing everything from the flowers and greens they'd already selected to twinkle lights and lanterns for the garden, and crystal vases stuffed with more twinkle lights for the inside. Table centerpieces would be branches (surrounded by flowers and greens, of course) with candle lanterns hanging from them. By the time he was done, Anne was practically drooling.

Even Laney looked impressed. "I love it," she said, a huge smile on her face.

Anne's savings account was probably in trouble, but so what? She'd find the extra money somewhere. And anyway, they weren't *that* far over budget.

Yet. They still had to order food, had to buy the wedding dress, the favors and the gifts for the bridesmaids.

Anne saw the proverbial writing on the wall and it was all in dollar signs. Okay, so she'd be paying for this wedding for the next five years. She'd gladly do whatever it took to make sure the day turned out to be exactly what her daughter had always dreamed of—especially after shooting down the Vegas idea.

Ah, guilt. The perfect present for the mother of the bride.

Fifteen

Laney, Having to Choose

"I don't get why you don't want me to come," Drake said as he and Laney jogged side by side around Green Lake on Saturday after her shift at the coffee shop.

"I told you, it's not that I don't want you to come, but it's just girls." Guys never went along when their fiancées went bridal-gown shopping. She'd watched enough episodes of *Say Yes to the Dress* to know that. "Even my dad isn't going." And if anyone should be there, it was Dad, since he and Mom were paying for it. "Anyway, it's bad luck to see me in my wedding gown before the wedding." That was a silly superstition and not very practical for taking pictures, but the drama of waiting until the big moment appealed to Laney.

"My brother saw his wife. They had their pictures taken before the wedding."

Laney tried another tack. "You'd be bored."

"Seeing you all dressed up? No way."

"You're so sweet."

Drake always said stuff like that. She was marrying the best guy ever.

"So, come on. Let me go with you."

Laney grinned over at him. "Uh-uh. You need to be surprised," she added with a teasing smile.

He shook his head. "I don't get why you're looking for a wedding dress anyway. I thought you were gonna wear shorts."

"I changed my mind."

Actually, her mother had changed her mind, but Mom was probably right about this. Getting married was major, and she might regret it if she went for casual.

Drake was frowning now. They weren't going to fight about this, she hoped.

"Come on. Don't be mad," she coaxed.

"I'm not mad. I'm just…"

"What?"

"I don't know."

Guy-speak for *I don't want to talk about it.* "What?" Laney pressed.

"I hate being left out of everything like I don't matter."

She stopped running. So did he. A cyclist whizzed past them.

"You do matter," Laney said. "You should know that. You're the most important person in my life."

"Yeah? Then how come I don't get to be involved in anything? How come you don't even ask me what I think?" He wiped his sweaty brow and looked away.

Two women jogged past them, laughing about something.

"I haven't even seen the place where we're getting married," he continued.

"I've shown you pictures."

He gave a snort of disgust. "Big deal. I thought we were gonna go up there. You've gone up twice without me."

She moved closer and put a hand on his chest. "Come on, babe. That was to order flowers. What guy is into flowers?"

"And cake. You ordered the cake. I'm into cake."

"Okay, I'm sorry. I didn't think it was that important to you."

"Well, it kinda is. I mean, *I'm* getting married, too. Someplace. Someplace I haven't seen."

Now Laney's stomach hurt. She hugged him and laid her head on his chest, hoping that would take away the hurt for both of them.

"It's not that I want to tell you what to do or anything," he said, wrapping his arms around her. "I just want you to care what I think."

"I do care," she protested.

"Yeah, right," he said sullenly.

They were getting married! This was supposed to be fun. Why wasn't she having fun? Maybe because her period was right around the corner. She always felt bitchy before her period.

That was it, of course. She'd be back to normal in a few days.

Meanwhile, though, she had to get back to normal with Drake. "How about we go up there the first weekend in May? I think they have some festival then. It'll probably be lame, but we can check it out, maybe do some rock climbing. I'll show you the park on the river, and we can go to the rafting place and talk to them about renting a raft for the wedding."

Mom had forgotten to add that to their list of things to do when they'd gone to Icicle Falls. She'd probably be glad to see that Laney had taken care of it. Not that she was worried about Mom right now. It was Drake she wanted to please. She looked up at him, hoping to see the smile back on his face.

It wasn't yet, but he nodded in agreement. "Okay. Fair enough."

"And to make things even, I won't go with you when you and the guys pick out your tuxes."

Now he did smile. "I'm not doing that without you. I don't wanna screw it up."

"It's hard to screw up renting a tux. But you'd find a way," she teased and started jogging again.

"That's why you have to come with," he said, falling in step with her.

They completed their jog in perfect harmony, so she should've been in a great mood later that afternoon when she picked up her best friend, Autumn, to go wedding-gown shopping. But she found herself feeling mildly grumpy. What bride felt grumpy about shopping for a wedding gown? Oh, yeah, one who had PMS. Oh, well. Trying on wedding dresses was bound to put her in a good mood.

It *was* just PMS, wasn't it? "It's not that I don't like everything we decided on," she said as she and Autumn drove to meet her mom and aunt and grandma at the bridal shop in the U district that her mom had suggested.

"What's with this 'we' stuff?" Autumn scolded. "It's your wedding. Who's in control?"

"I am," Laney insisted. She was. She was having her donut cake and she was getting married on the river.

"I guess," Autumn said dubiously. "Your mom's really sweet, but sometimes she kinda takes over."

"Well, she's not taking over today. *I'm* the one wearing the wedding gown. And the bride is always right. That's what Mom says."

"Sure. If you say so."

She did say so. And yeah, okay, maybe her mom was a little controlling. But Autumn should talk. Her mom still got on her about cleaning their house, even came over every other week with her Pledge and dust rag to check that it was done right. Mom never did stuff like that. She hadn't told Laney what to do since she moved out.

Only since she got engaged.

No, she hasn't, Laney reminded herself. *She's just made suggestions.*

Well, she wasn't going to be making any suggestions about Laney's wedding gown. Laney wanted the decision to be hers and hers alone. She wanted to fall in love with the perfect gown for her big day.

Autumn dropped the subject, and they picked up the two other bridesmaids, Drake's younger sister, Darcy, and Laney's other close friend Ella, who'd recently gotten engaged.

"I don't know how you guys are pulling this together so fast," Ella said to Laney as they drove down Forty-Fifth. "There's so much to do."

"It helps when your mom does it for a living."

"I'm impressed," Ella said. "Gordy and I aren't getting married until next February, and I'm about to have a nervous breakdown."

"Go to Hawaii and get married on the beach," said Autumn. "That's what I want to do when *I* get married."

"That's what I want to do, too," said Darcy. She was the youngest of them all and had just broken up with her boyfriend, so Laney suspected a wedding on the beach at Kauai would be a ways off.

"Too expensive," Ella said. "Half the family wouldn't be able to come, and my mom would have a shit fit."

"It's not about your mom," Laney told her, and Autumn pretended to choke on the Diet Coke she was drinking.

"Tell that to her," Ella retorted as they pulled up in front of Here Comes the Bride. Even though they were ten minutes early, Mom's car was already parked in front of the shop. They walked in to find her standing in front of a rack of size-six gowns along with Aunt Kendra and Grammy, in earnest conversation with the saleswoman.

"Let's set this one aside," Mom was saying, pointing to a low-cut gown with sheer sleeves.

"Not taking over at all," Autumn said under her breath.

"Shut up," Laney whispered back, and Autumn smirked.

Having heard the little bell over the door, Mom looked over her shoulder and smiled at Laney. "Hi, sweetie," she called. "Are you ready to play princess?"

That was what they'd called it when Laney was a little girl and dressing up in pillowcases, lace and bits of organza and anything else Mom had lying around. This time she'd be dressing up and it would be for real. The last time they'd done anything like this was when they'd gone shopping for her prom dress. The dress shopping had been fun but things had gone downhill fast.

She remembered how Mom had tried to control

her prom night and ruin all her big plans with Drake. "Someday you'll understand," Mom had predicted right before the fight got really ugly. She was an adult now, and she still didn't understand.

The memory of the prom-night battle didn't exactly sweeten her mood. But she smiled and went over and dutifully kissed everyone.

"Hi, girls," Mom said to the bridesmaids. "I'm so glad you could join us today. Maybe we can find your dresses, too."

"Wow, you are efficient," Ella murmured.

"We don't want to put it off too long in case we need alterations," Mom told her. To the saleswoman, she said, "This is my daughter, Laney."

"Hello, Laney," said the woman. "I'm Glenda. My assistant, Rose, and I will be happy to help you find the perfect gown today."

The perfect gown. Laney's bad mood melted. "Thanks."

Mom held up the one she'd been looking at. "What do you think of this one?" she asked Laney.

It was okay, but… "I don't like the long sleeves," Laney replied.

"Up in the mountains it could still be chilly in the evenings," Mom said.

Grammy pulled out a gown weighed down with ruffles. "Here's a nice sleeveless one."

Laney wrinkled her nose. "Too ruffly."

"Oh," Grammy said, surprised, and put it back.

"Told you," Aunt Kendra said to her.

"This is nice." Autumn lifted a simple satin gown with a sweetheart neckline and a full skirt from the rack.

"Nice" didn't come close. It was freakin' awesome. "I love that," Laney breathed.

"How about this one?" Aunt Kendra asked, pulling out a gown with cap sleeves.

It was pretty, too, trimmed with lace and sequins, but she didn't love it the way she did the first one.

"Why don't we set you up in a dressing room and you can try these on," suggested Glenda. She called over her assistant, who took one of the gowns. Then she smiled at everyone else. "Ladies, if you'd like to go on over to our seating area, we'll bring your bride out in a minute."

"Try this one on, too," Mom said, handing over the long-sleeved gown.

Laney frowned. She'd already said she didn't like it. "No, I don't want that one."

"Just try it on," Mom urged.

"Okay." But she wasn't taking it.

"Hey, here's one," said Ella, holding up a lacy number with seed pearls, a full skirt and a long train.

"I'll try that one on, too," Laney decided.

So, off she went to the dressing room, with Glenda right behind her.

The first gown she tried on was the one with the sweetheart neckline. She felt like a princess in it. Glenda fluffed out the skirt and Laney turned and smiled at her reflection. Drake would love her in this.

Glenda ushered her from the changing room to where her family and friends sat in a grouping of comfy chairs.

"Oh, wow," said Aunt Kendra. "You look great."

Grammy's expression was slightly pained and Mom was half smiling.

Laney would never fight with her grandma, but Mom was a different story. "What?" she demanded. As if she didn't know.

Mom almost jumped. "Nothing."

"You don't like it."

"No, it's very nice," Mom said and managed a long-suffering smile.

"You don't like my tat showing." And if she wore her hair up, the one on her neck would show, too. But so what? She happened to like her body art, even if her mother didn't.

Mom sidestepped the issue. "We don't have to buy the first dress you try on. Let's see what the others look like."

"Fine," Laney snapped. With a swish of her skirt she whirled around and marched back to the changing room.

Next came the gown with the capped sleeves. "I like the first one better," said Autumn.

"Me, too," Ella chimed in.

"Yeah, me, too," said Laney.

"It's a very pretty gown," Grammy said, and Laney noticed her grandmother didn't say *she* looked pretty in it.

The third gown got slightly more positive reviews but Grammy still wasn't oohing and aahing and neither was Mom.

"Let's see the long-sleeved one," Mom said.

Keep an open mind, Laney told herself as she returned to the dressing room.

One look in the mirror confirmed it; this wasn't the gown for her. It was definitely a princess gown, but one a dated Disney princess would wear.

"My goodness, she's beautiful," Grammy gushed when she came out to model it for the others.

She shook her head. "It's too old-fashioned."

Grammy disagreed. "That's not old-fashioned. That's classic."

"The tat will still show," Laney said. So if that was Mom's issue, what was the point of getting it?

Her mother studied the gown and tapped her finger to her lips thoughtfully. "It's not bad."

Oh, just what she wanted, a gown people would look at and say, "It's not bad."

"Don't do it," cautioned Autumn.

Autumn was right.

"We've got all afternoon," Aunt Kendra said. "I say try on every gown they have in your size."

And so she did, with Glenda and Rose scurrying back and forth, their arms full of lace and organza and satin. None of the gowns did it for her like that first one. "I want to try that on again," she said to Glenda as her assistant bore away yet another gown.

The woman nodded and helped her into it. She looked at her reflection. Oh, yes, this was the gown she wanted. She went back out. "This is the one."

"It *is* nice," said Grammy.

"If that's the one you want, that's the one you should get." Sadly, it wasn't Mom who said this. It was Aunt Kendra.

"Let's look a little more," Mom suggested.

"I've tried on every friggin' gown in the place," Laney growled.

"I know. But there are other shops."

"Mom, my tat's gonna show. There's nothing you can do to hide it." Maybe her mom would like her to get married in a white body bag.

"Sweetie, you want to be sure," Mom said.

"I am sure." She loved the gown. She could see herself in it, walking through the woods to that raft on the river. This was what she wanted to be wearing in her wedding pictures.

"I still think we should look around a little more."

"Until we find something *you* like. I thought this was my wedding." Why was Mom being like this? She was spoiling everything.

"It is, but I don't think that's the best gown for you."

"This is the gown I want."

Mom sighed, and in that sigh was a world of disapproval.

"Oh, never mind." Laney stormed off to the dressing room. Never mind the friggin' gown. She'd get married in shorts (lowriders!) and a bikini top. Maybe she'd even get another tattoo before the wedding. A tramp stamp. Mom would love that.

Just as she was leaving, she met her mother coming into the changing area with still another gown. "Here's one we missed," Mom said. It had a sweetheart neckline…and a long-sleeved lace jacket to go with it. Yet another attempt to cover the hated tattoos.

"I don't want to try it on," Laney snapped. "I don't want to try on any more wedding gowns. In fact, I don't want to get married in a gown, after all," she added.

"Oh, come on, Laney. Don't be like that," Mom said, following her out of the changing area.

"Like what?"

"Stubborn," Mom said, irritated. "Just try this on."

"No. I'm done." Laney grabbed her purse. "Let's go, you guys," she said to her bridesmaids.

"Laney, quit acting like you're twelve," her mother scolded.

"I'll quit acting like I'm twelve when you quit treating me like I'm twelve," Laney called over her shoulder as she made her way to the door.

"Oh, boy," Ella said.

"That went well," added Autumn. "But hey, I don't blame you. It's your wedding."

Somebody needed to explain that to Mom.

Sixteen

Anne, Mother in Crisis

"Really, Anne," Julia said as they trooped back to Anne's car. "What were you thinking?"

"What do you mean what was *I* thinking?" Anne countered. "I wasn't the one who threw a fit in the bridal shop."

"No, you were the one who caused it," Julia said sternly.

"I certainly was not." Anne unlocked the car and they got in, her mother riding shotgun in the front passenger seat. "Laney was being stubborn and uncooperative," Anne said and shut her door with a bit more force than necessary.

"She found the gown she wanted," Julia pointed out.

"Mom, do you want her parading down the aisle with that tattoo sleeve showing? Not to mention the one on her neck." Although, actually, the one on Laney's neck was kind of cute. Not that Anne would ever tell her.

"The sheer sleeve didn't hide it anyway," Kendra said from the backseat. "You'd need heavier material, and you're not going to find that in any summer wedding collection."

"We could look online," Anne said. "Or…" Oh, she didn't know. And right now that wasn't the issue. Her daughter was mad at her. No, make that furious. Well, darn it all, she wasn't exactly happy with Laney, either. This should've been fun, a memorable outing. It hadn't been fun and it'd been memorable in the worst kind of way.

"I hate to say it, but the baby Momzilla is growing," said Kendra.

"I am not a Momzilla!" Anne almost shouted.

"What on earth is a Momzilla?" Julia demanded.

"It's what we call an out-of-control mother of the bride," Kendra explained.

"Momzilla," Julia said, trying out the word. She nodded. "Yes, Anne, I think you were a bit of a Momzilla today."

"I was not! I didn't tell my daughter what wedding gown to buy or refuse to pay for a gown I didn't like."

"Only because you're not a full-grown Momzilla yet," Kendra said.

"You may not have done that but you certainly balked at getting the dress your daughter picked out," said Julia. "You might as well have told her you wouldn't buy it."

Anne frowned at her mother. "So, you want her to walk down the aisle with the mermaid in full view of everyone?"

"What does it matter?" Kendra argued. "It'll be family and friends at the wedding, and they all know she's got a sleeve. Heck, half the women at the wedding will have tattoos."

"Call her and tell her to get the gown," commanded her mother.

Anne scowled at the traffic in front of her crawling down Forty-Fifth. "I don't see what's wrong with going to another shop and seeing if there's anything else."

"Well, then, your eyes are closed," Julia said shortly. "Laney loved the first gown, and none of the ones she tried on lit up her face like that one did. Your sister made a good point. Everyone coming to the wedding knows about Laney's tattoo. They've all gotten used to it. So you may as well let her have the dress she wants."

"Twenty years from now, when she looks back on her wedding pictures, what's she going to think?" Anne asked.

"That she got to have the dress she wanted," Kendra answered. "Come on, sis. Give it up."

"Easy for you to say. You haven't gone through this yet," Anne grumbled.

"Well, *I* have," said Julia. "And if you think I wanted to see my oldest daughter married in the courthouse, you can think again."

"I *know* you didn't want me getting married in the courthouse."

"*You* didn't even want you getting married in the courthouse. But you married the man you loved in the dress you picked out, and I was there to support you. It was your decision and I had to live with it. In the end, that's all a mother can do. Unless, of course, she wants to become a Momzilla," Julia added, obviously enjoying her new word.

"It's a gorgeous dress," put in Kendra, "and Laney looks beautiful in it."

"She didn't even try on the one with the jacket," Anne muttered.

"If I get like this when my daughters get married, somebody shoot me," Kendra said from the backseat.

"You will," Anne predicted. Maybe it wouldn't be over a gown, but it would be about…something. Suddenly she had empathy for the Laurel Brownes of the world. Being the mother of the bride wasn't easy.

Both her mother's and her sister's final words to her when she dropped them off were to call Laney and tell her she could have the dress, which left her feeling self-righteous and misunderstood.

She drove home, her eyes stinging with tears. She hadn't actually said not to buy the dress. All she'd wanted was for her daughter to be open to different options. How was that so bad?

Laurel Browne's words haunted her. *"We never fight."* But they had, and over something as inconsequential as goldfish.

When it came to mother-daughter disagreements, Anne had seen it all. She'd seen mothers and daughters get into it over everything from whom to include on the guest list to what flavor cake to serve. She'd always watched with smug tolerance, assuring herself that when they planned her daughter's wedding, there'd be none of that. She and Laney were too close for such nonsense, and although they might not have had the same taste in fashion, they certainly shared the same taste in weddings. They always had.

Until now. Now it felt as if every choice was a challenge and every decision her daughter made a surprise. And not necessarily a pleasant one.

Okay, so Laney was her own woman now. And Anne

had no problem with her daughter making her own decisions. This was her wedding, a once-in-a-lifetime event (well, theoretically), and she wanted only to make sure Laney got it right, that she had no regrets later. Was that so wrong?

She came home to find Cam grading papers. "How'd it go?" he asked.

"Not good," she said and proceeded to give him a blow-by-blow account of what had happened.

"Not good," he agreed. "What are you going to do about it?"

She knew what she wanted to do. She wanted to implant a chip in her daughter's brain so she'd make the best choices.

No, she was trying to make her a Stepford Bride. She was trying to make Laney not be Laney.

The realization was horrifying and humiliating. Laney loved her mermaid tat, considered it part of her artistic expression. If Anne was ashamed of that, wasn't she also ashamed of her daughter?

She was proud of Laney, proud of how well she was doing, what a talented young woman she was. Did the tattoo matter so much? Obviously, it bugged her, but why? Because she thought people would judge her for her daughter's extreme tattoo and consider her an inferior mother? And what did that say about her? She suddenly felt selfish and small. This was her daughter's big day. It was about Laney, not Anne, and if Laney wanted a sleeveless dress, then she was going to get a sleeveless dress.

Anne called the dress shop and caught Glenda just as they were closing. "We're going to take that sleeveless dress with the sweetheart neckline."

"It is a lovely dress," Glenda said encouragingly. "And your daughter will look beautiful in it."

"Yes, she will." Laney would look beautiful in anything.

"My daughter has a tattoo," Glenda said. "She went sleeveless with her wedding gown, and you know, it looked fine."

Anne sighed and gave the woman her charge-card information.

"Good decision." Cam nodded in approval when she hung up.

"It *is* all about her," Anne said as much to herself as him.

"Yes, it is."

"I guess I'd better call and tell her she can pick up the dress." Compromise. They all had to compromise. Hadn't she told herself that a while back?

She called Laney's cell but, big surprise, her daughter wasn't picking up. She was probably off somewhere with a voodoo doll marked "Mom," sticking pins in it. Hopefully, she'd listen to Anne's voice mail message.

"Hi. It's Mom. I just wanted to let you know that I've paid for the wedding gown you liked." Loved. Laney had loved it, and every bride deserved to have the wedding gown of her dreams. "You can pick it up anytime. I'm sorry we quarreled, sweetie. I want you to be happy and have the wedding you want." And there was still so much to do between now and the big day. She added a verbal PS. "Oh, and by the way, have you sent out the save-the-date announcements yet?" Okay, that sounded a little…critical. "If you haven't, I'll be glad to help you."

"Interesting way to end an apology," Cam observed as she ended the call.

"We have to stay on top of things."

"Yeah, I see how well we're staying on top of things for our anniversary."

She decided to ignore that remark. They'd get to it eventually, when she wasn't feeling completely wrung out. Planning a wedding had never been so stressful.

Of course, she'd created much of the stress herself. How tangled mothers' and daughters' lives got! She could still see her own mother's face when she announced that she and Cam were getting married at the courthouse ASAP.

1990

Julia stared at Anne as if she'd just announced a death in the family. "You what?"

It was only the two of them, seated at the breakfast table with cups of coffee and banana bread left over from the day before. Anne gripped her mug tightly. "Cam and I are getting married next week at the courthouse," she repeated, smiling insistently.

"Anne," her mother protested, "that doesn't make any sense. You wanted a church wedding and a big reception. You don't even have a ring yet."

As if she didn't know. "We're going to look at rings tomorrow."

Julia shook her head. "I don't understand. You two have been an item since high school. Why the rush all of a sudden?" And then a disapproving look took over her face. "Anne Marie Wellington, are you pregnant?"

Anne was still trying to compose her answer when

her mother said, "You are," in tones that were just as disapproving as her expression. "Oh, Anne, what were you thinking?"

That I love him. Obviously, she hadn't been thinking about getting pregnant. They should've waited until they were married to have sex. Too late now. Anyway, she wanted Cam's baby, wanted to have something of him to love while he was so far away.

"How am I ever going to tell your father?"

Anne bit her lip. She had no idea, but she hoped it was when she wasn't around. He'd be as disappointed in her as her mother was. "I'm sorry," she said in a small voice.

Julia expelled her frustration in a long sigh. "We raised you better." Now she was shaking her head. Okay, so they'd messed up, but her mom didn't need to carry on as though she'd committed the crime of the century. Women who weren't married got pregnant all the time. They even moved in with their boyfriends.

"Mom, I'm sorry, but I love him."

This inspired another long sigh. "I know. Still, there's still no need to rush like this."

"Yes, there is. He's shipping out in a few weeks. We want some time together before he goes. If he doesn't come back…" Her throat tightened and she couldn't finish the sentence.

"You're going to regret this haste." Her mother went on as if she hadn't spoken. "All those dreams you had, those plans, all the times we talked about your wedding. All these years your father's dreamed about walking you down the aisle."

That was when Anne realized she wasn't the only

one who'd had to give up a dream. Her mother had been anticipating a wedding, too.

This was not how she'd planned to start her married life, but she couldn't turn back the clock. Anyway, she'd meant what she said. She did want as much time as possible with Cam, wanted to give him some happy memories to take with him. Maybe things hadn't turned out according to plan—the old plan—but they'd make the new plan work.

She said as much to her mother and Julia came around the yellow Formica kitchen table and hugged her. "You're right. We love you, and we love Cam, too."

"And what about the baby?" Anne asked.

"Of course. We'll love the baby to pieces." Her mother frowned again. "I just wish… Oh, never mind," she said brusquely. "We'd better go shopping for a dress this afternoon."

And so they got right down to the business of getting Anne ready for her courthouse wedding. Her mother said nothing more about her disappointment and helped her pick out a dress and bouquet. Her father hugged her and told her he'd be happy to give the bride away, and so they made the best of things. On her wedding day her parents hosted a family dinner featuring standing rib roast and baked potatoes. And that horrible cake the neighbor made. *At least it's a wedding cake*, she thought.

Her parents gave Cam and her two entire place settings of fine china and a check for a hundred dollars. Other friends and neighbors, upon hearing the news, sent gifts, as well, but Anne's courthouse wedding hung over the day like a black cloud. She'd disappointed her mother; there was no denying it. Still, if she had it to do over, she'd probably make the same choices. The bottom line was that she loved Cam and he loved her. And later that night, when they were in their motel room at Ocean Shores, wrapped in each other's arms and listening to the crash of waves on the beach, she was able to sigh happily. Thank God, she thought, that even when life wasn't perfect, when daughters weren't perfect, there was usually a plan B.

In the end, weddings were about the bride and groom, Anne reminded herself now. Yes, she planned weddings for a living, but she had no business telling her daughter what gown to wear.

No more Momzilla, she vowed. From now on she'd back off—but there was nothing wrong with offering guidance.

Seventeen

Roberta, Mother of the Year

It had taken a while after the last wedding mishap for mother-daughter relations to return to normal. Roberta had not reacted well when Daphne dropped the wedding cake; she'd be the first to admit it. But honestly, what grown woman tripped over her shoelace? Anyone would've reacted the way Roberta had.

Maybe not. Muriel Sterling, Daphne's new guru, would've hugged her and kissed her frosted face, told her accidents happened. But Muriel Sterling wasn't running a business where cake was a necessity. And Roberta thought she'd shown considerable restraint, all things considered. All she'd said was "Oh, Daphne." All right, she'd also tagged on "For heaven's sake!"

With one little phrase she'd hurt Daphne's feelings. Again. It seemed she was always upsetting her daughter. But that same daughter kept her in a near-constant state of upset, as well. Years of worry over Daphne's relationships and her future security had grown every gray hair on Roberta's head.

If she didn't accomplish anything else in this world, Roberta needed to get Daphne's life sorted out. Then she could stop worrying.

Somewhere along the mother-daughter timeline, Daphne had turned from a well-loved child to an obsession. Obsessions were exhausting.

This day was going to require yet more emotional energy. Hank Hawkins would be arriving soon to put the fishpond in order and do some planting, and Roberta needed to find a way to get her daughter gone. It shouldn't be too hard, since this was Daphne's day off. Surely she'd want to go have a latte or something.

Roberta had already taken her morning walk, eaten her granola and was on her second cup of coffee when Daphne made her appearance in the kitchen, wearing a ratty old T-shirt, the circles under her eyes testifying to a poor night's sleep. Even in her rumpled state she was a beautiful woman.

"You look tired," Roberta greeted her.

"I didn't sleep well last night," Daphne said, pouring a cup of coffee. "I kept having these awful dreams. I was back with Mitchell and he wanted me to have a threesome with him and Betty White."

"Betty White?" What was happening to her poor daughter's subconscious?

"And Betty dragged me to Macy's to shop for a black negligee for her. We couldn't find one and Mitchell got mad and said he was leaving. But he came back and set the house on fire with me in it." Daphne rubbed her forehead. "I hate him, Mother. I truly hate him."

"Well, you'll soon be rid of him," Roberta said, hoping that was a comfort.

Daphne frowned into her coffee cup. "The sooner, the better."

"Meanwhile, there's nothing to take your mind off your troubles like a day of shopping."

"I don't feel like shopping. There isn't anything I need."

"Well, I need something."

"Like what? I asked yesterday if you needed anything and you said no."

"I forgot I'm almost out of Metamucil," Roberta improvised, "and we could use some more double-A batteries. And maybe while you're at the drugstore, you could pick up my prescription." She was bound to have some prescription or other waiting. She always did. "Oh, and why don't you get us a couple of lattes."

Daphne was looking at her with a mixture of perplexity and irritation. "Anything else?"

Nothing Roberta could think of. She wished she'd sent something to the dry cleaner. "That should do it." She hoped.

"All right," Daphne said. "I'll go as soon as I have breakfast."

Her daughter took forever with breakfast, putting together an omelet and then sitting down to eat it while reading the copy of *People* she'd brought home the day before. Hank would be here any moment.

"You're not done yet?" Roberta said, coming into the kitchen to check on Daphne's progress for the third time.

"What's the hurry?"

"I'd like to get my prescription as soon as possible."

That worked. "I guess I'd better get dressed, then," Daphne said, shutting the magazine.

"I'll clean up." Roberta took her plate. "You go get ready."

Daphne had just left the house when Hank arrived. Whew, Roberta had gotten her daughter away from temptation in the nick of time.

And a good thing, too. Hank Hawkins was a fine specimen of manhood; he was also polite and hard-working. But he would never do. Being divorced made him a very poor risk, especially for Daphne. Honestly, at this stage any man would be a poor risk for Daphne.

She must have run her errands on winged feet because it seemed Hank had barely started working and she was back. With plants.

She handed Roberta her usual plain latte. "They didn't have a prescription for you at Johnson's."

"I forgot—I already picked it up," Roberta lied. "What's this?" She pointed to the box of pansies Daphne had set on the kitchen table.

"I stopped by the nursery. They were on sale. We've got a few spots in the flower beds where they'll fill in nicely."

Roberta wasn't sure if she was pleased or irritated that her daughter was making landscaping decisions for her.

She was still trying to decide when Daphne said, "Since Hank's here he can get them in the ground for us right away."

"I'll do them later," Roberta said.

"Mother, you don't want to be out there on your hands and knees. That's why you hired a gardener. Remember?"

Roberta wished she'd never confessed how tired she was of yard work.

"Don't worry," Daphne said. "I'm just going to take him these plants. I'm not going to ask him for a date."

Roberta scowled at her daughter's departing back. Really. When had Daphne become such a smart aleck?

And why had she returned home so quickly? Had she known that Hank was coming over? Roberta certainly hadn't said anything. She hadn't known he'd be coming by herself until the day before, when he'd called and told her he had to change his regular day due to a dental appointment. She'd automatically agreed to the change, forgetting that it would be Daphne's day off.

She should've called him first thing in the morning and canceled. Or asked him to send someone else. All this forgetfulness. Perhaps she had a subconscious desire to match her daughter up, a longing for one of them to grab the romance brass ring.

No, no, no. Everything Daphne grabbed turned into something smelly. There would be no grabbing going on here at Primrose Haus, especially with a man who already had one strike against him. That made four strikes between the two of them—a very bad combination of numbers.

Roberta could hear voices outside the kitchen. She stole over to the back door and opened it a crack. Then she leaned in for a listen.

"Met any interesting lesbians yet?" Hank asked.

Roberta blinked and shook her head. She must have misheard. She pressed her ear closer to the door.

"I saw someone at Zelda's who looked interesting," said Daphne.

What? Since when did Daphne decide she preferred women to men?

"Uh-huh," Hank said. Even through the door Roberta could hear his skepticism.

"You know, I was where you were. Emotionally, I mean."

"Oh, really?"

"Yeah. After my wife told me I was too boring to bother with and left me for another man."

"Your wife left you for another man?"

Daphne sounded shocked. So was Roberta. She'd always thought Hank was a nice man. How sad that his wife hadn't appreciated him, and it was a pity he and Daphne hadn't met earlier, before Mitchell the ogler came on the scene.

"Yep," Hank was saying. "Some cowboy she hooked up with when she went to the Ellensberg rodeo with her girlfriends. I guess he gave her a wilder ride than I could."

Daphne said something, but it was so soft Roberta couldn't be sure what. It sounded like "I'm sorry."

"I used to think it was all on me. Then I realized it wasn't."

"My husband left me for another woman. Well, more than one. He was a rat and I already know it had nothing to do with me. Except for the fact that I picked him in the first place. When it comes to men, I'm not a good chooser."

"What makes you think you'll have any more success with women?"

Roberta shook her head again. Honestly, what kind of conversation *was* this?

"Okay, the truth is, I don't want to be with anyone," Daphne said. "I like being on my own."

No, she didn't. Poor Daphne. Cupid had given her a raw deal. She deserved better.

Maybe Hank Hawkins was better.

Oh, but a fourth husband? Was that even worth considering? Roberta was still mulling it over when the kitchen door opened suddenly, taking her by surprise and nearly toppling her onto the back porch.

"Mother! What are you doing?"

Roberta willed away the guilty flush on her cheeks. "It was hot in here. I was opening the door for a little fresh air."

"You were eavesdropping," Daphne said in disgust.

"I was not."

Daphne crossed her arms. "Really, Mother."

"I don't know why you're getting after me," Roberta said, opting for wounded dignity. "I simply happened to be passing by the door. I must say, I didn't know Hank's wife left him for someone else."

"There's a lot of that going around," Daphne said bitterly.

"It's too bad you didn't meet someone like him sooner."

She could have if she'd listened to Roberta and used one of those online dating services everyone was talking about. From what Roberta understood, you filled out a detailed questionnaire and then were given any number of perfect matches. But, as usual, Daphne had to do things her own way. And look where it got her.

Daphne frowned. "We're not going to start talking about my horrible taste in men, are we?"

Roberta had no desire to go down that long and winding road. "I have no intention of talking about your past mistakes."

"Good," Daphne said with a nod, "because that's a subject I'd rather not discuss if you don't mind." With that she picked up her latte and walked out of the kitchen, leaving Roberta feeling frustrated.

As usual. She'd made a verbal misstep somewhere in the conversation and now Daphne wasn't happy with her.

Well, she wasn't always happy with Daphne, either, but at least she cared, which was more than she could say for her own mother.

"I'm only doing this for your own good." The words came back to haunt her. Oh, yes, her mother had the right words for every occasion—not that learning her daughter was about to become an unwed mother was much of an occasion—but her actions spoke so much more loudly.

1961

"If you're going to refuse to tell me who the father is, then I have no choice," Roberta's mother snapped. "Although I can guess, and that young man should be held accountable."

"You can't guess anything," Roberta said, determined to be stubborn. There'd been that period of time she'd been with another boy. The baby could be his, couldn't it? And just now, she wished it was. Any other boy would have done the right thing.

They were in the living room, the perfect living room with its crushed-velvet furniture and expensive drapes, the living room where her mother liked to entertain friends for coffee. (If you could call the rich, snobby women she cultivated *friends*.) Roberta huddled in a chair, her tummy churning. Her grandmother, who'd been summoned from her little house up on Tenth Avenue, perched on the couch, trying to calm Roberta's mother with phrases like "These things happen" or "Helen, darling, please try to get hold of yourself."

Nothing could calm her mother. She paced the room like a caged animal while Roberta sat in a wingback chair, her hands tightly clasped. If her father had been alive he might have tempered her mother's wrath. He certainly would have hugged Roberta and told her he still loved her and that it would be all right. But Daddy had died when Roberta was ten. Her mother had played the brave, grieving widow to the hilt, although Roberta sometimes wondered if she even missed him. Had she ever really loved him? Did she know what it was to love someone? Did she know what it felt like to have your heart broken?

Not that Roberta loved Gerard anymore. She hated him for being so selfish, hated him for leaving her in this mess. She'd rather be alone the rest of her life than forced to marry such a selfish creep.

Of course, her single state made it oh-so-inconvenient for her mother, who worried more about what people would think than her own daughter's broken heart.

"Well, you can't keep it."

"What do you mean?"

"The baby. If you won't tell me who the father is, then you'll have to give it up for adoption."

Give up her baby? She might have hated Gerard, but she already loved this little life growing inside her. How could she give it away? "No," she protested.

"What are you planning to do?" her mother asked contemptuously. "Waddle around town with a big tummy, a walking advertisement for what not to do? Do you want people laughing behind your back? Do you want every respectable man to cross you off his list? Men don't marry girls who get themselves into this kind of mess."

"Then maybe I don't want to get married," Roberta shot back. Brave words but she did want to get married. She'd never imagined herself alone.

"Don't talk foolishly," her mother scolded.

"This is a short time in your life, dearest," her grandmother put in. "I know it's…awkward."

Was that what you called this horrible feeling of rejection?

"But we can get past it," Grandma finished.

"There's a home outside Seattle, in Dunlap," her mother said. "They take in girls who find themselves in this situation. Your father was from California. We'll say you've gone to visit family down there. No one will be the wiser."

"I don't want to go to some…home and stay with strangers."

"You can't stay here, Roberta. How would it look?"

Roberta didn't have an answer for that.

"I'm only doing this for your own good."

They were going to turn her out, send her off to some jail for unwed mothers, hide her away like a leper. "I won't go," Roberta said stubbornly. "And you can't make me."

"Oh, yes, you will," her mother said, pointing a finger at her. "You've gotten yourself into this mess and now you'll have to deal with the consequences."

Roberta jumped up. "I won't! You can't make me." And with that she ran from the room. Upstairs she slammed her bedroom door to emphasize how strongly she felt.

But slamming doors and protestations did no good. Her mother swept everything aside and made the arrangements. And if that wasn't bad enough, she kept Roberta home under virtual house arrest.

The following week, as she and Roberta sat at the kitchen table, she broke the silence by announcing, "It's all arranged. You'll be going to the Florence Crittenton Home for Unwed Mothers. Your grandmother and I will take you the day after tomorrow."

The day after tomorrow, she was getting shipped off to some…place, to live with strangers, other girls who found themselves in the same mess. Well, she wouldn't do it. Her mother could make all the arrangements she wanted, but Roberta wasn't going to go along with it, like…like a sheep headed to the slaughter.

Except what choice did she have? Only one.

"Roberta?"

She looked up to find her mother regarding her with a stern expression. "Did you hear what I said?"

"Yes, Mother." Let her mother think she was going along with this.

"Good. Pack a few clothes tonight. I'll bring you more as you need them."

Maternity clothes, of course. Oh, she'd done this all so wrong. She should be married, sitting at her own kitchen table, talking about the baby, making plans. Gerard had cheated her out of that. But he wasn't going to cheat her out of being a mother. Neither was her own mother.

"May I go out tonight to say goodbye to my friends?"

"You may go out and see your friends as long as you

stick with our story. You'll be visiting your father's relatives in California."

"Yes, Mother."

Roberta told her friends she was leaving, all right, but she told them the real reason. She and her best friends, Nan and Linda, sat on Nan's canopy bed and discussed what Roberta should do.

"I have ten dollars in my purse," Nan said.

"And I have six," added Linda. She frowned. "That's not enough for bus fare and a place to stay."

"Or food," Nan added. "I know! I'll tell Daddy that Linda and I want to go shopping tomorrow. He'll give me some money."

"Jilly just got her allowance. Let's call and ask her to come over and bring what she can," Linda said.

"We can't let too many people know about this," Roberta cautioned. "Someone will tell my mother."

"Jilly won't," Linda said. "I've got the car. I'll go pick her up. Oh, and she's the same size as you. She can put some clothes in her train case and tell her mother she's spending the night with me."

Meanwhile, Nan was up and rummaging through her jewelry box. She came back holding a gold locket. "Take this. If you need to you can pawn it. If not, keep it to remember me by."

Roberta's eyes filled with tears. She had such good, caring friends. If only she had a mother who cared as much. She took the necklace and hugged Nan. "Thank you," she managed around a throat constricted with emotion.

Once the money was collected, there was nothing left to do but say goodbye to her friends at the bus station.

"Don't forget to change buses," Nan told her. "In case the police come looking for you."

"Or your mom hires a private detective," Linda said.

"And if anyone asks, remember all I told you was that I was going to visit family in California."

Nan was crying now. She pulled Roberta into a fierce hug. "Oh, Bobbi, I'm going to miss you. Are we ever going to see you again?"

"I don't know," Roberta answered.

One thing she knew for sure—she'd never see her mother again.

She'd relented and gone back to visit when Daphne was two, hoping that once her mother saw her pretty blue-eyed granddaughter with her golden curls, she'd repent her heartless behavior. But her mother had refused to even come to the door. Roberta had stood on the porch of the large brick colonial, her daughter's hand in hers, knocking and then ringing the doorbell, telling herself that her mother simply hadn't heard her knock. But then she'd seen the living room curtain twitch. Her mother knew she was there, knew it was her standing on the front porch. She still didn't let Roberta in.

"She's ashamed," said Roberta's grandmother, who'd been overjoyed to see her. Grandma had fed her tea and ginger cookies and held Daphne on her lap, exclaiming over what a sweet child she was. She'd listened with interest as Roberta told her about her new life in Icicle Falls, how well she was doing at the bank. Grandma had even said she was proud of Roberta.

Her mother never did. Oh, she finally heard from her. Grandma had passed on Roberta's mailing address, and Roberta had received a letter a month later. But it hadn't been filled with kindness and forgiveness. Instead, it had been a diatribe, all about how Roberta had disappointed and humiliated her. She'd tried to help her and Roberta had thrown that help right back in her face. And then she came waltzing home, bold as brass with a baby in tow, and expected her mother to welcome her with open arms? Wicked, ungrateful girl!

The very memory of that letter could still open the dam of emotion. Her mother had been the most selfish creature alive. At least she'd had her grandmother, who sent presents every Christmas and chocolate bunnies at Easter. Grandma had even come to Icicle Falls to visit once before she died, bringing a handmade dress for Daphne and pictures for Roberta of when she was a little girl and her father was still alive.

"It's important to hang on to the good things from the past," she'd said. "Your mother… Well, I'm sorry. She's my own daughter but sometimes…" Grandma didn't finish the sentence. No need. Roberta understood.

And now she *really* understood. Daughters didn't always turn out the way a woman wanted. But all daughters deserved to be loved.

And helped. Even when they drove their mothers nuts.

Eighteen

Daphne, the Wiser Woman

Today she was going to court to finalize her divorce. Again. For the third time. There would be no haggling over child custody or fighting over who got the cat. Mitchell had his things and Daphne had hers. The house was in her name, so she'd keep that to do with as she pleased. As for the time-share they'd bought two years ago, against her lawyer's advice, she'd told him he could have it. She didn't want to go anywhere that would remind her of Mitchell.

"We're ready," Shirley had said on her last office visit.

Yes, as far as all the paperwork went, they were. But Daphne wasn't ready emotionally. She didn't want to go to the courthouse and see her failure officially recorded.

Still, to the courthouse she went. Into Room 3 with its rows of hard, wooden benches and the judge's throne of judgment looming above it all. She saw two people, each on opposite sides of the room, conferring with their lawyers in whispers and scowling at each other. Another lone man in a three-piece suit didn't seem any happier to be there. But she saw no sign of Mitchell. She didn't know whether to feel angry or relieved. She'd seen him at the pretrial conference, and that had been enough. She never wanted to see him again. Still, what did it say about her that he couldn't even bother to show up for their final court date?

She sat at the back of the courtroom, waiting her turn, watching as other people stood before the judge alongside their lawyers and officially ended what had started as happy unions. Ages ranged from twenties to fifties. How many church weddings were represented here? Had these couples lit a unity candle, poured sand into a glass vase? Promised to love, honor and obey, stay together in sickness and in health? Had any of them tried three times and failed?

Three weddings, three disasters. She probably held the record in Icicle Falls for more romantic failures than anyone else. And yet, each time she'd started out with such hope, such an air of celebration.

Her first wedding had been fit for a princess; her mother had seen to that. Even though Mother had her doubts. Why hadn't Daphne herself had any doubts? Oh, yes, because she was an idiot.

"You're still so young," Mother had said. "Why don't you wait a little longer?"

The answer to that had been simple. She was tired of waiting to have sex. Her mother had warned her about jumping into bed, telling her that often ended badly. When Daphne decided to jump into marriage instead, Mother flipped on the caution light again, and that was when she'd finally shared the truth about her own mistake and Daphne had learned that the daddy she'd always thought was dead was very much alive.

Daphne had tried to contact her birth father, wanting to see him, maybe develop a relationship with him. He couldn't have been as awful as her mother had said.

It turned out that he *was* as awful as her mother had said—a selfish man who didn't want to be reminded of his youthful indiscretion, as he so kindly put it. So she'd decided that, after all those years, she didn't need a father anyway, not when she had Johnny. He was more than enough for her.

Johnny was good-looking and fun and she could hardly wait to start their new life together. He had a job with a construction company in Seattle and a line on a cute little apartment in Magnolia. He was ready to go and so was she, so she plunged heart-first into marriage.

Her bridesmaids had dressed in pink, her favorite color, and she'd carried pink tulips. She'd read that tulips signified passion and that had certainly described her relationship with Johnny. Even the cake had been a mass of pink—pink frosting, pink roses, pink doilies underneath. Roses for a rosy future. But that rosy future lasted only five years, which was probably longer than it should have taken for Daphne to realize that her husband loved booze more than he loved her. Or their daughter.

So then came Fred, good solid Fred. And once again, there'd been a wedding on Primrose Street, a June wedding with lots of flowers and candles and a fancy sit-down dinner. The guest list was a little smaller than for wedding number one, but it had been lovely all the same. Daphne had gone with blue this time, the color of trust and peace, and she and Fred had vowed to be faithful all the rest of their days, to stay together in sickness and in health, for better or worse.

Somehow they'd neglected to add "in boring times and through the everyday grind" and Fred had started drifting like a sailboat with no anchor. And speaking of sailboats, he'd had to go and buy one. At first it was expeditions to the San Juans. Next thing she knew, he was talking about sailing around the world.

"But Marnie's in middle school," she'd protested. "We can't pull her out of school. And I have to work."

"We can homeschool her. You can quit your job."

"Fred, what will we live on?"

"We've got some money in savings, and I'm going to write a novel."

This was what came of marrying a man who was twelve years older. He'd been ready for a midlife crisis and she hadn't. He filed for divorce and sailed off without her. She was still waiting to see his novel on bookstore shelves or the internet.

Single parenthood was no fun, but she managed. Then Marnie graduated from college and moved out of the house and the place seemed so…empty. When Marnie moved to New York, Daphne figured she'd learned her lessons in love. She was ready to try again. And, lo and behold, along came Mitchell, charming lovable Mitchell. They got married in Seattle, at her house. Just family. She wore a gold cocktail dress because she'd read that gold was the color of success and triumph, and she'd carried a small bouquet of orchids and stephanotis to represent joy and marital happiness.

As she stumbled down memory lane her eyes began to leak tears, not so much for the loss of Mitchell but the loss of hope. *Don't cry*, she told herself, but somehow her tear ducts didn't get the message. In fact, they began to produce tears at an alarming rate. *Don't cry, don't cry, don't cry.*

Her lawyer passed her a tissue, and that small kindness made the tears flow all the harder. She slipped out of the courtroom and rushed to the women's bathroom. It was old-fashioned, with black-and-white tiles on the floor and ancient windows, and her wails echoed like a banshee's. *Don't cry, don't cry, don't cry.*

Another woman came into the bathroom. She was wearing jeans and a T-shirt and a scowl. She smelled of smoke. It could've been from cigarettes or plain old anger. "Whoever he is, he ain't worth the tears," she growled at Daphne.

Daphne wanted to explain that she wasn't crying over Mitchell. She was crying over lost love, over the sad fact that she'd probably be alone the rest of her life and never have sex again, even though fifty was the new forty and that made her forty-three. Instead, she swallowed a sob and nodded. Then she splashed cold water on her face, took a deep breath and went back to Room 3.

"Are you okay?" Shirley whispered when Daphne slid back onto the chair beside hers.

"I will be," Daphne whispered.

She spent the next half hour watching other people's marriages dissolve, and then it was her turn to go stand in front of the judge. Still no Mitchell.

Nobody seemed to need him anyway. It took less than ten minutes for the state of Washington to put its seal of approval on the end of her marriage.

Outside the courtroom she hugged Shirley and thanked her for all her help.

"Now, get out there and enjoy your single life," Shirley said.

"I will," she promised.

The first thing she did to enjoy her new single state was to sit by the river and have a pity party. She didn't need any noisemakers. She was making enough noise herself boo-hooing. It was wrong; it was unfair. She'd never wanted to be single.

But, she finally reasoned, being single and happy (she'd get there eventually!) had to beat being married and miserable. She wished she felt happier about no longer being miserable, and she said as much to Muriel Sterling when she went to her house later to put in a couple of hours. She set up some signings for Muriel's upcoming release, a book of chocolate recipes and small-town reminiscences. Muriel had told her she could take the day off, but Daphne realized she needed the distraction, needed to do something to feel good about herself.

"Transitions are hard," Muriel said as she and Daphne settled at her little dining table with mugs of chocolate mint tea and a plate of brownies.

"After this many divorces I should be used to it," Daphne said with a grim smile.

"It's a loss. I don't think anyone ever gets used to loss."

"When it comes to men, I don't seem to be very smart," Daphne confessed.

"Oh, I wouldn't say that." Muriel nudged the plate of brownies closer to Daphne.

She'd been eating way too many carbs lately. She shouldn't.

Wait a minute. Why not? So what if she'd gained a couple of pounds since coming home to Icicle Falls? Who cared?

She took a brownie and bit off a good-size chunk. "Oh, wow. These didn't come out of a box."

Muriel smiled. "They're my own special recipe. Chocolate—it's one of life's small pleasures."

Small pleasure was better than no pleasure. Daphne took another bite.

Muriel picked up a brownie and examined it. "You know, a lot of life is about starting over."

"I've got that market cornered. But no matter how many times I start over, I can't seem to get it right." Daphne sighed. "I hate being a failure."

"We all fail. It doesn't make us failures. You're only a failure if you quit trying, and I suspect you're a long way from quitting. In fact, I think you have a very good future in store."

"I wish I could believe that."

"You can't judge your future by your past, Daphne. You know, there's a Bible verse I recently discovered. It talks about not calling to mind the things of the past, about God wanting to do something new in you."

Forget the past? How did someone do that? Her past was like a big neon sign flashing Loser.

Muriel studied Daphne for a moment. Then she said, "Would you be willing to do something for me?"

Daphne looked at her suspiciously. "What?" Was Muriel going to suggest she take some self-improvement course, or stand up in the middle of a service at Icicle Falls Community Church and ask everyone to pray her out of loser purgatory? Go on *Dr. Phil* and get psychoanalyzed? Become a marathon runner?

"Start telling yourself, 'From now on, every choice I make will be the best choice for me at this time.'"

Daphne made a face. "I don't know."

"Just try it," Muriel urged. "It'll take the pressure off. Every decision doesn't have to be perfect. It just has to be right for you at that particular moment. You're a kind, intelligent woman, Daphne. I think the only thing stopping you from living a happy life is that you've programmed some wrong information into your brain. It's chipped away at your confidence. A lack of confidence makes us not want to try anymore, and I don't want to see you give up trying, not when you still have so much life to live."

Was Daphne's big problem a lack of confidence?

"What can it hurt?" Muriel asked.

Nothing. Daphne gave an assertive nod. "You're right."

"Everything you've experienced, both good and bad, has taught you things, made you wise. Now you need to draw on that wisdom," Muriel finished with a smile. She offered Daphne the plate of brownies.

Okay, she didn't need to keep self-medicating with carbs. "No, one was enough," Daphne said.

Muriel smiled. "Probably a wise decision."

"It's the best choice for me at this time," Daphne said with a grin.

After finishing up with Muriel, she made another wise decision. She was going to do something positive to celebrate her freedom from the rat of the Western world. She'd buy herself a present.

With this in mind, she made her way to Hearth and Home, one of her favorite shops in Icicle Falls. Daphne had always loved decorating and prettying up her house. Granted, she wouldn't have her house much longer, but she had a room, and she'd find something to put in it to remind her of new beginnings.

The shop wasn't large, but Gigi Babineaux, the owner, had stocked it with lovely things—an eclectic selection of unique and vintage furniture, candles, paintings and statuary.

"Daphne, I heard you were back in town," Gigi said.

Like everyone else, she'd probably heard why. "It's nice to be home."

"You look good."

"I feel good." Daphne was shocked to realize that was no lie. She walked by a gilded mirror and caught herself smiling. This was the day her divorce was final. She shouldn't have been smiling.

Oh, yes, she should. She was done with being miserable and brokenhearted. That was the old Daphne. The new Daphne was truly free to begin again.

Suddenly she saw just the thing to commemorate her new life. She drifted over to an ornate buffet where an amethyst glass vase imprinted with butterflies beckoned. Butterflies. Was there any better symbol of transformation, of new beginnings?

Daphne looked at the price tag. Whoa. Would purchasing this be a wise decision, the best decision she could make in that moment?

Yes, she decided. It would. This was a landmark day, a turning point in her life, and buying the vase would be a good way of reminding herself that she was indeed capable of making wise decisions. No more falling for the wrong man, no more letting neediness or loneliness rush her into a relationship she'd live to regret. She picked up the vase and marched to the cash register.

"I almost took this home myself," Gigi said as she rang up the purchase. "I love butterflies. And fairies."

Gigi herself reminded Daphne of a fairy queen with

her long, white hair and diaphanous blouse worn over her jeans. She was older than Daphne, probably nearing retirement age, a slim, small woman who favored bangles and dangly earrings.

"My divorce was final today," Daphne confided to the fairy queen. "I wanted to get something to mark that I'm starting over."

Gigi approved. "Great choice," she said. "How are you settling in?"

After her shrink sessions with Muriel... "Fine."

Gigi nodded. "Good. It's not fun having to pick up the pieces, but you will. I did. Moved here ten years ago after getting rid of my abusive husband. I've never been happier. Still, it's an adjustment. If you ever want to talk, let me know. I'm always up for a break at Bavarian Brews."

"Thanks. I might take you up on that," Daphne said. She'd take Cass up on her offer to go out for drinks, too. She needed to start hanging out with more people.

Gigi wrapped her purchase in several layers of tissue paper and Daphne went on her way.

But she didn't go home. She wasn't done celebrating yet. The mention of Bavarian Brews made her realize she needed to toast her new beginning.

She'd just picked up a blended coffee drink oozing with caramel and topped with toasted coconut when a male voice rumbled, "Yours looks better than mine."

She knew that deep baritone. The butterflies on the vase she'd purchased migrated to her chest. She glanced over her shoulder to see Hank Hawkins standing behind her with a to-go cup of coffee.

He held it up. "I take mine plain."

She would *not* allow herself to be interested in how

Hank Hawkins took his coffee (or anything else about him), but it would be rude not to make some polite conversation. "I like black coffee now and then, too, but it's more fun when you dress it up. Is this coffee-break time?" she asked, noting his grass-stained jeans and the flannel shirt he wore over a T-shirt. He sure knew how to fill out a T-shirt.

"Yup. How about you?"

"I'm finished working for the day. Just stopped by to celebrate." Or did she mean medicate? No, no, no. She was celebrating. Mitchell and the heartbreak he'd caused were going to be nothing but a distant memory.

"Celebrate the end of work?"

"Nope, the end of my marriage."

He took a step closer. "So, you're a free woman."

She backed up. "Free forever."

"Forever's a long time."

It was getting hot in here. She undid the buttons on her sweater. She noticed him watching, and that made the hot flash hotter. She took a big sip of her cold beverage. "So is being in a bad marriage."

He nodded. "I know what you mean, and I don't blame you for not wanting to try again. I sure didn't want to."

She noticed his use of the past tense but decided not to comment on it.

"But a bad marriage is a little like hitting your thumb with a hammer."

Or your head.

"It hurts like the devil at first, but after a while your thumb recovers and you forget the hurt. Then you're back swinging the hammer again."

"Have you forgotten the hurt?"

He smiled. He had a very sexy smile. It was definitely hot in here. She took another gulp of her drink.

"It's in the past. No sense living there. I'm ready to pick up the hammer again."

She knew what that translated to. He was ready for another relationship. She wasn't. The time would never be right for her. *From now on every choice I make will be the best choice for me...* The best choice she could make right now would probably be to scram.

"Not all men are jerks," Hank said.

"No. Only the ones I'm attracted to."

But Hank Hawkins didn't seem like a jerk at all. He seemed like a nice, trustworthy man.

Looks could be deceiving, Daphne reminded herself. It was time to go. "I'd better get home."

He saluted her with his coffee. "Have a good one."

She would. Her life had no way to go but up. *I'm not going to worry about past mistakes, no matter where I've made them*, she told herself.

Her mother must have seen her coming. She opened the front door for Daphne as she came in bearing her new vase. "How did it go at court?"

"Fine," Daphne said, walking in. "I'm a free woman, and from now on I'm going to make better choices."

Mother gave a satisfied nod. "I know you will, dear. What's that you've got?"

"I'll show you." Daphne started for the back parlor where they did all their living.

"No, no. Show me here."

What on earth was that about? Was her mother getting eccentric in her old age? But Daphne complied, setting down the bag and pulling her vase out of the tissue paper.

"Oh," Mother said, her voice filled with awe. "How lovely."

"It's my divorce present to me," Daphne said.

"Butterflies," Mother said softly. "How appropriate."

"I thought so," Daphne said, pleased that her mother got the symbolism.

"Well, put that away where it won't get knocked over and then come on back to the parlor. I have something for you. It's an early birthday present," Mother added, suddenly looking like a woman who'd just learned where the Easter bunny hid his cache of Cadbury eggs.

Very mysterious. Daphne put her vase on the dresser in her bedroom and went back downstairs to see what her mother was up to. She entered the back parlor to find Mother bent over some kind of animal carrier. "What on earth?"

Mother stood up and turned around. She was holding a black cat.

"That looks like…" No, it couldn't be.

"Milo," Mother said. She walked over to Daphne and placed the cat in her arms. "I know your birthday isn't until later in the month, but I thought you should have him now."

The animal purred and snuggled up against her shoulder. Oh, yes, they were meant to be together. Still, her mother's views on pets had been pretty clear.

"But we don't want animals here." So, was this gift another subtle nudge for Daphne to find her own place? "And you were worried about people with allergies."

"I'm aware of what I said," Roberta said crisply. "But I reconsidered. We'll find a way to work around the allergy problem. Anyway, I think we could use the company around here, don't you?"

Daphne didn't know what to think.

"This is your home, too," she added.

It was such a simple statement but it meant so much. Once more she found herself with tears in her eyes, but these were the best kind of tears, the kind that sprang from a healing heart.

"Thank you," she said, giving her mother a one-armed hug and a kiss on the cheek. Milo seconded her thanks with a loud meow.

"You've had a rough time of it these past few months, but things will get better now. A strong woman can get through anything."

Her mother was testimony to that. She never spoke much about her own mother, but the lack of communication between the two of them had said it all. Roberta Gilbert had single-handedly carved out her successful life here in Icicle Falls.

Daphne wasn't her mother, and yet she must have inherited that independence gene. All she had to do was find it. And she would, because from now on she was making wise choices, the right choices—for her.

Nineteen

Anne, Queen of Disaster Relief

Outdoor weddings were lovely…as long as it didn't rain. Anne looked at the cloudy sky covering Lake Washington like a dome of doom and sighed. It had been sunny all day and Anne had begun to hope that the weatherman was wrong. Why couldn't the rain have held off a little longer? She'd reminded the bride and her mother that end of April was not a good choice for cooperative weather. In Seattle anything before the Fourth of July was a risk.

But Felicity had her heart set on an outdoor wedding, and her mother, Trina, had her heart set on giving Felicity anything she wanted. "She's my only baby," Trina had said. "I want her to be happy."

Anne could understand that. Although she did encourage the bride to have a plan B.

"It won't rain," Felicity had said blithely.

"If it does, I guess we'll have to squeeze into the basement," her mother had said with a helpless shrug.

Later she'd confided to Anne. "I don't know how we'll fit everyone in the house."

"That's something to consider," Anne had responded diplomatically.

Mother and daughter did consider it, and the bride-to-be stuck to her plan for an outdoor wedding. They cut the guest list, but not enough, since even after that her mother worried about where they'd put everyone.

Planning the event had been easy. Both mother and daughter had been delighted with all of Anne's ideas, making it a snap to take care of ordering the cake and flowers and finding the DJ and caterer, renting the chairs and the tent and the dishes and linens. Now all sat in readiness waiting for the bridal party to finish with photos in the garden and on the dock.

Anne blinked as something wet hit her in the eye. This was followed by another something wet splashing her cheek. Oh, no. Here came the rain.

The photographer was finishing up, and Felicity and her groom and their posse began horsing around on the dock, the guys pretending to push the girls off and the girls squealing in mock horror. Ah, the energy of youth. They seemed oblivious of the darkening gray clouds and the spatter.

The mother of the bride wasn't, though. She hurried over to Anne, her face a study in motherly concern. "Oh, Anne, you were right. This was a bad idea. I wish I'd never let Felicity talk me into this."

Anne was never one for I-told-you-so. "What would you like to do?"

"Felicity will want to wait and see if this blows over."

Maybe it would, but not in time for the wedding to take place outdoors. They'd have to move the ceremony inside. Anne looked over to where Felicity stood on the dock, laughing. A speedboat decorated with flowers bobbed next to it, ready for the father of the bride to motor the couple to an undisclosed wedding-night location. She felt sorry for Felicity and her mom. They'd taken a gamble and lost.

Trina shook her head. "She wanted an outdoor wedding so badly, and she wanted it this weekend."

Anne knew why. Trina had told her. Felicity had wanted to honor her older sister, who had died in April twelve years earlier from childhood leukemia. Later in the evening the wedding party planned to toss their flowers on the lake in honor of her.

When Anne had brought up concerns about the weather, Felicity had insisted that the day she'd picked would be sunny. It had to be. The universe couldn't be that cruel.

It had been all Anne could do not to say, "Oh, yes, it can. In fact, the universe doesn't care two figs about you or any of us."

1997

Anne burrowed under her blankets on the couch and turned up the TV, ignoring the ringing phone. She knew it would be her mom calling to check up on her, but she didn't want to talk to anyone, not even Mom. All she wanted to do was stay here forever watching soaps on TV and feeling sorry for herself. She'd been doing a pretty good job of it, too. So far, forever had lasted three months. She barely cleaned; she served sandwiches and canned chili for dinner, and let her business slide, leaving Kendra, who'd only recently come on board, scrambling.

"We can try again," Cam had said after her first miscarriage, holding her in his arms and kissing the top of her head.

But now she was convinced it didn't matter how many times they tried. They were never going to have another baby.

"It's a blessing in disguise," her grandmother had said after each miscarriage. "Something must've been wrong with the baby. This is nature's way of telling you to start again."

No, it was nature's way of taunting her. She'd always thought they'd have at least two children, maybe three, or even four. She'd longed to hear the thunder of feet as her children raced up and down the stairs, longed to hear giggles and see sisters and brothers playing together in the backyard. She felt cheated and angry, and she felt especially angry at God. This was her third miscarriage. How could He let this happen?

"How is it that any bad thing happens?" her mother had responded earlier in the week when Anne was venting her anger. "There are no guarantees in this world. You know that. All we can do is enjoy the good things that come our way and accept the bad."

Well, Anne didn't want to accept the bad. Her arms ached to hold the little one who'd tried so hard to hang on inside her. She felt the loss as surely as if she'd carried the baby to term. Now she was in deep mourning, her husband and daughter mere figures, blurred and moving at the dark edges of her grief.

The phone rang again. She turned the volume on the TV even higher.

Later in the day she was still on the couch when her mom let herself in with the spare key Anne and Cam kept under the flowerpot out front. "I don't want to see anyone," Anne greeted her and burrowed deeper under her blankets.

"I know." Her mother sat down on the opposite end of the couch, settling Anne's feet in her lap and starting a foot massage.

"It's not fair," Anne said bitterly.

"I know. But you still have a living daughter."

Anne pulled her foot away. "What's that supposed to mean?"

Her mother calmly took back her foot and resumed rubbing. "I'm only agreeing with you."

"No, you're not. You're trying to teach me a lesson."

Julia smiled. "Things always had to be fair when you were growing up. I had to make sure you and your sister both got the exact same number of cookies for your after-school snack, the exact same number of gifts at Christmas. And, oh, the complaints when she was allowed to stay up as late as you on special occasions."

"I don't know where you're going with this."

"Going? I'm simply agreeing with you. It's *not* fair. It's not fair that you still have a healthy, happy child when so many women all over the world wind up with none. Come to think of it, it's not fair that you have such a kind, loving husband who's always there for you. Or such a nice house. And plenty of food on the table."

"Now you're going to lay a guilt trip on me for feeling the way I do?" Anne demanded, incredulous.

Julia stopped the foot rub. "No, sweetie. Remember, I had a miscarriage between you and Kendra and it broke my heart. But I couldn't stay brokenhearted forever. I still had a child who needed me. And after losing the baby, well, you became even more precious."

Anne had been too wrapped up in her grief to remember what she still had.

"I'm not saying you shouldn't mourn this loss," her mom continued. "All those hopes and dreams, gone, the little one finished before even getting a chance at life. It's horrible. But at some point you have to go on. You can't lie on this couch forever. And you can't let yourself become bitter. It's not fair to your husband and the child you have."

Anne chewed her lip, taking that in and yet wishing she didn't have to.

"You still have so much to be thankful for," Julia said gently.

"I don't want to be thankful, damn it!" This was followed by a storm of tears and a maternal shoulder to cry on. And hugs. And a quiet prayer together.

An hour later, Anne got up and made a real dinner for her family for the first time in three months.

Dinner wasn't all she made. She made an attitude adjustment, too. She reentered life with a vengeance. She and Cam took tango lessons and started scheduling a monthly date night.

On their first night out, as they sat in a little Italian restaurant in lower Queen Anne, enjoying pizza and Chianti, she thanked him for being so patient and understanding. "I know you always wanted to have more kids."

"But I've got you and Laney, and I'm okay with that, Annie. In fact, I'm more than okay. I think I'm a pretty lucky guy."

"And I'm a lucky woman," she said.

He raised his glass to her. "We've got a lot to be thankful for, babe."

Yes, they did, she thought as they clinked glasses. Cam and her mother were right. In spite of what she'd lost, she could still be thankful for what she had.

Now the wind had arrived, whipping the water on Lake Washington into whitecaps and tearing at the pretty white tent. While the groom and his grooms-men carried chairs into the basement, Anne, the bride and her mother and aunt all went into a wedding huddle.

The bride began to cry, her eyeliner running. "I can't believe this! Where are we going to put everyone?"

"We'll make it work," Anne promised her. The basement was roomy and finished and had a fireplace, perfect for a floral arrangement. The bride and groom could take their vows in front of it. They'd have to forgo the tables and squeeze chairs along the walls. A number of guests would have to stand, and in the interests of squeezing everyone in, the bride would have to don a raincoat and make her entrance via the patio door.

"Good idea," said the aunt after Anne had shared her ideas. "We can do this."

"Go fix your makeup," Trina said. "We'll take care of everything."

And they did. With Anne supervising, everyone got busy preparing for plan B. The bride patched up her makeup and found her smile again, even as the rain beat on the windows.

The guests came and the basement got hot with all the bodies in it. So hot, in fact, that the bride fainted just before saying, "I do." Father fretted while the groom carried her to the nearest chair, and a friend of the family who happened to be a doctor helped revive her. A door was opened and a gust of wind blew in, along with a neighbor's dog, who insisted on greeting one of the guests with his muddy paws. In spite of all that, the bride and groom finished their vows and the guests enjoyed their salmon, getting their food from the upstairs kitchen and spreading throughout the house to eat with their plates on their laps.

As the evening continued, the wind blew away the clouds and the night cleared up enough for dancing on the soppy lawn and, most important, for the bride and her bridesmaids and the groom and his groomsmen to cast their flowers on the water in memory of the bride's sister.

"For a while there I wasn't sure I'd be able to say this," Trina said to Anne, "but it was a wonderful wedding."

"Your daughter's a wonderful girl."

They turned to watch as, in the middle of the lawn, the groom spun his new bride in a circle, both of them laughing.

Bride and groom happy, mother of the bride happy—mission accomplished.

Twenty

Laney the Tour Guide

"I was thinking we should get together on Saturday after you're done with work and wrap up a few more things for the wedding," Mom said.

Laney found herself suddenly clenching her cell phone and walking faster on the treadmill at the gym. "I forgot to tell you. Drake and I are going up to Icicle Falls this weekend."

Normally, she would've told her mother. She told her mother practically everything and they talked every day. But lately all they talked about was the wedding, and she was tired of talking about the wedding.

What was wrong with her? What kind of daughter didn't want to talk with her mother about her wedding?

If only Mom wasn't acting quite so…in charge. It had taken a fight in the middle of the stupid bridal shop for Laney to get the gown she wanted. Of course they'd made up, but things hadn't felt quite the same since. Autumn's words kept sneaking back into her mind every time Mom called to go over stuff. *"It's your wedding.*

Who's in control?" Sometimes it didn't feel as though she was at all.

Not that her mom didn't ask what she wanted or what she thought. She did. But then when Laney told her, Mom seemed to find a way to shoot it down or change her mind.

And poor Drake—he'd really been left out. It seemed as if somehow things got decided and were a done deal before he even heard about them. That wasn't right. A lot of guys couldn't care less, but he wanted to be involved.

Well, this weekend he would be. It would be their time together. They'd check out the river, go dancing and, if the weather cooperated, get in a little rock climbing on Sunday before coming back to Seattle.

"That's a good idea," Mom said, bringing Laney back to the moment. "I'm sure Drake will love it up there."

Laney hoped so. It was his wedding, too, and she wanted him to be excited about it. Actually, she wanted them both to be excited about it.

She *was* excited. Yes, she was!

"We can do more next week," Mom said. "We need to get out those save-the-date cards."

"I already sent them out," Laney said. Her mom had almost made her crazy pushing to get those done. She hadn't been this much of a slave driver since back in Laney's junior year of high school, when Laney was applying at colleges. *"It's your wedding. Who's in control?"*

"And now people will be expecting invitations. You know they should go out two months in advance. We don't want to wait too long."

Everyone already had the date on their calendar, so Laney didn't see what the big deal was, but she said, "Don't worry, Mom." She shouldn't be dragging her feet like this. She should just sit down and do it. And she would. Next week. Or…when she had time. "I gotta finish my workout, Mom."

"Oh. Well. Okay."

They said their I-love-yous and then ended the call. Laney turned off her cell phone and upped the speed on the treadmill. She and Drake were going to have fun this weekend. He'd love Icicle Falls. Everything would get done and her wedding would be perfect. And she'd never been happier in her life.

She reminded herself again how happy she was once she and Drake were in his truck and on their way up the mountains to Icicle Falls. There were still some patches of snow on the ground but the evergreens were in their full glory. The sun was the center of attention in a cloudless, blue sky. In short, it was a beautiful day to be heading for the mountains.

She'd taken the day off, so they'd left at nine, which put them in Icicle Falls in time to have lunch at a burger place called Herman's Hamburgers. They passed by a life-size wooden figure of a woman in a traditional German dirndl as they entered. She was holding a platter bearing a hamburger. The little sign hanging from her neck said Willkommen in Herman's.

"Okay, what's with that?" Drake asked.

"It goes with the theme," Laney explained. "You know, it's supposed to look like a Bavarian village up here. That's what Mom says."

"Whatever."

He might have been unimpressed with the German

theme of Herman's but he loved the burgers and garlic fries. After that they moved on to Gerhardt's Gasthaus, where Laney had found a bargain. This time they encountered real people wearing dirndls and lederhosen.

"Weird," Drake said under his breath.

The lobby was all dark wood and carved wooden chandeliers with lights made to look like candles. A mounted deer's head hung on one wall, watching them with glassy eyes. Another wall bore a coat of arms with a lion on it. Stepping into their room was like going back in time, with old furniture and some ornate wooden…things that reminded Laney of *The Lion, the Witch and the Wardrobe.*

"Where's the closet?" Drake asked.

"I think this is it." Laney opened the doors on the thing and found a rack and hangers. "Yep."

He came to stand behind her. "You don't see that at Motel 6."

"It's kind of cool."

"I guess." It wasn't hard to tell from his tone of voice that he didn't agree with her. "Let's get out of here."

On their way out, they poked their heads into the little bar, taking in the huge wine casks and the decorative steins on the wall. Two old guys sat on bar stools, talking to another old guy who was pulling beer from the tap. "A real hot place," he observed.

"We're not gonna be here tonight," Laney assured him. "There's dancing at the Red Barn."

"The Red Barn? I'm guessing they don't do rap there."

"Uh, country?"

"Yee-haw," he mocked.

"I've heard it's a fun place."

"There's gotta be someplace here that is," Drake said.

They made their way down the main street through the throng of tourists, watching the goings-on at the center of town. The aroma of sizzling bratwurst drifted over to them from the hot-dog place farther down the street, mixed with the tempting smells of waffle cones from the nearby ice cream and candy shop. A German oompah band was set up in the gazebo, playing accordions and yodeling, and in the middle of the street a gigantic maypole had been erected. Performers in traditional German costumes danced around it, wrapping it in colorful ribbons.

"Seriously weird," Drake muttered as they passed.

"I saw this online," Laney said. "It's to celebrate May Day."

"I thought that's what people say in airplanes when they're gonna crash," he joked, eyeing the dancers as if they were some strange species. "I guess."

So far he wasn't exactly in love with the town. She shouldn't have let her mother talk her into getting married in Icicle Falls.

Mom didn't talk you into this, she told herself. *You decided you wanted to get married on the river.* And wait till Drake saw the river. Once they got down to the Wenatchee, heard the whoosh of water speeding past and saw the swirling, white eddies crashing around the boulders, his smile grew. Visiting Adventure Outfitters was like going to guy playland. They had kayaks stacked outside the building, river rafts and giant inner tubes down by the river, and inside she and Drake found all manner of outdoor sports equipment and toys.

"Oh, yeah," Drake said with an appreciative smile. "That's what I'm talking about."

There was only one person in the store, and he was pulling life jackets out of shipping boxes and stacking them on a display table. He was older than them, maybe toward the end of his thirties, dressed in jeans and a flannel shirt. His hair was long and shaggy, and he was already getting some wrinkles, probably from spending too much time on the river.

He gave them a friendly nod. "Hi, there."

"Cool stuff," Drake said, gesturing around him.

"We try. You interested in booking a river rafting trip?"

"Actually, we came to talk about booking a raft for June," Laney said.

"Smart to do that now," said the guy. "June is a high-demand month."

"We want to get married on one," she explained.

"Serious?"

"Serious."

"Hey, Mick, come on out here!" he called. He thrust a calloused hand at Drake and then Laney. "I'm Darrell."

A man who looked her grandpa's age emerged from a back room. He was tall and skinny and he had dark hair shot with gray. Judging from the salt-and-pepper stubble on his chin he hadn't bothered to shave that morning.

"These guys want to get married on one of our rafts," Darrell told him.

The old man nodded. "Never had anybody get married on a raft before." He rubbed his grizzled chin, contemplating. "You wanna go down the river on it afterward?"

"Sure," they both said.

"Well, come on down and I'll show you what we've got."

The rafts were definitely rustic. Laney could almost

see her mother cringing. But they could fix one up with flowers and it would look great. Anyway, it would be fun to shove off on the raft after the ceremony, better than a horse-drawn carriage. They could meet everyone at the reception after.

Details were discussed, and Drake laid down a deposit, and then it was time to visit Primrose Haus.

He wasn't quite so enthusiastic about that. "It's kind of old-lady looking," he said as they pulled up in front of it.

"It's a Victorian. It's supposed to look old," Laney said, and suddenly she was aware of the garlic fries gurgling around in her tummy.

"Hey, I'm okay with it," he said. "It's just, well, it's not Vegas."

She sighed. "You're right." Obviously, he was still stuck on Las Vegas.

"It's not too late to change your mind, you know," he said.

Yes, it was. "This will be great," she insisted.

"Which one of us are you trying to convince?"

"I don't need convincing," she said and rang the doorbell. Nobody came. "That's strange. There are cars out here." One of them was a PT Cruiser with a gingerbread boy and girl painted on the panel, along with the words Gingerbread Haus, the bakery that was going to do her cakes.

She rang the doorbell again. A moment later the door was opened by Daphne, one of the women she'd met when she came up with her mother. She was somewhere around Mom's age, a little bigger in the butt and boobs but really pretty with perfectly highlighted hair and perfect makeup. She reminded Laney of those older models you sometimes saw on the cover of *People* with headlines like She's Turning Fifty and Still Turning Heads.

The woman gave her the kind of friendly uncertain smile people used when they were sure they should know you but couldn't remember who you were.

Laney introduced herself. "Hi, I'm Laney. My mom and I were up here last month. June wedding."

"Oh, of course, and this must be your groom."

"This is him," Laney said, hugging Drake's arm.

Drake reached out and shook her hand. "Hi, I'm Drake."

"I'm Daphne. Come on in."

"I thought maybe I could show Drake around," Laney said.

"Oh, sure. We're setting up for a wedding this evening, so things are a little crazy, but I'd be glad to give you the tour," Daphne told her.

"Super. Thanks," Laney said and followed her inside. Behind her she was aware of Drake looking around, and she began to see the decor through his eyes. Fussy girl-stuff like you might find in a museum or on an episode of her mom's favorite show, *Downton Abbey*. Laney had liked it when she and Mom came up, but now she couldn't help wondering how comfortable her groom and his friends were going to be here.

"This is where we usually have our receptions before the nice summer weather hits," Daphne said, opening a pocket door and showing them a huge room with a crystal chandelier. Fancy chairs were scattered around the room, and there was a fireplace with a marble mantel at one end.

A table clad in white linen and edged with flowers had been set up in another corner, and the older lady

Laney and her mom had met earlier was helping the woman who owned the bakery set up a wedding cake on it.

"It's like a castle," Drake said, and Laney wasn't sure whether or not he meant that as a compliment.

Their voices echoed across the room, catching the older woman's attention. She smiled and made her way over to them. "Well, hello. I do believe this is one of our brides."

"It's Laney," said Daphne. "And Duke."

"Drake," Drake corrected her, and she blushed.

"Of course. Drake. Great name."

"Thanks," he said in a tone of voice that asked if it was so great why didn't she remember it.

"Let me show you the grounds," Daphne said next and led them outdoors.

It was too early for much of anything other than the primroses to be in bloom; even so, the grounds were impressive, with statues and a fishpond and that rose arbor Mom had wanted them to get married under. The rose arbor would be nice once it had flowers blooming but Laney preferred something more exciting.

Like a *Pirates of the Caribbean*–style ship.

No, like a raft on the river. "By summer it'll be gorgeous out here," Daphne said, "with the lavender and honeysuckle and the lilies and peonies."

Drake didn't say anything, so Laney filled in the empty conversational space. "It's really pretty."

"The whole house is," Daphne said with a smile. "My mother's held a lot of weddings here, including mine." Her lips slid down at the corners. "And my daughter's," she added, bringing the smile back full-force.

Her wedding must not have turned out so well. Laney sneaked a look at her left hand. No ring. That sucked.

That won't ever be Drake and me, she told herself. They'd been together long enough to feel confident it would last. He was kind and fun. He knew that she was grumpy in the morning, that she could get pissy when she was PMSing and that she wasn't very good with money. And he loved her anyway. He knew what turned her on and what turned her off. And she knew what turned him on. (Anything!) She'd learned that he was easygoing but also anal about saving money, and they'd already talked about having a budget when they got married. Ick. But it was probably a good idea because he wanted to budget for big things, like cross-country camping trips and a house. And if it made him happy, then she was willing to write down how much money she spent at her favorite clothing consignment shop. Right now he was trying to act all chill, but she could tell he wasn't excited about having their reception here. "You don't like it," she said once they were back in the truck.

"It's okay."

"Just okay?" How could they have the reception here if he didn't like the place?

"I don't think that house is really us."

What *was* really them? Tents and log cabins and houses with modern colored-glass lights hanging from the ceilings. Old leather furniture and flea-market coffee tables.

And mountains and rivers. "Did you like the idea of the raft?"

"Oh, yeah!" He turned to face her and pulled her to him. "Hey, if you want to get married up here and have the reception at that house, then that's what we'll do. I want you to be happy."

"I want you to be happy, too."

"You know what—you're the bride and it's more important for you to be happy." It was such a Drake thing to say.

She hadn't sent out the wedding invitations yet. Like he'd said, it wasn't too late to change her mind. Two different images battled there—one of her stepping off a raft in her beautiful dress and coming to a big reception with all her friends and family at the fancy Victorian, the other of her and Drake in Vegas. The two of them, their parents and a couple of friends, no one to clap when they walked down the aisle or dance at their reception or blow bubbles as they ran for their car. But there would be glitz and glamour and excitement. She gnawed on her lower lip.

"Hey," he said, touching his forehead to hers. "If this is what you want, this is what we'll do."

It *was* what she wanted, what she'd always wanted. She'd gotten sidetracked with the idea of going off to Vegas and getting married on the Treasure Island wedding ship. But this was the wedding she'd dreamed of when she was a little girl. Mom was right. If she abandoned that vision, she'd be sorry.

Still, she didn't want Drake to have any regrets, either. She gave him one last chance. "Are you sure?"

"I'm sure. I love you, babe. I want our wedding to be your dream come true."

How had she lucked out, finding such a great guy? She thanked him and kissed him, then said, "Okay, let's do it."

With the issue finally settled, they went on to enjoy

the amenities of Icicle Falls, eating dinner at Zelda's, one of the town's most popular restaurants, going dancing at the Red Barn and learning how to two-step. Although Drake had poked fun at country music, he'd enjoyed himself and even talked about getting a cowboy shirt, which made Laney laugh.

"Yeah, gauges and cowboy shirts really go together," she teased.

"They could," Drake insisted. "Why not?"

That was Drake, always full of crazy ideas. Was getting married on a raft going to be enough for him?

Twenty-One

Roberta, Letting Go

Mayor Del Stone dropped by on Monday to discuss his daughter's wedding, armed with a last-minute to-do list from his ex-wife in Oregon. "Mandy wanted me to check on a few things," he said as they sat down in Roberta's parlor with coffee and raspberry coffee cake. (Del never turned down a treat and he had the girth to prove it.) "She said she sent you an email yesterday, but hadn't heard back."

Roberta checked her emails twice a day. "I didn't see anything." Of course, Del's wife had sent her so many over the past few weeks she wouldn't have been surprised if one had fallen through the cracks.

"She changed the recipe for the nonalcoholic punch." He handed over a piece of paper with a recipe printed on it.

That had been in a previous email, and Roberta already had it in the Stone-Woodhouse file. "Yes, I've got that," she said politely.

He nodded and consulted his list. "My daughter

changed her mind about the flowers. She wants star-gazer lilies and…" He squinted. "Stepha—"

"Stephanotis," Roberta supplied.

"That's it." He beamed as if he was a teacher and she an exceptionally bright student.

"Stephanotis symbolizes marital happiness." Daphne had carried it in her bridal bouquet at her third wedding. Obviously, it took more than flowers.

"Anyway, can you let Heinrich know?"

"Certainly."

"Mandy wants to make sure we can all get here for pictures at two instead of three. She thinks three will be cutting it too close."

"That's fine," Roberta said.

"And she wants to make sure all the decorating will be done by then."

"That won't be a problem."

"Okay, what else?" He consulted his list. "Oh, and you're ordering an extra case of champagne, right?"

"Yes, Del, that's been done."

He nodded, looking the slightest bit sheepish. "Mandy is a perfectionist. I tried to tell her you've got everything under control, but she doesn't listen to me."

Roberta could understand why. Del was something of a blowhard and it wasn't worth listening to two-thirds of what he said. And, if you asked Roberta, he wasn't the most competent mayor the town had ever had. If he was, the potholes on Pine Street would've been fixed by now.

Still, he'd managed to glad-hand enough people to get himself reelected. And his daughter's wedding was going to be the social event of the season. Every member of the Icicle Falls Chamber of Commerce had been invited as well as the mayor of Portland, all the Icicle

Falls town councillors and even a state representative. This was definitely an important wedding.

"Del, you know you're in good hands with us. No need to worry."

At least, she hoped not. Her bunion surgery was scheduled for Wednesday and there was no way she'd be up and around by the wedding. But Lila would be covering for her. Daphne was going to help, too.

Daphne. Was she ready for prime time?

Roberta thought back to the mishaps that had occurred since her daughter had come aboard the *SS Wedding Special*. She'd better postpone her surgery. Daphne wasn't hopeless, of course, but if she was going to be helping with the business as she kept insisting, she needed a few more weddings under her belt before taking on one of this magnitude.

Roberta assured Del again that everything would go smoothly and, after one more serving of coffee cake, showed him to the door. Then she got on the phone to the surgeon's office, informing the receptionist she'd like to postpone her surgery.

Wouldn't you know? Daphne picked that very moment to come home. "What are you doing?" she demanded as she set a bag of groceries on the kitchen counter.

"Let me call you back," Roberta said and ended the call. She felt like a child caught doing something naughty, which was ridiculous.

"Why are you canceling your surgery?" Daphne asked. "You've been waiting to get this done for a month."

"I don't think this is a good time."

"Why on earth not?"

Here was where it got sticky. How did she tell her daughter she didn't trust her not to make a mess of this wedding without sounding as if she didn't trust her? "There's simply too much going on."

Daphne's big blue eyes narrowed. "I saw Mayor Stone driving away just now. Was he here talking about the wedding?"

"Er, yes."

"You don't think Lila and I can handle this alone."

"It's an important wedding, Daphne. I think I should be there."

Daphne sighed in disgust. "Mother, we can handle this."

She would have Lila there, and Lila was the soul of efficiency. But if Daphne happened to spill appetizers on the mayor's daughter...

"I promise not to go anywhere near the bride with food," Daphne said, reading her mind. "Or anyone else, for that matter. I'll stay in the kitchen and help the caterers plate the dinner. And I won't go near the cake," she added, managing to smile at her mishap.

Roberta could smile now, too, although at the time she hadn't been smiling. They'd had to call Cass and make a slapdash substitution. But Cass had pulled it off. Besides, anyone could trip. Although Roberta never had.

"Mother, you need this surgery. There'll never be a convenient time. You'll always have weddings booked and each one will be important."

But probably not as important as this one.

"I know it's hard to delegate, but if you could bring yourself to trust me, I promise it'll all be fine. Everything's already ordered and organized. What could go wrong?"

Any one of a hundred things. However, Daphne was right. It wasn't easy to get in with the surgeon Roberta had scheduled. If she gave up this date, she'd probably be sorry.

"You can't do everything yourself," Daphne said gently. "It's not good business. That's why people have assistants."

"All right," Roberta said. "I'll let you girls handle it."

"Good." Daphne's tone of voice implied that it was about time Roberta came to her senses.

As if Roberta had no grounds for concern. Well, then, let Daphne demonstrate her efficiency. "You can start by checking with Ed York to make sure he got my message about ordering another case of champagne."

Daphne already had her phone out and was typing on it. "Done," she said a moment later.

The quickness of it made Roberta blink. "And I'll need you to go over to Lupine Floral and see what they can give us that incorporates stargazer lilies and stephanotis instead of roses."

"I can do that."

Wait a minute. What was she thinking? She could do this herself. "On second thought, I'll look after the flowers."

"Mother," Daphne said sternly. "I can go over there. You must have other things to do."

Actually, she did. She had a pile of paperwork waiting for her and several calls to make.

"Trust me," Daphne urged.

"All right. I do have several other things I need to take care of today."

"Then take care of them. I've got this covered," Daphne said. She kissed Roberta on the cheek and then went back to putting away groceries.

"Thank you, darling," Roberta said.

As she went to her little office, she reassured herself that Daphne could indeed handle this, then tried not to think about how she'd neglected to order the invitations for her own daughter's wedding on time.

That was then. This is now, she told herself. Her daughter had emerged from her latest romantic rough patch and had her wits about her once more. All would be well.

But maybe Roberta should still postpone that surgery.

In the end, Roberta had her surgery on the original date. Daphne drove her over the mountains to Virginia Mason in Seattle and brought her home again, where she did an excellent job of caring for Roberta, as well as keeping the house running smoothly. They set Roberta up in the back parlor on the sofa with her foot propped on pillows (and Milo to keep her company) so she wouldn't have to use the stairs.

"I'll be happy to bring food up to you," Daphne had offered, but Roberta had nixed the idea.

"I'd feel too isolated stuck up there." She didn't want to feel so cut off from what was going on in the rest of the house. And she wanted to be within hearing distance when Daphne was on the phone, handling last-minute wedding details.

This arrangement created almost as much work for her daughter as if they'd ensconced Roberta in her room, but Daphne never complained about having to run up and down stairs fetching fresh clothes, toiletry items or whatever book Roberta wanted. Could a mother ask for a better daughter?

And Daphne was certainly proving to be helpful, especially in the kitchen, Roberta thought as she enjoyed a shrimp salad Daphne had made for lunch. Maybe it wasn't such a bad idea having her daughter live with her. For the most part they'd settled into a comfortable routine and were getting along quite well. Maybe having her more involved with the business wasn't a bad idea, either. Perhaps someday she could take over. Perhaps now Daphne would, at last, come into her own and shine. Yes, Roberta should have suggested this long ago, groomed her daughter from the start. Or at least after her second divorce.

Well, it wasn't too late. Daphne could learn the ropes now. Roberta smiled at the pleasant vision of Daphne becoming one of the town's movers and shakers, working with the chamber of commerce, helping plan festivals. Even running for mayor someday. There was so much she could do if she'd develop a little more confidence in herself.

The girl could succeed if she had a mind to. All she needed was some motherly assistance, which Roberta was happy to offer every time the phone rang.

"Mother!" Daphne said after Roberta had insisted on talking to a woman who called about having a fall wedding at Primrose Haus. "I'm perfectly capable of answering questions about price and availability."

"Of course you are," Roberta agreed, "but I'm not helpless here. I don't want to sit around like a lump watching TV all day." Her foot was beginning to hurt and she popped another pain pill. And she was getting sleepy. The surgery had really taken it out of her. She needed a nap. "I think I'll shut my eyes for a few minutes, though. I know you'll see to everything while I do."

"Good idea," Daphne said, placated. She kissed Roberta on the forehead. "Have a good rest. I'll take care of everything."

And she did.

So when the day of the mayor's daughter's wedding came, Roberta wasn't the least bit worried. Lila had things well in hand, and Daphne had sworn that every detail had been attended to, including shutting Milo in her room so he wouldn't get underfoot.

That didn't stop Roberta from putting on the special boot the doctor had prescribed for her and hobbling out to the reception room to see how things were coming along. Daphne had run to the store to pick up some Sweet Dreams chocolates (a last-minute request by Del), and Heinrich, the creative genius from Lupine Floral, had arrived himself to fuss with the flowers rather than leaving it to his partner, Kevin. In addition to the bridal bouquet and boutonnieres, he'd made small elegant arrangements for the tables, a larger one for the bridal party's table and two for the front parlor. They were all exquisite concoctions of greens, baby's breath and...roses. With not a single stargazer lily to be seen. And where was the stephanotis? What had gone wrong?

Daphne was supposed to have dealt with this. One quick visit to the florist—that was all she had to do. Roberta could feel her blood pressure rising like a jet taking off from the runway.

She looked at her wristwatch. It was edging toward

noon. The bridal party would be showing up for pictures at two. Oh, dear.

She hobbled over to Heinrich as fast as she could. "Heinrich, these are beautiful," she began.

He beamed, obviously pleased with the compliment.

"But where are the stargazer lilies and the stephanotis?"

He stared at her, befuddled. "Lilies?"

"Yes. The bride changed her mind and wanted lilies instead of roses. Daphne was supposed to let you know."

Heinrich went from befuddled to horrified, placing a hand to his chest as if he was about to have a heart attack. "This is the first I've heard of it."

Roberta was sure *she* was going to have a heart attack. "The bridal party will be here at two. Can you fix these before then?"

He frowned. "That's like asking Michelangelo to hurry up and finish *David*."

Oh, great. Of all times for Heinrich to remember he was an artiste.

He also remembered he was a businessman. "But for you I'll move heaven and earth." He picked up the huge arrangement from the buffet table, obscuring his entire head from view. "I'll take these back to the shop and fix them."

"Of course I'll pay for the flowers you've already used," Roberta said. She'd have to eat the cost; there was no getting around it.

"I wouldn't dream of it."

"No," she said adamantly. "The one who makes the mistake should be the one to pay." And sadly, that one was her. Or rather, her daughter. Honestly, if she couldn't count on Daphne to do this, how could she count on her to take more responsibility for the business?

This was why her daughter had never climbed the ladder of success, Roberta thought as her blood pressure continued to soar through the clouds and into the upper stratosphere. Daphne was incompetent. Sweet and well-intentioned but incompetent. And this was the last wedding she was going to help with. Ever.

She was hobbling out of the room when the culprit came home, bearing two pink shopping bags filled with boxes of Sweet Dreams chocolates. Roberta's displeasure must have sat like a billboard on her face because Daphne's brows knit and she asked, "What's wrong?"

"The flowers," Roberta said through gritted teeth.

Daphne looked around in surprise. "They're not here yet."

"They were here. They were here wrong."

"I don't understand."

"The lilies," Roberta said, her voice rising. "Heinrich had no idea he was supposed to substitute them for the roses. And there was no stephanotis, either."

"How can that be?"

There was only one explanation. "Daphne, you obviously forgot to contact Lupine Floral."

Daphne shook her head. Emphatically. "No. I didn't."

"Well, they weren't in the arrangements," Roberta said testily. It wasn't going to do any good to stand here and argue with her daughter. She started to hobble off.

"Mother, I did go over there."

"Never mind. It's been taken care of." But this was the end of Daphne helping. Every time she "helped," it was not helpful.

"You don't believe me."

The hurt and accusation in her daughter's voice were like fingernails on a chalkboard. *Don't say anything you'll regret!* Roberta took a deep breath and turned around. "Darling, I'm sure you meant to call or drop by. I do that, too, think I've done something when I haven't gotten around to it."

"No." Daphne frowned. "I went over there and talked to Kevin. I'm not completely incompetent, you know."

"Of course you're not." Roberta wished she'd postponed her bunion surgery. "Anyway, as I said, it's all taken care of now." So there was no need to be upset or to fuss at her daughter. But there was certainly cause to wonder what else would go wrong at this wedding.

"I'm glad it is." Daphne's voice was as cold as the Wenatchee River during spring runoff. "But it should never have been a problem in the first place."

Oh, no. She wasn't going to get the last word. "Why can't you just admit you made a mistake?"

"Because I didn't! And why do you always have to believe the worst of me?"

"Oh, Daphne. I do not."

"Yes, you do. And I'm tired of it." With that, Daphne marched full steam ahead into the kitchen to arrange the chocolates on tiered china serving dishes.

Roberta fell onto the nearest chair, exhausted, unhappy and irritated. Really, at her age she shouldn't have to cope with disagreements and emotional undercurrents. She shouldn't have to walk on eggshells, worrying about hurting her daughter's feelings. Life had been so much simpler before Daphne and all her drama had returned to Icicle Falls.

Was Daphne right? Did Roberta always believe the worst of her? Wanting to help her daughter improve

A Wedding on Primrose Street

her life didn't mean Roberta saw her as a *complete* failure. She'd been a wonderful mother. Marnie was well-
adjusted, happy, successful, and Daphne could take all
the credit for that. In addition to raising a lovely daughter, she'd held down the same job for years. She'd been
a responsible adult with no addictions or bad habits.
Well, except the habit of making poor choices when it
came to men. Of course, Roberta was in no position to
throw stones, not from her glass house.

Still, it was a mother's job to advise her daughter.
And once in a while, when the daughter had fumbled a
simple task, a mother should be allowed to feel a little
frustration without said daughter climbing on her high
horse. Especially since that daughter had fumbled more
than one simple task here at Primrose Haus. But, oh,
no. Here she was, once again, the cruel, wicked mother,
making her daughter's life miserable.

Darn it all, Daphne drove her crazy.

Roberta continued to stew in her emotional juices
for several minutes. Then she hobbled past the kitchen,
where the atmosphere was decidedly frosty, to the back
parlor sofa. She'd barely gotten settled when the phone
sitting on the TV tray next to her started to ring. The
last thing she wanted was to talk to anyone, so she ignored it. She wished she could ignore the fact that her
daughter was in the next room, hurt and angry.

Daphne picked up the kitchen extension. Roberta
could hear her talking. "Hello, Heinrich. Yes," Daphne
said, her voice softening. "No, no problem. It could
happen to anyone. But would you mind explaining to
my mother?"

A moment later she was standing next to Roberta,

holding out the phone. "Talk to Heinrich," she said brusquely.

"I don't want to talk to anyone right now."

"Well, I want you to talk to him."

Roberta took the phone with all the eagerness of someone reaching for a rattlesnake and said a leery hello. Heinrich had probably returned to the shop and discovered his cooler had no lilies.

"My darling, I am so sorry," he said.

No lilies. The bride was going to come unglued. Del would want a discount.

"This is all our fault."

"You have no lilies," she said weakly.

"Oh, we have lilies. And I'll be able to make your arrangements, but I needed to call and apologize right away. Your daughter did talk to Kevin, and he meant to tell me, but then Hildy Johnson came in and talked his ear off and it went right out of his head. Of course we'll fix this, no extra charge."

"Thank you, Heinrich. I appreciate that."

So Daphne had indeed taken care of contacting the florist. Roberta felt ill. She'd been so determined to blame the problem on Daphne's incompetence that she'd refused to believe her. Why did she always assume the worst about her daughter?

Maybe it was programmed into her by her own mother. *"I'm disappointed in you, Roberta. I raised you better."..."Don't think you can come back parading your illegitimate child here. I won't have it. I won't have you humiliate our family any further."*

She'd failed to meet her mother's expectations, and her mother had written her off like a bad investment. She'd never planned to do that with her own daughter, and yet how many times did she find herself feeling disappointed in Daphne? And how many times did that disappointment show? Maybe none as badly as today.

She hobbled her way to the kitchen, where Daphne was busy with the chocolates. It was a short but painful trip, painful on so many levels.

Daphne didn't turn to look at her. "Did you get it all sorted out?" she asked.

Very diplomatic. "Yes." Roberta came closer, setting the phone on the counter. "Daphne, I'm sorry."

Daphne didn't say anything. Instead, she shrugged as if to say it didn't matter and kept on putting out truffles. No "I forgive you" was forthcoming. No hug. Not even any eye contact.

Well, she deserved as much. "I'm terribly hard on you, aren't I?"

Daphne hesitated a moment, then returned to the task at hand. "I know I'm not the overachiever you wanted me to be."

"Possibly not," Roberta admitted. "But we don't all have to be overachievers." *And we don't all have to be perfect.* "You're a generous, kindhearted woman."

"Apparently, that's not enough." Daphne picked up the tiered plates and left the kitchen.

"Daphne, wait." Roberta hobbled after her.

Daphne didn't wait. Instead, she picked up her pace.

Roberta gave up. It was obvious that her daughter didn't want to talk to her. Her foot was hurting now. She needed to sit down. She needed a pain pill. She wished there was a pill that could make her a better mother.

Twenty-Two

❧❧❧

Daphne, the Queen of New Beginnings

The mayor's daughter got happily and memorably married. The bride was beautiful in her designer gown and her mother, also in a designer dress, was pleased with everything, especially the flowers. The house was packed with family and friends, movers and shakers, and everything went smoothly.

Except for a slight catering crisis thanks to a horde of party-crashers. Daphne saved the day by whipping up some fast and easy appetizers, consisting of crackers and shrimp dip, as well as baking the mini quiches they stored in the big freezer in the basement for such emergencies. She halved the chicken, covered it in sauce and made an extra salad. Lila complimented her on how well she'd handled the situation. Her mother thanked her for all her hard work. It wasn't enough to make her want to stay.

Later that night, with Milo on the bed next to her, she spent some time on her laptop checking out rentals in Icicle Falls. She found a couple that would work, and just as she had when she'd first come home, she went to sleep with tears on her pillow.

The following morning was Mother's Day and Marnie called her on her cell phone while Daphne was still in bed, trying to ignore Milo, who was climbing on her chest, insisting it was time to get up. "Happy Mom's Day," she sang.

"Honeybee, this is a nice surprise," Daphne said, sitting up in bed.

"Why should you be surprised? It *is* Mother's Day."

"Yes, but you already sent those chocolate-covered strawberries on Friday."

From Sweet Dreams Chocolates, of course. They were big and juicy and gorgeous, not to mention pricey, and Daphne had enjoyed sharing them with her mother and Lila.

She'd also enjoyed showing off her daughter's good taste and thoughtfulness. With Marnie, there was a lot to brag about. Unlike her mother, she was doing everything right. She was succeeding in her career. She'd waited until her late twenties to get married and had picked a nice, stable man from a solid family, one with no history of divorce or bad romantic choices. Marnie's life was as close to perfect as anyone's could get. And so was she.

"That doesn't mean I don't want to talk to you on Mother's Day," she said now. "Are you still liking Icicle Falls? 'Cause if you're not, you could move out here with us."

"Oh, your husband would love that, having his mother-in-law underfoot."

"He thinks you're great. So do I."

That little bit of flattery gave Daphne's sagging spirits a much-needed lift. Someone appreciated her just as she was. Of course, maybe that was because she felt the same way about Marnie. She'd never tried to improve her, never hounded her to do more and be better. She'd let Marnie find her own path and become her own person, and she'd exceeded Daphne's expectations. That was more than Daphne could say for herself and her mother.

"What are you two going to do today?" Daphne asked.

"We're going to celebrate."

It wasn't their wedding anniversary. "Did Alan get a raise?"

"He got something," Marnie said, her voice mysterious.

"Okay, I give up. What are you celebrating?"

"You're going to be a grandma."

"A grandma?" Marnie was pregnant? Her baby was having a baby. Lately life had been serving her a lot of lemons. Here was the lemonade that made it all worthwhile. "Oh, honeybee, that's fabulous. When are you due and what are you having?"

"We don't know yet. I just took the pregnancy test."

"Wow," Daphne breathed. "I'm so happy for you."

"You'll come out and help when the baby's born, right?"

"Just try and keep me away."

"I knew you'd say that," Marnie said, a smile in her voice. "Tell Grandma, okay?"

"I will." She had a few things to tell Grandma this morning.

They'd planned to go out to brunch at Zelda's and Daphne had made a gift basket for her mother. She'd been looking forward to the day. Now, not so much. She loved her mother and she knew her mother loved her, but at the moment Daphne didn't exactly like her. With a sigh, she got out of bed.

"Carpe diem," Mother would say. Seize the day, never waste a minute. It was how she managed to accomplish so much. Maybe Daphne should have carpe diem-ed more. Maybe then she would've been a success story, too, like her mother and her daughter. Or maybe success sometimes skipped a generation.

After she'd showered and dressed, she grabbed the gift basket from the dresser and went downstairs to check on her mother, Milo racing ahead of her. She found Mother already up and seated at the kitchen table with her coffee mug, her leg propped on the chair opposite her.

"Good morning," she said. It was tentative, more a question than a greeting.

Daphne set the basket on the table, then bent over and kissed her cheek. Her mother always smelled like Chantilly. "Happy Mother's Day." The words felt awkward and stiff.

"Oh, my. This is beautiful." Mother leaned forward to inspect it. "Chocolates, dusting powder, bubble bath and, oh, I see the latest Vanessa Valentine novel. Daphne, you have such a gift for creativity. You know, you could…"

Daphne cut her off. "Start a gift basket business."

"Well, you could."

"There are any number of things I could do. But right now, I'd like to let the dust from the divorce settle, find out what it's like to be on my own. I've never spent much time doing that." And that could be part of the problem. She'd always been with a man, always felt she needed a man in order to be happy. What she really needed was to learn how to be happy, period.

Mother nodded. "You do have talents. You should explore them."

And then become wildly successful. Anything less wouldn't measure up. Daphne fed Milo, then sat down at the table. "I've been thinking."

"Yes?"

There was an eagerness in that one-word prompt. Was her mother just waiting for her to say she was ready to move out? Probably. Her decision would come as a relief to both of them. "I think it's time I got my own place. I'm going over to Mountain Meadows Real Estate to check out a couple of places this afternoon."

To Daphne's shock, Mother didn't seem relieved at all. Instead, her face fell like a ruined soufflé. "I don't understand. I thought you were happy here. If this is about last night…"

Daphne shook her head. "It's about more than last night. It's about how we work together. Or rather, don't work together." Her mother looked as if she wanted to cry. What was that about?

"Other than our misunderstanding yesterday, I thought we were getting along quite well."

She couldn't be serious. "Mother, we've done nothing but aggravate each other ever since I arrived."

"That's not true," her mother insisted, opting for deliberate blindness. "Don't move out, Daphne. Don't leave, not like this."

There it was again, that moment where her mother looked old, vulnerable. "I'm not leaving Icicle Falls." Not yet, anyway. Although knowing she had a grandchild on the way made the idea of moving east very tempting.

"I was wrong not to believe you," Mother said in a small voice. "I've been wrong about a lot of things." Her gaze dropped to her hands, and she smoothed the skin on them, as if to smooth away the years. "I've done so many things wrong. I'm afraid I turned out to be like my mother, more than I want to admit." She sighed deeply. "I was never good enough for her. She was a hard, selfish woman who cared more about what other people thought than she did her own daughter." Mother lifted her gaze and Daphne saw tears glistening in her eyes. "I hope I'm not that woman. Daphne, I love you, and I'd like to think that's why I've always wanted so much for you. But maybe there was some pride in there, too. Maybe I wanted you to become the most successful woman ever so I could show my mother she'd been wrong to disown us. Either way, I'm afraid I haven't been a very good mother to you." She shook her head. "What a sad thing to realize on Mother's Day."

Now Daphne felt tears flooding her own eyes. Yes, her mother had interfered in her life at every turn, given unrequested advice and often been irritated with her. But she'd always been there for Daphne, offering a shoulder to cry on, lending her money when she needed it, buying extravagant presents for both Marnie and her. She hadn't been a perfect mother but she'd tried. And she'd cared.

"You *have* been a good mother," Daphne insisted. "We're definitely not the same, though. I can't be a version of you. I'll never accomplish as much or be as successful."

"Or as fussy and nitpicky."

Daphne smiled at that. "I hope not."

"I have to admit that when you first came back I thought living together would be a terrible idea. You're right—we are different, and those differences frustrate me sometimes. And, as you may have noticed, I like my independence. But I'm getting older and I could use some extra help around here." She reached across the table and placed a hand on Daphne's arm. "And I enjoy the company."

"You do?" She had a funny way of showing it.

"Darling, I really am sorry about last night. Let's start over. Could we do that?"

The truth was, Daphne didn't want to leave. She might be fifty-three, but she still wanted her mother's approval. She wanted to try again. If... "Mother, do you think you could be a little less critical?"

"Yes, Daphne. Please forgive me. It's hard to accept your child for who she is when she's not who you want her to be, especially when you see..."

"So much potential," Daphne finished with her, and they both smiled.

"But you know," Roberta continued, "I never measured up in my mother's eyes, even though I always made the honor roll. She wanted me to marry the 'right' kind of man, increase her status. She wanted me to display nicely, like her Dresden figurines. I didn't choose well, and she couldn't forgive me for that because I ruined the facade." Mother sighed. "We could have had a happy life together if she'd ever given us a chance, if she'd seen beyond herself. She didn't, though. She never really saw my heart. I don't want to be like that with you."

Over the years there'd been the occasional mention of

Daphne's grandmother but no more than that. When she was small, her great-grandmother had come to see them a couple of times and sent presents at Christmas, and she hadn't questioned the fact that no other family was part of their lives. But when Daphne got a little older she began to ask questions. Her mother had dodged them with excuses such as "Grandmother's busy" or "Grandmother isn't well enough to come and see us." Daphne finally lost interest in the ghost grandma she never saw, and it wasn't until she was fully grown that she learned her mother and grandmother didn't get along. No more details were forthcoming. Hardly surprising, since she hadn't learned about her bumsicle father, either, until she became engaged to Johnny, of whom her mother strongly disapproved. After the way her mother had dribbled out information over the years, her intimate confession this morning felt like a landslide of sharing.

And it explained a lot. "I wish you'd told me more of this over the years," Daphne said.

"I should have. But honestly, Daphne, I don't think I really made the connection between my behavior and hers until now. That doesn't make me a very wise old woman, does it?"

Milo rubbed against Daphne's legs and she picked him up and cuddled him next to her, considering what her mother had said. "I think wisdom comes with experience and with figuring things out. I'd like to believe I'm wiser now than I was a year ago."

"I hope I'm wiser now than I was a day ago," Roberta said.

"Wise or not, I love you."

"Can you love me enough to stay?"

Words Daphne had never thought she'd hear, they

poured like a healing balm over her wounded feelings. "It's what I wanted all along," she said softly. "You've always been there for me. I want to be there for you now."

Daphne rarely saw her mother cry. Roberta Gilbert was too strong for tears.

But not today. They flowed in twin rivers down her cheeks. She picked up her napkin and touched it to her eyes. "Daphne, darling, you truly are a wonderful woman."

Daphne gave her a wistful smile, and she, too, picked up a napkin and dabbed at her cheeks. "Even if I don't always keep the kitchen as clean as you'd like," she added in an attempt to lighten the moment.

"There's more to life than cleaning, isn't there?" Mother said, and it was all Daphne could do not to ask, "Who are you and what have you done with my mother?"

Later that morning as they sat in Zelda's enjoying omelets, crepes, strawberries and champagne from the Mother's Day buffet, Daphne revealed Marnie's good news.

"A new baby in the family," her mother said happily. "Oh, how much fun we'll have spoiling her."

"Or him."

"Oh, dear. If it's a boy I'll have no idea what to do with him."

Maybe that wouldn't be a bad thing.

They were just finishing up when Hank Hawkins came in with his mother, a slight woman with salt-and-pepper hair and a stooped back. How had such a small woman produced such a large man?

The large man looked even better in a Sunday suit

than he did in his work clothes. His jaw was freshly shaved and smooth and his dark hair slicked back. He cleaned up well.

Someone must have turned up the heat in the restaurant. Daphne took a long drink of orange juice in an effort to cool down.

He smiled at the sight of her and her mother and led his own mom in their direction. "Happy Mother's Day, ladies," he said, stopping at their table.

"Thank you, Hank. Nice to see you, Sal," Mother said to the woman.

"Is this your lovely daughter I've been hearing so much about?" asked Sal.

Hank suddenly looked as if he was the one having a hot flash.

"This is my daughter, Daphne," Mother said and introduced Sally Hawkins.

"Pleased to meet you," Daphne said. She caught a whiff of Hank's cologne, some kind of woodsy virile scent, and she knew she couldn't blame the heat she was feeling now on misfiring hormones. Her hormones were just fine, thank you, and ready to hook up with some nice testosterone.

"How's the breakfast?" he asked.

"Very good," Daphne replied. The best breakfast she'd ever had with her mother. Today was a celebration of new understanding and, hopefully, a new beginning. She smiled across the table at Mother, who beamed back at her.

"It certainly looks delicious," Sal remarked. "Aren't we blessed to have wonderful children to take us out?"

"We certainly are," Mother agreed.

"I guess we'll see you around," Hank said. The look

he sent Daphne promised he wasn't about to give up chasing her.

Maybe that was fine with her, after all. Maybe somewhere in the distant future her heart would heal and she'd dive once more into love's choppy waters. "I'm sure you will."

Hank and his mother went back to the reception area to check in with Charley Masters, who was busy seating people. Then, as she led them to their table, he winked at Daphne, turning her internal thermostat even higher.

"He really is a nice man," her mother said. "Not that I'm encouraging you to start dating." This was followed by a guilty expression. "Of course, I don't want to tell you what to do."

"Of course not," Daphne murmured. Her mother would probably never change. She'd interfere in Daphne's life and try to run the show as long as she drew breath. But here was one area she didn't need to worry about. Daphne had finally learned her lesson about love. "I'm in no hurry to start dating. I'm doing fine on my own. And I think that things are only going to get better," she added. Because from now on, she'd be making wiser choices, choices that were right for her.

Actually, she'd already started. Moving to Icicle Falls had been one of the smartest decisions she'd ever made.

Twenty-Three

Anne, Distracted Wife and Loving Mother

The family gathered at Anne's house for Mother's Day, and talk naturally turned to how the wedding plans were progressing.

"We still have so much to do," Anne said as she passed around slices of chocolate cake. "Invitations need to go out."

"I'm working on that," Laney said vaguely.

"They should go pretty soon." Her daughter shouldn't be procrastinating, and she shouldn't have to keep nagging.

"They will," Laney said curtly.

"At least the save-the-date announcements went out, so people will have it on their calendars," Kendra reminded Anne.

"Bring the invitations over here," said Julia. "We can all help you and have the whole thing done in an evening."

"Good idea," Kendra said.

Laney didn't say anything.

Anne went on with her list of unfinished business. "The bridesmaids still need to get their dresses. Laney, when are you and the girls going shopping?"

"Probably next week," Laney said, digging into her cake.

She was more interested in the cake than she was in talking about her wedding, and Anne found that disturbing. Lately, Laney seemed rather cranky, too, which was also disturbing.

But hardly uncommon. Planning a wedding could be stressful, so the crankiness was understandable. The lack of enthusiasm, not so much. In fact, it was downright mystifying. When she was a tween and a teen she'd been fascinated by what her mother did for a living, wanting to see pictures and check out links to various sites right along with Anne. Now, when it counted, she wasn't focusing on any of it.

"I want to get my flower-girl dress," Coral, Kendra's oldest, announced.

"Me, too," her little sister, Amy, chimed in.

"Don't worry," Kendra told them. "You will."

"And the bridesmaids' gifts. Have you decided on them yet?" Anne had sent her a couple of different links to check out.

Laney heaved a long-suffering sigh. "Not yet."

"Who's going to be your photographer?" Julia asked.

"I don't know yet, Grammy," Laney said. "I still have time."

"Not as much as you think," Anne cautioned. "We really need to get going." She hated to push, but honestly, they had a lot to do.

Laney made a face. "Jeez, Mom. Stop already."

Stop? As if she was, somehow, being unreasonable

in trying to get her daughter moving? "Laney," Anne said sternly.

"Good cake," Cam said, and everyone else at the table happily went along with the change of subject.

Anne sat and stewed. Happy Mother's Day. Hmmph.

"I only want our daughter's wedding to turn out well," she said to Cam after everyone had left. It seemed she'd said that a lot over the past couple of months.

"Everything will get done," he reassured her, leading her over to the couch.

"When?"

"Before the wedding," he said, slipping an arm around her and pulling her close. "Stop worrying."

"Easy for you to say," she grumbled. "All you have to do is show up."

"And, when it comes right down to it, that's all you have to do, too. This is Laney's wedding. She can plan it."

"I know," Anne said. "But the problem is, she's not. She's letting things slide. She needs help."

"Maybe she doesn't want help. Maybe she doesn't care about some of those things."

"Then she shouldn't be having a wedding. She should just elope." Wait a minute. What was she saying?

Cam grinned. "Yeah, I can picture you allowing *that* to happen. Seriously, Anne, let some of this go and make her do the heavy lifting." He disappeared into the spare room that served as their office and then returned with his laptop. "Let's do some planning of our own. How's that sound?"

It sounded better than fretting over her daughter's lack of motivation. "Sure."

He opened the computer and they went online, comparing cruises. "This one with Holland America looks good," he said.

At that moment Anne's cell phone rang.

"Don't answer it."

"It's Laney." Of course she had to answer it.

Cam sighed and slumped against the sofa cushions.

"I'm going to make an event on Facebook instead of sending out all these invitations," Laney told her.

"Sweetie, I think that would be tacky, and not everyone we know is on Facebook. Anyway, Grammy, Aunt Kendra and I are going to help you. Remember?" Since they'd paid for the invitations, it seemed silly not to use them. Cam picked up the remote and brought the TV to life. An action film roared onto the screen and Anne moved to the kitchen. "We'll do it one night this week. Between all of us we can have it finished in no time."

"I guess," Laney said dubiously.

"It'll be fun." Anne tried to encourage her. "Meanwhile, check out the links I sent for your bridesmaids' gifts."

Now her phone was telling her she had another call. She glanced at caller ID. "That's Aunt Kendra. I'll talk to you later," Anne said. As she switched from Laney to Kendra she could see her husband channel surfing, waiting patiently for her to return to planning their anniversary. "What's up?"

"I was going to ask you that. Is Laney ticked at you? She seemed kind of grumpy at dinner today."

"Pre-wedding stress," Anne said. "You know how that goes. But she's fine. I was talking to her when you called."

"Okay. Just thought I'd ask."

She was barely off the phone with Kendra when her mom checked in, also wondering about Laney.

By the time she wandered back into the living room, Cam was involved in a TV show. Or pretending to be. She could tell by the expression on his face that he was miffed. "Okay, now where were we?" she said in her cheeriest voice, sliding next to him.

"*We* were obsessing about our daughter's wedding and ignoring our husband."

"I'm sorry. But, Cam, these things take a lot of planning."

He turned to her, his face solemn. "Anne, I get that you want to help, and I know this is your business, but you don't need to do it 24/7. And like I said, you need to let Laney do some of it herself. It's her wedding."

"I agree. And I am, but planning a wedding is complicated."

He shrugged and turned his attention back to the TV. "Tell me when you're done."

"I'm done now," she said and put a hand to his chin, forcing him to look at her.

He obliged, but he was still frowning.

"Come on now. Don't be mad. This is important. This is our daughter."

He sighed. "You're right. I'm sorry."

"Kiss and make up?"

The frown disappeared. One kiss was all it took to make him forget about the action on the TV and switch his attention to the action on the couch, which started heating up pretty fast, clothes slipping off and Anne slipping into a horizontal position. It was nice to lie here and enjoy her husband's caresses and kisses. She didn't have to spend every second thinking about the wedding to-do list.

Except it was such a long one and they had so many things to check off. Crud, and when she was talking to Laney she'd forgotten to bring up the subject of "wedding favors."

Oh, no. Had she just said that out loud? Judging by the look on Cam's face she had.

"Now, that's funny," Kendra said the next day as she and Anne perused dresses in Macy's, looking for Anne's mother-of-the-bride dress.

"Oh, yeah. Cam was laughing. I hope my marriage survives my daughter's wedding."

"Your marriage could survive a zombie apocalypse."

Anne pulled out a champagne-colored dress with a nipped-in waist and pleated skirt. It was love at first sight. "I like this."

"Oh, yeah. Try it on."

She did, and the love affair grew stronger. "I'll take it." Oh, that everything would go as smoothly.

But it didn't. It seemed that there was constantly something new to deal with, both at work and on the home front.

The bridesmaids finally got their dresses. So did the flower girls. When Kendra's husband was supposed to be watching them, the girls put on the dresses and played wedding, which somehow resulted in Amy ripping her dress and Coral getting chocolate all over the bodice of hers.

Laurel Browne had two more meltdowns before her daughter's wedding, and on the night of the actual wedding, the caterer was short-handed, the booze ran out and three of the goldfish on the dinner tables did the dead-fish float.

In the end, though, Laurel was so happy with the flowers, her daughter and her new son-in-law that she hugged Anne and thanked her. "Didn't it turn out beautifully?" she gushed.

"Weddings usually do," Anne replied sagely.

She reminded herself of that as she hurried around trying to cover all the bases for Laney's upcoming nuptials. The invitations finally went out, but Laney continued to avoid some of the more minor details.

"Sweetie, you have to decide on wedding favors," she told Laney during one of their many phone conversations.

"I don't know," Laney said, not for the first time.

"What about the bracelets?" Laney had talked about giving away some kind of bracelet since she liked making jewelry. Although now, even with the help of her bridesmaids, Anne doubted she'd be able to get them ready in time.

"No. I changed my mind."

Nice of her to tell her mom. "Okay, then, what about the bubbles?"

"I think using all those little plastic bottles wouldn't be very environmentally responsible. People might not recycle them."

At this rate they'd never decide. "Okay, let's go with the M&M's with your names on them. Everybody likes chocolate." And heaven knew Anne could use some right about now.

"I guess that'll be fine."

She guessed. "Is there something you'd rather have?"

"No, that'll work."

Her daughter's enthusiasm was underwhelming. This was really beginning to bother Anne.

When she said as much to Cam, though, she didn't get the support she wanted. Considering his earlier comments, she shouldn't have been surprised.

"Like mother, like daughter," he said.

Anne frowned at him. "What's that supposed to mean?"

He frowned right back at her. "It means that's pretty much the reaction I'm getting from you about our anniversary. If you don't want to do the cruise, Annie, just say so."

"Okay, fine. I don't want to do the cruise," she said and then shocked both herself and her husband by bursting into tears. Oh, no. Where had this come from?

He was instantly apologetic, wrapping his arms around her and kissing her forehead. "I'm sorry, Annie. I didn't mean to make you cry."

"It's not you. It's just that…"

"I know. You're all caught up in Laney's wedding."

"It's not that I don't want to celebrate our anniversary," she said with a sniffle. She did. Of course she did. "But I'd like to have the time and energy to enjoy planning it. I know you wanted to take a cruise, but I'd rather go up to the mountains and have a getaway, just the two of us, rather than be stuck on a boat with a few hundred—or thousand—other people."

"Don't tell me. Let me guess. To Icicle Falls."

"That's not as exciting as a cruise, is it?"

"I don't need to go on a cruise."

"But you want to." He'd been the one to bring it up.

"Not that much. I thought you wanted it."

"*You* suggested it. I agreed it would be nice to get away," she said with a shrug.

He frowned and shook his head. "After twenty-five years, our communication should be better."

Or she should say what she really wanted more often. But she hadn't done that from the very start of their marriage. She'd set the pattern and, for the most part, they'd lived by it. Not that she didn't enjoy the same things Cam did or that she had a problem going along with his ideas, especially when they were great, like those dance lessons they'd taken years ago.

Still, she did have a few dreams of her own, and maybe she should start sharing them more. She sighed. "If I was a rich woman, I'd buy a little cabin on a lake where we could go for weekends, or up in the mountains where we could hike, take the kids for Christmas. But I'd settle for a weekend somewhere quiet." She smiled. "Of course, we could do that *and* a cruise."

He dismissed her compromise with a wave of his hand. "Forget the cruise. I was trying to think of a big-ticket item you'd enjoy and that's what I came up with. I don't care what we do. I just want to give you something special for our twenty-fifth, something to make up for the fact that you never got your big, fancy wedding."

"But I got you. That's what matters," she said, "and our daughter will get the big, fancy wedding." She studied his face. "Are you disappointed?" Maybe he was; maybe he was simply trying to cover it up. Probably not, though. That was her modus operandi.

"Whatever you want. We can decide on something after we get the kids hitched."

She took his face in her hands and kissed him. He was such a good man. "I know I've been…"

"Absent," he supplied. "But I understand, and I'm sorry I was a jerk. You're doing this for our daughter."

In spite of the fact that their daughter didn't seem to appreciate everything she was doing.

She wound up confessing as much to Roberta Gilbert when she made a day trip to Icicle Falls on the flimsy excuse of deciding where she wanted the flowers to go. Really, she just needed the R & R. There was something about seeing those mountains standing guard over the town that eased the stress from her mind and body. The quaint frescoes on the buildings, the hanging baskets and storefront window boxes filled with flowers made her smile. And visiting with Roberta was better than a shrink session.

"I sometimes wonder if my son-in-law would like a picture of me so he can throw darts at it," she said. "He and Laney originally wanted to go to Las Vegas to get married."

"It's a popular place," Roberta said diplomatically.

"I talked them out of it," Anne admitted.

"If they wanted to do it that badly I doubt you could have."

"My daughter always wanted a big, fancy wedding."

"Most girls do."

Anne set aside her teacup. "I plan weddings for a living. I shouldn't be this stressed."

"Oh, I'm not so sure about that," Roberta said. "It's different when it's your daughter."

"You're right," Anne said with a sigh. "I don't think my husband understands that. He's trying, but I don't think he really does. I only want her to be happy."

Roberta freshened Anne's tea. "Of course you do.

It's what every mother wants for her daughter. There's nothing wrong with that."

"I should be enjoying this a lot more," Anne said and helped herself to a lavender–white chocolate scone.

Roberta chuckled. "My dear, I've come to the conclusion that anything involving a daughter is a mixture of pleasure and pain. However, you'll both get through this, and as long as the bride is happy and comes away with good memories, that's what counts. Sometimes a woman can get so sucked into all the wedding hustle and bustle, she forgets there'll still be life *after* the wedding."

Anne nodded. Roberta was so right.

"Go home, take a break and take a deep breath," Roberta advised. "Everything will turn out exactly as it's supposed to. We haven't lost a mother of the bride yet."

Anne couldn't help smiling. She'd said as much to a few mothers of brides herself.

She decided it was time to follow Roberta's advice. She called Cam. "I'm on my way home. I'll pick up Chinese."

"Works for me," he said.

Three hours later she walked in the door with their premade dinner and found Cam had a bottle of wine chilling. "Everything set for the big day?" he asked.

She nodded. "Yes, it's going to be fine, and I'm done stressing about the wedding. In fact, I think we should plan what we want to do for our anniversary."

"Nope," he said, pouring her a glass of pinot grigio. "Don't need to. I've already got it figured out."

"You have?"

"Most of it. I have a few details to work out, but don't make any plans for the weekend after Laney's wedding."

Just like that he'd gone ahead and planned what they were going to do for their anniversary? Without asking her? She put down her glass and frowned at him. "Well, don't you want my input?"

He picked up the glass and gave it back to her. "Now, don't look at me like that. Trust me. You're going to like this."

She put the glass down again. "How do you know?" She was the planner, not him.

"I know," he said, sounding both mysterious and cocky. He slipped his arms around her. "I know what you like," he added and planted a kiss on her neck.

"Yeah?" He was doing a pretty good job of showing her right now.

"Yeah." He touched his lips to her shoulder.

"Prove it."

"If you insist," he said and set about doing exactly that.

They abandoned the Chinese takeout in favor of satisfying a different appetite, and this time Anne didn't worry about her daughter's upcoming wedding. She did have one moment when she wondered if they'd ordered enough champagne, but she wisely kept that thought to herself.

Twenty-Four

Roberta, New and Improved

It was the second Saturday in June, a perfect day for a wedding with only a few wispy clouds floating in a blue sky. But no wedding was happening at Primrose Haus today. Thanks to a runaway bride, the wedding had been canceled.

This was such a rare thing Roberta almost didn't know what to do with herself. Daphne suggested a play day.

"We can start by going over to Bavarian Brews and getting a latte," she said.

"I can't remember the last time I did that," Roberta confessed. She also couldn't remember the last time she and her daughter had gone out and done something fun, just the two of them. It seemed that for the past few years, Roberta had been too busy most weekends to get away, and whenever Daphne had come up to visit, she'd either been with Marnie (always a good thing) or a man (never a good thing).

Bavarian Brews was packed with locals chatting

or texting on their cell phones, and tourists wearing novelty hats from the hat shop and armed with digital cameras, ready to shoot pictures of the town's colorful main street and the surrounding scenery. The place was fragrant with the aroma of freshly brewed coffee, and looking at the different concoctions the baristas were making with various combinations of chocolate, coconut and caramel made Roberta's mouth water.

Del Stone and Ed York were there, and after picking up tall orders of coffee, they stopped by to say hello. Del once more thanked Roberta for giving his little girl such a great wedding. "I'll wager you'll be hearing from Representative Wattle. His daughter just got engaged. I told him he couldn't pick a better place."

"Thank you, Del. That's very sweet of you." Del would have her vote in the next election, whether or not those potholes on Pine Street got fixed.

He elbowed Ed. "You and Pat should've done it up right and gone to Roberta for your wedding."

Roberta couldn't have agreed more, especially considering how many years they'd all known one another and how much business she'd given both of them. She'd hoped to get invited to the wedding.

"Pat's daughter insisted on us getting married at her house. It was a small wedding, just family."

At least it wasn't a case of not making the cut. "You have to do what your children want," Roberta said. "I'm happy for both of you," she added to show there were no hard feelings.

"I feel pretty lucky finding a woman like Pat," Ed said. "What they say is true—love is better the second time around."

She'd have to take his word for it.

"After my first time around, I'd sure hope so," Del said heartily.

Roberta shook her head at Del. "You forget I've met your wife."

He smiled good-naturedly, then wished them a nice morning as he and Ed moved off to stake out a table by the window, which offered a view of the street and its various shops as well as Sweet Dreams Chocolates, the town's pride and joy and source of all things chocolate.

"Mother, have you ever thought about dating?" Daphne asked when they settled at a table with their lattes.

"Oh, goodness, Daphne. Why would I want a man at this point in my life?"

Daphne shrugged. "Companionship?"

"I have plenty of companionship with you and Lila and my friends at the chamber of commerce. Besides, no real man ever measures up to the ones in my Vanessa Valentine books. You've learned that firsthand. Although there may be a few out there who come close," she mused, seeing Hank walk up behind Daphne. A shame they hadn't met earlier, before they'd both messed up their lives.

"Hello, ladies," he said, making Daphne jump.

Roberta would've liked to shoo him away, but that would be rude, so she forced herself to ask, "Would you care to join us?"

"Don't mind if I do." He seated himself next to Daphne, whose face was suddenly flushed. "I'm surprised you're not at Primrose Haus getting ready for a wedding."

"The wedding got canceled," Roberta explained.

"Uh-oh. Did the groom have cold feet?"

"Nope, the bride did," Daphne answered. "She'd been married before. She probably decided not to jump off the cliff again."

"You can't fly if you don't take a leap," said Hank.

Roberta could see where this conversation was going, right into three's-a-crowd territory. What to do? Her first inclination was to stay at the table like a two-legged guard dog, make sure Daphne didn't do anything foolish.

But she'd resolved not to interfere in her daughter's life or tell her what to do, and Daphne had assured her she wasn't going to rush into anything, that she was learning to be happy on her own. Was it really so foolish to have coffee with a nice, hardworking man, a man who, like Daphne, had gotten a raw deal on love? Anyway, if the two of them were going to wind up together eventually, there was nothing Roberta could do to stop it.

So, no guard-dogging. "I think I'll go back to the house. My foot is hurting." Actually, her foot felt pretty good these days. She was off the heavy-duty painkillers and down to ibuprofen, fitting in her morning walks again. She hadn't taken a walk yet today. Maybe she'd do that.

Daphne nodded and began to get up.

Roberta waved her back down. "Stay put, darling. Finish your latte." *Start your new life.*

"We were going to spend the day together," Daphne reminded her.

"We can do that tomorrow." Then, before Daphne could say anything more, Roberta slipped out of the coffee shop.

It was around ten in the morning and by now downtown was buzzing with visitors checking out the various shops. It made Roberta happy to see so many people in town. She could remember when she'd first arrived and the place was almost a ghost town. Thanks to the cleverness and hard work of its people, Icicle Falls had come back to life in a big way.

She caught sight of a couple around her age, holding hands as they entered Gilded Lily's women's apparel. Their easy familiarity suggested they'd been married for years. The woman had probably said, "Look at that cute dress in the window," and he'd most likely replied, "Why don't you go try it on?"

Roberta sighed. If she hadn't been so bitter, so unwilling to give love another chance, that could've been her. But after two bad experiences she'd given up.

Ah, well. She'd still had a good life, a satisfying life. She'd made something of herself, something her mother should have been proud of. Sadly, her mother never got past her disappointment, valued her pride above her daughter's feelings. Roberta had her faults as a mother, but at least she'd never done that.

She'd done other things wrong instead, always pushing Daphne to do more, be more. Sadly, no one offered parenting classes back when she was raising Daphne. Roberta hadn't had any help. She'd been completely on her own. And she'd stayed on her own, never hearing from her mother, never seeing her again until the end.

2004

Roberta's old friend Nan had kept in touch over the years, mostly with Christmas cards and a few phone calls. One day she'd called to tell Roberta that her mother was dying. "I know you don't care if you ever see her again," Nan had said, "but she's all alone in that place. It's pathetic, really. I think she's sorry she never mended fences with you."

She'd had her chance. Actually, she'd had more than one. Roberta's grandmother had known where she was. Anytime her mother wanted to contact her, she could have. But she hadn't. So let her die alone, choking on her pride.

And what will you choke on someday? came the thought. *Resentment? Bitterness?* Roberta had tasted enough of those emotions over the years. She had to admit that now, at sixty, she'd lost her appetite for them.

And so, on a mockingly beautiful spring day, she made the two-and-a-half-hour drive to Seattle. She didn't tell Daphne she was coming or why. Daphne would've wanted to accompany her, to meet the woman she'd never known and offer Roberta her support. But Daphne still knew very little about her grandmother, and that was for the best. The woman had poisoned Roberta. She hadn't been going to let that poison touch her daughter.

The care facility smelled like a nasty combination of urine and disinfectant. A couple of ancients sat in wheelchairs at the side of the hallway, one a grizzled man who was muttering to himself, the other a woman with sparse gray hair and a caved-in chest, who held out a beseeching hand to Roberta. She had blue eyes and a button nose and in spite of the wrinkles Roberta could tell she'd been pretty in her younger days.

She stopped and took the woman's hand. "How are you?"

"Have you seen my daughter?" the woman asked. "She's supposed to come and see me. It's my birthday."

How many of her own mother's birthdays had Roberta missed? If this woman had been her mother, she wouldn't have missed a single one. "I'm sure she's coming," she said in an effort to comfort the woman.

The sweet face changed into a mask of anger. "She never comes."

The accusation and bitterness hit Roberta like a red-hot poker. "Maybe there's a reason." *Maybe you're like my mother, a selfish, judgmental shrew.*

Or maybe this woman was simply lonely and unhappy. Roberta softened her voice and gave the woman's hand a squeeze. "I'm sure she'll come," she said again. Daughters did. Eventually. Even when their mothers didn't ask for them.

The woman on duty at the reception desk pointed her down the hall to a different wing. Room 27, which her mother was sharing with another patient, a woman in the throes of agony. Roberta could hear her groaning from outside the room. When she entered, she had to catch her breath at the sight of the shrunken form in the other bed. This slack-jawed, sleeping cadaver hooked up to a morphine drip couldn't be her mother. Her mother had been plump, with carefully maintained brown curls and polished manners, always dressed to the nines.

But this was how it ended if you lived long enough. You found yourself riding out your last days in a rickety shell of a body. *This will be you someday.* Except she'd have a daughter who'd come to visit her and comfort her. She'd have a daughter who cared.

She could have been a daughter who cared. She should have tried harder to forge a new relationship with her mother, should have brought Daphne to see her. Guilt overrode the resentment as she pulled up a chair next to the bed and laid a hand on her mother's arm.

"Mother?"

The cadaver slept on.

Roberta tried again, gently tapping the arm, wrinkled and spotted with the bruises of age. "Mother?"

The eyes opened and the head turned. The woman squinted at her as if trying to place her.

"It's me, Roberta."

"Roberta." The sound came out faint and raspy. "What are you doing here?"

"I came to see you."

"I'm dying."

"I heard."

The lips turned down at the corners. "Did you come to see if you're in the will? There's nothing left, you know." The cadaver let out a tired breath and shut her eyes again.

"I didn't come for anything other than to see you and tell you I'm sorry."

The eyes stayed closed. "After all these years?"

"I'm sorry you could never forgive me. I'm sorry we never had a relationship, that you never got to see your granddaughter grow up."

A tear leaked out of one eye. "It could have been different."

"Yes, it could have," Roberta agreed.

"If only you'd listened to me."

So the fault was all hers. Even now, on her deathbed, her mother would bear no blame for those many years of estrangement. "All I wanted was your love."

Another tear slipped out. "I always loved you. You... disappointed me so."

She had; there was no denying it. She took her mother's limp hand and squeezed it. "I'm sorry."

"Why didn't you say that...years ago?"

"Perhaps I was waiting to hear that you still loved me."

Her mother gave no indication of having heard. A breath seeped out and she turned her head away. "I'm tired."

So am I, thought Roberta. Yes, she'd disappointed her mother but her mother had hurt her deeply. What a sad mess. They should have had a relationship all these years. Her mother should've come to Icicle Falls to spend weekends and see Daphne performing in the Sunday-school Christmas pageant or watch her graduating from high school. She should've been there for Daphne's wedding, should have held her great-granddaughter. Roberta should have come over to Seattle to take her out to lunch. So much they could have done, so much they'd missed. "I wish it could have been different between us," she said.

Too late for that now. The only thing it wasn't too late for was forgiveness. Bitterness was exhausting, and she'd carried hers long enough. "You were never there for me, but I forgive you. I learned from your rejection. My daughter isn't perfect and we've had our problems, but at least she knows I love her."

The eyes stayed shut and the mouth pressed together in a tight, thin line. Her mother obviously had no more to say.

But that was okay. Neither did Roberta. This time the tears were hers. She couldn't help crying for what they'd lost all those years, but she also felt like a woman

who had just survived a deadly disease. The fever had
finally broken. Now she could truly heal. "I'll do whatever I can to make you comfortable."

"Thank you." The words came out so faintly Roberta
almost wondered if she'd imagined them.

She gave her mother's hand one final squeeze.
"You're welcome."

Before she left, she made arrangements to have her
mother moved to a private room. She lasted another
two weeks and then she was gone. Roberta saw to it
that she was buried at Washelli right beside her father.

"I hope you rest in peace," she said to her mother
when she stood at the graveside. She knew now that she
could live in peace.

Roberta gave herself a mental shake. This was such
a lovely day. She had no intention of wasting even a
minute of it revisiting the past. Instead, she decided
to enjoy the moment at hand and take a walk up Lost
Bride Trail. She might not make it all the way to the
falls, but the scenery would be beautiful and she could
look for lady's slippers. She'd bring her walking stick,
a bottle of water (and an ibuprofen) and take her time.

Half an hour later found her on a wooded mountain path, surrounded by evergreens and ferns, walking through dappled sunlight, taking in the earthy scent
and breathing the fresh mountain air. It had been ages
since she'd walked this trail. She really needed to get
out more, have more fun.

She eventually made it up to Lost Bride Falls. By
the time she got there, she was definitely ready for a
break. She sat down on a little wooden bench by the
scenic outlook to rest her foot and enjoy the sight of

water cascading over a rocky outcrop. What a history that waterfall had. She wondered what had happened to Rebecca Cane, Joshua Cane's mail-order bride, who'd mysteriously disappeared so many generations ago. Had she run away with his younger brother, Gideon, or had Joshua truly killed the two of them in a fit of jealous rage, as so many people had speculated? The lurid story of the disappearing bride had, over the years, turned into something positive. Legend said that any woman who caught a glimpse of the ghost of the lost bride under the falls had a proposal of marriage waiting for her in the near future.

Roberta had never seen the ghost.

She took off her hiking shoe and rubbed her aching foot, then gulped down her painkiller. Even though it was a relatively easy hike, it was probably longer than she should have attempted. She'd go home, kick off her shoes and relax with her latest romance novel.

She'd just put the shoe back on when two strangers came up the path. They were both good-looking men, lean and fit, wearing T-shirts, jeans and hiking boots and carrying water bottles. Roberta judged the younger one to be somewhere around Daphne's age. The other was probably in his seventies, with white hair and plenty of lines to show he'd logged in some hours out in the sun. He resembled a younger version of Clint Eastwood. Roberta had always adored Clint Eastwood.

The younger man said hello, then got busy taking pictures of the falls with a camera that looked very expensive. The older man smiled and said hello. "Nice day to be out," he added.

"Yes, it is," Roberta said.

He strolled over to where she sat. He was a tall man.

Put him in a cowboy hat and poncho and give him a cigar and he could *be* Clint Eastwood. "Great view."

"You'd be hard put to find a better one anywhere."

"Do you live here?"

It had been about a million years since a man had been interested, but Roberta hadn't forgotten the signs. "I do," she said and introduced herself.

"My name's Curtis White. This is my son Brian."

"Good to meet you," Brian said and continued to take pictures.

"Mind if I join you?" asked Curtis.

"Not at all." She scooted over to make room on the bench, and he sat down, causing a flutter in her chest.

"We came up with some friends to do a little fishing and hiking."

"This is the place to do it." Roberta couldn't help herself; she had to check his left hand for a ring. Bare-naked. A bare-naked Clint Eastwood. *Really,* she scolded herself, *at your age.* Well, what was wrong with feeling the cold embers stir at her age? She wasn't dead yet.

But just because he wasn't wearing a ring didn't mean he wasn't married…

He was checking out her ring finger, too. "Have you lived here long?"

"For years."

"Lucky you," he said. "I've always thought it would be nice to retire over here somewhere, have a cabin, fish every day. Never got around to it."

"It's not too late."

He smiled. The man had a great smile. "You know, you're right."

They chatted for a few more minutes, long enough for him to confirm that she was single and find out she was in the business of providing brides and grooms with a place to get married. She learned that he was a retired banker and had been a widower for five years. And he was in town until Monday.

"Would you like to have dinner with me tonight?" he asked.

"Oh, I couldn't. You're up here with your son."

"And his brother. They won't miss me."

"You can say that again," teased the son.

"Well…"

"I hear there's a restaurant that offers traditional German food. I haven't had schnitzel since I was stationed in Germany. Do you like schnitzel, Roberta?"

"I do, as a matter of fact."

"Well, then, let's make it a date."

Roberta suspected Daphne would have plans for the evening, so why not? They agreed to meet at Schwangau at six. Then, with his son finished taking pictures, the two men said goodbye and made their way back down the trail. Roberta watched them go and wondered what silliness had prompted her to accept a date at this age. Clint Eastwood, that was what.

"Silly woman," she muttered and rose to her feet. Her back was stiff from sitting, and she paused to stretch and take in the view one last time before starting back. The waterfall was a gorgeous, roaring thing, with rainbows dancing in its waters and in that little cave behind the falls… What was that? She saw the figure for only a few seconds. It looked vaguely like a woman in a long gown.

The lost bride!

She blinked and looked again. Of course there was

nothing. "Honestly, Roberta, you really are a silly, old woman."

By the time she was halfway down the trail she was limping and chiding herself for walking so far. Then she remembered Curtis White and decided her hike had been worth the pain. But she could hardly wait to get home, pop another pill and put her foot up.

When she got to the house Daphne was back. "I thought you'd be out with Hank," Roberta said.

"No. I came back looking for you. Where'd you go?"

"I went for a hike."

"It hasn't been that long since you had the surgery," Daphne protested. "And you said your foot hurt."

"I thought exercising it would do me good. Anyway, the doctor said I could walk on it now."

"A little. Not a hike. Where'd you go?"

"Up Lost Bride Trail."

"Oh, Mother," Daphne said, her voice a mixture of disgust and worry.

"I'm fine," Roberta assured her and went to the kitchen, trying not to limp noticeably. She got some water and washed down a pain pill.

"I can tell," Daphne said. "Let me get you some ice."

Roberta hobbled to the back parlor and sat on the couch. Daphne was right behind her, carrying a gallon freezer bag filled with ice and wrapped in a towel. She helped Roberta prop up her foot, then laid the ice on it, over the towel. "You're a good daughter," Roberta told her. She was beautiful, both inside and out, and Roberta was glad she'd come home.

"Thank you," Daphne murmured.

"Now, tell me how you managed to get away from Hank. You know he's not going to give up until you go out with him." Whether that was a good or a bad thing remained to be seen.

"I told him I'm not rushing into anything."

"Very wise. I have a feeling he'll wait."

Daphne shrugged. "I do, too. He's taking me to Zelda's for dinner. We're just going out as friends," she hurried to add.

Roberta wished she'd had the good sense to find a male friend to do things with. Maybe she had that afternoon.

"Do you mind? I know we talked about spending the day together."

"I don't mind at all," Roberta replied. "I have plans for tonight myself."

"You do?"

"I'm going to dinner at Schwangau."

"Oh? With who?"

"A very nice man I met while I was taking my walk. He's up here with his sons."

Daphne looked incredulous. "You met a man?"

Roberta scowled. "Old people do make friends, you know."

"I know. It's just that, well, I'm surprised. All these years, you never dated."

She had, for a brief time when Daphne was little, only a casual date or two with a couple of the locals. And then that disastrous affair...

1967

Nobody knew about it. He was a salesman from Seattle. He'd stopped at the diner, soon to become Pancake Haus, for a coffee on his way home from Coulee City and they'd struck up a conversation. Conversation had led to dinner, and afterward Roberta had given him a kiss and her phone number. How fortunate that she'd popped in for a bite on her lunch hour that day!

The next month he came back and rented a small cabin and Roberta got a babysitter. He took her to dinner, to a different restaurant this time, one in nearby Wenatchee, and then back to the cabin, and suddenly her dull life began to sparkle. Love at last!

A month later he was in town again. Janice Lind took Daphne for the night so Roberta could supposedly have a getaway with a girlfriend, and Roberta returned to the secluded cabin.

On Sunday morning she made him bacon and eggs. He reached across the small wooden dining table and said, "It's been a wonderful weekend."

She thought so, too, and went to take his hand. That was when she spotted it, the barely discernible band of white on his left-hand ring finger. Surely she should have noticed that before. "You're married."

Guilt flashed across his face and she pulled her hand away. He tried to cover it with an earnest look. "I am, but it's over."

"Until you go home to Seattle?"

"It's not like that, Roberta. We don't get along. She…"

"Doesn't understand you." The oldest lie in the book.

"It's true," he insisted. "We're separated."

Roberta had no desire to play that game. She'd already been used once. She wasn't going to allow herself to be used again. She could almost hear her mother sneering, "Foolish, wicked girl," as she walked out of the cabin and back to her single life. She was better off alone. The only man a woman could trust was the kind she met between the covers of a book.

"I was running a business," she told Daphne now. *Protecting my heart from further injury.* She'd tried to protect her daughter, too, but Daphne had never listened. She'd kept believing there had to be a good man out there somewhere. Maybe Daphne had been right all along. Maybe Roberta simply hadn't encountered one until now.

"And only this morning you said you didn't want a man in your life."

"A woman can change her mind, can't she?"

"Absolutely, and it's about time," Daphne said now with a smile and an approving nod. "I hope you have a great evening."

"I do, too." It had been years since that disastrous, short-lived affair, and Roberta hadn't been on a date since. She was a female Rip Van Winkle waking up after years of sleep. What was she going to wear? What was she going to say? Was this a bad idea?

Bad or not, she went to Schwangau. She donned a pair of cream-colored slacks, her favorite pink top and floral jacket and her comfiest shoes, and sailed out the door, feeling as nervous as a young girl going on her first date.

Seeing Curtis White waiting for her in the lobby of Schwangau, wearing black jeans and a button-down shirt with a dark blue tie, set her tummy doing flips. She couldn't remember when she'd found a real, live man so attractive.

"You look lovely," he said.

Lovely, at her age. She could feel herself blushing.

"And you look... Has anyone ever told you that you look like Clint Eastwood?" *What a silly thing to say!*

He didn't seem to mind. "I get that a lot," he said with a smile. "Normally, I clean up better. I'm afraid I didn't realize there was a dress code at this place. This is the only shirt I had with me. I had to borrow a tie from the maître d'."

"You clean up just fine." Roberta told him. Now, there was an understatement. She should pinch herself to make sure she wasn't dreaming. Except she didn't want to wake up. At this point in life, a woman deserved a good dream or two.

The dream only improved as the evening progressed and they shared a bottle of Riesling and life stories (Roberta's highly edited). Curtis confessed to a love of old fifties doo-wop groups, and then she did sneak a quick pinch. This *had* to be too good to be true.

Nothing vanished. It was still evening and she was still in a fancy restaurant with a great-looking man. "How about breakfast tomorrow?" he asked as they left the restaurant.

"I think I could manage that."

Breakfast was even better than dinner, so they decided on lunch, including his sons and her daughter. "He kind of looks like Clint Eastwood," Daphne whispered as he and his sons walked into Zelda's.

"He thinks I look like Audrey Hepburn," Roberta whispered back. "The mature version," she said with a smile. Of course, other than being slender, she didn't look anything like the famous actress, but she wasn't about to disabuse the man. Let him have his fantasy.

Later that day, after their children had discreetly drifted off, they took a walk on the bank of the

Wenatchee River, admiring the view of sparkling blue water wending its way past a forest of pines and firs. He took her hand and said, "Roberta, I've had a wonderful time this weekend."

A little gremlin landed on her shoulder and whispered, *Here's where the letdown begins. He'll say, "But now I have to go back to my real life."*

"I hope you have, too," Curtis went on.

"It's been lovely," she replied, careful to keep her voice neutral.

"I'd really like to do this again."

"You would?"

He looked surprised. "Wouldn't you?"

She smiled. "Yes, actually, I would. But let's take it slow," she added, picking up her daughter's new mantra.

He smiled back. "Okay. But not too slow. I'm not getting any younger, and I'd like to cruise the Greek isles before I die. That isn't the kind of thing a man wants to do alone."

"I'd like that, too," Roberta said. She was sure she would.

"Glad to hear it," he said and kissed her.

It was a kiss filled with both tenderness and promise, and probably the best kiss Roberta had ever had. Maybe life began at seventy-one.

Twenty-Five

❧❧❧

Anne, Mother of the Guest of Honor

The Sunday before the wedding weekend Kendra hosted a bridal shower for Laney. It was a balmy afternoon with the kind of blue skies that made Seattleites ecstatic, and the temperature hovered somewhere in the low seventies. The same pleasant weather was expected for Icicle Falls the next weekend.

In addition to family, Laney's bridesmaids, Autumn, Ella and Darcy, were present, along with her coworkers at the coffee shop and several friends from church. Laney was all dolled up in a green sundress that complemented not only her hair but also the mermaid swimming up her arm.

"She's going to be a stunning bride," Mrs. Ostrom, the pastor's wife, said to Anne as she made the rounds with Laney, saying hello to everyone. Mrs. Ostrom was pushing seventy. She either had no problem with tattoo overload or was too polite to say anything. Probably the latter.

But it was proof of how much everyone loved Laney,

and knowing that made Anne happy. Right now it would've been impossible to be unhappy. It had been a race to the bridal finish line, but everything had finally come together.

"You have been busy, haven't you?" Cam's mother said to Laney as she hugged her. "Planning a wedding so quickly."

"I had a lot of help," Laney said, smiling at Anne.

"The best," added Julia, who'd come over to greet her daughter and granddaughter.

Anne smiled at her mother's praise. She was still smiling when Aunt Maude approached, but she felt the smile getting a little stiff. Aunt Maude was one of Cam's aunts, the polar opposite of his mother. She was tall and skinny with a lack of bustline that she accentuated with a horrific blouse in a wild purple print. To complete her ensemble, she wore a faded black, crinkly skirt from a long-gone fashion era. She tried to distract from the wrinkles growing on her face by dyeing her hair a color of red found nowhere in nature. To complete the look, she showed off her perpetual frown with bright red lipstick. She was a walking sour lemon and purveyor of doom.

"Laney, you seem tired," she said, patting Laney's arm.

"She's been busy, Aunt Maude," Anne said.

Aunt Maude shook her head. "Girls these days, they take on too much. I blame it on the women's movement."

No one quite knew what to say to that—and remain polite. Julia turned to Laney and Anne. "Let's get you girls some punch. Excuse us, Maude." As they walked over to the refreshment table, she muttered, "Who invited that woman?"

"I couldn't not invite her, Mom," Anne said.

"*I* could have."

Once everyone had had an opportunity to chat and enjoy a glass of punch, Kendra started a game that involved unscrambling letters to form words that all had to do with weddings. "I love this kind of game," Cam's mom enthused.

"Good for your brain," agreed Maude, who'd taken a seat next to Anne. "Did you know that an estimated 5.2 million people now have Alzheimer's?"

There was some cheery news. "Where did you hear that?"

"I can't remember," Maude replied. "You know, one of the signs is losing your sense of smell," she informed Anne.

Just what she wanted to talk about at her daughter's bridal shower. She found herself surreptitiously sniffing her wrist to see if she could detect the perfume she'd sprayed there earlier. Whew. Her brain was still okay.

They moved from the game to eating, with Kendra's terrier, Barney, posing hungrily in front of various guests, hoping for a handout. "Barney, no!" Kendra commanded. "Don't anybody feed him."

Cam's mother, who was about to share some of her prosciutto, drew back her hand, making Barney whine. Not that he should've been remotely hungry, since he'd already begged several handouts when Kendra wasn't looking.

Kendra the social director soon moved on to the purpose of the shower, giving the bride her gifts. With Autumn on one side, writing down who gave Laney what, and Darcy on the other, forming a ribbon bouquet for the wedding rehearsal, Laney set to work, dipping into gift bags and opening boxes containing everything from margarita glasses to dish towels. The ribbon bouquet began to swell.

"A baby for every ribbon you break," teased Drake's mom.

Laney said she liked kids, then with a grin yanked off a ribbon, letting it snap apart. Ella folded and stuffed wrapping paper in the ginormous gift bag that had contained a cashmere blanket from Julia.

Barney found this all fascinating. And appetizing. Perhaps it was the fact that he'd been denied that final treat earlier or maybe he was simply being a dog. Whatever the cause, the four-legged garbage disposal, who'd managed to snarf cake off an abandoned plate, now developed a fondness for wrapping paper and began noshing on a piece that hadn't made it into the bag.

Anne watched in disgust as he shredded a bow of pink curling ribbon. "Should he be doing that?" she asked Kendra.

"What?" Kendra turned and saw the last of the paper about to go into Barney's mouth. "Oh, Barney, no!" She took away what was left of it and Barney slinked off to a corner where, later on, as Laney was thanking all the guests for their presents, he threw up both the wrapping paper and his earlier snacks.

"Eeew," said Autumn, wrinkling her nose.

Aunt Maude shook her head. "It's a sign."

"Oh, really, Maude," Julia said, sounding disgusted.

Maude refused to be put in her place. "When things go wrong at a bridal shower, things will surely go wrong at the wedding."

Anne had never heard that before. "Is that a real saying? Where did you hear it?"

Maude shrugged. "I don't remember."

"And how's your sense of smell?" Julia asked, sneering.

Maude harrumphed and took herself off to the refreshment table for another helping of lemon dessert.

"That woman," Julia said, shaking her head. "She's a regular encyclopedia of misinformation and nonfacts. I never heard such nonsense in all my life."

That's what it is, nonsense, Anne told herself for the rest of the afternoon. When Cam asked how the shower had gone, she replied, "Great." It had been a lovely shower and Laney was going to have a lovely wedding.

She continued to tell herself all evening long, and again when she lay in bed, thinking of everything that could possibly go wrong. Finally, around one in the morning, she took a melatonin tablet to help herself sleep. One wasn't going to do it. She took another and finally drifted off.

And went to Laney's wedding. But instead of wearing her mother-of-the-bride dress, she was prancing around in some skimpy showgirl outfit and sporting a huge, feathery headdress that was so heavy she had trouble holding up her head. This made it hard to keep her balance, and when a groomsman wearing an Elvis-style white rhinestone jumpsuit escorted her down the aisle, she found herself weaving back and forth like a woman who'd had too much champagne.

She toppled into her seat. Cam should have slipped in beside her but he was nowhere to be seen. Instead, Kendra's dog, Barney, jumped up onto the pew, pink wrapping paper hanging from his jaws.

She looked up front and there stood Drake in raggedy pirate garb, a patch over one eye. The "Wedding March" began to play, but it wasn't wedding music. Instead, Elvis, the King himself, appeared, dressed in a white rhinestone jumpsuit, and began to sing "All Shook Up" backed by the Flesh Eaters, who wore zombie makeup. And here came Laney in some kind of serving-wench outfit. Where was her wedding gown?

Anne tried to stand up and demand her daughter march right back down the aisle and put on her gown, but the heavy headdress propelled her forward and she fell on her face. Barney leaped off the pew and began tugging at the headdress, growling playfully.

"What a disgrace," hissed Aunt Maude, who'd seated herself directly behind Anne. "The woman can't even plan her daughter's wedding. I knew this would happen. Didn't I say this would happen?"

The woman seated next to Maude seemed to be her twin. She whispered back, "I heard they wanted to go to Vegas and Anne put a wrench in it."

"I did not," Anne protested, trying to struggle to her feet.

"Get that woman out of here," said the minister, who looked suspiciously like Jack Sparrow. "She's messing everything up."

"I'm the mother of the bride!"

Drake pointed a finger at her. "She's a Momzilla. Get her out of here."

"I'm going to be your mother-in-law. You can't do this to me!"

But they did. Two burly men in white rhinestone-encrusted tuxes dragged her down the aisle, past the guests. Some stared at her with pity. Some giggled. One fellow showgirl laughed out loud.

"Sorry, sis," Kendra called. (Why was she dressed like a zombie?) "I'll save you a donut."

Down the aisle they went and into the foyer. They pushed open the church door and hurled Anne out.

But there was no sidewalk to catch her. The church gripped the edge of a cliff and she found herself falling, screaming as she went.

She awoke before she landed, Cam gently stroking her arm. "It's okay, Annie. You're having a bad dream."

Bad dream? There was the understatement of the century.

"You all right now?"

She swallowed and willed her heart to stop doing the Indianapolis 500. "I'm fine."

It was just a dream, she told herself. But what did it mean?

Nothing. She was simply suffering from the combined effect of too much melatonin and too close proximity to Aunt Maude. Everything was fine and the wedding was going to be perfect. Anne closed her eyes and snuggled back under the covers.

But she never got to sleep again. Maybe that was just as well.

Twenty-Six

Laney, Ready for the Big Day

"**J**ust think," Autumn said to Laney as they wiped down counters at the coffee shop, "it's almost your wedding. Tonight we'll be at the Red Barn, dancing with cowboys at your bachelorette party."

It was hard to believe. After all the discussion and planning, the big day was only forty-eight hours away. Everyone would be meeting at the waterfront park for the ceremony, then going back to Primrose Haus for the reception. There would be food and flowers and dancing. No bright lights, no noise and crazy excitement, but they'd have the stars in the sky and they could make their own noise. It would be exactly the wedding she'd dreamed of when she was a little girl.

"Ben told me the guys still don't know what they're going to do up there for Drake's bachelor party," Autumn said. "I think hang out at the river, sit around and drink beer. Talk about boring."

Laney shrugged. "It's not Vegas." Okay, that sounded kind of...off. From the corner of her eye, she could feel

Autumn studying her. "I'll take out the garbage," she announced and ducked into the alley behind the coffee shop. It was wrong not to feel more excited about all of this, especially since her mom had worked so hard on pulling everything together for her. And everything had been pulled together perfectly, right down from the donut cake to the DJ. (The Flesh Eaters weren't happy that they'd been bumped from playing at the reception, but Drake had told them about the open-mike night at Zelda's on Sunday, and they were planning to make an impression on the residents of Icicle Falls and maybe get a future booking.) Laney had a wedding gown she loved and was marrying her best friend. That was what mattered, not where or how they got married. Anyway, it was too late to change her plans now. Everything was ordered and everyone was coming.

Autumn was happy to keep the wedding conversation going when Laney came back in. "Are you sorry you guys aren't going to Vegas?"

Laney concentrated on putting a new liner in the garbage can. "My mom's right. This is better."

"For who?"

"For everyone."

"It's not your mom getting married," Autumn reminded her.

Why was she always saying stuff like that? "I know," Laney said. "But this way our family and friends can come."

"They could've come to Vegas. I just got a Visa card. I could go. So could Ben." She grinned. "Let's go."

"Oh, sure," Laney said. "I'm gonna take off for Vegas two days before my wedding."

"I would. If that's what I really wanted."

Laney bit her lip.

"Don't be a wimp, Laney, not when it's something as important as your wedding."

"I'm not being a wimp," Laney insisted. "I want this." She liked Icicle Falls. She liked the river. She liked the old-fashioned house on Primrose Street. So did Drake. Well, sort of. He liked the river, anyway. This was going to be fun, the best of both worlds. They'd have the fancy wedding here and then go to Vegas for their honeymoon. She set aside the image of Drake and her on the Treasure Island pirate ship, shook her head in an effort to erase the beautiful pictures she'd seen on the website.

But she'd *wanted* to get married on that ship. Primrose Haus was beautiful, but in the end, it was just a house and the yard was just a yard. She frowned and told herself to cut it out. Her mom was right, she thought again. She'd have no regrets about the wedding they'd planned.

Your mom will have no regrets about the wedding you've planned.

Where had that come from? It was as if Autumn was still talking to her.

Well, she wasn't listening. Canceling things now would be totally selfish and unfair to her mother.

And so the wedding party left Thursday afternoon for Icicle Falls. Friday morning after breakfast they'd all go rock climbing. At some point during the day, her parents, grandparents, aunts, uncles and cousins would arrive, along with the rest of the guests who would trickle in. There would be a rehearsal on Friday night and then a dinner party for the immediate family and bridal party. Saturday was the big day. It was going to be like Christmas, only better. Yes, she *had* made the right decision.

They checked into the Icicle Creek Lodge and Drake's best man, Ben, said, "This place is something else." Since he'd leaned over to Drake and lowered his voice, she knew he hadn't meant that in a good way.

"It ain't Vegas, that's for sure," Drake whispered back, echoing her earlier words.

Her stomach started churning and that made her cranky. They got to the room and instead of being charmed by the mountain view, she saw fussy furniture she'd never pick and curtains at the window that made her think of her grandmother. Those were antiques. Valuable antiques. And the lace curtains were pretty.

Except she didn't like lace curtains.

This was her bridal suite. This was where she'd spend her wedding night. She burst into tears.

He dropped their suitcases and took her by the arms. "Laney, what's wrong?"

"I don't want to do this," she wailed.

He looked at her in concern. "You don't want to get married?"

"No."

"You don't?" He sounded horrified.

"No. I mean, no, that's not it. I want to get married, just not here. But it's too late."

"No, it's not. Tell me what you want."

She shook her head. Too late, too late. She'd blown it. She'd let herself get talked into something that wasn't her and Drake. Yeah, this had been her when she was ten, when she was sixteen even, but she wasn't six-teen anymore. Somewhere along the way, her tastes had changed. Her mom had meant well, but she'd been wrong and now they were stuck.

He led her into the room and settled them on the bed. "Talk to me."

"We should have gone to Vegas," she said between sobs. "I'm sorry, Drake."

He tucked a finger under her chin and raised her face to look at him. "Hey, don't be sorry. I told you I'd do whatever you wanted."

"I know, and I thought I wanted this. What I really want is to go to Vegas."

He brightened at that. "Yeah? Then we'll go to Vegas."

"Are you crazy? We can't do that now! It's too late to cancel the reception. My parents have spent all this money."

"We'll pay them back."

"My mom would be so embarrassed." The very thought of humiliating her mother made Laney cry even harder.

There was a knock at the door, and Autumn and Ella ducked in, together with their boyfriends. Darcy and Drake's other pal, Gordy, hovered behind.

"What's wrong?" Autumn asked.

"Laney doesn't want to do this," Drake explained.

"She doesn't want to get married?" Ben asked, shocked.

"No, stupid," said Autumn. "She doesn't want to get married *here*. I told you all along this was a mistake," she scolded Laney. "You're such a wimp."

Good old Autumn, always a comfort. Laney glared at her.

Unaffected, Autumn pulled out her cell phone. "Let's check on flights to Vegas. I bet we can get a red-eye."

"I can't go to Vegas," Laney protested. "It'd be wrong."

"Well, then, what are you going to do?" Autumn demanded.

"I'm going to call my dad." She didn't dare tell her mother what she was thinking.

Her father answered his cell phone on the second ring. "Laney girl, are you guys up there now?"

"Yes, and, oh, Dad, this is all wrong."

"What's wrong?"

His voice was suddenly worried. Great. He was going to be mad; Mom was going to be upset. "Never mind. I shouldn't have called."

"Yes. You should have. Tell me what's going on."

"I don't want to do this."

"You don't want to get married?" he asked, shocked.

"I don't want to get married here. We should've gone to Vegas. I should be happy about this wedding, but I'm just so…unhappy."

"Aw, Laney, why didn't you say something earlier?"

He had to ask that? As if he hadn't been there, seeing all the work Mom was doing, how important this was to her? "Mom." That was as far as she got, but that said it all. She started crying again.

"I know. Your mother really wanted this for you. Sometimes I think that in doing it for you, she's enjoyed planning the kind of fancy wedding we didn't have."

He suddenly stopped talking. Had they lost the connection? "Dad?"

"Don't do anything just yet, Laney. Stay up there. And don't worry. I've got an idea."

Twenty-Seven

Anne, Mother of the Bride-to-be

Friday morning Anne and Cam got into their trusty little Kia and, after a quick stop to grab some coffee, made their way up the mountains to Icicle Falls. "Don't you love it here?" she gushed as they passed the Willkommen in Icicle Falls sign. "I don't know why we don't come up more often."

"Weddings."

"Oh, yeah, that." Her wedding business did cut into their getaway time. Maybe she should start easing up on her work schedule, take advantage of being empty nesters.

Laney's wedding felt like the apex of her career. It was as if this was what she'd been waiting for all these years. An insistent itch was finally getting scratched.

"Well, this is the most important wedding I've ever planned." She laid a hand on Cam's leg. "Can you believe it? Our daughter's getting married." She felt like a kid on Christmas Eve. *Tomorrow you get to unwrap your presents!*

Cam just smiled.

"Drake's a sweet boy. They're going to be so happy together."

Cam nodded, and Anne turned her attention to all the shops as they drove through town. There was the Mad Hatter, a shop that specialized in novelty hats; there was Local Yokels, a shop featuring all kinds of Northwest treats—everything from smoked salmon to huckleberry jam. They passed Big Brats, the restaurant stand that sold great bratwurst, and Gilded Lily's, the women's clothing shop. She and Kendra would definitely have to do some shopping later, after they'd caught up with Laney and her posse.

They drove on through the town and then down Icicle Creek Drive, where the shops were replaced by woods and an occasional glimpse of Icicle Creek. Off through the trees she noticed a cleared area surrounded by a split-rail fence. A couple of llamas peered out at her. Looking past that, she could see some cabins scattered about—a camp of some sort. The road took a small jog and they wound up on a smaller, private road. Holly Road. It led to the Icicle Creek Lodge, a timbered affair that offered views of Icicle Creek and, beyond that, the mountains.

"Isn't this charming?" she said as Cam pulled up in front of the lodge. "What a fabulous place for a wedding night."

"Annie, I hate to break it to you, but I think they had their wedding night long before this," Cam said.

She frowned at him. "Some things a mother doesn't want to know." Anyway, she was in no position to judge, a fact she'd reminded herself of many times once her daughter moved out.

Her story had turned out fine, and so would Laney's. She wouldn't have a grandchild as soon as her own mother did, though, that was for sure. Laney would be going back to school, and she and Drake had dreams of taking a cross-country camping trip and, after that, buying a house. Ah, young love with all its plans and dreams.

Plans and dreams weren't only for newlyweds. She and Cam had plenty of time left for some of their own. He'd refused to share any details about what he had in mind for their anniversary, but whatever it was, she'd be ready to relax. Organizing her daughter's wedding had taken a lot out of her.

They went inside the lodge and checked in. "We should go see how the kids are doing," she said to Cam as he pocketed their room key.

"They were going rock climbing," he reminded her. "They're probably not back yet."

Good point. "Well, then, later." Meanwhile, they could get some lunch and kick around town as they waited for Kendra and her family.

She'd reserved the private room at Schwangau for the rehearsal dinner, so, wanting something different, they wandered over to Zelda's, one of the other popular restaurants in town. It was less pricey and more hip, decorated with a mixture of Northwest contemporary wood trim and art-deco decor. All the waitresses wore Roaring Twenties headbands and served up everything from salmon and trout to salads with mountain blackberries.

Charley Masters, the owner, seated them and stuck around a few minutes to chat. "Your daughter's having her reception at Primrose Haus? Great place," she said. "I got married in Vegas," she added with a wink. "Different strokes."

The very mention of Vegas made Anne shudder, but she smiled and nodded.

"Anyway," Charley concluded, "I hope you folks enjoy your stay."

"We already are," Anne told her. "I love this restaurant," she said after Charley left to go seat another couple.

Cam smiled. "I think in your present mood there isn't anything you *wouldn't* love."

"True," she admitted. "I'm on a wedding high." She had checked and double-checked every detail. Everything was in order. All she had to do now was enjoy the party.

They'd just finished lunch when Anne's cell phone rang. "We're here," Kendra said. "Where are you guys?"

"We're at Zelda's, finishing lunch. Come on over."

Ten minutes later, Kendra and her family entered the restaurant. The girls were bouncing with excitement. At the sight of their aunt, they let out squeals and dashed for the table.

"Inside voices," their mother scolded, taking off after them, "and no running."

The running turned into hops. Coral was the first to reach the table, but Amy was the first to share the news that they'd had a flat tire on the way up. "And Daddy swore."

"Sounds like you had a fun trip," Anne said, greeting her sister.

Kendra rolled her eyes. "Family fun. Can't beat it. Is it five o'clock somewhere? I think my man needs a drink."

"He needs two," her husband said, coming up behind her.

They slid into the bench opposite and then squeezed in the girls on each side of the table. "Have you seen the bride and groom yet?" Kendra asked.

Anne shook her head. "They're out rock climbing. We figure we'll catch up with them later this afternoon."

"Can I wear my dress to the practice?" Coral wanted to know.

"Not after what happened last time you put it on. It's jeans and T-shirts for the river tonight and your church dress for the party after."

"I like parties," Amy announced.

"That's good," Anne said, hugging her, "because we are going to party tonight."

Roberta's crew was taking care of the seating for the ceremony tomorrow and the other reception details, so all Anne had to do was watch her beautiful daughter take her wedding vows. Life was good.

After a leisurely visit at the restaurant, the men took the girls to the little amusement park that had recently opened at one end of town, giving Anne and Kendra a chance to prowl the shops. "Well, you did it," Kendra said as they examined the antiques and collectibles in Timeless Treasures. "You finally got your perfect wedding."

"My daughter's perfect wedding," Anne corrected her.

"One and the same." Kendra gave her a playful nudge. "Ooh, look at this china mug. I think I need it."

They found several more things they needed as the afternoon wore on—bath bombs from Bubbles, gingerbread boys and girls from Gingerbread Haus and, of course, chocolate from Sweet Dreams. "I may as well get a large box of truffles," Anne said, "since I'll have to share with Cam."

"I'm hiding mine," said her sister.

They met their husbands and the girls at the Tea Time Tea Shop, where they indulged in purchasing some lavender sugar cookies and chocolate mint tea to take home, and where Anne had a last-minute confab with Bailey, the shop owner who was catering the wedding.

"Roberta's got it all under control. Remember?" Kendra reminded her as they left.

"I know." But once a wedding planner, always a wedding planner.

They got back to the lodge to learn that their parents had arrived.

"Where's Daddy?" Kendra asked once Julia had let them in.

"Off to buy some German beer and check out that sausage place we saw when we drove in." She grimaced. "He does love all that wurst, but it doesn't love him. I'm sure he'll have heartburn by the time he comes back. Where's our bride?"

"She and Drake and their friends were going rock climbing," Anne said. "I guess I'll call her and see if they're back yet." All she got was voice mail. "She must be out of range."

Laney was still out of range at four thirty. "They should've been back by now," Anne fretted as she and Kendra and the girls hung out in Julia's room. "We've got the rehearsal in an hour."

"Try her again," Kendra suggested from their mother's bed, where she was stretched out beside Julia, watching reruns of *Love It or List It*.

Anne did, and again it went straight to voice mail.

"Where is she?" Maybe she'd fallen and was stuck in some rock crevice with a broken leg. How would they find her?

Anne was pacing the floor, leaving a frantic message for Laney to call her, when Cam appeared in the doorway, his brother-in-law behind him. "Looks like we're all here," he said. He cleared his throat. "So now would probably be the time to tell you."

A feeling of foreboding began to sneak up on Anne. "Tell me what?"

"There's been a slight change in plan."

"What's wrong?"

"Well, um, nothing." He cleared his throat again. "Laney and I have been talking."

"Is she back from rock climbing?"

"I don't think so."

"Cam, you're being awfully mysterious," Anne said.

"Well, like I said, there's been a change in plans."

This couldn't be good. Anne braced herself.

"Laney and Drake really want to get married in Vegas."

"Vegas!" Julia repeated.

Anne felt suddenly light-headed. She fell onto the bed opposite her mother. "Vegas?" With Elvis impersonators and the showgirls with the feathers and the chapels of love. And the pirate ship! "Vegas," she repeated, anger roaring through her like a tsunami.

Cam sat down next to her and put an arm around her shoulders. "She had an...epiphany."

"An epiphany! An epiphany is something *good*. An epiphany is not...running off to Vegas the day before you get married." She shot off the bed and went to search through the store bags. "Where's that chocolate?"

"Annie, calm down," said Cam. "They haven't run off. They're still here. They just don't want to get married here."

She had to be hearing things. In fact, she had to be hallucinating. Or dreaming. Yes, she was dreaming, that was it. She shook her head, pinched her arm. Nothing seemed to work. She was standing in the same room, hearing the same shocking news.

Stuffing chocolates in her mouth. "Why can't I wake up?"

"Have another chocolate," Julia urged. "And give me one, too."

"Let me see if I've got this straight," Anne said as she plopped down on the bed and handed over the chocolates. "They're still here but they're not getting married."

"That about sums it up."

"I want to wear my dress," Coral said and burst into tears. That set Amy off, and she started crying, too.

"Oh, boy," muttered Kendra. "Come on, girls. Let's go take a walk." She and her husband ushered the girls out of the room.

Julia stayed behind to comfort her daughter with hugs and more chocolate.

There was no comfort to be had. "I saved for this for years," Anne said, wiping at her eyes. "I wanted her to have something special. And now, just like that, we're canceling the wedding?"

"Actually, we're not," Cam said, and now he was smiling.

She blinked. "I don't understand."

He crossed the room to kneel in front of her and take

her hands in his. "There's going to be a wedding here tomorrow, babe. Ours."

"What?"

At that moment his cell phone rang.

"It's Laney, isn't it?" Anne said as he answered it. Their daughter wasn't calling her mother. Probably too afraid. That made Anne both sad and angry.

Cam nodded at her. "Yes," he said to Laney, "I told her. Hang on." He handed over the phone.

"Don't you dare say anything you'll regret," Julia cautioned. "Remember, daughters don't always do what their mothers want."

A not-so-subtle reminder of her own past wedding choice. Anne took the phone and said hello. It was impossible to keep the disappointment out of her voice.

"Mom, I'm sorry. Please don't be mad," Laney begged.

She found it hard not to be. She'd gone to so much trouble to make sure her daughter had a memorable wedding. "Laney, I don't understand."

Laney sighed. "I just… I don't know. We got up here and I realized getting married at the house on Primrose Street wasn't what I really wanted. Neither did Drake. If we went through with it, if Drake and I didn't get married in Las Vegas like we talked about in the first place, I'd always be sorry. I didn't want to have any regrets."

Anne bit her lip. Okay, she understood about regrets. But she couldn't help wishing her daughter had figured this out sooner.

"I tried to want what you wanted for me, Mom. I really did. But the wedding you planned, it wasn't us, even with the raft."

Anne knew she had only one person to blame for how

this had turned out, and that was herself. She'd been so determined to give Laney the wedding she'd never had, the one she thought Laney should have, she'd blinded herself to what her daughter truly wanted. And that was something very different from what Laney had talked about when she was younger. Her tastes had changed; they'd veered away from Anne's. Laney had become her own woman and Anne had ignored that.

Still… "If you get married there, a lot of your family and friends won't be able to come."

"But Drake and I will be there and that's what really matters," Laney said. *I'm marrying Cam, and that's what really matters.* Anne's words to her mother floated at the back of her mind.

"I'm sorry I ruined all your plans for me. It's not that I don't appreciate how hard you worked and how much time you spent, but the wedding you planned is the one *you* always wanted. So Dad came up with the perfect solution. You're going to be the bride tomorrow. And I hope I can be your maid of honor."

Anne could barely speak, choked up as she was. This was all so much to process. "That would be lovely," she managed.

"Thanks for understanding," Laney said, and Anne could hear the relief in her voice.

Better late than never. Here Anne did this for a living, yet when it came to her own daughter she'd been clueless. How pathetic was that?

"This is going to be fun," Laney continued, all excitement now. "Happy anniversary."

Anne smiled. "Thanks, sweetie." Okay, so things weren't going according to plan—well, *her* plan, anyway—but her daughter's happiness was what counted.

"I know Dad's excited about this and I am, too. Oh, and by the way, you don't have to get married on a raft. We canceled that part."

Thank heaven.

"I love you, Mom."

"I love you, too." And because she did, she couldn't stay mad, especially since she was the one who'd created this problem. But it was all working out. Her daughter was getting the wedding she wanted.

And it looked as though, after twenty-five years, so was Anne. Everything had changed so fast, she had wedding whiplash. She handed Cam's phone back to him. "I don't know what to say."

He smiled at her. "Say 'I do.'"

Twenty-Eight

A Wedding on Primrose Street

It was the best kind of day for a wedding—warm weather, blue sky and the sun shining on the bride… who wore a champagne-colored dress with a nipped-in waist and pleated skirt and flowers in her hair. She carried the bouquet that had been ordered for her daughter, and she and her husband were remarried under the rose arbor.

"Do you take this woman for another twenty-five years?" Pastor Ostrom asked the groom.

"I sure do," Cam said.

"And how about you, Anne? Do you pledge yourself to Cam?"

"I do," she said, her heart full.

"Then I pronounce you still husband and wife. I hope your next twenty-five years together are as wonderful as the first twenty-five," said the minister, beaming at them. "You may kiss your bride," he said to Cam.

Cam was happy to oblige. He dipped Anne backward and gave her a photo-op-style kiss, while the professional photographer recorded the moment for posterity…just like every friend and family member present who had a cell phone.

It had been a little embarrassing announcing to all the guests that there'd been a change in plans and they were here to celebrate a different bride and groom, but no one complained. More than one relative was thrilled about Laney's new plan to go to Vegas and begged to be included. "Wish we'd done that," said one of Drake's cousins. "Our wedding was boring." She rolled her eyes. "I let my mom plan most of it. Dumb."

Laney and Anne both said nothing.

Now, with the ceremony over, everyone went to the bar to get down to the serious business of partying.

The crab cakes, Brie and smoked salmon bruschetta, and pulled-pork sliders were a hit, as was the dinner, which consisted of three-cheese stuffed chicken, accompanied by tossed salad, a lobster-pasta salad and crusty rolls. And everyone raved over how clever and cute the donut cake was. The DJ had car problems halfway up the mountain and was still waiting for a tow truck, but the Flesh Eaters were in town and had brought their instruments along and were happy to fill in until he got there. So Cam and Anne did their opening dance to "Give It to Me, Baby, Hard, Hard, Hard," an original song by the lead singer.

"Congratulations on twenty-five years of marriage," Roberta's daughter, Daphne, said to Anne as she proffered a tray of champagne glasses. "These days that's quite an accomplishment."

"It can be done when you've got a good man," Anne said, taking a glass and smiling up at Cam.

"You give me hope," Daphne said with a smile.

"By the way, where's your mom? I haven't seen her," Anne said.

Daphne grinned. "She's in Seattle, visiting a new friend. She said to give you her best wishes."

"Champagne!" boomed Aunt Maude from behind Daphne, making her jump and the champagne glasses rattle. "I love champagne." She took a glass and Daphne slipped away to serve other guests. "Didn't I tell you something would happen?" Maude demanded.

Maude was *not* getting invited to Vegas. "Yes, you did," Anne said. "And isn't it terrific how it all turned out?" Maude scowled.

Julia came up just then. "I think it's time to cut the cake," she said, rescuing Anne and Cam from Aunt Maude. "Well, darling," she said as they made their way to the cake table, "how are you enjoying your wedding?"

Anne smiled up at Cam. "It's wonderful."

"Yes, it is," Julia agreed. "But then, how could it have been anything else with my lovely daughter planning it?"

"Thanks, Mom," Anne murmured.

Cam shook his head and frowned. "I wish I'd known twenty-five years ago how badly you wanted a fancy wedding."

She laid a hand on his arm. "I meant what I said back then. The most important thing to me was marrying you. And under the same circumstances, I'd do it all over again."

Not that she wasn't enjoying her fancy twenty-five-years-after-the-fact wedding. She was. But the simple fact remained. A marriage was about the two people who were making a commitment to each other. How they did it wasn't half as important as *why* they did it. Everything else was just frosting on the wedding cake.

Later that night Cam carried Anne over the threshold into the bridal suite at the Icicle Creek Lodge. "I'm a lucky man," he said, setting her down and putting his arms around her.

"And I'm a lucky woman," she said, reaching up and putting her arms around his neck.

"Thank you for marrying me again."

"I'd marry you again and again and again," Anne said and kissed him.

"Same here." He led her farther into the room, where a bottle of champagne sat next to the king-size bed. The nightstand held a small box of Sweet Dreams chocolates. An envelope sat on one of the pillows.

"You thought of everything."

He picked up the bottle and popped the cork. "I did. I'd actually reserved this room for next weekend, when I planned to bring you up here."

"That was what you'd planned?"

He nodded.

"We can still use it next weekend," she said coyly.

"I don't think we'll need it."

Of course, it would be silly to come back again so soon, she told herself, especially in light of the big blow-out party they'd just had.

"Open the card."

She did, and out fell a magazine clipping. She picked it up. It was from some sort of real-estate brochure and featured a rustic mountain cabin perched alongside a river. "What's this?"

"Since we bagged the cruise, I thought we might like to make a down payment on a cabin up here instead. Now that we're empty nesters we can afford it. We may even get it paid off by the time we retire," he added with a grin. "I've got a couple of places in mind and a real-estate agent lined up to show us around. Actually, she was lined up for next weekend, but we moved it to tomorrow."

"A cabin?" Could she have heard correctly?

"Please tell me I got it right this time."

"More than right," she said, then threw her arms around him and kissed him.

The champagne was forgotten. Who needed bubbly when you had a handsome man kissing you?

Later that night as they snuggled together on the big bed, she relived the whole evening. It had been everything she'd ever dreamed of, a perfect wedding—just as Laney's Las Vegas adventure would be perfect for her. Most important of all, the day had been a celebration of love. And in the end, love was all that mattered.

* * * * *

Acknowledgments

I had such a good time writing this book! And I'd really like to thank the wonderful people who helped me along the way. Thanks as always to the "brain trust": Susan Wiggs, Anjali Banerjee, Kate Breslin, Lois Dyer and Elsa Watson. And a very special thanks to Megan Keller, event designer and owner of A Kurant Event in Seattle, Washington, for giving me a glimpse into the life of a wedding planner. (I'm sure there are some things I didn't get right, but that's my fault and not hers.) I've seen Megan in action and she plans fabulous weddings! Thanks to my good friend Theresia for the wonderful recipes. Everything you make is fabulous!

Finally, a big thank-you to my agent, Paige Wheeler (you're the best!), my insightful and lovely editor, Paula Eykelhof, and all the wonderful people at MIRA who work so hard to turn stories into books and dreams into dreams come true.